CW00821306

THE SANDS SHALL WITNESS

WALTER HURST WILLIAMSON

WHWILLIAMSON.COM

Published by Walter Hurst Williamson

ISBN: 979-8-35093-080-1

Cover design, illustrations, maps and interior formatting:
Mark Thomas / Coverness.com

This book is dedicated to my parents.
My selfless and encouraging father, Mark,
and my creative and inspirational mother, Sally.

GERMAN SOUTHWEST AFRICA

1903-1905

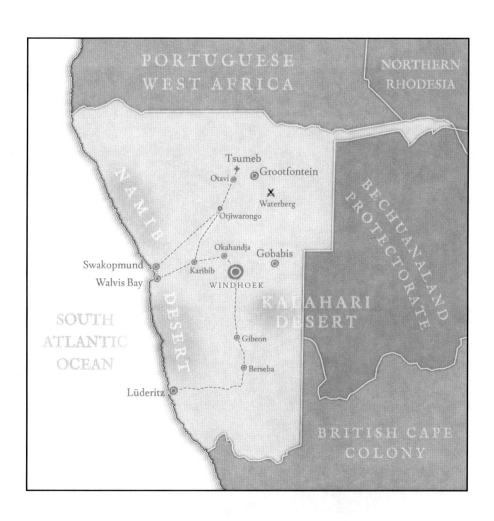

BECHUANALAND PROTECTORATE

1903-1905

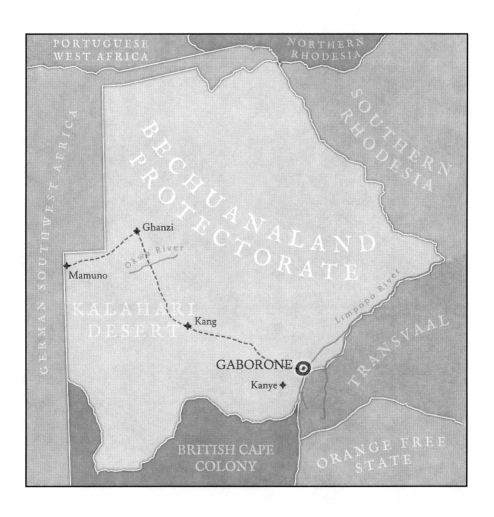

PROLOGUE

I *f it was possible, his blistered lips bothered him even more than the cracked, dry sores on his cheeks. He licked them, though his dry tongue did little to help with the pain. The thin borders of shade around him evaporated like steam, and in a few minutes, his stained trousers and boots would be exposed and baking in the blinding sunlight once more.*

A slight tremor nearby had woken him, and he'd jerked awake in practiced terror. He scanned the burning horizon for a few petrified seconds, but nothing stirred. He was alone. For the last two days, he'd had a terrible feeling that something was stalking him. He'd drift off to sleep for an hour or two but was always awakened by that same familiar panic. But once again, he'd awoken to the vast emptiness of the Kalahari, alone except for the wind and sand.

He would never be able to fall asleep again now. He had to shut his eyes before the sun rose each morning; the heat was too much for him to bear awake. Only the occasional ostrich or lone, desperate gnu bothered to stir in such heat, and now that he was awake, he would be confined to hours of stifling misery.

He dared not move from the little shelter the knotted tree branches above him offered. The sun had not yet risen half its way into the sky, yet already the heat battered him like violent waves. Sweat stung his eyes, and the salt from it clung to his damp clothing like a parasite. He blinked away the latest droplets and tried to pull his mind away from the torment of the sun.

He'd fallen off his horse yesterday, and the stupid beast had spooked and run off with the last of his rations. He was still trying to follow the mare's trail, but he knew it was hopeless. He hadn't caught her yesterday, and now she was as lost in the maze of dunes as he was. He would never find her. And if the rest of the division's dragoons did not find him soon, they would both die alone.

He cursed the God of Africa and Conrad Huber and tried to will himself back to sleep. When the sun finally fell behind the hills of sand, he would force his weary legs back underneath him and toil to reach the end of the purple-hazed horizon. The end never seemed to come, but he would press on once more across the endless orange dunes, for another day at least, until either the sun or the stalking menace killed him.

CHAPTER ONE

APRIL 1903

Georg was late. Very late. Conrad reached into his coat pocket for his watch and suppressed another groan. He'd expected his cousin to be late; he was used to it by now. But today, Georg was exceptionally late.

Quarter 'til one. Not good at all.

Conrad re-pocketed his watch and unfolded his newspaper for the sixth time. Reading usually helped to steady his nerves, but if Georg did not arrive soon, Conrad doubted that leafing through the choppy write-ups of the Hamburg Fußball club's latest disasters would calm his frayed nerves.

Today was the start of a grand adventure for Conrad, and he'd be damned if his carefree cousin was going to cause him to miss it.

The *Calypso,* currently preparing to depart without him, was a magnificent ocean liner heading for Walvis Bay, a small English colonial port city in the midst of Southwest Africa, the German Empire's newest colony.

Deutsch-Südwestafrika, affectionately known in the Colonial Office's diplomatic corps as the DSWA, was currently a subject of great personal interest to Kaiser Wilhelm II. An area roughly one and half times the size of Germany, the colony was home to the *Deutsche Kolonialgesellschaft,* whose massive mining operations sent fat shipping convoys of copper, gold, and platinum home to Germany month after month.

Although only a few thousand Germans lived in the colony at present, Conrad had seen hundreds of advertisements in the papers back home in Aschaffenburg extolling the vast extent of free farmland available for every colonist, the clean and orderly streets of the colony's new capital city, and the exotic landscapes of bright sand beaches and jungles teeming with elephants and hippopotamuses.

The colony was the latest crown jewel of the Empire, and it would be the saving grace for Conrad and his mother.

The Huber family tree had always more or less drifted between humble circumstances and minimal prosperity, but that had all changed when Conrad's uncle, Johannes Huber, took over his father's single grocery store.

A born businessman and investor, in twenty years, Johannes Huber had turned his father's small village store into a well-connected commercial fiefdom. Johannes now owned seven more grocery stores throughout Hamburg, two steel mills in Frankfurt, and was an invested partner of a new munitions factory near Berlin.

Conrad's father, Ekkehardt Huber, however, had been called to a very different sort of life. A Lutheran minister in Aschaffenburg, Ekkehardt was what Georg called "a methodical man" or, when he'd had a few pints of beer in him, "a tough old bastard."

Ekkehardt Huber saw the world in black and white. What was good with the Lord was written in the Bible. Anything else, well, there was scant room in his household for it.

Conrad had spent his entire life in a quiet, three-room village home whose peeling paint had always reminded him of a snake trying to shed its skin. He'd received a decent enough education. The Lord expected young men to be scholars after all. Yet when Father had suddenly caught pneumonia last year and died, the nineteen-year-old Conrad had been left alone to support his mother.

There was little work to be found on the surrounding farmsteads for a

2

young man with a sharp mind but a weak back. Tall and gangly, Conrad was a good worker but an awkward laborer. Without his round-framed glasses, he could scarcely see ten feet in front of him. His long arms gave him a wide reach when he worked a scythe in autumn wheat fields, but he lacked the disciplined muscle of the other farm boys, and he would soon fall behind. He was nervous around animals, and none of the horses, oxen, or donkeys in the surrounding farms would let him harness them to a plough.

Worst of all, he suffered from painful asthma attacks that often left him panting heavily by mid-morning. Twice in his first week as a farm hand, he'd had to be carried home by two other men and laid out on his bed like an ailing child. He was undoubtably the worst farmer there had ever been.

Yet, for several months, he had managed to hold on and keep himself and his mother afloat. But when the harvest was in at last, and the winter planting finished, Conrad found himself unemployed once again. As the days had grown shorter and the first frosts hardened the soft country roads, he had feared that he and his mother would starve.

Until he'd received a telegram from Uncle Johannes.

In Berlin to inspect his investment in the munitions factory, his uncle had stopped on his way home to have lunch with an old friend of his, Herr Karl Kleinschmidt. And, as the telegram said, their conversation had shifted to the recent growth of Germany's African colonies. Herr Kleinschmidt mentioned an opening for an aide to the Commissioner of the DSWA, and Uncle Johannes had recommended Conrad for the post.

It was more than a bit fantastical. Conrad knew nothing about the German Colonial Office or Southwest Africa, but the last of the harvest money was nearly gone, and no one had offered him any work in weeks. So, with a train ticket purchased by Uncle Johannes and wearing his father's old, worn church suit, Conrad had journeyed to Berlin and arrived promptly at the Colonial Office on the appointed day.

Uncle Johannes had seemed relaxed and confident when he'd met Conrad at the train station.

"Not to worry, my boy," Johannes said as he treated Conrad to breakfast at a nearby café. "Why, it's all practically been arranged. You'll do marvelously!"

When, at last, the hour of the interview came, Uncle Johannes had taken Conrad by tram to the *Reichskolonialamt*, the Imperial Foreign Office palace that sat next to the Brandenburg Gate and overlooked the Tiergarten. Conrad had never seen anything half as grand.

Uncle Johannes walked Conrad up the stone steps to the huge wooden doors of the palace, flanked on either side by two *Gardes du Corps*, the German royal guardsmen. His uncle had shaken his hand, opened the door, and given him a gentle push with a wink.

But as Conrad walked across the palace's marble-tiled floor, he felt out of place with every *click-clack* of his father's dress shoes that seemed to echo above the general chatter and humdrum of the bustling officials. He gave his name to a prim receptionist at the base of the main stairwell, who scrutinized him with a frosty gaze before she rose from her seat with a curt, "This way, please."

As he followed the receptionist up the stairs, a few well-dressed men bid him good morning and tipped their hats. But Conrad could see in their eyes that they were surprised to see someone dressed so unfashionably within the confines of the Colonial Office. In his father's tired, provincial suit, no one would've confused him with a footman or a butler, much less someone who was interviewing for an important foreign posting.

All this did nothing to calm Conrad's nerves as the receptionist whisked him into a large corner office overlooking Pariser Platz and motioned for him to sit across from one of the fattest men Conrad had ever seen.

"Your 10:00 interview, *Botschafter*," the receptionist said to the seated man.

"*Danke*, Hilda," the large man wheezed.

The receptionist gave the man a short bow and left the room, closing the door behind her. Conrad barely had time to glimpse the gilded nameplate on the big man's desk: *Herr Karl Kleinschmidt*, before the ambassador turned his full attention on him.

"So," Herr Kleinschmidt began at once without any formalities. "You're interested in going to Africa, are you?"

That was ridiculous. Two weeks ago, Conrad had been turned away for a job as the village train depot's groundskeeper on account of his weak chest. He wasn't sure he could even pinpoint Germany's colonies on a map, let alone help the Colonial Office administer them.

After a moment, Conrad seemed to realize that he'd been asked a question and hastily responded.

"Y-yes sir," he sputtered out hastily. "I believe I am."

Gott, Conrad thought to himself. I believe I am? What a foolish thing to say.

Herr Kleinschmidt gave Conrad a long, appraising look, as though inspecting a horse with minimal prospects that he was hesitant to buy.

Conrad tried to avoid the intensity of the diplomat's scrutiny by studying the decor of his office. Herr Kleinschmidt's walls boasted pictures of himself elaborately dressed, shaking hands with a colorful assortment of characters against every variety of far-off landscapes imaginable.

In one, the bemedaled diplomat was shaking hands with a huge man covered in furs and mounted on horseback. Its caption read: *Mongolia, 1897.* Another showed Herr Kleinschmidt as a front-row member of a German delegation at what looked like an international conference, seated next to the late Chancellor Otto Von Bismarck himself.

On his desk, Herr Kleinschmidt had a variety of exotic trinkets: an ornate letter opener with a gold handle, a photograph of himself receiving his first Imperial commission from Kaiser Wilhelm II, and most intriguing of all, a large ivory horn decorated with an etching of the Prussian victory over the French at Sedan.

"I see no reason to waste words with you, Herr Huber," Kleinschmidt said after a moment. "We've had very few applicants for this posting. Your uncle speaks quite highly of your intelligence and your work ethic."

Conrad nodded along dumbly. Kleinschmidt was a heavyset man with a great white mustache, which, Conrad could not help but think, made him look like an elaborately dressed walrus. His voice was deep yet raspy as though speaking was an effortful task, but one that he thoroughly intended to undertake.

Herr Kleinschmidt pressed on, with a slight wave of his enormous hand.

"The post is yours if you'd like it. It's a two-year assignment, and you'll receive a sizable bonus at the start of your second year. Just be warned, Herr Huber. Africa is not for everyone."

Conrad was stunned. He'd been fretting all night on the train, and all the way to the Colonial Office, that he'd have to endure a lengthy, rigorous interview that he was laughably unprepared for. Yet now he'd been offered the job after answering only one question and being given a once-over by a man who looked as though he could barely stand. What had Uncle Johannes said?

Why, it's all practically been arranged!

"Th-thank you, Herr Kleinschmidt," Conrad managed to say.

"Don't thank me," Kleinschmidt said with another dismissive wave. "Commissioner Leutwein's got a real mess on his hands down there, and I need someone there as soon as possible. Someone who is not afraid of a little hard work and a few bad-tempered natives.

"I'll make the arrangements to secure the necessary paperwork. Our next supply ship leaves in three weeks. Hilda will book you a cabin aboard the *Calypso*. I'll have all the preparations finalized and delivered to your uncle's residence in Hamburg in a few weeks' time. I'm sure you'll do the Kaiser proud."

With that, Herr Kleinschmidt leaned back in his leather chair, which squeaked under his immense weight, and produced a finely carved pipe from his desk drawer that was probably worth more than Conrad made in a year.

As Kleinschmidt sprinkled several generous pinches of tobacco into the pipe's chamber, Conrad stood to leave, his head still spinning from how fast he'd apparently climbed the social ladder. He was sure he must've set a world record for transformation from laborer to Imperial diplomat in the span of fifteen minutes! As he began to walk out of the office, he tried to steady himself, somewhat dizzy from the vertigo of his newfound luck.

"It was an honor to meet you, Herr Kleinschmidt," Conrad said graciously as he left. "You won't regret this, Your Excellency!"

"I'm sure I won't," Kleinschmidt said with a smile that was courteous and also indicated he wished to be left alone with his pipe.

As Conrad bowed and turned around to leave this ornate office, Kleinschmidt spoke up between puffs.

"Oh, Herr Huber," he added with an air of detached amusement. "I'd invest in some khaki if I were you. It's damn hot down there."

*

And thus, Conrad's life was changed in an instant. And it seemed to continue to change every day. His mother was finally persuaded to leave the tiny house on the outskirts of Aschaffenburg. She moved in with Uncle Johannes' family at the Huber's summer house in Frankfurt. Although she piously protested the whole time as her few personal effects were transferred to her new home, Conrad thought Georgina seemed happier in the large home than she'd been in ages.

Uncle Johannes's generosity seemed to know no bounds. He'd taken real joy in his nephew's appointment to his new post while modestly insisting that he'd had nothing at all to do with it.

He'd purchased Conrad a new steamer trunk for the journey and also, at no small expense, several crisp, new khaki shirts and trousers that a British associate of his claimed were the finest of their kind available for tramping around the African bush. Among his uncle's various other gifts were a brand-new, tailored black suit and a silver pocket watch that had belonged to Conrad's grandfather.

Johannes's eagerness was touching, but Conrad felt more than a little uncomfortable. He was unaccustomed to sleeping in a large feather bed and wearing starched, white shirts that made his neck chafe. And with each new trinket or present that Johannes and Aunt Clara pressed into his hands, he began to feel more and more like an imposter realizing someone else's fairytale.

When the day of his departure finally arrived, Conrad was both excited for the adventure that awaited and relieved to escape his aunt and uncle's home. He kissed his mother goodbye, and then headed north by train to the port city of Hamburg to meet up with Uncle Johannes' eldest son, his cousin Georg, who would escort him to the *Calypso* and see him safely aboard.

At least, that had been the plan.

But now it was a quarter till one, and the *Calypso* was due to sail with the tide.

Damn him, Conrad swore to himself.

His cousin Georg was perhaps the most amiable person Conrad knew, but his joviality made him constantly tardy and, even at the best of times, hardly reliable. A handsome, albeit slightly pudgy young man, Georg was a womanizing socialite who smoked and drank more than anyone Conrad had ever met.

It was only when the call to muster sounded at his barracks each morning that Georg became the model German soldier: strong, efficient, and cool under fire, to hear his military friends boast of him. Through his new involvement in the munitions industry, Johannes had purchased his carefree son a commission in the German army, and, much to everyone's surprise, Georg had prospered there. Rising quickly through the ranks, he was now a captain in the Imperial artillery regiments in charge of his own battery of six field guns.

But as he was off duty for the week to see Conrad off, he was typical, lovable, aggravating Georg, who at this moment might keep Conrad from catching his ship.

Conrad refolded his newspapers and checked his pocket watch again.

Ten till one.

Conrad glanced quickly down at his heavy steamer trunk and several other suitcases piled beside him on the street outside the quaint hotel where he and Georg had spent the night.

Georg had insisted that he and Conrad rent a room for their final night in Hamburg. They'd spent the better part of it slipping in and out of bars where Georg seemed to know everyone. Georg and his small army of friends had bought Conrad drinks, and a pretty redhead named Sofia, urged on by Georg and the others, had even danced with him and sat in his lap at the table. It had been by far the best night of Conrad's life.

But when Conrad had rolled out of bed late this morning, his head pounding like a thunderstorm, Georg was nowhere to be found. Conrad had changed quickly, eaten a quick meal at the hotel restaurant, and asked the hotel bellhop to bring his luggage to the street curb.

Conrad checked his watch again and swore under his breath. He was regretting turning down the night clerk's offer to arrange a carriage for him in the morning.

As the seconds began ticking away loudly in his mind, Conrad folded his hands together and began to count to one hundred. His mother had taught him this trick after the first time she'd found him behind the house, collapsed in a heap and struggling to breathe. The doctor had arrived to diagnose Conrad with asthma and had mentioned that if Conrad were a continually nervous child, his asthma would only get worse and might perhaps kill him.

That night as she tucked him into bed, Georgina had told Conrad to fold his hands together over his chest and count to one hundred. She had called it a game, though Conrad had never thought it much fun.

"By the time you reach one hundred, your worries will all be gone," his mother had assured him.

He'd fallen asleep that night before he'd made it halfway, but he still sometimes found himself counting in his head whenever he felt his heart racing and his breath turning shallow.

Eins...zwei...drei...

By the time he'd counted to seventy-two, he was about to abandon his luggage and make a run for the docks when an open-aired carriage made a wild, fast-paced turn around the corner up the street. Conrad shouted in surprise as Georg yanked back on the reins and brought a magnificent two-horse team to a stop in front of the hotel.

"Conrad!" Georg's little sister Frieda shouted in greeting from the back.

A small blonde head popped up from the carriage next to Frieda. It was their four-year-old brother.

"Connie!" Justus shouted happily, waving his tiny hands rapidly.

Conrad smiled in surprise to see his cousins and waved back as Georg leapt down from the driver's bench and grabbed Conrad in a strong embrace. Although nearly a foot shorter than his cousin, Georg's every movement radiated energy. Conrad's thin frame appeared smaller when the two stood side by side.

"Good morning, Connie!" Georg said with a big smile. "Are you ready for this grand adventure of yours?"

"Yes," Conrad replied with a hurried politeness as he looked down at his watch yet again. "If I haven't already missed it."

"Ahk!" Georg called as he handed the bellhop a few marks and started to lift Conrad's luggage into the carriage. "You worry too much, cousin! I've rented us the fastest horses in Hamburg. We'll be at the docks in plenty of time! I just needed to pick up my sister and baby brother at the train station. They couldn't let you leave without seeing you off properly!"

"This is so exciting, Connie!" Frieda said as Conrad and Georg hoisted the heavy steamer trunk into the carriage. "Do you suppose you'll see elephants out of your bedroom window? Oh, Ara Egger just returned from her father's embassy in Togoland. Is that near Southwest Africa? She's been going on and on about these bright pink feathers she showed me that belonged to some funny-looking bird called a flamingo. You'll be sure to bring me back a present, won't you, Connie?"

"What about the lions?" little Justus piped in his limited speech, pronouncing the German word, *löwe*, with a few extra e's. "Don't get eaten, Connie!"

"Hush now, you two," Georg said as he and Conrad climbed up onto the driver's bench of the carriage. "Your poor cousin's already nervous enough without you badgering him."

Georg slapped Conrad on the back and shot him an impish smile.

"Onward, then?" Georg asked.

"Please," Conrad replied, resisting the urge to check his pocket watch again.

Georg cracked the reins, and the two horses leapt at his command and rattled down the cobblestone streets of Hamburg. Conrad clung to the small driver's bench, his slim frame shaking with the vibrations. Georg chatted as he tore past slower carriages and responded amiably each time someone on the streets cursed his reckless driving.

Frieda and Justus took turns pouring questions into Conrad's ear over the clatter of the hooves. Conrad tried to answer them pleasantly, still clutching the small bench and trying not to think about the time.

After a few stressful minutes and several attempts at checking his watch, Conrad let out an anxious sigh as Hamburg's grand dockyard came into view with row after row of dreadnaughts, steamers, and luxury liners lazily bobbing up and down in port.

Each moment after that passed painfully. Each ticking second felt to Conrad as if an ant was burrowing and crawling beneath his skin. The elderly customs official dropped Conrad's papers before he could stamp them, and the dockside porters Georg hired seemed to take a lifetime to locate the right ship for his luggage.

But at last, Conrad found himself at the correct dock, the *Calypso*'s proud steel hull pulling at her moorings in the swelling tide. She seemed as eager as Conrad to set sail for the wilds of Africa. Two small tugboats pulled up alongside the *Calypso*, their captains impatient to begin pulling the great ship out to sea.

"Good thing you got here when you did," the Port Master told Conrad as he walked the last few feet down the long gangplanks. "I've just finished my inspection. She'd have left without you if you'd been another minute late. Up you go."

The Port Master beckoned up to the *Calypso*'s main deck and Conrad nodded, turning around to give his cousins one last goodbye.

Yet as he hugged little Justus and gave Frieda a kiss goodbye, the reality of what he was about to do suddenly sunk in. The past three weeks had flown by in such a blur that Conrad had never really considered that he was *actually* being shipped out to Africa!

The *Calypso* was going to take him out of poverty, but it was also going to take him over seven thousand miles away to a world he knew absolutely nothing about.

I can't go to Africa! Conrad suddenly wanted to scream. God, I could die out there!

But then Georg clasped his shoulder and whispered in Conrad's ear too low for Frieda and Justus to hear.

"Courage," he said. "You'll be all right."

Georg then broke off with a smile.

"Go on now, Conrad!" he teased. "Those horses cost me far too much for you not to get yourself aboard that ship!"

Conrad laughed, his tensions and fears mercifully dulled for a moment. He nodded to Georg, who grinned broadly. Then he raced up the gangplank before his brief courage failed him.

The *Calypso*'s deep whistle sounded as Conrad stepped onto the ship's main deck, the sailors not even waiting for his last step as they began to rapidly pull in the gangplank.

No turning back now, Conrad thought.

The whistle blew out another long note, and the mooring lines were tossed off. Conrad stuck his hands in his jacket pockets to calm their shaking. His right hand struck something heavy. From inside his coat pocket, Conrad pulled a small bottle of *Obstwasser*. He uncorked the stopper and took a quick sniff. The sharp tang of sweet fruit was so overpowering it nearly knocked him over the railings.

Pear schnapps, Conrad recognized instantly. Good lord, this stuff's rare!

A third whistle blew as the two tugboats began to slowly shepherd the *Calypso* out of the port.

Conrad turned back and looked over the *Calypso*'s railing down at the wharves now fading quickly behind the ocean liner. Georg stood waving at him with his siblings and laughed when Conrad waved back and pointed at the small, glass bottle in his hand.

"A gift from me!" Georg called up from the docks. "Don't drink it all at once! And try not to get eaten in Africa!"

Conrad laughed back, and he waved at the disappearing docks until his arm was sore and they faded from sight. The other passengers and crew bustled around the deck in all directions, but out on the open, gray water with Germany growing smaller and smaller in the distance, Conrad felt suddenly, truly, alone.

Once again, he found himself counting.

Eins...zwei...drei...

"Well," he said aloud after a moment. "Here I go."

Taking a long pull from the bottle Georg had adroitly slipped him, and his throat burning with the taste of pear, he went to find his cabin.

CHAPTER TWO

MAY 1903

"They're right whales," Erik said over the wind. "Southern right whales to be exact."

The *Calypso* cut effortlessly through the mild morning surf as Conrad watched the pod of whales roll playfully over the water's surface. Erik had said they might spot a whale or two on the final morning of their voyage as they approached the shore, but the ocean liner's passengers had great luck: an entire family of the creatures began trailing the *Calypso* just after sunrise.

"They're quite odd fish, really," Erik said to the small crowd of spectators gathered around him. "Sometimes they'll trail after us for hours, thinking the *Calypso's* one of them! Only give up when one of the bigger ones gets wise enough and gives us a bump."

Conrad watched a particularly large whale blow a high stream of water in the air before tearing himself from the railing.

"You'll remember our arrangement, Erik?" Conrad called as he began to move away from the small, cheering crowd and toward the ship's aft deck.

"Aye-aye, Herr Huber!" Erik shouted back in mock salute before returning to his collection of awed passengers.

Conrad shook his head fondly as Erik continued his impromptu lecture on the habits of southern right whales. Most anything that came out of Erik's mouth was complete fantasy, but Conrad had to admit the young, sunburned sailor had a flair for showmanship. He also knew more about Walvis Bay than Conrad, despite being about three or four years younger. Erik had experience, real or imagined, and either was more than Conrad had, so he procured Erik's services as a guide and porter for a few of Uncle Johannes' marks.

The *Calypso*'s aft deck was relatively deserted, as many of the passengers were either still bemused by the whales or scurrying below deck to gather their possessions before the ship reached port. When Conrad had first stepped out onto the upper deck this morning, Walvis Bay had only been a small brown and gold line in the distance. Now, as he made his way towards the bow of the ship, the English settlement was fully in view.

Nestled in a vast expanse of bright orange sand dunes, Walvis Bay seemed almost like a child's creation perched precariously close to the sea's edge. The dunes rose and fell before the *Calypso,* dwarfing the wooden steeple of the Anglican church in the town's main square, and casting an imposing shadow over the small brick-and-mortar homes and shops.

"Looks as though the dunes might push it right into the water, doesn't it?"

Conrad had not seen the man next to him on the aft deck at first, but he immediately recognized the friendly tone of Eugen Fischer. A tall, slim man, Fischer had studied medicine and history in Berlin and received a doctorate in experimental medicine and anthropology from the University of Freiburg three years prior.

Nearly thirty, Fischer had sharp features with an aristocratic nose and a well-trimmed, pointed beard. Yet despite his fine wardrobe and congenial smile, the faint, musky smell of old paper and ink always seemed to hover around Fischer, as though his research stayed draped over him like an undershirt.

Finding himself seated next to Eugen Fischer at dinner during their first night aboard the *Calypso* had been a stroke of luck for Conrad. Although a highly regarded medical prodigy, Fischer too knew next to nothing about their mutual destination.

Fischer was heading to Southwest Africa as part of a field research expedition he'd organized to test a new theory of human behavior with his partner, the famous Dr. Theodor Mollison. But given that the renowned anthropologist and financer of their expedition had been quickly confined to his berth due to frequent bouts of seasickness, Fischer found himself at loose ends on the long voyage, and he and Conrad had become daily companions.

"I was just thinking the very same thing, Dr. Fischer," Conrad replied. "I suppose I expected an English colony to be…grander. Walvis Bay looks more like a town of pebble sandcastles on a beach than a bustling port."

Fischer laughed as he reached into his coat to pull out a small photograph.

"That's Africa, I suppose," he said. "Our captain showed me this photograph he took of the German port, Swakopmund, a few miles from here. It might be prettier than Walvis Bay, but the captain assured me their docks were too small for a steamer of our size. Far simpler to immigrate through the English port and then clear German customs on the other side, strange as that may sound."

Conrad looked at the photograph Fischer had handed him and nodded in agreement. Swakopmund, while charming with neat rows of German-styled cottages, looked more like a coastal resort village than a proper port city. No doubt a ship of the *Calypso*'s size would have overwhelmed its small dockyard.

"What is making all that ungodly noise?" Fisher suddenly asked as Conrad returned the photograph to him. The deep, bellowed breaths of the whales had been replaced by a steady cawing over the dunes. As Fischer asked the question, a large black bird landed right next to them on the ship's railing, startling several nearby sailors, and nearly knocking a shocked Fischer overboard.

"*Verdammt nochmal* that nasty thing!" Fischer swore as Conrad helped him to his feet. "What the hell is that monster?"

The large bird cocked its head to the side and stared at Fischer as if in disbelief that the incident could've possibly been its fault. About the size of a sleek goose, the bird was completely black except for the outlining area of its mouth that announced its prominence in a vibrant shade of orange. Its feathers looked velvety, almost as though dipped in oil. But its most bizarre feature was a sack-like bulge at the top of its gullet that vibrated at a constant, rapid pace.

"It's a Cape cormorant," Erik said, dutifully drifting over to the aft deck now that the whale-watching crowd had been captivated by something else. "They're native to this part of Southwest Africa. They build their nests just on the other side of these dunes in perfect circles that stretch for miles in the sand. They flock to the coast this time of year to breed. There are so many of the creatures that they have to build their nests out of pecking range of one another. See here, this one is vibrating his neck, almost in the way a dog pants? It's to keep himself cool in the heat."

The cormorant, as if insulted by this discussion of its anatomy, took off from the railing with a loud squawk and headed towards the sand dunes.

"You're going to want to shed those coats, gentlemen," Erik added once the cormorant had gone. "The bird has the right of it. Cool enough out here on the bay, but on a bad day with people shoving and jostling about, the customs office can feel like an oven once we make port."

Most passengers heeded Erik's advice and hurried back to their cabins to change into something more suitable for the city streets. But a few stubborn traditionalists remained on deck, determined to greet the savageness of Africa with the strict and proper coat and tie of the civilized world.

Fischer straightened a crease in his shirt where the cormorant had caused him to stumble.

"I suppose I'd best rouse Theodor and see if I can't manage to get him to keep something down before we disembark."

The young doctor offered his hand in a warm goodbye, which Conrad shook reluctantly. He had never met anyone as educated as Dr. Fischer before. Fischer had been fascinating to listen to as he recounted great moments in scientific history over dinner. He had been rather mum on the subject of his medical research in Southwest Africa, and Conrad had not wanted to be rude by pressing the matter. He had greatly enjoyed talking with Fischer and felt he would miss his company a great deal.

"Listen, Conrad," Fischer said before they parted. "If they ever give you a holiday away from the Commissioner's Office in Windhoek, why not come visit Theodor and me in Lüderitz? It's a fair trek, to be sure, but I'm to understand this colony has a passable railway system, and I'm sure I could acquire a bottle of two of something decent."

"I'd love to!" Conrad replied, hoping the fear of being left alone in a few moments was not too apparent in his voice.

"Splendid!" Fischer said. "I'll send a telegram to the Commissioner's Office once we've gotten ourselves settled. *Viel Glück*, Conrad!"

Fischer disappeared below deck to attempt to revive his infirm partner as Conrad turned to stare back at the fast-approaching shoreline.

He'd retire to his cabin in a moment to exchange his suit jacket for one of the crisp khaki shirts that Uncle Johannes had insisted on purchasing for him, but for some reason, he found himself wanting another few moments alone on deck.

The morning's sun had nearly risen to its peak, lighting the sandy orange shore before him in a friendly sheen. The cormorant's calls grew louder, and a soft, gentle breeze blew lightly over the ship. For the first time since leaving Hamburg, Conrad felt his worries and dread give way to excitement.

"Best get ready, Herr Huber," Erik said beside him. "Don't want to keep the dockhands waiting!"

*

If Walvis Bay had seemed like a small and lonely outpost from the *Calypso's* decks, amidst its bustling docks and crowded streets the town seemed like a strange metropolis. No sooner had Conrad changed into his khaki shirt and trousers and double-checked that all his belongings were stowed and accounted for than the largest man Conrad had ever seen walked into his room on Erik's heels.

"We've docked, Herr Huber," the redheaded youth announced proudly. "This is Christoph. He will take your things to the customs building."

Before Conrad could respond, the giant of a man swung Conrad's heavy steamer trunk onto his shoulder with a deep, short grunt. Christoph's head barely cleared the ceiling of Conrad's small cabin. Yet despite his size and height, Christoph moved gracefully, scooping up another of Conrad's bags in his free hand before heading for the ship's gangplank and the customs office below.

As Conrad followed Erik down the gangplank, he was amazed at the dockhands they passed. Conrad had seen dark-skinned men before, albeit briefly around the docks of Hamburg in the few days before his departure, but he had never seen so many of such different shades. Most of the men in Hamburg had been light-skinned Turks and Arabs, but Christoph's skin was the color of burnt coffee. They passed another dockhand scrambling up the gangplank to assist a different passenger with their luggage, and this man was short and thin, with a complexion that reminded Conrad of cinnamon.

"They all come in from their villages when a large ocean liner arrives," Erik informed him as they both passed through customs. "Dozens of 'em. Scores, really. Damara, Nama, Kavango, Tswana, Himba, Ovambo, and Herero. I couldn't begin to tell them apart to tell the truth. I think Christoph here is a Kavango from one of the nearby fishing villages. I don't know about the others. The big man is always standing around the docks every time the *Calypso* docks, and we've struck up a small partnership, you might say."

Conrad couldn't see how Erik would have known anything about Christoph, much less struck up a business partnership with him. Christoph did not strike Conrad as the conversational type.

"Is his name really Christoph?" Conrad asked Erik discreetly as the big man ducked inside a small building at the end of the pier.

Erik shrugged.

"I wouldn't know," Erik said indifferently. "He probably had some tribal name once that you and I couldn't begin to pronounce. The missionaries have been slowly straightening all that out, though. More baptized Christophs and Wilhelms running around now than cow herders in loincloths, at any rate. Easier to tell the Christian darkies from the savage ones, that's for sure."

Erik went inside after Christoph. Conrad followed close behind.

After a short stint in the stuffy and crowded customs office, a sweaty and curt secretary stamped Conrad's passport and waved him through the exit. Conrad followed Erik and Christoph out into the tightly packed dirt roads.

The sounds of the city hit Conrad like a wave.

As Erik led them down the main square, Conrad turned his head in every direction, feebly trying to establish his bearings. All around him Africans shouted, cooked, cursed, bartered, and laughed, while small packs of white Englishmen in bowler hats and starched shirts smoked cigars and strode absently down the main streets. Conrad could not make any sense of the hubbub.

He'd envisioned arriving in Africa hundreds of times since leaving Hamburg. He'd imagined himself gutted and roasted by a pack of roving cannibals, worshipped by people who had never seen a white man, or left abandoned in the sheer wilderness, the sole survivor of a terrible shipwreck on an unforgiving coast.

But amidst the civil congestion, Conrad felt completely confused by his first glimpse of Africa. Everywhere the crowds were moving, teeming, never leaving the same scene in his view for longer than a moment. Conrad could not find a single African clad in the long raffia robes that dominated the advertisements for the Kamerun colony. Instead, on one side of the street clusters of old Black men in coats and trousers held court around their favorite market stands. The rival vendors shouted at and laughed with another as younger men stoked large, boiling vats of sweet-smelling fruit and small boys spooned a hot, red liquid into their customers' bowls.

Several tall women dotted Conrad's view as well, their dark skin bolded by the rich, vibrant hues of their long, Victorian dresses. Each sported a matching headboard as well, a pronged, cloth headpiece that mirrored the swirling patterns of their dresses. They reminded Conrad of bull's horns.

Children were running everywhere, and the few white policemen Conrad saw watched the chaos in detached indifference.

He could never pick an individual out from the masses for long before they were swept away by someone even stranger.

Along one street, a group of men they passed might've been from another world. Most stood nearly naked, a thick loincloth their only attempt at clothing. Each loincloth had a small "tail" that covered the men's backsides and Conrad stared open-mouthed as Erik led him past them. These men stood apart from the rest of the dockyard, several of them eyeing the new arrivals with undisguised contempt. One of them met Conrad's eye and held his gaze challengingly.

"Herero," Erik explained as he touched Conrad arm and hurried him along the street. "They're not the friendliest of natives."

After a period of weaving through the dusty streets, Erik sensed Conrad's fading energy. He whispered something to Christoph, who nodded his understanding and continued on with Conrad's luggage in what Conrad could only assume was the direction of the train depot. Despite the weight of Conrad's trunk, Christoph lumbered on through the mass of people, his massive neck and arms slick with perspiration.

According to Herr Kleinschmidt's assistant, who had sent Conrad a frustratingly terse telegram from before departing Hamburg, he was to meet a Mr. Beaunard Hertzog at the train station in Walvis Bay. Mr. Hertzog would accompany him by overnight train to Windhoek and then escort him to the Commissioner's Residence, where Conrad would be living for the duration of his tour.

Of course, he thought, these instructions were all rather useless if he died of a stroke shortly after arriving.

"Perhaps a short respite from all the excitement, Herr Huber?" Erik asked with a veteran smile at Conrad's reaction to the pulse of the city.

Conrad opened his mouth to respond, but both his nose and mouth seemed caked in dryness. His words caught in his throat.

"Christoph will take your bags to the train," Erik continued, not waiting for a response before he began dragging Conrad down a nearby alley. "He'll find Mr. Hertzog and send him our way while we raise a drink to celebrate your safe arrival in Africa!"

Conrad merely nodded. At that moment, the offer of a cold beer was too alluring to refuse.

Ducking and squeezing between the press of buildings, stalls, and foreign sailors seeking refuge from the chaos, Conrad followed Erik through the blessedly shaded alleyway, finally arriving at a small café tucked up between a leatherworker's shop and a slightly hidden Lutheran church.

In other circumstances, Conrad might've protested the foul odor of tanned leather, but once he stepped into the shaded awning, he collapsed into a chair at the first open table. A tough-looking Black woman with broad shoulders and a stained apron walked up to Erik with a grimace as they sat down, saying nothing as Erik ordered two beers. Conrad suppressed a sudden groan. If the beverages were anything akin to the rest of his experiences in Africa so far, well, at least it would be wet.

The woman set down two generous glasses of golden lager overflowing with thick foam. Conrad gawked at his beer, and Erik laughed.

"You were expecting rhino piss, maybe? You are in *German* Africa, Herr Huber! Beer is one thing you shan't have to settle for here. Oh, no—Windhoek alone has six beer halls!"

Conrad took a small, hesitant sip.

It was delicious. He began to gulp down the thick lager thirstily, but Erik reached out a hand to stop him.

"Easy now, Herr Huber," he explained. "Too much too quickly will make you miserable."

Conrad nodded, a little embarrassed at his own rudeness. Erik just shrugged knowingly.

The two sat and talked for an hour or so in the quaint alley café. Conrad sat mostly in silence while Erik regaled him with long, winding stories of all the ports he'd visited from Gabon to Singapore. Conrad felt himself begin to relax. Everyone in the packed café was speaking either English or German, and with a second lager in front of him and the Lutheran church bells ringing above, he might have been in some back alley of Hamburg.

Perhaps this won't be so bad, Conrad thought. If there are such established towns here, then maybe I won't be exposed to anything too wild or dangerous. After all, I am not a soldier, and the Commissioner could hardly expect me to....

"I sink dis must be de place, ja?"

Conrad turned in his chair to see Christoph's enormous frame filling the alleyway and a small, blond man heading towards him.

"Are you Herr Huber?" the man asked as he approached their table.

"I am," Conrad said, barely having time to stand before the man shook his hand with great enthusiasm.

"*Willkommen* to Africa, Herr Huber," he said in a singsong voice that echoed off the café's brick walls. "I am Beaunard Hertsog, de oferseer of de railway construction for dis colony. It is a great pleasure to be meeting you."

Beaunard was so energetic, Conrad nearly laughed with relief as he shook the small, white man's hand. Erik had told him a few days ago that the man he was supposed to meet with in Walvis Bay was a Boer, a descendant of the first Dutch farmers to settle in Southern Africa and who had named the town Walvis or Whale Bay. One of the most prominent businessmen in the colony, Beaunard made up for his short stature with boundless energy and a love of all things commercial.

Conrad had been prepared for all of that, but he was forced to suppress a chuckle every time Beaunard began to speak. The usual fast-paced Dutch was hardly noticeable in the colloquial rise and fall of Beaunard's Afrikaans. His voice sounded like a wood instrument playing a scale. Conrad could almost see each word bopping up and down a metered score as Beaunard's octave rose and fell with certain words.

But as humorous as the man's voice might be, Conrad was immensely glad to have found him and returned his eager handshake.

"The pleasure is all mine, Mr. Hertzog."

"Oh please," the small man said as he smiled warmly. "Call me, Beaunard. But if you are ready, Herr Huber. I sink we had best be going if we are to catch de train."

"I'll leave you here then, Herr Huber," Erik said as he stood to leave. "Christoph will see you and Mr. Hertzog to the train. I wish you a very pleasant tour of Africa."

Conrad paid for their drinks and bid Erik farewell, handing him the few promised marks, which Erik pocketed masterfully in one quick, smiling movement.

"Shall we?" Beaunard asked happily.

"After you," Conrad replied with a nervous grin.

Following Christoph through the crowds, they made good time and arrived at the train depot five minutes before the train was scheduled to leave. Conrad peeled off several marks and tried to hand the stack to Christoph, but the big man took only three notes and handed the rest back to Conrad.

"Too much," Christoph said in a voice so deep it might've frightened thunder.

Conrad was about to insist that Christoph accept more, but the giant had already turned to leave without another word.

"All aboard!" the conductor yelled.

Conrad hurried aboard behind Beaunard and found that his luggage had been stowed neatly in the storage compartments at the front of the car. The train car was opulently adorned in leather seats and smelled of cigar smoke and brandy. Every soul in the first car was white, and Conrad recognized one or two from the *Calypso*.

As he settled into a comfortable chair across from Beaunard, Conrad could make out Christoph's large frame amongst a group of Black porters wading back into the press of the main crowd. Conrad wasn't sure but he thought he saw Christoph hand two of his three notes to a small, ragged-looking child before disappearing out of view.

"Will you take some wine with me, Conrat?" Beaunard asked, snapping Conrad's attention away from the window. "It is such a long, warm trip and some chilled wine will help keep us cool."

"Oh, um, yes thank you," Conrad answered. "I'd love some."

Beaunard smiled and motioned at the train car's attendant, who returned smartly with two glasses and a bottle of wine.

"To Africa!" Beaunard said, pouring them both a tumbler.

"To Africa," Conrad replied.

CHAPTER 3

MAY 1903

"Pardon me, sir, but Herr Hertzog requested I wake you when we were an hour away from the Windhoek station."

Conrad opened his eyes slowly and nodded at the elderly attendant who had just shaken him awake. The old man had light brown skin that faded effortlessly into his clean-pressed, tan uniform and a tidy shock of silver hair that peeked professionally from beneath his cap.

"Thank you, Mikal," Conrad said through a gaping yawn. "Is Beaunard awake yet?"

"Attending to some matters with the conductor in the next car forward, Herr Huber. He should return momentarily."

Conrad nodded through another yawn and caught a glimpse of his disheveled reflection in the window.

"Um, Mikal," Conrad started hopefully. "I don't suppose there's anywhere I might…."

"I've a basin of warm water and a razor at the back of the car, Herr Huber," Mikal answered, producing a small washcloth from behind his back and handing it to Conrad. "The railway's smooth for the next few miles, sir, but I'd advise you to make quick work of a shave before the track gets rougher near the outskirts of the town. Would you care for a bit of breakfast this morning, Herr Huber?"

Conrad rose from his leather seat and blinked a few times.

"I don't suppose you have any tea, Mikal?" Conrad asked sheepishly, embarrassed by how quickly he was getting used to having someone wait on him.

He'd found maids and butlers suffocating in his uncle's home, but now that he was alone in Africa, he found himself clinging to this small privilege like a life preserver.

"As luck would have it, Herr Huber," Mikal replied with a soft smile and a wink. "I happen to have some red bush tea I think you'll enjoy, sir. It's brewed from leaves that grow right alongside these tracks. It's a bit strong, but add a pinch of sugar, and I believe it will do nicely."

Mikal left to fetch the tea, and Conrad made his way past several still-sleeping passengers to the basin. He took Mikal's advice, grooming himself as best he could with the soft rocking of the train car. He made quick work of the stubble, relishing the feel of the hot water and cotton towel against his skin. When he returned to his seat, he found Beaunard waiting for him.

"*Guten Morgen*, Conrat!" Beaunard said cheerfully. "Dit you sleep well, I hope?"

"Wonderfully," Conrad replied, returning Beaunard's smile. "The wine was an excellent help." Beaunard had been right about the wine. After the two of them had polished off the bottle, they had both slumped euphorically into a dreamless sleep that had lasted clear through the warm night. Their train had departed around six the previous evening, and now, nearly twelve hours later, the sun was rising in an orange and pink sky.

Beaunard chuckled, an odd mix of humming and singing.

"It is a goot fix for a long trip, I sink," he said, pleased. "But it will be much better once I make de improfements to de track next year."

Beaunard had opened his window, and a cold, desert breeze washed over Conrad, flushing the last remnants of sleep from his limbs.

Mikal returned with the red tea, and Conrad wrapped his cold fingers around the hot cup. He thanked Mikal, who smiled back and left to wake the remaining passengers.

As Conrad sipped his drink, Beaunard chatted amiably about the state of the colony's rail lines. Commissioner Leutwein had hired Beaunard as the railroad overseer the previous year, and the small Afrikaner had already launched a series of aggressive expansion plans.

"I tell you, Conrat," he said, pride animating his whole face. "We shall be able to travel from any station in de colony to efen the smallest village within fife years! Dat will give de pompous English and French engineers in Africa a goot thrashing!"

Conrad nodded along politely, until something caught his eye.

As the train rounded a bend in the track, a series of large, fenced-in structures slowly came into view outside the sprawling outline of Windhoek. The fences were made of tightly layered barbwire, and each of the four structures he saw appeared to have several guard towers and an imposing front gate.

Conrad's heart beat a little faster. They must be approaching a public safari park, he thought, with a collection of African wildlife corralled for the public in elaborately constructed pens.

But instead of the elephants, giraffes, and lions Conrad expected to see, the train sped quickly past the sun-lined, dark faces of hundreds of Africans.

Conrad slowly put his tea aside, craning his neck to keep looking behind him as the train rapidly put the fences behind it.

"Beaunard," Conrad finally asked when the barbwire was out of view, his voice crackling slightly with shock. "What were those?"

"Hmm?" Beaunard replied, turning back to Conrad from a newspaper he'd begun reading. "What waz what?"

"Those…prisons," Conrad answered, somewhat bewildered. "Who are those people in them?"

"Prisons?" Beaunard asked, looking genuinely confused for a moment. "Ah, you mean de camps."

"Camps?" Conrad asked.

"Yes, yes," Beaunard explained as though he was discussing some trivial affair. "Dis is where we keep de *Hottentots* who make lots of trouble for de colonial authorities. Sey are a bit of an eyesore, I admit, but a necessary burden for the time being."

Conrad could feel a small lump beginning to form in his throat.

"Necessary?" he asked hesitantly.

"Oh, ja I'm afrait," Beaunard said nonchalantly, as he folded his newspaper. "Nine years ago, dere was de Hottentot rising under Hendrik Witbooi."

"Hottentots are what we call the darkies down here," a kind-looking gentleman added when he saw Conrad's look of confusion.

Conrad nodded, not knowing what else to do.

"I believe Witbooi and his followers were Nama, but who really knows with Hottentots," the man continued. "Anyway, that Witbooi is a nasty thing. Shot his brother over the chiefdom of some small village near Windhoek, I believe, and started building up a small army of bandits and thieves. Wasn't long before he went around calling himself the 'King of Great Namaqualand'.

"His followers finally got bold enough to attack the garrison at Hornkranz a while back. There was some nasty fighting for a few months, but the Commissioner eventually bought Witbooi off after the fighting at Gurus in '94. Now the Hottentot and his men work for the *Schutztruppe*, helping round up other insurgent tribes."

Beaunard gave Conrad a jovial slap on the back.

"We need de camps to keep de Hottentots from making trouble. But not for long, ja? You are here to help Commissioner Leutwein with dese nasty Nama."

The other gentleman chuckled as he excused himself and went to check his luggage. Conrad swallowed hard, trying to push down the lump in his throat.

Beaunard seemed to notice Conrad tense and patted his knee as Mikal arrived to clear away their breakfast.

"Do not worry, Conrat," he said nonchalantly. "We are joking with you. Sey are not all bat, de Nama. Why, Mikal, you are a Nama, ja?"

"Yes, Herr Hertzog," Mikal replied cordially. "I am."

Mikal cleared away the dishes as the train began to slow. Beaunard slipped his paper into his bag and got to his feet.

"Shall we go meet de Commissioner?" he said cheerfully.

Conrad felt his stomach churn.

*

The Commissioner's Residence was enormous. Schwerinsburg, one of three large, castle-like estates that surrounded Windhoek, reminded Conrad of the great American cotton plantations he'd seen in photographs. A grand porch wrapped around the main house, offering a shaded veranda for important visitors who might come to call on the Commissioner. The house itself was modest in its design, a few brightly painted shutters and enough extra bedrooms for five or six guests. But situated on a shady hill overlooking the rest of Windhoek, the Residence seemed somehow grander than a Schloss.

A stone wall surrounded the Residence grounds, which included a small garden with a gurgling fountain and an impressive bloom of pink and blue hydrangeas. A coach house and stable were visible behind the main house, as well as a few manicured cottages for the Commissioner's aides and their families.

When their train arrived at the station, Beaunard arranged with the station conductor for Conrad's luggage to be delivered to the Residence. Then, suggesting they stretch their legs a bit, he led Conrad into town.

If Walvis Bay had been chaos, Windhoek itself seemed a sanctuary of order and civility. Though small, Windhoek was one of the few towns in this part of the world to have been laid out on a grid. The influence of German architecture was abundant.

The whole place felt new. Its buildings shone brightly in the sunshine, and its brass doorknobs and freshly painted window frames had not yet been worn away by the creeping sand.

As they approached Schwerinsburg's main gate, Conrad and Beaunard were met by two enormous, red-haired hounds who leapt down from the front porch.

"*Hallo*, Gustavus and Ivan," Beaunard cooed at the big dogs as he opened the gate.

The two dogs recognized Beaunard instantly. They jumped playfully around him, each vying for a pat on the head and the scraps of his breakfast that Beaunard produced from his trouser pockets.

"Sey are Rhodesian lion dogs," Beaunard explained as he scratched the ear of the one called Ivan. "Sey are de best hunters in de worlt. Sey can smell a lion from nearly two kilometerz away! A personal gift to de Commissioner from de Kaiser himself."

Beaunard walked past the two dogs and up onto the main porch, continuing to list the wondrous attributes and mannerisms of Leutwein's pets. With the little man gone, Gustavus and Ivan both turned their attention to Conrad.

The two dogs looked similar to a British Labrador except for an odd streak of dark fur on their backs, ridge-like, that cut against the rest of their orange-brown coat. Conrad held his breath while the two dogs sniffed the air around him to see if he was worth the trouble of exploring further. After a brief once-over, the two seemed to deem Conrad unworthy of their attention and loped off toward the back of the house. Conrad breathed a sigh of relief and hurried onto the veranda after Beaunard.

A young Black boy answered Beaunard's knock on the Residence door, his voice cracking with angst.

"The Commissioner's in a meeting with the garrison commander, sir," the boy told Beaunard. "But I can bring you up to the office when he's done."

"No need," Beaunard replied with a sudden, terse wave of his hand. "We can fint the Commissioner ourselves."

Beaunard's coolness surprised Conrad, but the young footman seemed to be relieved at his dismissal and quickly fled down the hall.

"Well," Beaunard said, turning back to Conrad with warmth and cheer. "*Willkomen* to your new home, Conrat. Woult you care for a whiskey? Leutwein always keeps de cabinets well stocket."

Beaunard laughed at his own jest and, with the ease of familiarity, departed down the hall without waiting for Conrad's reply.

Left alone in the grand house's reception hall and not wanting to make eye contact with the fearsome-looking buffalo mounted above the doorway, Conrad wandered slowly into the next room. Beaunard's chirping voice floated down the halls, dulled only by the clanking of crystal glassware from somewhere in the house.

Conrad, only half-listening to Beaunard's patter, found himself in a library majestically adorned with shelf after shelf of leather-bound books and a rack of antique and exotic-looking firearms. A full lion's skin lay draped triumphantly over the mantel. Conrad glanced out the window and breathed another sigh of relief that Leutwein's hunting dogs had not found him more interesting.

Thick, green drapes blocked out much of the hot daylight, giving the room a pleasant, restful air. Conrad noticed a small figurine on a nearby table. The figure, which looked as though it were made of clay, had been painstakingly carved into a monstrous creature, half woman and half python. He picked up the statue, wondering as he studied it if Frieda would consider such an odd totem a more impressive present than Ara Egger's flamingo feathers.

As he was about to return the strange object to its proper place, Conrad heard someone crying. He followed the sound back out into the hallway, where he found the young Black servant crying softly by the main staircase.

The boy tried to pull himself together when he saw Conrad, and he wiped his nose on a coat sleeve several sizes too large for him.

"Did you need anything, sir?" the boy asked him through half-sobs.

Conrad was nonplussed. He had little experience with children, having only been around Frieda and Justus for a few weeks at his uncle's house; he'd never seen either of them cry before.

"Er...no, I'm fine, thank you," Conrad said.

Perhaps the boy wanted to be left alone. He remembered hiding from other boys in Aschaffenburg when he had cried, not wanting any of them to think he was weak.

"Are you alright?" he asked the boy after a moment.

The boy did not answer. Conrad guessed from the way he had fled so quickly from Beaunard that the boy was frightened of the Afrikaner.

"Do you know what I do sometimes when I'm scared?"

The boy still did not speak but shook his head in reply.

"I like to count to a hundred," Conrad told him. "By the time I'm done, I've forgotten what it was I was scared of. Do you want to try it with me?"

There were still tears in the boy's eyes, but he nodded slowly and began to count with Conrad.

"*Eins…zwei…drei…*"

When they got to ten, the boy stopped and looked down at his feet.

"What's the matter?" Conrad asked him.

"I don't know how to count any higher in German," the boy said, looking down.

Conrad could see the boy was about to burst into tears again. He knelt to the boy's height and placed his free hand on his shoulder.

"What's your name?" he asked him.

The boy looked hesitantly at Conrad as if unsure if Conrad could be trusted.

"Petyr," he said after a long pause.

"Well, Petyr," Conrad said. "It's nice to meet you. My name is Conrad. Would you like me to teach you how to count higher in German?"

Petyr nodded.

"All right then," Conrad said. "After *zehn* comes *elf.*"

"*Elf,*" Petyr repeated, his pronunciation harsh as he struggled with the unfamiliar tongue.

"Good," Conrad said. "Then comes *zwölf.*"

When they'd counted to twenty, Petyr seemed to calm down a little as he tried to remember each new number. Conrad realized he was still holding the statue in his hand, and he guided Petyr toward the library.

"That's very good," Conrad told him. Then after *zwanzig* comes…"

As they stepped back into the library, Conrad realized they were not alone. A woman stood watching them appraisingly. Conrad suddenly felt as though he had done something wrong.

The woman was dressed as a maid, but she moved quickly about the room as though it were hers. She bent over the tables of knick knacks, dusting and polishing each item efficiently, with practiced skill. Though her thick dress obscured a good deal of her body, her lithe movements suggested slim, graceful limbs, and her hands and cheeks were a deep, umber brown.

She was tall, almost the same height as Conrad, with a swan-like neck and a short, boyish head of woolly black hair.

She had clearly heard Conrad talking to Petyr in the hallway, and now that they had entered her domain, she paused in her work and watched the two of them with analyzing coolness. Petyr's face was still puffy from crying, and the woman examined Conrad with deep-set eyes that shocked him. Although her skin was brown, she stared at him with pale blue eyes that seemed to accuse him of several things at once.

The woman had been humming as she worked, and the song's haunting tune still hung in the room like a whisper. As he was trying to think of how to explain to the woman that he had not made the boy cry, his hand slipped, and he dropped the statue in his hand.

The snake woman hit the floor with a loud crash and shattered at Conrad's feet.

Petyr bolted from the room.

The woman continued to stare at him with baffling hostility.

Conrad remained frozen in place. It was as though he were standing face to face with a great, angry cat, peering at him with alarming interest. He wanted to apologize, but his words caught in his throat. He could only look down dumbly at the expensive rug and the broken pieces.

"Goot news, Conrat," Beaunard sang as he entered the room with two generous glasses in hand. "Leutwein has improvet his stock! Sey have de..."

Beaunard stopped abruptly at the sight of the woman. His brow furrowed when he noticed the broken bauble on the floor. The woman met his gaze defiantly.

"*Domme doos!*" Beaunard, red-faced, cursed in his native tongue. "Look what you haf done now, you foolish woman! Get out of de room when your betters are present. Be gone!"

Conrad didn't know what a '*doos*' was, but given the circumstances, he couldn't imagine that it was a flattering term. He opened his mouth to protest, but his voice caught in his throat. He was frozen, too embarrassed to admit that he had been the one that had broken the statue.

Beaunard handed Conrad one of the whiskey glasses, despite the early hour, and dismissed the woman with his free hand. The woman's eyes glinted. For a moment, Conrad thought she might inform the little Boer man that it was Conrad who had broken the Commissioner's knickknack. Instead, she ignored him and finished dusting the last bookcase with deliberate slowness before leaving the sunroom.

"*Entschuldigung*, Conrat," Beaunard said, taking a sip of his drink to calm himself once the woman had left. "I apologise. Between you and me, Leutwein does not keep a tight enough leash on dese Hottentots. Sey can so easily forget seir manners."

Beaunard gestured somewhat theatrically toward the door.

"Especially Sybille."

Conrad nodded nervously and sat in one of the great armchairs across from Beaunard, his head still spinning. The fatigue of the ocean voyage and train trip across the DSWA, the talk of rebellious natives, his fearful encounter with the two lion-hunting hounds, the small boy's tears, breaking one of the Commissioner's artifacts, and now Beaunard's unsettling dislike of everyone they'd encountered in the house so far was all a bit too much to contemplate at the moment.

A wonderful start to his African tour!

Conrad folded himself into the armchair, enjoying its momentary respite and concentrating on the feel of the whiskey glass in his hand.

As Beaunard concluded his graphic description of a bull elephant he'd observed mating with a female, he suggested that they venture upstairs to see if the Commissioner's meeting had concluded. Conrad regretfully pried himself from the chair and followed Beaunard up the main staircase.

No sooner had they made it to the top of the stairs, however, before they nearly collided with the Commissioner's previous appointment, a broad-shouldered man in a crisp khaki uniform. His white skin was taut and tanned, and his nose bore the pronounced hook of a veteran fighter who had survived more than his fair share of fights.

"Ah, *hallo*, Major Baumhauer," Beaunard said warmly as he sidestepped to avoid bumping into the man.

The major, red-faced and obviously dissatisfied with the conclusion of his audience, barely nodded in return.

"Major, dis is Conrat Huber," Beaunard continued unabashed. "He has come to be de new aide to de ommissioner."

Major Baumhauer scowled, but he shook Conrad's hand and greeted him with a curt "*Guten Morgen*, Herr Huber" before continuing down the stairs and out the door.

"*Oh liewe*," Beaunard sighed in now-released exasperation. "Sat man is impossible. We best make sure Leutwein is still alive."

Conrad followed Beaunard closely, worried yet *another* surprise might accost him if he did not find Leutwein soon.

The Commissioner was at his desk, a wet cloth draped over his eyes and a barrage of expletives cascading from his mouth.

"Damn these soldiers," he said blindly as Beaunard and Conrad entered the room.

"Beaunard, I'm surrounded on all fronts. Indigenous insurgents, trigger-happy soldiers, and a Kaiser 7,000 miles away who has no sympathy for the patience required to rule His colonies."

Leutwein removed the cloth from his forehead to reveal a pair of etched, gray eyes and a smartly combed mustache. The Commissioner was not as small as Beaunard, but he was slightly built, with pale skin and a manicured presence that seemed at home behind a desk.

The Commissioner donned a pair of tortoiseshell glasses. When he spoke, his voice was clear yet pallid, as though it belonged to an intelligent, exhausted man.

"Is this our new charge?" Leutwein asked, collecting himself and standing to greet Conrad more formally.

"Ja, indeed, Theodor," Beaunard replied. "Dis is Conrat Huber."

"It is an honor to meet you, Herr Leutwein," Conrad said, trying to muster as much ceremony amidst the chaos as he could. "I hope to make you proud, sir."

Leutwein shook Conrad's hand and patted him twice on the back in an avuncular manner.

"Please, call me Theodor," he said, "After all, we shall be working very closely together for some time, and I think you'll find that formalities just get in the way in this house.

"Now, let us put all the unpleasantness of *my* morning behind us and welcome the newest member of my staff to the DSWA properly! You'll stay for lunch, Beaunard?"

"I would not miss it for de worlt, Theodor," Beaunard sang, draining the last of his whiskey and following Leutwein towards the dining room.

*

Conrad was silent throughout most of his welcome meal. Beaunard and Leutwein had much to discuss before Beaunard returned to the railroad's northern field office in Tsumeb, and Conrad's mind was still swirling too much for him to manage anything other than listening.

The colony's new railways were expanding rapidly, but one of Beaunard's overseers continued to report trouble with the locals along the newest rail line between Tsumeb and Grootfontein. Beaunard, who had already traveled to the northern township twice to settle disputes between the natives and his workers, was confident that he could resolve the matter permanently this time, without Leutwein's assistance.

This seemed to relieve Leutwein somewhat, and the two men began chatting amiably with one another, occasionally remembering to bring Conrad into their conversation. Leutwein now and then offered a cross word about the Schutztruppe, the colonial soldiers under his command, but Beaunard did not encourage the Commissioner by responding. Conrad sensed there might be more to the Commissioner's confrontation with the Major this morning than Beaunard had let on. But the little Boer man was clearly not in the mood to debate that with Leutwein this afternoon. Instead, Beaunard shifted the topic to the German government's latest frustrations with their Ottoman allies while Conrad tucked in hungrily to a rack of braised lamb chops in a thick gravy.

Despite not understanding a word of Beaunard's railings against the Sultan's inability to persuade Chinese Muslims to stop attacking Western shipping, Conrad found himself completely enthralled by his first meal in the Commissioner's Residence. Beaunard and Leutwein toasted Conrad often in honor of his safe arrival, and their gossip about the colony and the European theatre cheered the dining room's imposing, dark blue walls, and opulent chandelier.

But while Beaunard and Leutwein's snippets about who was who in the colony and the inner workings of native politics were intriguing, the real point of interest of the afternoon was Sybille. She moved around the room like a hostess, only leaving for brief moments to fetch another decanter or clear away dishes, busying herself with the same steady authority that Conrad had observed earlier.

Whenever Leutwein asked her for something, Sybille would smile sweetly and serve the Commissioner with doting attention. But with Beaunard, Sybille was cold and efficient, and it was clear that Beaunard was certainly not a welcome guest in *her* house. The two made no effort to hide their animosity toward one another, though Leutwein pretended not to notice it.

Conrad appeared to fall somewhere in the middle of these two camps. Sybille spoke very little to him, but her penetrating blue eyes watched him constantly. Whenever he caught her staring at him, Conrad could not force himself to meet meet her eye, knowing that she must be making up her mind as to which of her two camps to put him in.

Conrad muttered a silent prayer that she would not sort him into Beaunard's camp. Though he'd done a poor job of trying to prevent that by not owning up to having broken the statue.

At some point late in the evening, after the lazy luncheon had slipped into a lavish supper followed closely by several cheery schnapps toasts, Leutwein announced that he was retiring for the evening. He gave Conrad instructions to meet him for breakfast at sunrise. Conrad, exhausted, readily agreed and bid the Commissioner and Beaunard goodnight.

The small boy-servant was waiting for Conrad in the main hall, and Conrad followed him to his own lodgings within the Schwerinsburg compound, a sparsely decorated cottage with a screen door and peeling green paint. But Conrad hardly noticed as he thanked the boy and collapsed on his cot-like bed without bothering to undress.

He'd been in the DSWA a scant two days and was already thoroughly overwhelmed and terrified of Africa.

"*Gott rette mich*," he whispered into his pillow, trying desperately to remember the psalms his father had made him memorize as a boy. "God save me."

CHAPTER 4

JULY 1903

The next two months passed quickly.

Leutwein proved to be a meticulous man. He kept excellent records and harbored a keen love for precise instructions, so Conrad found it relatively easy to step into the demands of his daily routine.

Each morning, Conrad rose an hour before the Commissioner and made a quick triage of any mail or telegrams that the butler, a thin Ovambo man named Herman, had laid out in the kitchen for him. Conrad then sorted all correspondence into that which Leutwein needed to address as soon as possible, and those that could wait until he had a spare moment, usually after his luncheon or in between his afternoon appointments.

Conrad was also expected to compile a short oral brief for Leutwein on the minor events of the colony that appeared in the headlines of the Windhoek paper or in a telegram from Berlin. The old man's eagle eye didn't miss much, but his brisk efficiency had a soft side as well, and he made a point of sending a congratulatory telegram on a local mayor's birthday or arranging a round of drinks at his own expense for some of his favorite merchant captains when they returned to Walvis Bay.

And finally, sometime between his own light breakfast and the few minutes he found to hastily groom himself to the polished standards of an Imperial aide, Conrad reviewed Leutwein's list of appointments for the day. In particular, he made a mental note of ones likely to be tiresome for the Commissioner.

Meetings with Adolf Grober, the homely mayor of Windhoek, were often short and civil. Conferences with any of the numerous officials from the colony's mining company, the Deutsche Kolonialgesellschaft, would be well-lubricated with lager from the town's breweries. Leutwein always ended those meetings in good spirits and, more often than not, would ask Conrad to cancel his appointments afterward.

Meetings with the Schutztruppe officials proved more difficult for Conrad to manage. The Commissioner typically left those meetings in a foul mood and with a searing headache. Conrad had been correct in assuming that there was a history of bad blood between Leutwein and the Imperial security troops, or more accurately, between Leutwein and Major Baumhauer. And as Beaunard explained subtly to Conrad one evening, the reasons why were more complicated than just a typical rivalry run afoul.

Prior to Germany's unification, Leutwein had been a prominent major in the Prussian army. When he had, at last, resigned his commission, his political connections had gotten him a post as a lead diplomat in the Colonial Office in Berlin.

In the gilded halls along Wilhelmstrasse, Leutwein had quickly made a name for himself among the Kaiser's top officials for his long, eloquent speeches advocating the need for "colonialism without bloodshed" in Southwest Africa. The age of gunslinging explorers was over, Leutwein argued, and Europe did not need another Henry Stanley leaving a trail of dead and mutilated Africans halfway across the continent.

The Kaiser had been impressed with Leutwein's military record and was eager to install a new Commissioner somewhere in Africa to reverse Germany's blemished reputation abroad. In 1891, British and French journalists had chastised the Kaiser in newspaper spreads from Dakar to Hong Kong for his brutal suppression of the Hehe rebellion in East Africa. Kaiser Wilhelm II was a proud man, and he was still fuming over the accusations and the smug reproofs he had received from the other colonial powers.

When the previous Commissioner of the DSWA, Curt von François had resigned three years later, the Kaiser, ignoring the recommendations of his senior colonial officers, had appointed Leutwein to the post. As the Kaiser toasted Leutwein's success at lavish receptions in his Berlin palace, von François' former deputy and expected replacement, Major Baumhauer, was informed by curt telegram that he should organize an escort to meet the new Commissioner in Walvis Bay in two months.

When Leutwein arrived, the two men were civil toward one another at first. But that lasted only a few months. The trouble began as a series of Nama revolts erupted.

The Nama had endured particular persecution by von François' troops. So, when Leutwein had arrived advocating non violent prosperity, albeit under colonial rule, the Nama leader Hendrik Witbooi had wasted no time in testing the new Commissioner's strength.

It was unclear if Witbooi had attacked the German garrison at Hornkranz, or if the German garrison had attacked Witbooi, but as soon as the firing stopped at Hornkranz, skirmishes seemed to break out across the colony all at once. Witbooi had somehow escaped the cannon fire at Hornkranz and had fled into the bush. Over the next two years, he organized a devastating guerilla war whose campaigns mocked the Schutztruppe and embarrassed the Kaiser and his new peace-touting Commissioner.

In a desperate attempt to discourage further bloodshed, Leutwein had, he himself admitted to Conrad, overcompensated.

When at last Witbooi surrendered, and to appease the German public's ire, Leutwein established a series of prison camps on the outskirts of the colony's new capital where he sent all captured Nama rebels to serve prison sentences. He had hoped, perhaps too naively he conceded, that the visible threat of imprisonment and public humiliation might tamp down the enmity of most of the hostile tribes.

However, the camps' initial goal had backfired, and the Nama rebels' treatment at the hands of the guards had only sown more distrust among the natives and driven other tribes to rebellion. After three more years of suppressing revolts from Tsumeb to Seeheim, Leutwein abandoned hope that his public prisons would ever bear fruit. And as revolts spread, the Schutztruppe officers petitioned for permission to take over control of the camps to hold their own increasing number of captive natives.

Leutwein had begrudgingly agreed.

During a spell of relative calm, Leutwein had tried to make the peace last. He gathered the leaders of the three largest tribes in the colony, the Nama, the Herero and the Ovambo in Windhoelk and offered up a series of compromises.

Leutwein agreed to establish civil mayoral posts in Windhoek, Otjimbingwe, Okahandja and Keetmanshoop to curtail the influence of local German commanders and to halt all German farming expansions for two years. Leutwein also agreed to decrease the size of the Schutztruppe over a period of five years, which the Herero leaders had insisted upon and which had infuriated the Schutztruppe officers.

All three of the native delegations who had accepted Leutwein's proposals signed an official treaty agreeing to disarm. As an extra show of good faith, Leutwein had retired his Commissioner's uniform and stated that he would meet with all indigenous leaders in civilian dress going forward. He had shaken hands with all the chieftains in the main hall of the Residence and sent a copy of the treaty back to the Colonial Office in Berlin to be ratified by the Kaiser.

But enforcing his compromises with the indigenous tribes without the approval of his colonial officers had proven far more challenging than Leutwein had foreseen. Despite his illustrious military career, the colonial soldiers did not seem to respect Leutwein much. They were outraged by his lenient native policies. The Schutztruppe were hardened soldiers serving in hostile territory, outnumbered and thousands of miles from civilization. Yet here was the leader of the colonial government retiring his military uniform, giving promises and concessions to Hottentots.

On top of the unrest among the security troops, Leutwein's absence from Berlin had begun to erode his stature with the Kaiser. A new, influential wing in the German Colonial Office did not support the Commissioner's policies.

Germany was the great industrial leader of the world. Peace was one thing, but how would it look to the rest of Europe and the United States if a Kaiser's representative bent to demands from savages? There was enough trouble for the Empire to deal with already in Kamerun and East Africa. Far better to force the Hottentots out of the DSWA, or, in the opinion of the rising extreme wing within the Colonial Office, far better to just quietly eradicate the most troublesome tribes and be done with it.

Dietrich Baumhauer, a career diplomat with the ear of the Kaiser, was a leader of the new wing in the Colonial Office and, as it turned out, the older brother of Major Sören Baumhauer. When Leutwein had submitted his treaty with the Nama, Herero, and Ovambo for approval, it had been delayed by intense resistance from Dietrich Baumhauer and his followers. Herr Kleinschmidt had eventually been able to convince the Kaiser to ratify the treaty, but not without considerable effort.

While Dietrich criticized Leutwein's every action in Berlin, Sören created trouble by harassing local chieftains and continuing to authorize land permits to German settlers in Herero and Nama lands. Most recently, he had imprisoned in one of Windhoek's camps the sons of a Nama chieftain who had defaulted on a small debt to the colonial government. Leutwein had released the boys shortly after their imprisonment, but the damage was done.

To Conrad, the colonial government in Southwest Africa seemed to be on shifting sand. Yet still, for the past two years, Leutwein had managed to contain the Baumhauers' meddling and keep the peace in the DSWA.

*

Amidst this backdrop, Conrad was kept constantly busy. After Leutwein had risen and received Conrad's morning reports, Conrad served as the Commissioner's messenger, scribe, and on a few occasions, political confidant. And once he'd gotten past the shock of his rather unorthodox reception in Africa, he found the work enjoyable.

Leutwein had taken to Conrad right away, eager to have a sharp, albeit young and inexperienced assistant. The Commissioner would often step into the small corner closet down the hall that served as Conrad's office, wanting his opinion on whether a sentence in Leutwein's weekly report to Berlin was too contrite, or if Conrad thought it prudent to interfere with a local dispute between two Zwartboois chieftains near Swakopmund.

Usually, Conrad had no background to respond to any of Leutwein's questions, but so long as he gave a thoughtful answer the old man seemed pleased.

Southwest Africa had its advantages, Conrad found. The sharp chill of the dry night air gave Conrad merciful relief from his asthma. Where Germany's damp summer nights had often left him breathless, the desert plateau around Windhoek was cool and dry in the evenings. Conrad found that he could walk around Schwerinsburg's gardens for hours without discomfort in his lungs.

Windhoek itself was a bustling town with several businesses that dotted the main square and Kaiserstrasse charmingly. Twelve green springs surrounded the city outskirts, which provided a pleasant escape from the midday heat. An imposing hillfort, Alte Feste, overlooked the capital and gave the citizens the promise of security from the wilderness that surrounded them.

The appearance and mannerisms of the natives he encountered while walking the streets were new to Conrad, but after a brief period of adjustment, he found them intriguing.

Herero women wore long, hooped dresses that resembled the old Victorian-English style but with bright, patchwork colors of oranges, blues, greens and grays. The Ovambo men were deeply religious but friendly. They would sit in their faded overalls and capes, brewing a strong liquor from jackal berries and buffalo thorn and peddling it from wooden stalls along the streets.

The Damara brought their cows to market with loud singing and fanfare, converted Kavango Christians milled about the square spreading the word of Jesus Christ to any who would listen, and the few mixed-race Baster farmers who ventured into the capital lounged on the outskirts of the crowds, holding their well-dressed families apart from the masses and watching the chaos with disapproving frowns.

And, on top of it all, the lager in the beer halls *was* exceptionally good.

Conrad was also pleased that he not ended up in Sybille's bad graces. From the night of his arrival, he had had few occasions to speak with her, considering how busy Leutwein kept him. But he had already decided not to ask Sybille for anything that he could not get for himself. He found being waited on as insufferable in Africa as he had in Uncle Johannes' home. And truth be told, he was more than a little afraid of her.

Once, he did try to strike up a conversation with Sybille in her native language. But as he felt the force of those azure eyes, he tripped over his tongue like a flustered schoolboy.

She had entertained his bumbling when he'd confused the word hello, *Kora*, with marriage, *Kupa*. She'd corrected him politely enough, and Conrad had quickly excused himself, leaving the room with crimson ears.

After that incident, he resolved to practice native languages with anyone but Sybille.

Although Schwerinsburg boasted housing for up to seven aides and their families, Conrad was the only one currently serving in the DSWA. That was undoubtedly why Herr Kleinschmidt had been so eager to see him under way.

There had been three aides the previous year, but the most senior man had been recalled to Berlin to assist with an Imperial delegation to Paris, another had been appointed to a more elevated post in Kamerun, and the third, Herr Janson, had had such a dismal time adjusting to life in Africa that Leutwein had nearly considered it a small blessing when his wife took ill and Janson requested an extended leave to return to her in Germany. Janson's leave had technically expired two months earlier, but Leutwein had made no effort to track the pitiful man down.

That left Conrad as the only aide to the Commissioner for an entire colony.

One particularly pleasant afternoon in July, Conrad was returning home to Schwerinsburg from the Mayor's Residence with the expense reports for the city's railway maintenance that Leutwein had requested. Ordinarily, Herr

Grober would have sent the reports over with one of his servants later in the evening, but Leutwein had wanted to compile his financial reports to Berlin tonight—before the Baumhauers could insinuate that he was derelict for having submitted them later than his counterparts in Togoland and Kamerun.

Conrad had been glad of the chance to stretch his legs and visit with the mayor's plump and pretty wife, Frau Grober, who always made sure Conrad left with a package or two of chocolate biscuits.

On a whim, Conrad decided to bring Leutwein's young footman, whose name was Petyr, along. This was partly because the boy knew nearly every nook and cranny in the city and was an excellent guide and partly because Conrad knew that Petyr had a ravenous sweet tooth. Bribing the boy's affection with biscuits, if perhaps a tad improper, couldn't hurt to ensure he had at least one steadfast ally within the Residence.

Well-rewarded with Frau Grober's sweets, Petyr became quite chatty, and Conrad learned a great deal about the boy and everyone else in the house as they walked home.

Petyr was an Ovambo orphan. His parents had brought him to the city when he was too young to remember anything else. If he had other relatives, he did not know where they lived. Sybille had found him crying beneath a pile of blankets in the marketplace the day after both his parents had died from wasting sickness. Taking him home with her, she had cleaned him up and gotten him a job as Leutwein's footman. Erwin the cook, from Grootfontein in the north, was always grumpy and best left to himself. Maxine, a soft-spoken maid who liked to wear ribbons in her hair, was a Nama from near Walvis Bay.

Both had been hired by Leutwein at Sybille's recommendation.

On Sybille's own history Petyr had said very little, but Conrad was hoping that a few more chocolate biscuits would loosen his tongue.

They decided against taking Kaiserstrasse home as the sun was beginning to set, and Petyr knew a more direct way home to Schwerinsburg, south of the main square that would keep them clear of the evening rush.

They soon came to a bar that Conrad thought resembled something like a cowboy's saloon. The structure was dilapidated, though it could not have been more than a few years old. The street here was barely a dirt pathway and what scant other buildings there were around the bar were not much more inviting.

A few saddled horses were tethered to a rail by a water trough, and several men sat on a dusty porch, drinking beer and playing cards.

"We'd better go back, sir," Petyr said as he saw the men on the porch and began to turn back the way they'd come. "Kaiserstrasse is this way."

"Don't be silly," Conrad said, gently grabbing Petyr's arm to stop the boy's retreat. "It's nearly dark, and you said we were almost there a moment ago."

Conrad had no wish to dally on the long loop back to Kaiserstrasse. Not only because Leutwein wanted his reports as soon as possible, but also because of whatever manner of nightly stalkers they might meet on the outskirts of the main city. A leopard had been spotted in Windhoek last week. Conrad had no desire to meet it in some dark alleyway because Petyr wanted to dawdle on the way home.

Perhaps next time he'd bring Gustavus or Ivan along for good measure, if he could even figure out how to leash one of them.

"Now, what's gotten into you?" Conrad asked, having finally stopped Petyr from backing away.

Petyr hesitated for a moment.

"Those are the Witboois' men, sir," he said, his voice shaking a little. "We should go back the other way before…"

"*Was machst du denn hier?*"

Conrad had not heard the man behind him approach. He turned and looked for who had spoken.

The man looked about Conrad's age, but any resemblance stopped there. The man was not especially tall, but he was as thick as an oak tree, and his coal-black skin and angry features made him look like a livid panther. He jabbed two sun-beaten and cracked fingers into Conrad's chest and repeated his question.

"What are *you* doing here?"

Conrad wheezed slightly from the strong thump on his chest, but he swatted the other man's hand away.

"Going home if you don't mind," Conrad replied sternly.

He was tired and in no mood for the man's bullying. Conrad made to walk past him, but the man blocked his way.

"I mind," he said belligerently.

Conrad had been in several fights as a boy, although his lanky frame had ensured that he'd won very few of them. The man squaring up in front of him was a solid mass of muscle, and judging by the prodding he had already received, Conrad had no delusions of besting him in a fight. He was wondering how far he and Petyr might make it at a full-on sprint when one of the men on the bar's porch intervened.

"No, you don't, Albert," he said in a calm voice that defied protest. "He's one of the Commissioner's aides, boy. You've got no problem with him."

Conrad turned to face the man who'd spoken and instantly wondered how he had not seen him before. The man sat apart from the rest on a short stool and appeared to have no interest in the half-empty beer bottles or tattered playing cards that lay around the others. He sat as straight-backed as a Prussian general and seemed to observe his cavorting men with an air of detached amusement.

Hendrik Witbooi was a plain-looking man, but his ordinary complexion could not quite camouflage the dominating disposition that Conrad could sense from the street. God had not made Hendrik particularly striking, but Hendrik carried himself as though he were invincible. He spoke German flawlessly, and his voice carried across the small side street with the certainty of one who was accustomed to being obeyed.

"My boy's not very polite, sah," Witbooi told Conrad. "He ought to know his betters."

The uniform of the self-proclaimed King of Namaqualand was covered in dust and horse sweat, and a rifle stood propped up against his chair. But despite the roughness of the men around him and the thick dust that hung in the air, Witbooi appeared as proper as if he were at an audience with the Kaiser. He stood politely and tipped his slouch hat in greeting to Conrad.

Conrad tipped his own hat in return, then waited with some small satisfaction as Witbooi's iron gaze fell on Albert. It was a frank look of disappointment and impatience, and it came from a man who, in a moment, seemed able to channel a commanding air that was equal parts King, rebel and father.

Albert flinched under his father's stare and, quelled, obeyed and removed himself from Conrad's path.

A small part of Conrad's brain registered that the other men on the deck all sat in silence, as if they were afraid to move without Witbooi's approval. Hendrik was a force, Conrad realized.

"Welcome to Windhoek, Herr Huber," Witbooi said formally. "It's a pleasure to meet you. Tell Commissioner Leutwein, Hendrik says hello, sah."

Conrad nodded acknowledgement.

"Of course, Herr Witbooi," he said, and took Petyr's arm.

Hendrik Witbooi smiled at Conrad and then returned to his seat. It seemed the moment of tension had gone. Witbooi's men returned to their card game and Conrad turned to hurry Petyr along.

As they brushed past Albert Witbooi, Conrad wondered with detached fascination if Hendrik would have let Albert beat him to a pulp if he hadn't recognized him. As that thought crossed his mind, Albert caught Petyr's arm and said something rapidly that Conrad could not understand.

Conrad had not mastered more than a handful of words in very few of the native tongues. He thought Albert was speaking Ovambo, but it could just as easily be Nama for all he knew.

He made a grab for Petyr's other arm, fearing that Albert intended to harm the boy, but stopped short. Albert's tone was more inquisitive than threatening. Petyr, though clearly afraid, was able to mumble some quick reply, and the burly man nodded and let him go.

Conrad breathed a sigh of relief and swept Petyr along the road at a brisk pace. When they'd finally put the broken bar and the Witboois out of sight, Conrad stopped to collect himself.

"Are you all right, Petyr?" he asked, giving the boy a quick once-over.

"Yes...I'm okay," Petyr stammered, obviously shaken.

Conrad cursed himself for not listening to Petyr when he had said they should turn around. The boy knew the ins and outs of Windhoek far better than he did: his desire to take a shortcut home had nearly gotten them both assaulted. At least Petyr wasn't hurt. Nor was he for that matter.

"What was that all about, I wonder?" Conrad asked out loud, not really expecting a response.

But Petyr, soon feeling restored with another of Frau Grober's chocolate biscuits, answered.

"Well, Witbooi's men hate the Germans. Lots of folk are saying that Hendrik's getting tired of being sent after his own kind. The Commissioner made peace with Hendrik before by recognizing him as King and giving him a commanding role in the German army. But the Major only uses Hendrik's men to flush out other Nama rebels."

Petyr paused just long enough to chew. His chest puffed out like a school instructor lecturing an ignorant pupil.

"People think that the Major just hates Black folk and that he creates false reports of rebels in a village and then sends Hendrik's men out to bring them to the camps, so they won't resist. The Major treats Hendrik like a dog—and everyone can see that Hendrik has been patient long enough."

Petyr looked up and down the alley, as if afraid of being overheard.

"There are even those saying that for every Nama that Hendrik has to turn over to the Major, he makes a tick mark on a piece of paper. And they say that one day soon he's going to rise up again and kill ten Germans for every one of those ticks."

Petyr talked freely, not seeming to register the weight of the gossip he was repeating. Conrad felt a small chill at the mention of killing Germans, but Petyr continued on, oblivious.

"But Hendrik won't mess with you since you work for the Commissioner," Petyr added. "Hendrik doesn't like the Commissioner since he beat him in war, but lots of the other chiefs do trust Leutwein. And Sybille says Hendrik won't risk a rebellion again if he doesn't have the other chiefs' support. He can be a brutal warrior, but he's also a very clever…"

Petyr paused as if trying to remember an unfamiliar word.

"*Politician*," he finished.

Conrad made a mental note to check all of this with Leutwein when they returned home. Petyr spoke as though everything he said were common knowledge. But if any of it were widely known among German social circles, Conrad clearly hadn't been informed.

Leutwein dealt with strains between the local people and German settlers on a daily basis. To Conrad, it seemed as though a peace of sorts had been reached. However, listening to Petyr talk, he wondered if the natives' resentment was far worse than Leutwein realized.

"And Albert," Petyr continued, "he hates Germans because a soldier shot his parents when he was a kid. Hendrik's not his real daddy. He was his Mama's chieftain, so since Albert doesn't have anybody else, Hendrik adopted him."

Petyr shivered as though he suddenly realized something frightening.

"He'd have killed you, though," Petyr said. "If Hendrik hadn't stopped him, and there was no one else around to see him…he'd have killed you."

Conrad felt the warmth drain from his hands, and he quickened their pace.

"And what did Albert want from you?" Conrad asked, trying to change the subject away from the thought of his own murder.

"Oh," Petyr said as though he'd only just remembered that Albert had spoken to him. "Albert's been asking Sybille to marry him, and he wants me to talk to her for him."

Whatever Conrad had been expecting Petyr to say, it certainly hadn't been that.

"Really?" was all Conrad could manage in reply.

"Mhmm," Petyr said, popping another biscuit in his mouth. "Albert's been asking for a while now, but Sybille doesn't like Albert. She thinks he's a bully and that he drinks too much, so she keeps refusing him."

Then, as if remembering something that had been repeated to him, he added, "Sybille says it's a shame none of Hendrik's principles rubbed off on Albert."

Conrad slipped the rest of the chocolate biscuits into his coat pocket.

He walked with Petyr in silence for a while, brooding over his first encounter with the Witboois. The sun disappeared behind the mountains in the distance. Conrad mumbled a silent prayer that the leopard would stay away from the town this evening as the indigo twilight edged deeper into night. Nearly being assaulted by the adopted son of a jaded auxiliary had been quite enough excitement. Conrad was in no mood to endanger his life twice in the same day.

Suddenly, Conrad heard a woman's muffled cry escape from a nearby alleyway. He turned and looked in the direction of the sound. Down the far end of the alley, Conrad could just make out her silhouette. But instead of a leopard, two men in the khaki uniforms of the Schutztruppe gripped the woman by the arms. One hastily clamped his hand over her mouth.

Perhaps an arrest, Conrad thought, trying to counter the horrid alternative already forming in his mind. The Schutztruppe did, sometimes, arrest natives inside Windhoek. Still, they hadn't recently since the trouble over the arrest of the Nama chief's sons.

But as one of the men shoved the woman up against the side of the building and the other began to fumble with his belt, there was no doubt as to what was happening.

"Petyr, go get Leutwein," Conrad said without thinking as he took off down the alley. "Now!"

Petyr nodded and ran down the road towards Schwerinsburg. Conrad only hoped for the boy's sake he didn't fully comprehend what was happening.

"You there!" Conrad shouted at the garrison troops as he ran. "*Halt!*"

Either the Schutztruppe men didn't hear him, or they were too engrossed in their current pursuit to pay him any mind. One man had succeeded in unfastening his trousers and began to tear at the woman's clothes while the other held her firmly against the wall.

"*Halt*, I said!" Conrad shouted again.

The two soldiers were both big men and one had a pistol hanging prominently from his belt.

Scheisse, Conrad thought to himself as he, lacking a better alternative, lowered his shoulder and rammed the trouserless man with his full weight.

The man tripped over his own clothing and crashed to the street with a grunt of surprise. Conrad's momentum sent him flying over the stunned solider, and he landed on his shoulder with a loud pop. Pain shot through his arm as he rolled onto his back in time to catch the second man's boot in his ribs. The man holding the woman released his grip on her and now rounded on Conrad, kicking him repeatedly as the other soldier got to his feet.

"*Du Arschloch*!" the second soldier curses as he made to kick Conrad as well. "You asshole!"

As the trouserless soldier made to strike Conrad, the woman threw herself at him, scratching at his face in a wild fury.

"Ack! You miserable bitch!" the man roared, throwing a blind punch that caught the woman right in the mouth. Blood spurted from the blow, but the woman made no sound. She lunged at her attacker, who hit her again with the full force of his strength. The woman bent over in pain and before she could recover, the soldier grabbed her and threw her roughly to the ground. Seizing the distraction, Conrad rolled away from the man and staggered to his feet. The second soldier, recovered too, came at Conrad with a savage right hook.

Conrad dodged the blow and dove at his assailant, his momentum tackling the two soldiers into one another. All three of them careened onto the ground, landing in a heap.

Conrad heard a second pop in his shoulder, and he cried out again. His vision blurred, and he felt someone grab him by the collar and hit him hard in the chest. He curled up in pain, trying to avoid a second blow, while the woman beside him slashed, kicked, and bit at her attacker with impressive vitality. Conrad felt the alley growing even darker as the salty taste of warm blood filled his mouth.

Suddenly a shot ran out high above the melee. Then a second, and a third. The armed soldier reached for his own weapon just as a fourth shot rang out, this one much closer to the Schutztruppes' heads.

Petyr? Conrad thought through the clouded fog of his throbbing head. No, there was no way he could have reached Leutwein so quickly, and there was no way that Leutwein would be firing a gun so recklessly in the city.

A group of male voices shouted something in what Conrad thought was Nama. The two German soldiers fled, quickly disappearing into the night.

Conrad lay motionless on the ground, wheezing heavily and trying to regain control of his racing heartbeat.

He coughed as he rolled onto his side, spitting up blood and trying to force as much cool air into his heaving lungs as possible. He tried to look around to find the woman, but as he lifted his head he came face-to-face with the barrel of a rifle and Albert Witbooi looming mercilessly over him.

Albert's eyes were white with rage. He had six men with him, none of whom were Hendrik.

"You gonna die now, German," Albert said slowly as he pushed the muzzle of his rifle up against Conrad's chin.

Conrad tried to speak, but no words came.

Anyway, he thought detachedly, there wouldn't be any reasoning with someone like Albert. He would either die because of a misunderstanding or for no better reason than that Albert had found him alone. He shut his aching eyes and prayed he wouldn't feel the bullet.

All of a sudden, the woman began shouting fiercely at Albert. Conrad opened his eyes and was astonished to see Sybille, half-naked and her mouth dripping with blood, screaming inches from Albert's face. In the darkness of the alley and the chaos of the fight, she had been unrecognizable: now, despite her swollen face and shredded clothing, Sybille's frame stood unmistakably between him and Albert.

Conrad had no idea what she was saying in her native Herero, but whatever it was, it gave Albert pause. He clearly was not used to a woman defying him so aggressively. Few men were. He stepped back, abashed like a chastised puppy, and his men shuffled their feet uneasily. Conrad gave a silent prayer of thanks that he was not the object of her fury.

Albert cast a menacing glance as Conrad slowly forced himself to his feet, but when Albert tried to point his rifle at Conrad again, Sybille swatted it aside and continued to berate him.

Sybille was at least a head taller than Albert, and despite her near nakedness it was evident that she intended to fly at him if he defied her. Albert and his men might've had guns, but they were no match for Sybille.

A siren sounded in the distance, and the muffled sounds of soldiers' boots began to thunder toward the alleyway. The gunfire had sounded the alarm at the town's garrison fort, Alte Feste. Albert's men began to fidget fearfully. Two of them started to back slowly down the alley, and the rest looked ready to do the same. Albert swore, and with one last baleful glance at Conrad he shouted a quiet command in Nama. He and his men melted into the night.

⋆

In the Commissioner's office, Conrad sat with a wet, bloodied cloth pressed over his mouth and one arm in a soft sling. Leutwein, livid, lashed out across his desk at Major Baumhauer with a veteran officer's incredulous ire. Baumhauer stood before the Commissioner, red in the face, and cursed back at Leutwein in full measure.

"A group of wild Hottentots opened fire on two of my men, and you are going to do nothing?!" Baumhauer roared for the third time.

"Your men attempted to rape a native woman, a member of my own household staff, to speak nothing of their attack on an Imperial diplomat! *Mein Gott*, Major, do you have any idea who her father is? Do you comprehend what your prick-mad troopers have done?"

"They're just dumb savages, Leutwein!" Baumhauer thundered, slamming his fist on Leutwein's desk. "Ignorant, godless, barbaric savages, and you should have listened to me and finished them off a long time ago. They're murderers and villains, and now they've grown bold enough, on *your* watch, to fire upon my patrols in our fucking capital! I don't give two shits who her father is. He's a savage mongrel, and he should be put down like the rest of them!"

"Silence!" Leutwein shouted above Baumhauer, in such a rage his glasses fell from his nose onto the floor.

He was shaking with fury as he leaned to retrieve his glasses. He placed them on his face, breathing hard. His next angry words emerged slowly, like small spurts of steam from a kettle.

"Major. I will have those men court-martialed tomorrow and on the next boat back to Germany."

"Really, Commissioner?" Baumhauer said defiantly as he folded his arms in assumed triumph. "And which men would that be, then? So far as you've told me, the girl didn't get a good look at her attackers. Or do you want me to cut my ranks again, like you do every time these natives cause trouble?"

Leutwein snapped his head around to Conrad.

"Conrad," he barked, "did you see what the two men looked like?"

Leutwein's wrath had taken Conrad by surprise, but he removed the cloth from his mouth to answer.

Baumhauer shot him a deadly stare, eerily similar to the one he'd received from Albert Witbooi mere hours ago. There was no mistaking the threat in the Major's eyes, and Conrad nearly thought better of answering.

But then Conrad got angry. Those two men had attempted to rape Sybille! To hell with Albert and his men firing guns at German soldiers. Two Imperial soldiers, representatives of the Kaiser, had tried to force themselves on a woman. And here Baumhauer was trying to defend them! A woman had been assaulted by the men under his command, but all the Major seemed to care about was locking up those who'd come to her rescue. The callousness of the Major's affrontery and his accusations against Leutwein were appalling.

Despite his pain, Conrad stood and met Baumhauer's stare angrily.

"Yes, sir," Conrad replied to Leutwein. "Although it was too dark to see all of their features clearly, I'd be happy to assist the Major in identifying the culprits. I think you'll find one with a swollen left eye, and the other should have numerous scratch marks on his face."

Leutwein's lip curled slightly and were he not so angry at the moment, Conrad thought he might have laughed.

"I want them dismissed, Major," Leutwein commanded. "Now. Can I trust you to carry out that order? Or shall I accompany you to the barracks and put them on the boat myself?"

Baumhauer looked for a moment as though he might explode. Conrad's bravery receded rapidly. What if Baumhauer refused? Worse, what if he discharged the wrong men? Conrad didn't see how he could manage to avoid danger from Albert Witbooi, the Major, and two vindictive, armed soldiers still at large. The tension hung in the air a moment longer before the major finally spoke.

"They'll be court-martialed," was all he said before turning on his heel in a huff.

Leutwein collapsed into his chair like a popped balloon as he heard the front door of the Residence slam shut.

"I suppose it was Hendrik Witbooi's boy, Albert, who fired at the two soldiers?" he asked Conrad knowingly as he let out a heavy sigh.

"Yes, sir," Conrad answered, with some difficulty through his swollen mouth. "Sir, I'm sorry about all of this. I never should've..."

Leutwein pounded the desk, cutting Conrad off.

"You absolutely should have, Conrad," he said firmly. "If you hadn't come along...never apologize to me for doing the honorable thing. It's too damn rare on this continent. I can deal with Baumhauer and his lot. Go clean yourself up; I can manage the rest of this mess myself."

Conrad turned to leave, but Leutwein stopped him before he got to the door.

"And congratulations, my boy. Now someone with influence hates you. That officially makes you a member of the Imperial Colonial Office!"

Conrad smiled at Leutwein's jest. Once he had left to sort himself out and see if any of Janson's abandoned suits would fit him though, he found the truth in Leutwein's words unsettling. He knew he had done the right thing in saving Sybille. But he also understood that he had made a dangerous enemy. He wasn't sure how much longer he would be able to survive in Africa if he continued to make enemies among both the natives and the Schutztruppe.

*

The next morning, Major Baumhauer court-martialed and discharged Sybille's assailants. For good measure, Leutwein also had a quiet word with Hendrik

Witbooi, and the Nama King and his auxiliaries left the capital soon after on an extended patrol east of Windhoek.

A week later, Leutwein received a telegram from Herr Kleinschmidt, informing him that Dietrich Baumhauer's wing within the Berlin Office had formally petitioned the Kaiser. He had called for Leutwein's resignation.

CHAPTER 5

OCTOBER 1903

I f Conrad had expected Sybille to be gracious for his intervention that night in the alley, he was sorely disappointed. Quite the contrary, Conrad's actions had confusingly rewarded him with the same icy disdain that Sybille reserved for Beaunard Hertzog. In the days immediately following the attack, Sybille first ignored Conrad, then shunned him altogether. Next, she made it plain that she despised him, gazing hostilely at him whenever she saw him, and most recently, muttering something harsh in Herero whenever he passed her on the Residence grounds.

For weeks now, Conrad had been walking on eggshells around Schwerinsburg. He was completely at a loss as to why Sybille abruptly left a room whenever he came in or muttered what sounded like a cross word in Herero at him wherever they passed in the hallway.

It was Erwin who finally took pity on him.

Erwin was preparing Leutwein's breakfast, and the rest of the household staff had yet to rise. Knowing no one would overhear them, Conrad pleaded with Erwin to explain his mistake. Erwin's German was rough, and he seldom practiced it, but his deep voice spoke plainly, as one might talk to a child. He was stirring brown sugar into some oatmeal for Leutwein's breakfast as he spoke. "It's simple," Erwin told him. "If she been raped, only she know. But you save her, and now everyone talk about her.

"You think you save her, but now the whole colony knows she almost raped. People always talk. Now they talking more. They using her as martyr against the soldiers. Sybille rather been raped than be martyr. The camps be full of martyrs. She'd been raped, that's her business. But you save her and now it's everyone's business."

"That makes absolutely no sense," Conrad replied horrified, his stack of early morning telegrams and reports for Leutwein forgotten. "You're saying I should have let those men…have their way with her?!"

"No," Erwin replied simply. "But you save her, so everybody know. And now she hate you."

Conrad had no response to that.

He spent the next hour in the kitchen with Erwin, utterly confused, while the cook silently went about preparing the staff's breakfast. It was ridiculous to think Sybille should hate him for saving her…wasn't it?

The rest of the day passed in a blur as he hurried back and forth on errands to help arrange the dinner party scheduled this evening to celebrate a local Damara chieftain's eightieth birthday.

The Damara comprised some five or so different clans, and it seemed the guest list included well over half of them. Conrad couldn't tell the Arodaman from the Audaman, but the small, private party Leutwein had wanted organized at the beginning of the week had quickly escalated into a thoroughly grand affair. If the chieftain !Gai!ga was coming, his brother Iazrus had to be invited too. Iazrus scarcely traveled down from the Khomas Highlands without an entourage of at least twenty family members. Then there were !Gai!ga's four sons, Bayron, !Notago, Dantago and Charles. Of course, Charles never traveled without his wife, Lao, and their three daughters, Phenny, Taotite and Ivonne.

It had taken Conrad the entire week to finally compose the full guest list for Leutwein's "simple" birthday party. When the guests finally began to arrive on the day of the party, they arrived in fantastic, colorful droves. The men, proud-chested and swathed in tanned animal hides, and the women, chatting happily in flowing dresses of green, white, blue, and gold, each effortlessly balancing an elaborate *otjikaiva*, a flatboard headdress wrapped in matching cloth. Among the swirl of color and chatter, each family arrived with dozens of extra guests in tow, a small army of bickering and shouting children.

At any given time, there were half a dozen quarrels that Conrad was forced to try and navigate through the guests' broken German. Iazrus could not be seated next to his cousin Vilho, whom he claimed had stolen four of his best cows, yet Vilho had to be seated close to !Gai!ga, for his oldest daughter was set to marry !Gai!ga's youngest son next spring. !Gai!ga's wife despised her eldest son's wife, a sharp-tongued woman who never failed to meet her mother-in-law's scorn with sarcastic defiance, and on three separate occasions, Conrad had had to pull a lusty young couple, Surihe and Matawa, out of the coat closet before they were caught by Matawa's octogenarian husband.

But finally, at around eleven that evening with the lager flowing, guests laughing, and Erwin having miraculously stretched his pantry's supplies to feed an additional fifty guests, Conrad found a moment of respite and slumped tiredly against the main stairwell in the front hall.

His dour predecessor's borrowed suit was tight in the arms and miserably hot amongst the press of bodies. Conrad had been sweating profusely since noon. There were few Germans here tonight; only the occasional bank teller or shopkeeper could be spotted chatting politely enough with !Gai!ga, though Conrad noted that they mostly kept to themselves and would not acknowledge any of the other Damara. Mayor Grober had claimed he was nursing a flare-up of gout and was unable to attend, which Conrad was sure was a politely feeble excuse, and Beaunard was away overseeing a rail line's construction in the colony's far north.

It had been a chaotic day, but now Conrad removed his heavy jacket as the mix of African tongues drifted throughout the halls. The guests' voices rose and fell with shared laughs and stories; German and Damara intertwined in a pleasant cacophony that sounded rather like a distant song. Conrad enjoyed the blended voices from his temporary escape and took a long, deep breath. He sighed and closed his eyes a moment.

When he opened them, he found Sybille standing in front of him.

"You and I need to have a talk," she said in perfect German. "Do you have any idea what you've done?!"

Conrad was too stunned to reply. Sybille had never spoken a word of German as far as he knew, and now her German was flawless, with no trace of the throaty accent many Herero in Windhoek had. Her grammar was so precise Conrad might as well have been receiving a scolding from his own mother.

"Um…er," was all Conrad managed before Sybille launched into a tirade.

"Of all the foolish things, you barrel down an alley and attack German troops without even considering the consequences! Do you have any idea the damage this has done to Leutwein in Berlin? Do you even comprehend how serious this is? As if making the Major an enemy wasn't bad enough for yourself, because you told Leutwein what happened, the honorable fool wastes what little authority he had left over the Major—over me! Now the Major is looking for blood. Who is going to protect my people if the Schutztruppe are at war with the Commissioner?"

Conrad tried to retreat further into the woodwork of the stairwell, but Sybille continued to yell at him, her sharp voice miraculously unheard by the partygoers.

"To say nothing of what men like Albert Witbooi will do! Have you ever even seen a war, Herr Huber? Because that's what the men of this land want! People here have been biding their time, waiting for something to spark the fire, and you just handed it to them!

"Because Leutwin sacked those soldiers, you've given the people here a false sense of his power. People expect Leutwein to keep the army in check now, but he's more powerless than ever! With the Major here and his brother back in Berlin, no commissioner could retain authority for long! There will be real violence the very next time something like this happens. Leutwein won't be able to control the Schutztruppe's response!"

All the color had drained from Conrad's face as Sybille raged, her eyes flashing with lightning bolts of blue.

Mist, Conrad thought to himself. I didn't even realize she spoke German, let alone that she could analyze the political intricacies of the whole colony.

She spoke with penetrating accuracy. Conrad wondered fleetingly how it was that a native maid grasped so much about German politics, but he was too unnerved by her shouting to dwell on the matter for long. She was terrifying, and it was so hot in the house.

Sybille's eyes continued to flare.

"If you had left me alone, none of this would be happening! Leutwein wouldn't have needed to throw such an elaborate party for one of the most influential chiefs in the area to buy favor for when he can't control his own men next time! The Major wouldn't have convinced even more members of the Colonial Office that Leutwein should be replaced, and your ridiculous Kaiser wouldn't be listening to a pack of rabid, bigoted careerists.

"Leutwein's fighting for his political life, you *Dummkopf!* And if he goes, the next man the Kaiser will send will either be too incompetent to stop the Schutztruppe or be just as bad as Baumhauer."

Conrad swallowed hard. Between the heat and Sybille, he'd grown quite dizzy. Somehow, he had to escape the stairwell.

"You should have let them rape me; then it would have only been my burden to bear. But now the whole colony could go to war again because you couldn't stop to think! We're all doomed because you had to save...."

All of a sudden, desperate to stop the torrent of words, Conrad kissed her. It was just a quick tap on her lips, but he stared at her in guilty shock, his whole body rocking slowly back against the stairs like a brass clock pendulum.

Sybille was dumbstruck. She took a step back, her mouth half-open in surprise. Her tirade halted, she looked at Conrad with a wide-eyed expression that no longer seemed angry but was impossible to read.

Conrad had no idea why he'd done it; it had just happened. He'd been trapped and overwhelmed, and it hurt him that she should be so angry with him. He also realized that she might be right, that he might have doomed Leutwein after only a few months on the job. She'd been yelling at him, and without thinking, he'd pressed his sweaty lips to hers as if that were the only way to make her stop screaming at him.

For several moments, they stared at one another in complete shock at what had just transpired.

"Er…excuse me, please," Conrad said at last as he made his escape through the small gap that had opened up between them.

Sybille stood immobilized in the hall while Conrad made a beeline for the kitchen, passing through the sea of !Gai!ga's relatives. A German banker's eighteen-year-old daughter waved at him across the dining room, and Conrad hastily waved back, his face a vibrant shade of crimson, and his ears and cheeks burning.

In his retreat through the kitchen door, he nearly collided with Leutwein, who was visibly rattled himself.

"Oh, Conrad," Leutwein said as he quickly pulled Conrad further into the kitchen. "Just the man I was looking for."

The Commissioner was dressed elegantly for the evening. The tails of his dinner jacket flowed smartly behind him, his white tie immaculate, and his new silk shirt from Berlin gave him a dapper and gentlemanly look despite the heat.

!Gai!ga had presented Leutwein with what Conrad thought must be the Damara's version of a slender cane as a small token of appreciation for the Commissioner's throwing of the party. Conrad had noticed that all the men from every clan sported one in their right hand, even the young and healthy, and Leutwein had accepted the gift with gracious reverence. He'd even twirled the wooden cane a bit, imitating a posh Englishman on a Sunday stroll, and all the Damara had howled with laughter.

Leutwein had been wandering through the party with his new cane all evening, his face flushed with the warmth of a convivial host. But now Conrad noticed that Leutwein's fleshy hands were clutching the fragile cane tightly, trying to steady himself as though he had suffered a great shock.

"Erwin," he said to the cook as he led Conrad away from the door. "Step outside and see that no one wanders in here for a moment."

Erwin nodded gravely and left the kitchen to stand guard outside.

Great, Conrad thought to himself. Everyone in this house seems to know important things before I do.

Leutwein waited until the door had swung closed behind Erwin before he spoke.

"Conrad, I'm afraid there's been an incident."

Leutwein dug into his coat pocket and produced a crumpled telegram that he handed to Conrad as though it were on fire.

"It's from Beaunard," Leutwein explained dolefully. "Apparently, his attempts to quell the unrest along the new railway have been…unsuccessful."

Conrad read the telegram quickly, easily pairing Beaunard's heavy accent with his written words. If Leutwein's tone had not alerted Conrad as to the severity of whatever situation was at hand, Beaunard's uncharacteristic brevity, even within the bounds of a telegram, was a sign that something had indeed gone seriously wrong.

Theodor. Stop.
Railway near Grootfontein has been attacked. Stop
Explosive used, three injured Germans. One dead. Stop.
Hottentots responsible fled, but troopers from Grootfontein in
pursuit. Stop.
Come swiftly. Stop.
Beaunard.

"Someone tried to blow up the railway?" Conrad asked, astounded.

Beaunard had told Conrad that the local tribes in the north staunchly opposed the construction of the new railway between Tsumeb and Grootfontein and that they frequently engaged in delaying tactics to undermine the work. Beaunard claimed that he did not know why the locals were so incensed about this latest expansion, but he had been confident that their anger would blow over eventually.

So far, the locals had been relatively peaceful in their protests. A few times, the local women lay themselves across the unfinished track and refused to move. Sometimes young men grew bold enough to steal railroad spikes and hammers at night. But the women could be moved easily enough, and tools could always be replaced.

An attack with explosives, however…that was another matter entirely.

What was it Sybille had just said to him?

That's what the men of this land want! People here have been biding their time, waiting for something to spark the fire.

"Indeed, but keep your voice down," Leutwein replied gravely. "Go and pack a bag, and don't take too long about it. We are leaving in the morning. Keep smiling, though. I doubt word of this will have spread to the social circles of Windhoek yet. We don't want our guests to grow suspicious and start spreading rumors about why we're missing from our own party."

Conrad nodded dutifully, glad to have something to do to keep his dread at bay.

"Anything else, sir?" he asked while trying to calculate in his head how long it would take to arrive in Tsumeb by train.

"Ah, yes," Leutwein said, already heading for the door. "Go and fetch Sybille, will you? She'll be accompanying the two of us. I don't speak whatever language they use in Grootfontein, and I know even less about their laws and customs. Tell her what has happened and to pack a bag as well."

Conrad stood frozen in place.

"Is something wrong, Conrad?" Leutwein asked, one hand already on the swinging kitchen door.

"No, sir," Conrad managed. "Of course, sir. Right away."

Leutwein nodded and waded back into the fray of Damara society.

Conrad waited a moment until he was sure the Commissioner was out of earshot and then swore adamantly.

*

The train depot was frigid so early in the morning. One of the grooms had a carriage ready for them, and Conrad, Leutwein and Sybille had slipped out of Schwerinsburg's gate before first light.

None of them had slept at all the night before. !Gai!ga's family had been jovial and spirited well into the night. Conrad had only had a short time to pack and change out of Janson's borrowed suit after ushering the last of !Gai!ga's relatives out the door. That morning he took his seat up on the carriage bench next to the driver, a large Kavango native named Frederick; Leutwein and Sybille had climbed onto the main carriage bench. Conrad muttered a small prayer of thanks that no one said a word as their carriage headed for the train depot.

He was already dreading whatever Sybille intended to do to him if they found themselves alone again.

In the end, unable to face Sybille after he'd left the kitchen, Conrad had written down Leutwein's instructions on a piece of paper and sent Petyr to give her the note along with Beaunard's telegram. He knew he was being cowardly, but he was sure she would not be likely to make things easy for him.

It only took Leutwein a few brief minutes to identify himself to the sleepy station attendant and to secure passage for the three of them on the early morning train to Walvis Bay, about 400 kilometers away. Since Beaunard's new track extensions were not yet complete, the fastest way to Tsumeb was to take a train nearly halfway back to the English settlement. There they would transfer to a northern line in the small town of Karibib that would carry them to a second town that Conrad couldn't even begin to pronounce, where they would transfer again to a third line to reach Tsumeb.

After a short wait, the conductor ushered them past the small band of sleepy second-class passengers into the same first-class car Conrad had ridden to Windhoek his first day in the DSWA.

They were the only passengers in first class. Most wealthy Germans had either already arrived in Windhoek weeks ago off the last steamer of the season or had departed the colony on leave or holiday back to Europe. There was a slight possibility of a wealthy gentlemen or lady making the long trek to Walvis Bay on a short holiday elsewhere in the colony, but Leutwein's presence would have discouraged any objection to Sybille riding in first class.

Conrad looked around the car, hoping to see Mikal's friendly face, but he saw no signs of the elderly attendant. Leutwein said something about "seeing to the conductor," and ducked into the engine room. The train depot in Windhoek usually had a small attachment of Schutztruppe who combed each train before it departed, and Leutwein wanted to ensure that they would not check the first-class car this morning and thus alert Baumhauer to Leutwein's sudden departure from the capital.

Undoubtedly, the Major would hear of the attack on the railway soon, but Beaunard was the only man near Grootfontein with a telegraph machine: if all went according to plan, they would arrive in Tsumeb and be on their way by horse to Beaunard's work camp before the Major discovered that Leutwein was already en route.

With Leutwein gone, Conrad was left alone with Sybille. He had chosen a seat at the far end of the train car, hoping that instead of attacking him on the spot, she might be content to sit as far away from him as possible. But much to his surprise, she followed him and chose the seat right next to him, taking her seat without saying a word.

A few awkward minutes ticked by, and then the train began to lurch forward with a soft *click-clack click-clack click-clack* over the rough spokes of the track. The sun was just beginning to rise as they pulled out of the empty station, but the train itself was still numbingly cold. Conrad could feel the heat of Sybille's body next to him and resisted the urge to slide closer toward her.

Sybille sat next to him in haughty silence, making no move to either change to another seat or harangue him further. Instead, she ignored him, only casting a covert glance at him now and then.

Conrad had no idea what to make of the inscrutable woman sitting next to him. She was as much a mystery to him as on his first day in the Residence when he'd felt so spellbound by her movements.

In truth, he knew little about her. She had at one point been a maid in the household of Frau Grober, who gave her a glowing recommendation when Leutwein's elderly Ovambo housekeeper had passed away three years ago. She was said to be an excellent housekeeper— and to take an immediate dislike to almost everyone who entered the Residence.

Almost all the other natives in Leutwein's employ regarded Sybille as their unquestioned commander. Still, from what Conrad could see in the short time he'd been living among the household staff, few actually liked her. Only the cook, Erwin, seemed fond of her in his own grumpy way, and Petyr, whom she had rescued from the capital's streets, followed her around Schwerinsburg like a doting younger brother.

The rest of the staff was just as nervous around Sybille as Conrad was. One, a young native groom named Lucas, who always grinned shyly whenever Conrad passed him on the grounds, even volunteered that he thought that Sybille must be a spy for the Herero chieftains.

The encounter with Lucas had fascinated him at the time, though now Conrad considered such an idea ridiculous. Sybille lived at least eighty kilometers from her home village and under the Schutztruppe's vengeful gaze, she would have no way to send word to anyone.

But what had shaken Conrad for days after his cursory chat with Lucas was what the groom's fantasy of Sybille being a spy would mean. Conrad knew that hundreds of native women migrated to the colonial towns every dry season looking for work, just as Sybille did. In the short time that he had known her, he'd seen Sybille exposed to the likes of mercenary hangers-on, verbal abuse from Beaunard and countless other white colonists, not to mention nearly being raped by two men of the Schutztruppe. If Sybille *was* a spy, she was one who was truly dedicated to her cause.

And if Sybille was willing to put herself through that, what did that say about what else she was willing to endure for the sake of whatever greater purpose she served?

As he remembered Lucas' warning, he looked sidelong at Sybille, who was still doing her best to ignore him.

They sat in silence a few minutes more, Conrad thoroughly unsure what to make of Sybille's behavior. Then, slowly, as if she were stretching, Sybille placed her arms on the arms of her seat. She still acted as though Conrad were invisible, though she doubtlessly felt the heat of him as well.

Conrad froze a moment, then slowly placed his own arms on the edge of his seat. He paused again, casting a terrified glance at the Herero woman beside him to see if he'd made a fatal error.

But Sybille continued to look out the far window, evidently indifferent to his actions.

For some moments they stayed like that, their hands inches from one another. Conrad had no idea what could be keeping Leutwein away for so long. He wasn't sure if the rapid thumping he could feel was the melodic pounding of the train over the tracks or the nervous beating of his heart in his chest.

Say something you idiot, he thought. If she's going to attack you, best get it over with now than endure more agonizing silence. You could offer her an apology at the very least.

"Sybille, I…" he started, stopping as soon as she turned her piercing eyes on him.

She *was* still angry with him, he guessed.

But her eyes showed something else as well, something that was not *entirely* hostile. She still looked guarded, yet a part of her, unless Conrad imagined it, looked amused.

Sybille had dressed very plainly for the journey in a faded red dress with a small, white cap over her hair. The Victorian-style dress, favored by colonists and missionaries, had clearly not been made for her, though she wore it with grace. Whether from the hastiness of their departure or because she was expecting to be out in the DSWA's sweltering heat all day, she was not wearing an outer bodice. The linen fabric of her dress clung tightly to her body, and Conrad averted his eyes in sudden realization.

"Er…I'm…um…sorry about the…uh…"

His tongue twisted into knots again. Had he kissed her the night before out of sheer reflex or for some other reason entirely?

He opened his mouth again to try to form actual words but was saved as Leutwein at last returned from the engine room. He still looked distraught and exhausted but wore the smile of having won a small victory as he collapsed into the seat opposite Conrad and Sybille.

"The conductor is a friend of mine," he said with a raspy voice that betrayed his fatigue. "As far as the Schutztruppe will know from here to Tsumeb, this car is empty, and they needn't bother searching it. We should be in Tsumeb by tomorrow morning and at Beaunard's worksite before the Major even notices we've left."

Evidently assured of their clandestine departure, the Commissioner soon fell asleep, leaving Conrad and Sybille in an uneasy truce all the way to Tsumeb.

*

The "Gateway to the Northern DSWA," Tsumeb was as bustling and overwhelming as Walvis Bay, albeit with far fewer white faces.

"In Nama," Leutwein explained to Conrad, "I believe that 'Tsumeb' means either 'the city of moss' or 'the city of frogs.' I'm not quite sure which it is."

Conrad chanced a furtive glance at Sybille, but if she knew the correct answer, she did not bother to correct Leutwein.

"Though I think !Gai!ga was having fun with me last night," Leutwein said as they pushed toward the center of the village, fighting their way through the crowded alleys and streets. "I've never seen a frog in this part of Africa."

Sprawling behind the skyline of the busy mountain town stood a giant hill of green, a single mound of oxidized copper that shone so brightly in the noonday sun that it stung Conrad's eyes to look at. From a distance, the hill had appeared to be a large rock slathered in several layers of glittering moss. As they drew closer to the great mound near the center of town, they passed gang after gang of dust-covered African miners.

Tsumeb was a mining town, the colony's wealthiest in terms of raw materials. The ground here was tough and covered in polymetallic, volcanic rock from which the Koloniagesellschaft's army of indigenous miners painstakingly pulled out lead, silver, gold, arsenic, germanium, and of course, cart after cart of copper.

They were greeted at the railyard by an assembly line of tightly packed boxcars and covered wagons overflowing with these materials. It was clear that a new shipment of ore would be heading to Germany via Walvis Bay and Swakopmund very soon.

Equally clear as their small party left the train station was that with this shipment would come the miners' pay. Passing several vendors along the packed streets, Conrad noticed that no one appeared to be doing any business. Vendors chatted amiably with one another around their stalls as though they knew that there would be no business today and had only gone through the routine of opening their stalls out of force of habit. Soon the miners would be paid, however, and then they'd rush to buy as much as possible, to last until the next shipment.

Yet something else hung in the air around Tsumeb as Conrad followed Leutwein and Sybille through the crowded town square towards the headquarters of the Koloniagelsellschaft. While Windhoek may not have heard of the attack on the railway station yet, it was clear that it was all anyone in Tsumeb was talking about.

Several natives averted their gaze as Conrad passed by, but something in the air made Conrad quicken his pace. He and Leutwein were not the only Germans out and about in Tsumeb. They passed several German overseers and clerks hurrying along the packed streets. But they might as well have been, for Conrad felt as though every eye in Tsumeb was following his every movement.

Have you ever seen a war? Because that's what the men of this land want.

Sybille's words echoed in Conrad's mind. He felt himself pulling his cap down lower over his forehead as they came across a group of Schutztruppe on a street corner. However, the soldiers paid them no mind. Major Baumhauer's men in Windhoek might be hardened soldiers with the holstered confidence of the Alte Feste garrison and a full colonial regiment behind them, but the soldiers on the street corners here looked young and anxious.

Few in number, surrounded by Damara, Nama, and a few Herero, it was obvious that these Schutztruppe felt something in the air as well. No question, they looked frightened.

It took their small party nearly an hour to navigate the streets of Tsumeb and arrive at the Koloniagelsellschaft's office, a lavishly decorated white building situated on the edge of the main square. Most of the buildings and streets in Tsumeb were plain, wooden structures covered in layers of dirt and grime. But the headquarter building was a grand brick house with a freshly whitewashed wooden fence surrounding a lush courtyard.

Its French vice president, Monsieur Perrot, was smartly dressed in a crisp, navy suit that he obsessively smoothed and straightened as he paced. Conrad had met the man twice before when he had come to dine at the Residence and discuss some trivial dispute with an Ovimbundu chieftain from Portuguese Angola to the north. The charming M. Perrot had always been in good spirits during his visits to Windhoek, and he was rumored to be a host of some repute in his native Marseilles.

But today, the Frenchman appeared on edge.

"And another twelve miners did not report for work this morning," M. Perrot informed them for the third time. "I have made every inquiry of their supervisors, but they have all vanished without a trace. Just like the others!"

A dapper man in his mid-fifties, M. Perrot had a neatly trimmed gray beard and well-combed salt-and-pepper hair. His three-piece suit looked as though it had freshly arrived from Paris. His stylish brown bowler hat was impressively free of dirt or sand and hung at a perfect angle on a brass hat stand by his desk.

But as the mining president informed Leutwein of the growing unease in Tsumeb, he began to perspire, and his voice rose higher. He paused often to wipe his face with an embroidered handkerchief or to fidget anxiously with his tie.

Clearly, Conrad thought, M. Perrot was not a man used to the burden of day-to-day administration in an African colonial backwater.

The twelve miners' disappearance that morning was only the latest in a string of natives abandoning their jobs in the city and slipping away into hinterland villages. A total of fifty-three men and six women had already abandoned Tsumeb in the days after the bombing. M. Perrot was obviously distressed.

"What would you have me do, Theodor?" Perrot asked in his thick Marseilles accent as he paced. "I'm afraid to pay the miners for fear that more of them will leave after I do, but if I don't pay them soon, I will surely have a riot on my hands!"

Conrad had seen hundreds of men still heading towards the labyrinth of mines when he'd arrived early this morning. But the idea of fifty men deserting their posts clearly worried M. Perrot a great deal.

The Frenchman, who came from a well-off Marseille family, had been sent by his company to the DSWA as a figurehead, not a manager. He had been managing the *Rheinisch-Westfälisches Elektrizitätswerk* company in the Ruhr Valley competently enough for the previous few years, but he was laughably unqualified for the challenges of a colonial operation. Conrad already knew that only a third of M. Perrot's overseers spoke French. And he did not appear the kind of person who would bother himself with learning native tongues.

M. Perrot seemed in the habit of being uninformed of the daily operation of the company's mines and had evidently not considered the possibility that a worker rebellion might occur. Conrad wondered if, besides the obvious potential consequences of the railway attack, he was afraid of having to explain to his superiors in Berlin that their labor force was hemorrhaging.

M. Perrot was not "overly fond of the Blacks," as Leutwein had put it, or women for that matter. Leutwein had tactfully asked Sybille to remain in the lobby. She shrugged as though expecting nothing else, but as they followed M. Perrot's secretary up the stairs to the Frenchman's office, Conrad thought he caught a glimpse of bitter resentment in her eyes.

In the end, it took Leutwein an hour to calm Perrot down, then another hour to arrange horses for himself, Conrad, Sybille and, to Conrad's surprise, M. Perrot himself. Either he was eager to escape his present worries about paying his laborers, or he was too afraid to be left alone at the headquarters. Either way, the polished bureaucrat insisted on accompanying them to the site of the attack.

Traveling with them as well were five of the same Schutztruppe Conrad and the others had seen on their way to M. Perrot's office. If Major Baumhauer had heard of the attack already, he had not yet issued any orders to Tsumeb's smaller garrison. The five soldiers who mounted up nodded deferentially to

Leutwein as they formed a shallow escort around their party, glad of a chance to escape the tension of the town.

None of them said a word to Sybille, who rode behind Leutwein at the front of their small column.

Sybille adapted to her first time riding a horse with surprising ease. At first, she viewed her haggard gelding skeptically, but the old horse almost seemed relieved to have been dealt a lighter burden and gave her no trouble as she mounted sidesaddle. She must've observed Frau Grober and the other white ladies of Windhoek on their short, daily rides in the city park, for after only a few tries, she was able to mimic the sidesaddle posture reasonably well.

M. Parrot, eyeing Sybille disdainfully, complained that having to wait for a Hottentot to learn to ride a horse would unnecessarily delay them, and a few of the Schutztruppe had nodded in agreement.

"Why exactly are we bringing her along?" M. Parrot finally demanded.

"Well," Leutwein replied as he swung into his own saddle. "She's the only one of my staff who can speak the local language. I can either wait an hour for her to learn to ride or wait a year or more for you to learn the local tongues around Grootfontein. Which would you prefer, monsieur?"

M. Parrot reddened but said nothing more as Sybille took several practice laps around the stable yard.

After some initial wobbling in the saddle and dropping the reins once at a trot, Sybille could mind her horse well enough to keep pace with the rest of the group.

The same could not be said for Conrad, who had also never ridden a horse before. His long limbs dangled gracelessly out of the stirrups whenever the group moved faster than a trot. The two-day journey to Beaunard's camp between Tsumeb and Grootfontein left him saddle-sore and ill-tempered, and his strong-willed mare seemed equally frustrated with her rider's inexperience.

At night they camped along the completed stretch of railroad, each of the Schutztruppe taking turns standing watch for lions and native saboteurs. M. Perrot insisted on having one of the soldiers pitch a tent for him, but the rest of the group slept on the ground around the light of the campfire.

Sybille kept apart from the men and avoided speaking to any of them as she prepared a meager meal of salted beef and bread. When she'd served the last of them, she picked a spot at the edge of the fire and bedded down quietly for the night.

Conrad wondered if Sybille were frightened of being so near Schutztruppe men after what had nearly happened to her in the alley in Windhoek, but he observed that the soldiers with them were far too nervous to pay any attention to Sybille. They were frightened of what might lie beyond the firelight in the dark, and they kept their rifles close by.

Leutwein had told him that there were few lions in this part of the colony, but that did little to reassure Conrad.

He slept little, and by the time they arrived at the outskirts of the railway camp the next morning, Conrad had already muttered half a dozen prayers that he would never have to sit in a saddle again.

The rail laborer's camp was efficiently modest. Designed to pick up and move as work on the railroad progressed, it consisted almost entirely of open-air tents clustered in groups around small cooking fires. The climate in this part of the DSWA was quite arid, and while hot during the day, the temperatures dropped drastically after dark. Conrad shivered at the thought of spending frigid months in one of those tents.

The ground appeared to be as much sand as dirt for miles around. Scanning the well-worn campsite, Conrad guessed that progress on this part of the track had been painfully slow, even before the native attacks.

But when Conrad and the others dismounted, it was clear that no work had been done for several days. The men, easily a hundred in this camp alone, were almost all African. A cluster of German and Boer overseers sat apart from the others, drinking strong-smelling coffee around their own, larger fire.

At the sight of their party's arrival and the Schutztruppe rifles, the camp fell quiet.

Something was not quite right in the men's attitude. The railroad workers' interest in the newcomers seemed subdued. Conrad had hardly expected a savior's welcome when they arrived, but for as much as everyone in their party had been fretting and arguing over the bombing that had supposedly happened in this very camp, the men of the camp itself seemed…complacent.

Their calm suggested to Conrad that there might never have been such a catastrophe in the camp, or if there had, that it had already been dealt with.

Conrad's eyes darted from Leutwein to Sybille to the mix of Herero, Damara, and Ovambo rail workers. He paused on the cluster of workers closest to them. Conrad guessed that they were southern Ovimbundu drifters from their darker skin and isolated spot at the edge of the camp. They had all turned to look at Leutwein as their party had ridden into camp, but now they had returned their attention to absently stoking their fire and mumbling conversations that Conrad couldn't begin to understand.

But even if he couldn't understand these men, their body language and those of the other nearby men was than enough for Conrad to sense that something new had happened since Leutwein had received Beaunard's telegram. These men had already lived through the chaotic aftermath of the attack and now wore the casual, if not disappointed look of men who had already witnessed the conclusion of the strange episode.

Leutwein seemed to sense the laborers' attitude as well and suddenly looked even worse than he had for the past three days. He swung down off his horse and started towards the group of overseers, only to bump right into the powerful frame of Major Baumhauer.

The glasses perched on the crook of his nose fell to the ground, and all the color drained from Leutwein's face.

"*Hallo*, Commissioner," Baumhauer said with a wicked smile. "I'd have expected you yesterday. Was your train from Karibib delayed?"

Their train had not been delayed, and they had made excellent time to Tsumeb.

How had Major Baumhauer managed to beat them to Beaunard's camp? Conrad wondered, stupefied. And where was Beaunard?

As if Conrad's thoughts had somehow summoned the little Boer man, Beaunard appeared from behind the bulk of Major Baumhauer. He looked as gaunt and drained as Leutwein.

"Ah, Theodor," Beaunard said with a dispirited air. "You haf arrived."

"Indeed, they have, Herr Hertzog," Baumhauer answered for Leutwein. "Arrived just a few moments ago. The Commissioner's a tad late for the festivities, I'm afraid, but we managed all right in his absence, didn't we?"

Major Baumhauer flashed another malevolent smile while Beaunard said nothing.

Leutwein managed to pick his glasses up off the ground but was still too stunned to speak.

How had the Major managed to arrive before them, Conrad asked himself again.

News of the bombing had not yet reached the public in Windhoek, but somehow Baumhauer had gotten wind of its occurrence before Leutwein. The Schutztruppe had a telegraph station in Tsumeb but no soldiers stationed in Beaunard's camp; any news coming from the worksite itself would have had to pass directly through Beaunard's hands.

A sudden thought crossed Conrad's mind. Could Beaunard have changed his allegiance and informed the Major of the attack before Leutwein? One glance at Beaunard, and Conrad realized at once that that was impossible. The little Boer man looked tired and solemn, as much a defeated party in this series of events as anyone else.

Beaunard had tried to contact Leutwein in secrecy, but somewhere along the chain, their ruse must have been uncovered by either the Major or one of his men.

As though confirming his suspicion, Baumhauer continued to smile pleasantly at the new arrivals, making no effort to hide his enjoyment at their discomfiture.

"I received a telegram about the attack from the Lutheran mission at Gaub," the Major explained. "Paster Odo feared that the violence would spread to his mission and asked me to reinforce Tsumeb. I felt it best to deal with the incident personally. Shall we show the Commissioner our prisoners, Herr Hertzog?"

Not waiting for a reply, the Major began to walk back the way he had come.

"Prisoners?" Leutwein asked softly when the Major was out of earshot.

"Yes," Beaunard answered wearily. "De Major has been combing de local villages for days with de Schutztruppe garrison from Grootfontein. Sey have found de culprits of de bombings and sey have sem in custody here in de camp."

"How bad is it, Beaunard?" Leutwein asked, somewhat shakily as he forced himself out of his stunned stupor. "Four? Five?"

Beaunard hung his head and shook it slowly.

"No, Theodor," he said, defeated. "Sey haf thirteen…thirteen still alive."

*

Originally there had been twenty young men involved in the bombing of the rail line, Beaunard told them later. But three of the boys had panicked and run when the Major's patrols swept through their village. The Schutztruppe had run them down on horseback and shot them.

A fourth had managed to evade the Major's patrols originally, but while fleeing through the bush, his "luck had run out," as Beaunard put it, and he'd had been bitten by a black mamba snake. The Schutztruppe found his swollen body the next morning, half-picked apart by vultures and hyenas.

Three more men had perished after the Schutztruppe arrested them, though how exactly they had died in the army's custody, Beaunard did not say. But as soon as Conrad took one look at the remaining suspects, it was immediately apparent how the other three boys had died.

Each of the young men sat with their hands bound behind their back at the bottom of a large trench that Baumhauer had forced them to dig. The trench was nearly twice the height of a man but only just wide enough for two bound men to sit back-to-back. It was clear that these men hadn't received any food or water since being captured, and as Conrad looked down at them, he was horrified to see that each one of them bore multiple, swollen bruises and deep cuts across their bare backs.

They were all younger than he was, Conrad realized after a moment.

Beside him, Conrad thought he heard Beaunard make a dismayed noise that caught in his throat. Beaunard had no love for Hottentots, as he'd told Conrad explicitly several times. But he evidently was not fond of violence, nor of seeing young boys, even African ones, beaten.

M. Perrot clasped his hands together nervously. He was visibly uncomfortable, but perhaps no more so than when pacing in his office in Tsumeb.

Sybille made no sound, but her stricken face told Conrad everything he needed to know about what she was thinking. Her shoulders slumped as though under a great weight. No doubt she had been expecting something as awful as this, he thought. As she stood looking down at the boys, her normally stoic face betrayed resignation and despair.

Conrad expected Leutwein to snap at any moment, to eviscerate the Major where he stood and demand the boys' immediate release.

Yet, as Conrad turned to look at the Commissioner, he was appalled to see that Leutwein was as pale as a ghost. The Commissioner stood in silence, staring into the crudely dug pit with an expression that was impossible to read.

One of the boys looked up at Leutwein then, but rather than the scared face of a child begging for mercy, it was the proud gaze of a young man who knew his fate and was prepared to meet it with cold, hard defiance.

The Commissioner opened his mouth mechanically, knowing that he should say something to intervene, but the Major pounced before Leutwein could speak.

"That one's the ringleader in this little circus," Baumhauer informed those gathered as he pointed down at the boy staring up at Leutwein. "He and the others snuck into the explosives shed in the middle of the night like a pack of thieves, rigged and primed several sticks of dynamite together into a bomb, and then detonated it. I've made some inquiries in the surrounding villages. Their leader's father used to work in Tsumeb as an assistant to the mine surveyor. The father's dead now, but he must've shown his son how to rig the wire for explosives."

The young man continued to stare up at Leutwein as Baumhauer gave his detailed account of what had occurred. Conrad didn't know if the boy spoke German, but he seemed to understand that Leutwein was being informed of what he had done. The bound boy made no move to speak or offer any protest.

"I've told you over and over, Leutwein," Baumhauer continued, his words dripping with personal satisfaction. "You have shown these Hottentots far too much leniency. Now we are going to have to deal with the consequences. They are murderous, violent sub-humans, and this is what happens when you negotiate with them.

"And before you try to lecture me about their age or your damned gilded ramblings of compromise and patience, I've got a dead German citizen in the casualty tent. Two of the other wounded probably won't make it through the night. These bastards have confessed to everything I've told you, and the law is perfectly clear in the case of murder."

Down in the trench, one of the boys was crying softly, rocking back and forth as much as his bonds allowed. He was moaning words Conrad couldn't make out. Beside him, Sybille tensed as she craned her neck to hear him better.

"He's saying he didn't mean to kill anyone," she whispered to Conrad after a moment, her first words to him since their confrontation a few days ago. "They just wanted to slow construction on a part of the track they thought was deserted. But the fuse didn't light when they tried it, and the bomb didn't go off.

"Then those four men in the medical tent appeared on an unexpected patrol. One of the men saw them and tried to chase them away. One boy panicked and dropped his torch as he ran. As the workers chased the boys across the tracks, the bomb's fuse caught fire from the torchlight. That triggered the explosion."

Sybille fell silent. Conrad did not know what to say.

The railway camp was heavy with gloom. Only Baumhauer seemed triumphant. He stood beside the pit like an eager mastiff, waiting to pounce upon whatever feeble excuse Leutwein might try to challenge him with.

Even had these boys not meant to hurt anyone, they had killed at least one German citizen. The law in the colony was clear: The penalty for murder was death. Baumhauer was correct that Leutwein could do nothing to save them.

Beside him, Conrad felt Sybille shift once more as though she were weeping silently. He felt a strong urge to reach out to comfort her but quickly restrained himself. It would draw unwelcome attention, and something told him that the last thing she needed right now was comfort from a German.

Conrad looked to Leutwein, silently urging him to do something, to find some way not to let Baumhauer triumph. Murderers or not, they were just kids, not hardened war criminals. Surely, Leutwein would not hang a group of children?

Leutwein looked at the Major for a moment, then back at the trench. Conrad hoped he could see a plan trying to form itself behind Leutwein's blank expression and willed the man with all his strength to think of something. But after a moment, Leutwein sighed. Whatever he'd been imagining seemed to vanish like a puff of smoke, and Conrad was shocked to see an unfamiliar expression cross the Commissioner's face.

It was the look of a beaten man.

"All right, Sören," Leutwein conceded after a moment. "But not here. In Windhoek. We take them back with us by train."

Baumhauer nodded. He seemed somewhat surprised that Leutwein had offered no protest and agreed to this small concession eagerly. Carrying out the sentence for murder publicly, in Windhoek, was much preferable to executing the boys in this desolate railroad camp.

The Major began barking orders at both the Schutztruppe he'd brought up from Grootfontein and the five men Leutwein had requisitioned from Tsumeb, to secure the railroad and to form up an escort for the prisoners.

Leutwein straightened himself into a more composed state and started to walk back towards the horses, Beaunard trailing silently after him.

M. Perrot stood by the side of the pit, somewhat calmer now. Conrad had nearly forgotten he was there. M. Perrot seemed unaware of the political dogfight that had just played out in front of him, but he apparently grasped that the issue had been resolved for the time being. Conrad guessed that he was simply relieved that he would be able to report back to his bosses in Europe that their investments were still secure.

The Frenchman offered Conrad a cigarette from a handsome gold case he drew out of his pocket and lit one for himself. Then, with a polite, nonchalant tone, he cleared his throat.

"I always appreciate swift justice," he said, taking a long drag on his cigarette. "What is the typical penalty in the colony for such an episode?"

Conrad turned to answer Perrot, but it was Sybille who spoke first.

"Death," she said flatly, keeping all emotion from her voice.

M. Perrot shrugged, apparently unperturbed by the punishment. He seemed more annoyed at Sybille's response than by the sight of the boys half-buried in the trench beneath him. After another long drag on his cigarette, he crushed the burning remains beneath his expensive leather boot and walked casually after Leutwein.

Alone with Sybille, Conrad began to feel his chest tighten. He had not had an asthma attack since leaving Hamburg, but now a mix of shame and heat swelled in his throat. He began to wheeze slightly. Sybille stood impassively beside him, her face revealing nothing of the emotions Conrad were sure lay just behind her mask.

Conrad squirmed inside his khaki clothing, unable to look away from the boy sobbing in the pit and unable to leave her without saying something.

"I'm so sorry," he mumbled.

Sybille said nothing for a long moment.

"Why are you sorry?" she said coldly. "This is always what comes from white men in the end. For all their talk and trade, there is only blood and death for us in the end."

Before Conrad could respond, she turned on her heels, leaving him alone, gasping for breath at the edge of the pit.

*

The train ride back to Windhoek was even worse than the journey to Tsumeb. After a silent two-day horseback trek back to the mining town, Baumhauer had requisitioned an old steam engine to transport himself, Leutwein's small entourage, and the prisoners back to Windhoek. At M. Perrot's grateful insistence, the Major also added the Koloniagesellshcaft's private train car for the Schutztruppe's use on the journey. The immaculate Frenchman had shaken Baumhauer's hand as the Major climbed aboard the train and waved goodbye as the train pulled out of the station.

It was in one of the car's lavish seats that Baumhauer now dozed, having ordered the prisoners secured and locked up in a rusted boxcar ordinarily used for transporting cattle.

The Major and a few of his staff lounged comfortably as their train puffed across the bare hinterlands. Leutwein sat apart, deep in his troubled thoughts.

All through the lavish train car, the Schutztruppe men who accompanied them were having a grand time. While Baumhauer dozed, his men laughed and swigged whiskey from their canteens. It seemed to be a great game to them. They'd bested their foolish Commissioner, and if a few more natives were to hang because of their victory, so much the better.

Sybille chose a seat near Conrad and Leutwein. Fortunately, Baumhauer had so far been too busy enjoying his victory to notice her presence on the train or recognize that he'd been forced to court-martial two of his men after they had tried to rape her.

The Schutztruppe ignored them as well, in too good humor to notice the Commissioner's gangly aide and young Black servant woman in the back corner of the car. Conrad saw that Sybille kept one eye trained on the group of soldiers. He wished for her sake that she did not have to be here.

Although there would be a formal trial once they arrived in Windhoek, Conrad already knew that at least five of the boys, the gang's leader and his four brothers, would likely be hanged. Before leaving the worksite, Leutwein had wanted to ride to the neighboring villages and inform the families of the prisoners of the impending trial. Beaunard eventually talked him out of it.

The people of Grootfontein knew the laws of the German colony already, and God only knew if the villagers would understand the purpose of Leutwein's presence, or if they would react to his goodwill violently, even harm him. The situation was already horrible enough without adding fuel to the fire. Leutwein had begrudgingly relented. He mounted his horse to take the formal lead of the prisoner escort to Tsumeb, leaving Beaunard to attempt to smooth over the relations with the locals. He would report on the situation in person to Leutwein as soon as possible.

Conrad spent most of the long journey in a dazed silence, trying not to imagine the young men in the boxcar behind them being tossed against the hard metal walls of the car with each lurch of the train.

Sybille had told him that the native peoples in the colony only needed a small spark to push them toward rebellion. It seemed that the Major might just give them one.

Conrad swallowed hard to push his fears about rebellion, and war, out of his mind.

Sometime after they had changed tracks at Karibib and cut back eastward towards Windhoek, Conrad felt he had to say something to Sybille or go mad in the silence. She'd been looking absently out the window as they'd passed by dunes of burnt orange sand spotted with clumps of sagebrush and quiver trees.

"*Otjiwa*," Conrad offered in Herero, his voice cracking from disuse. "It's beautiful."

Sybille turned toward him and raised an eyebrow quizzically at him.

"Oh no," Conrad corrected hastily in German. "Not the…er…well. Not this mess. I…uh…meant that you…er, rather the colony…the country, it really is quite nice."

Sybille continued to stare at Conrad, who stumbled clumsily onward, growing more and more flustered.

"I just meant that they are nice to look at," he said, prattling on in both German and broken Herero. "*Eheke.* The orange sand. The amazing orange dunes. They're lovely. I've never seen anything like them before. I like them a lot."

Conrad took a deep breath to calm himself. He could feel his face and ears turning red.

"Sorry. Sometimes I feel like such an awkward duckling, just quacking away and spouting nonsense. Oh, a duck is like a cormorant only…"

"We have ducks here, Conrad," Sybille interrupted in crisp German.

Conrad's face flushed even deeper, and he wished in that moment that the train would derail and throw him out the window.

Sybille gave him a hard look, and then, after a moment, she surprised him by laughing. It was a quiet laugh so as not to rouse Baumhauer or his men, who had all fallen asleep in the train car. Still, it was a real laugh, and it gave Sybille's face a soft glow.

She'd worn a yellow dress today, this one too a long-ago-acquired piece of her wardrobe that had obviously been made for a much larger woman and hid her body amidst a loose curtain of faded cloth.

She laughed again and then gave Conrad a brief, shy smile.

"I think they are nice, too," she said.

Conrad smiled back.

For a long while they sat together, watching the endless orange sand pass before them as the evening sky rose above the dunes.

They were both too exhausted by the past few days to talk, but after a while, Sybille placed her arm on the arm of her seat next to Conrad. He stared at it for a moment, hesitating. At last, he placed his own hand over Sybille's, slowly interlocking his long fingers with hers.

Neither of them said a word as the train puffed its way across the desert, but they sat connected, their minds far away from the cold chill of the falling night and the long shadows of the approaching prison camps.

CHAPTER 6

NOVEMBER-DECEMBER 1903

The hanging was overall an anti-climactic, albeit gruesome, affair. Upon arriving in Windhoek, Leutwein had no choice but to turn the thirteen young prisoners over to Major Baumhauer, who sent them to the largest of the labor camps. Leutwein and Conrad scarcely slept in the days following their return from Tsumeb, as the Commissioner tried to delay the trial in any way he could. But at last, the official go-ahead arrived by telegram from Berlin, and Leutwein unhappily organized the trial of the ringleader, whose name Sybille had discovered was Berriz, and his fellow bombers.

As the Commissioner of the colony, Leutwein served as the judiciary authority for cases involving offenses to, or transgressions against, the Kaiser's government as well as German enterprises. But in the end, even with Leutwein presiding over the boys' fate, the trial itself was little more than a farce.

Leutwein could do nothing to save the boys whom Major Baumhauer had identified as having lit the fuse of the bomb that had killed the rail workers, Berriz and his four brothers. And it would have cost Leutwein too much influence back in Germany to let the other eight boys that the Schutztruppe had captured go free. As it was, relations with the northern chiefs were already damaged, whether the boys were freed or not.

Few officials attended the trial. Mayor Grober came only as required of a representative of the capital. Three senior Schutztruppe aides accompanied Baumhauer to the simple courthouse on the town's main square. None seemed to pay particular attention to the trial, apart from their brief accounts of their arrival at Beaunard's camp and how they'd assisted in the rounding up of the prisoners from the nearby villages. In their testimony, not one mentioned shooting the three boys who had tried to run away or the deaths of three others at the railroad camp. And as judge, it was not Leutwein's place to introduce the matter to the court.

In the end, the evidence was overwhelming. The proceedings lasted less than half an hour. Each of the prisoners was offered a chance to speak in his own defense. But whether sworn to secrecy by the leader of the group, the defiant-looking Berriz, or because they were too afraid to speak under Baumhauer's steely gaze, none of the boys said a word.

Conrad ran his hand through his hair nervously throughout the trial and rearranged his small stack of paperwork multiple times. His summary, in the fresh notebook he had brought with him to record the transcript of the trial for Leutwein, was pitifully succinct.

He had wanted to suggest Sybille as a court translator, but he knew Leutwein would refuse. While Sybille's word was good enough for the Commissioner's own informal use, the word of an African, and a woman at that, in Imperial Court would be worthless—even if she was the only translator in Windhoek who could speak the defendants' language.

So instead, Conrad sat in silence each time the sour court bailiff, an old ex-Schutztruppe colonial whom Leutwein reluctantly introduced as Herr Volker, stood before each of the accused and asked them gruffly in German if they had anything to say on their own behalf. When the boys said nothing, Herr Volker would repeat himself once in his mangled, broken Herero. Then a third time, in even worse Nama.

Met with silence again, Herr Volker would dismiss the prisoner and call the next one. Conrad wondered if any of the boys had understood his question at all.

Conrad's initial prediction proved accurate. Whether Berriz and his brothers had intended murder or not, they had clearly been the organizers of the raid on the railway. They had manufactured the bomb that had killed two Germans, the second man having died of his injuries before the trial.

And so, on an unseasonably chilly morning three days later, Berriz and his four brothers were marched out of the labor camp to be hanged.

Conrad had never witnessed a hanging before and had no desire to attend this one. But when Leutwein had asked him to accompany him to the city outskirts where the Schutztruppe had erected a large hangman's gallows, Conrad could hardly refuse.

Since returning from Tsumeb, Conrad had noticed an alarming change in Leutwein. He was still sharp, but his latest bout with the Major seemed to have taken something out of him. While the Commissioner rose each morning with military precision, it seemed to Conrad that he attacked his daily tasks with a little less vitality than the day before.

Conrad was also beginning to worry that Leutwein might continue to diminish under the increasingly volatile pressures of the colony and the growing hostility within the Colonial Office.

After a bone-chilling, pre-dawn carriage ride, they arrived at the outskirts of the camp the Schutztruppe affectionately referred to as the "Iron Palace." Leutwein read out his brief sentencing to a small group of Schutztruppe camp guards, Herr Volker, Mayor Grober, and the over 400 prisoners within the Iron Palace.

A strong wind blew over the proceedings, and Conrad had to strain himself to hear the Commissioner only a few steps in front of him. But those in the camp did not need to hear Leutwein to understand what was happening, and each dark face stared out at the gallows set up in full view. Every prisoner, old, young, male and female pressed up against the camp's barbed wire fence in a crush of bodies. All gazed dolefully up at the scaffold where Conrad now stood.

Conrad suddenly felt dizzy.

Everyone who described the hanging later said that it had been done well. The bodies had been pulled taut by an expertly hung rope, causing the prisoners' necks to separate instantly from the rest of their vertebrae without any of the awkward gasping and kicking that occurred in sloppier hangings.

Conrad could not remember seeing Herr Volker pull the lever and open the trap doors beneath the five boys' feet. He could not remember the sounds of the ropes being pulled tight and fragile bones breaking.

All he could remember was the sea of silent, ebony faces pressed against the rusted fence, the bitter morning cold, and the dried, sharp edge of a sagebrush bush against his face as he ran down from the scaffold and vomited into it.

*

For weeks afterward it seemed as though the colony was about to erupt into open war. The heightened tensions around Tsumeb had spread across the whole colony, and Conrad had felt sure that once word of the execution of the five Grootfontein boys reached the colony's hinterlands, half of the natives would rise up in vengeful rebellion.

Yet though Conrad spent weeks of sleepless nights and overwrought days in Windhoek's stuffy telegraph station waiting for news of violence, nothing happened.

A week stretched into a month. And still, no rebellion came. Slowly, the rage of the northern chiefs receded into discontented grumblings, and an eerie calm settled back over the DSWA.

M. Perrot continued to send frantic telegrams to Leutwein. He was still hemorrhaging workers, although most of his workforce continued to report to the mine day after day. The next few ore shipments departed for Germany without difficulty.

In fact, the only real excitement in the colony came when Otto Wolf, the elderly mayor of the central railroad town of Okahandja, announced that his heart condition of several years had worsened. The spindly old man, who had somehow managed to endure the colony's harsh climate for decades, requested immediate retirement to spend his remaining few years back home in Germany.

Leutwein thought about refusing Herr Wolf's request at first. The colony's "Gentle Wolf," so dubbed for his soft voice and agreeable manner, was well-respected among the Herero chiefs surrounding Okahandja. Perhaps even more importantly, he was one of Leutwein's few remaining allies in the colony.

But Leutwein could hardly deny the aging mayor's request. He was obliged to accept his resignation and send him back to Berlin with a paraded ceremony in the capital.

As soon as the train carrying Wolf to Walvis Bay departed, Leutwein began looking for a temporary replacement until the Colonial Office got around to appointing Wolf's successor. And after only a week's deliberation, Leutwein surprised Conrad by appointing Beaunard as Okahandja's acting mayor.

Beaunard was one of the few men left in the colony who had the managerial skill necessary to govern a town the size of Okahandja. Nevertheless, Conrad had been taken aback that Leutwein would choose such a polarizing candidate.

Okahandja and its surrounding bush areas were the traditional birthplace of scores of Herero chieftains. Many of those chieftains had opposed the construction of Beaunard's new railroads. Several had family members incarcerated in the Windhoek camps. Beaunard had made no secret of his distaste for Africans. Nor was it likely that any of the local chiefs would be willing to overlook his role in the hanging of the five Grootfrontein boys.

The appointment had also enraged both Baumhauers.

Dietrich Baumhauer had protested the appointment in Berlin, using it to fuel his campaign against Leutwein with relish. He made sure that it was widely circulated in the Colonial Office that Leutwein was losing his touch with the natives: now he had gone so far as to appoint a Boer engineer to a mayoral post instead of a German official!

Dietrich's vendetta against Leutwein intensified as he accused the Commissioner of everything from incompetence to cronyism. Conrad began to fear that the Baumhauer brothers might succeed in turning more members of the Kaiser's inner circle against Leutwein.

But for all the political infighting from the Baumhauers and their supporters, Beaunard's appointment went unchallenged by the Colonial Office. And once again, life around Windhoek slowly resumed normalcy.

Except with respect to Sybille.

For the first few weeks after the trial, she had avoided him. Not intentionally perhaps, given the rush of events around their trip back and return to Windhoek. Still, there was now a painful, nervous silence between her and Conrad that neither dared to or even knew how to break.

Around the Residence's other staff and Leutwein, Sybille was still her poised self. But on the rare times when the pair happened to bump into one another, Sybille spoke to Conrad in a rush. On more than one occasion rather than address him, she had hurried from the room without saying a word.

Generally, they exchanged a few polite, quick words whenever they found themselves in the same room alone. But there was always another chore Sybille needed to do, or another urgent matter that Conrad needed to attend to – providing each a quick escape.

It was an accident, Conrad told himself each time he invented a pretext to avoid being alone with Sybille. It had been the suffocating heat that made him kiss her at !Gai!ga's party. Anyway, he had just needed a way to get her to stop yelling at him. He couldn't be attracted to a Herero housemaid. Could he?

And in the train car, when he'd held her hand in the darkness, he had been merely comforting her. The horror of what they had witnessed had certainly shaken him too, and he'd only wanted to offer her some sense of solace. It would be ridiculous to think that Sybille might have read more into his actions than that.

Or perhaps not.

Perhaps Sybille had been so shell-shocked by the events in the rail workers' camp that she had lost her senses for a moment. Conrad could not think why else the haughty Sybille would have let him hold her hand. Grief made people act strangely, didn't it? Sometimes even surprisingly, inexplicably…needy?

There had been that time back in Aschaffenburg when his father had presided over the funeral of the town's prosperous wine merchant, Herr Acker. Conrad had seen the deceased's oldest daughter, Olga, kissing one of the local farm boys against the transept wall of his father's church. The boy, Noah, had been a year younger than the pretty Olga, with the patchwork beginnings of a red beard and a permanent layer of dirt embedded beneath his fingernails.

Yet at her father's funeral, Olga Acker, clad in a fine black riding habit and new white gloves, had clung hungrily to Noah's strong shoulders as though she were trying to quench an insatiable thirst.

In any event, Conrad now thought, it didn't really matter. Kissing Sybille was merely a reflex. There was no reason to think she had not sought his comfort for the same reason.

Whatever had passed between them on the train was clearly a mistake, and in the past. If Sybille chose to avoid him either out of disappointment that he had not done more or sheer embarrassment that she had let him see her grief, there was little he could do about it. And why should he want to do anything about it? He couldn't imagine someone more dissimilar from himself.

Sybille was, on the best of days, abrasive and assertive. Conrad had witnessed her merciless temper first-hand any number of times. She was too proud, too tall, too loud, and too...*foreign* to be any sort of match for him. And, after all, she was a household servant and he was an aide to the Imperial Commissioner.

Yet no matter how hard Conrad tried to erase the memory of the kiss from his mind, the feeling of her lips on his lingered.

*

One day, returning from an errand he'd run in town for Leutwein, Conrad had the strangest feeling that he was being watched as he opened the main gate to the Residence. He found Petyr in the front yard, trying to mend a fence post that one of Leutwein's dogs had broken. Petyr was still wearing his baggy footman's uniform, and a line of frustrated sweat was pouring down his face as he struggled in vain to move the broken wooden rail.

"Do you need a hand with that?" Conrad called to him.

Petyr looked frightened for a moment, as if afraid of punishment, but relaxed when he saw Conrad.

"I can't move it," he told Conrad fearfully. "But William said I have to or Leutwein will whip me."

Conrad frowned. William was a stable boy only slightly older than Petyr. Conrad guessed that William was the one who was supposed to be mending the fence. William was also a troublemaker and had obviously scared Petyr into doing his work for him. While Leutwein had never whipped any of his servants that Conrad knew of, Petyr had obviously believed William.

"Let me help you," Conrad said as he set down the package he'd been carrying and took off his suit jacket.

Between the two of them, they pulled the mangled fence post out of the ground and hammered the new one into place. Relief flooded over Petyr's face, and Conrad slipped him a chocolate bar he had bought in town. As Petyr ran off toward the stables, Conrad turned around to see Sybille watching from the Residence's porch. Her expression was unreadable, and before Conrad could say a word she disappeared back into the house.

After three more weeks of restless fretting and darting away from Sybille every possible moment, Conrad finally realized that not only had he enjoyed kissing Sybille and holding her hand on the train, he also wanted to do it again.

Sybille was not beautiful exactly. Her limbs were long and gangly, much like his own, and her striking azure eyes, which drew your attention the moment you looked at her, were set a bit too narrowly against her nose and gave her a self-commanding poise that was more aggressive than dignified.

Yet what fascinated Conrad about her was that she seemed to possess an infallible sense of honor hidden beneath her impertinent shell. Conrad had never met anyone with more self-determination than Sybille, a badge she bore like a martyr's cross. She'd been willing to suppress her own rape to save Leutwein's political position, and while she'd still been half-dressed and bloody, she had turned on her rescuers and shouted at Albert Witbooi to save Conrad.

He had absolutely no idea what to make of a woman like that.

She'd traveled to Tsumeb and stared into a pit of mutilated children, and still she had returned with Leutwein to the capital to resume her role on his staff.

If she could bear horrors like that and still maintain her pride and walk about the Residence with her head high with purpose, then Conrad had no doubt she could do anything she put her mind to. Despite her lot in life, she was impossibly strong. And perhaps, if nothing else, that was what Conrad liked about her.

Late one evening, while he was reviewing the last of a stack of deteriorating files Leutwein had asked him to copy, he went to the kitchen in search of coffee. Over the recent months, the Residence staff had grown accustomed to Conrad working late hours, so someone always made a habit of leaving a cup out for him.

On his way, he found Sybille clearing away the last of the dinner dishes. Mayor Grober had been at dinner that night, and, as they did at every meal, the man's careless eating habits had made a considerable mess of the tablecloth.

Sybille moved the dishes onto a tray on the sideboard and concentrated on trying to save the white tablecloth from Grober's numerous wine stains. She did not hear Conrad come in.

Conrad tried to say something to alert her he was there, but his voice caught in his throat.

Verdammt, he cursed to himself. Since coming to Africa, he'd already been beaten, bludgeoned, threatened and made to watch children hang. Surely, he could manage to speak to a servant?

Throwing up her hands in exasperation with the stains, Sybille turned to take the tray with the remaining plates and silverware to the kitchen. When she saw Conrad, she froze and nearly dropped the heavy tray.

"Er...*hallo*," Conrad managed to sputter. He felt as awkward as ever in her presence. But he had nothing better to say.

"*Hallo*," Sybille replied neutrally.

Well, this can't get any worse, Conrad thought as they both stood there, hesitating.

"Yes, well," Conrad started, looking around the room to avoid making eye contact with Sybille. "What happened at the party, and again on the train..."

Conrad saw Sybille tense, but he plunged on before she could say anything.

"That was...*unusual* for me," he said. "That is to say, I don't normally behave that way. Never...actually. Not that it wasn't special. It was...I..."

Sybille still hadn't moved. Conrad forced himself to meet her blue, impenetrable eyes.

"I wanted to apologize," he said as formally as he could as she stared. "With all that's happened lately, I suppose I lost control of myself for a moment. I want to say, well, that my actions were highly inappropriate. I want to offer you an apology."

For a moment, Sybille looked wary. But then, a small sound escaped from her throat, and she began to laugh.

Conrad's face flushed. He was already embarrassed to be having this discussion, and now to his shock Sybille was laughing at him.

He was simply trying to be civil about this whole strange business. He wanted to do the right thing and apologize. He especially didn't want them to spend the rest of his tour awkwardly trying to avoid one another. And here was Sybille laughing in his face.

"Now, wait just a moment," he said, lowering his voice so that any other lingering staff would not overhear them. "I hardly think…"

Abruptly, she crossed the short distance between them and kissed him. It was just a soft brush of her lips on his, but a small shiver ran down his spine and Conrad instantly forgot whatever it was he had been about to say.

Sybille stepped back from him but gave him a small smile. Outside the window behind her the last of the sunlight faded beyond the outskirts of the city. A sea of stars was beginning to emerge over the glow of Schwerinsburg's lamplight. Conrad smiled back at Sybille, lost in how her chiseled features softened when she smiled.

"You are sweet," she said as she gathered up the last of the dishes. "I don't usually behave that way either, you know."

Conrad made to help her finish clearing up, but she waved him away. The skittishness she'd shown over the past few weeks seemed to melt away all at once as if an unspoken question on her mind had finally been answered.

Once again, the room was fully her domain. In her presence, Conrad felt helpless, forced to watch her walk away from him. Still, the recollection of her kiss lingered on his lips.

"However," she said, walking past Conrad towards the door. "I *might* be persuaded to let you do it again."

She paused a moment and gave Conrad a look that was both coquettish and, he thought, a challenge. With that, she disappeared into the kitchen.

*

Clearly, unlike most German women and girls he knew, Sybille did as she pleased. If Conrad were honest with himself, confused as he was about this strange country and his role in it, he was happy for her to take the lead.

After their brief exchange in the dining room, the tension between them began to ease day by day into a warm, discreet dalliance. They were both inexperienced, giving their rendezvous a hurried, shy feel. But Conrad awakened each morning hopeful that he might steal Sybille away from her chores and have her all to himself for a few precious minutes.

It was not just the possibility of receiving a quick, covert kiss in Leutwein's garden or beneath the stairwell of the main house that excited Conrad, though he certainly enjoyed them.

When Sybille was not shouting or threatening someone, she was an utterly enchanting woman. He had long ago realized that Sybille was intelligent. But what he found even more attractive was that her intelligence seemed to make her such a sound judge of character. He admired her selflessness and the ways she looked after the other natives employed at Schwerinsburg, especially young Petyr, and she seemed to know every tradition and belief of even the remotest tribes in the DSWA.

And after only a few weeks of hearing her typically clipped, terse speech mellow beside the gurgling fountain and beneath the hot shade of a purple jacaranda tree, Conrad found himself enthralled by her.

"Do you believe in God, Conrad?" she had said one day as they stole a few restful minutes alone.

"I suppose so," he said, watching as her long fingers traced ripples in the fountain's pool. "My father was a preacher back home in Germany."

Sybille's eyes widened.

"Was your father a Lutheran minister?"

"Why, yes he was," Conrad replied. "Why do you ask?"

Sybille made a disgusted noise.

"The Lutheran minister who taught my father to speak German told him that God had set the white man in dominion over the Black to help educate and enlighten him. Do you believe that's true?'

Conrad was momentarily floored. Searching for something to say, he shrugged and tore his gaze away.

"I…well, I suppose there's quite a lot that most Africans don't know that most Europeans do."

Sybille gave a short, involuntary laugh.

"Yes, I'm sure," she said with breathtaking insincerity. "And yet while most Black men here know two or three profitable trades, all the white men I've met seem to struggle to cope with a measly amount of paper-pushing."

Conrad had no idea how to respond to this either, so he tried a sheepish smile.

"Well," he tried. "Surely not *all* the white men you know, I hope?"

Sybille stopped playing with the water and gave him a very direct look.

"Nearly all," she replied. "There are a few I haven't made up my mind about just yet."

Conrad shot her another foolish grin. As he leaned in to kiss her mouth, Sybille dipped her hand back into the fountain and splashed his face.

The water was warm and tasted of sand and algae. As he spluttered and wiped the water from his eyes, Sybille laughed and kissed his nose. He coughed twice and took a handkerchief from his jacket to dry his face. When he finally looked up, Sybille was standing fifty feet away on the Residence's veranda. She winked at him and blew him another kiss before she turned her back on him and slipped back inside the house.

Conrad was utterly smitten.

Once in a while, he wondered what his family would say if they knew that he counted down the hours until he could sit beside Sybille and hold her hand, secluded in their employer's garden.

He knew, of course, they would not approve. God forbid his mother should ever find out. It would've been hard to say what was more likely to terrify Georgina: that he'd kissed a woman before they were married or that the woman was a house servant, to say nothing of the color of her skin.

Conrad thought about confessing his relationship with Sybille in his letters home. He wrote his mother once a week, and he'd only received a few short formal replies. But he knew that as soon as he mentioned that he was involved with a native African maid, his mother would be on the next ship from Hamburg, with his uncle's blessing, to drag him home in disgrace.

In truth, these thoughts never occupied his mind for long. His family was thousands of miles away. While he knew his cousins loved him, Ekkehardt and Georgina had hardly been the most affectionate parents. It was hard for him to imagine a warm welcome for any woman Conrad found himself involved with.

Meantime, Conrad was alone in Africa, and he was lonely. And if Sybille didn't care, then neither did he.

Conrad grew accustomed to the feeling of Sybille's hand in his. The more discreet kisses they stole, the more he longed for their next encounter.

That same night he returned to his bungalow late at night to find Sybille sitting on his doorstep waiting for him.

"Leutwein is keeping you busy," she said as she stood up and brushed the hem of her dress. "Saving the colony, were you?"

Conrad smiled at her in the dark.

"Pushing papers mostly," he said mockingly.

"Careful," Sybille chided. "You'll ruin your eyesight trying to read in the dark."

"Really?" Conrad replied. "Well, I wouldn't want to do that."

"I should hope not," Sybille said, her storm-colored eyes flashing in the pale starlight. "Otherwise, you might miss a girl's subtle invitation."

Sybille tipped her chin up to invite a kiss, but before Conrad could respond, she became impatient and pulled his face to hers. They kissed softly in the darkness for a long moment, and Conrad relished the feel of Sybille's hot skin against his own. He wanted to stay like that forever.

Then, Sybille shocked him by slipping her tongue inside his mouth. He'd been surprised for a moment, and then responded, hesitantly teasing her tongue with his own. He heard Sybille moan softly, and Conrad thought he would melt in her arms.

But it was not enough for Sybille. She pressed herself closer to him and wrapped her arms around him. She stiffened suddenly, and Conrad was embarrassed that she must be able to feel his erection through his trousers. But after a moment's hesitation, Sybille pressed herself up against him again as if she wanted to feel it.

Conrad felt his breath coming in gasps and, hesitantly, he moved his hands up from Sybille's waist to the underside of her breasts. They were small and firm in his hands, and he could feel the soft flesh tingling beneath the thin cloth of Sybille's dress. His right hand closed over her right breast, and he felt her nipple stiffen at his touch. His thumb teased the tip of it and Sybille bit down hard on Conrad's lower lip.

He moved to explore her left breast, but before he could find her other nipple, she broke the kiss. They both stood there in the dark, panting as they looked at the outline of each other's faces.

"That was a *subtle* invitation?" Conrad asked with a nervous laugh.

Sybille was silent for a moment, and Conrad was afraid he had offended her. Then, to his astonishment, she snorted loudly and began to laugh.

"You don't know anything about how to charm women, do you Conrad?" she asked without malice.

"Er, well…" he said trying to read her face in the dark. "No, I suppose not. I don't really have much experience."

Sybille laughed again, and then pressed herself back up against Conrad's chest. She was a tall woman and her hair tickled Conrad's nose, and she forced her way beneath his chin.

"Good," she said simply.

Then she kissed him firmly on the mouth, turned on her heels and disappeared toward the servants' quarters.

Conrad hardly slept that night.

A few days later, Erwin caught them entangled in the kitchen early in the morning. Petyr grinned at Conrad knowingly a few hours later. After that, both he and Sybille were even more circumspect around one another.

The last thing either wanted was to be the subject of Windhoek gossip. There were no mixed-race couples in Windhoek, at least none that were publicly acknowledged. No question, for someone on the Commissioner's staff to be caught with a Black maid would be a damaging scandal. One that was the last thing Leutwein needed right now.

But more than what such a discovery would mean for him and Leutwein, Conrad could not bear for Sybille to become the object of gossip again. Nor did Sybille want Conrad to be knifed or gunned down in some back alley now that Albert Witbooi and his men had returned to Windhoek.

For weeks they found ways to meet without raising any suspicion, which was why Conrad was taken aback when Leutwein called him into his office one day and asked him how he and Sybille got along.

"Sir?" Conrad said, not sure that he had heard Leutwein correctly.

"How well do the two of you get along?" the Commissioner repeated across a desk buried beneath territorial maps and the morning's telegrams from Berlin.

The temperature had risen over the past few weeks in anticipation of the coming rainy season, and Leutwein's shirt was already wet with perspiration. His necktie hung in disarray from his collar.

"Er…we get along just fine, sir," Conrad replied, wondering in a silent panic which of the house staff or white visitors had discovered him with Sybille and reported him to Leutwein.

"Excellent," Leutwein said distractedly as he sorted through a stack of already-rifled papers. "I thought as much. In that case, I have an important task for you. Your first solo diplomatic foray, as it were. Pack a bag for a few days. I want you to escort Sybille home to her village outside of Okahandja and speak with her father, Samuel Maharero."

Conrad felt as though Leutwein were making fun of him. Take Sybille home and speak to her father? Surely this was a joke or even a disapproving command.

"Samuel Maharero, sir?" he stammered out.

"Yes," Leutwein explained patiently as he moved around to the other side of his desk. "Didn't know our Sybille had a famous father, did you? He's the Herero chieftain of Hochfeld. Quite possibly, he's our best chance right now at avoiding a full-scale war with the Herero."

Conrad was at a loss for words. What exactly was Leutwein getting at? Why were the Herero suddenly threatening war? And what exactly did Leutwein want *him* to say to a Herero chief?

"Samuel Maharero may be our last chance of preserving the peace," Leutwein repeated. "Of all the Herero chiefs, he is the most respected. He had a Lutheran education, and we get along. Some years ago, I decided to hire his daughter Sybille from Frau Grober as a token of good faith. Now, I've heard word that he has called a meeting of the Herero tribes a day's journey from Okahandja. I want you to accompany Sybille back to her village at Hochfeld and speak with her father as my emissary.

"Urge him to be patient. Tell him I know that the Herero are angry, but that violence will solve nothing. Tell him…I'm trying my best to hold the warmongers in Berlin back, but should anything else disturb the peace before I can smooth over the Colonial Office…"

Leutwein trailed off a moment, halting his frantic search for whatever document lay concealed beneath the clutter of his desk.

"The Kaiser has taken note of the recent events here, Conrad," Leutwein sighed. "The man is even prouder than Bismarck. He is…*displeased* that the natives are growing more hostile. He wants Germany to have colonies to rival those of England and France, and he won't suffer any resistance to German expansion. Togoland and Kamerun are of little interest to him right now, and after that business in East Africa, he's got little patience for anything that might threaten German prestige. He's got his eye on Southwest Africa. We need Maharero to help us keep the peace. That devil Dietrich Baumhauer has wormed his way into the Kaiser's inner circle, and I don't know how much longer I can stave off an invasion if we can't make peace with the Herero."

Leutwein's words hung heavily in the air. Conrad knew the political situation in Berlin regarding the DSWA was strained, but could the Kaiser be seriously considering *re-invading* the colony?

"I'd go myself," Leutwein said, renewing his search for whatever item he had misplaced on his desk. "But with things as tense as they are, I can't risk leaving Windhoek and having the Schutztruppe run amok while I'm gone. I need someone to go in my stead, Conrad, so I'm asking you."

Conrad thought he saw an almost pleading look in the man's eyes. The Commissioner was teetering on the edge of total collapse, and if Conrad failed him, he thought Leutwein might never recover.

"Of course, sir," Conrad replied.

Leutwein had shared too much in these few short moments for Conrad to make sense of. War, invasion, a long trip into the bush, Sybille's father. For the moment, Conrad was just relieved that his romance with Sybille had not been found out. In any case, how could he not oblige the Commissioner on the very first diplomatic mission he'd been given to handle on his own?

Leutwein gave him a relieved smile as he rifled through another pile of maps.

"Thank you, Conrad," he said. "You're a godsend."

*

Conrad knew almost nothing about Samuel Maharero.

When he and Sybille were alone, their conversations came in snatches. Sybille had told him little about her village, only that she returned home every November just before the rains came to care for her father. She'd never mentioned her mother.

She would return to Windhoek in late March at the beginning of the dry season, along with the scores of other young native women who flocked back to the capital to seek seasonal work as housemaids or seamstresses.

Sybille had been following this routine for six years since she'd first left her father's village at age eighteen.

Without Leutwein, the Schutztruppe train station officials were in no mood to kowtow to Conrad. As Conrad tried to purchase two first-class tickets northward, he was rudely told by a Schutztruppe private in a wrinkled uniform that the first-class car was already full. Conrad had yet to see a single person enter the car at the far edge of the platform, but he decided not to challenge the man and to hurry past the ticket counter.

Not wanting to be separated from Sybille in the whites-only, second-class cars, Conrad had purchased two tickets for third-class. The conductor at the Windhoek station had raised a questioning eyebrow at Conrad but shrugged after a moment and waved Conrad and Sybille aboard.

Unlike their empty train to Tsumeb, the train to Okahandja, 70 kilometers north of the capital, was jammed with the most bizarre, motley crowd Conrad had ever seen. The communal benches of the third-class car had long since been claimed by other passengers, who clung to their small oasis tenaciously. As the train began its long journey forward, Conrad and Sybille were flung unceremoniously into a sea of Africans in various states of dress and ill-temper.

They squeezed themselves into a small gap near the back of the train car, unable to find anywhere to sit down amongst the crowd.

Sybille motioned towards a bare-chested man adorned in a long skirt and a patchwork headdress that strung together a chaotic rainbow of peculiar-looking feathers. Many of the other passengers tried to give the man a wide berth, which only added to the congestion. Sybille whispered in Conrad's ear that the man was an infamous shaman, from a Damaranland village called Twyfelfontein, about 500 km northwest of Windhoek.

Only one person was willing to sit next to the shaman: a man whose ribcage practically poked through his torn shirt and who muttered incoherently to a brightly colored parrot with a collar attached to a worn leash on his shoulder. To the left of the bird man stood two Ovambo women in the garb of the Black Christian sisters of the small St. Catherine's nunnery in Windhoek. The nuns were attempting to read their tattered Bible despite the strenuous jostling of the train.

The two women cast a disapproving glance at the shaman and crossed themselves, and the shaman sneered wickedly back at them, revealing a set of crooked, rotting teeth.

Amid the bustle of passengers talking, gesticulating and arguing, Conrad received only a few curious looks. For the most part, however, as he struggled to keep his balance in the rocking railway car, he was ignored. For the few uncomfortable hours of the train ride, he was simply another oddity, just another part of the swirling mass of miserable camaraderie as the train lumbered slowly northward.

Some five or six hours later, the train pulled mercifully into the Okahandja station. Conrad managed to step down onto the platform and turn to help Sybille, but he wobbled unsteadily and nearly fell over as the grimacing shaman shoved roughly past him. Sybille stepped down nimbly and quickly led him toward the exit used by natives. She laughed as his knees nearly buckled beneath him again. He flushed with embarrassment as all the natives from their third-class car disembarked without trouble.

Surrounded by farmland, Okahandja was much smaller than Windhoek but felt far busier than the manicured capital. While over three-quarters of the town's population were normally white German settlers, at this time of year its dirt roads flooded with native men, women, and children, all making their way home to their local villages.

Black merchants shouted at passersby, hawking everything from roasting meat and steaming stews to colorful new clothes and Onyoka jewelry made from white mussel shells. Each stall owner tried to shout louder than his neighbors, each determined to attract the horde of workers traveling home with a season's worth of wages hidden within the secret folds of their clothes.

Conrad, struck by the lack of white faces in the crowd, wondered fleetingly if most of the town's German residents stayed indoors until the wave of migrants had passed.

In a few days, on his return trip to Windhoek, Conrad planned to visit Beaunard and see how he was adjusting to life as mayor. But for now, he and Sybille pushed their way through the crowds on the platform to hurry out of Okahandja as quickly as they could.

Okahandja now boasted a new garrison where Major Baumhauer had established a Schutztruppe command post. The Major had alerted his brother Dietrich in Berlin that local Herero activity in the colony's central region demanded a stronger security presence outside of Windhoek. After Dietrich pressed the matter with the war hawks in the Reichstag and the Colonial Office, Berlin had readily agreed to finance the new garrison.

The shadow of the new barracks loomed over the small-town square. Conrad could smell the peculiar aroma of fresh paint and gunpowder as he and Sybille hurried past.

The nearby Damara and Herero villages had all been loyal subjects of the colonial government. They had not taken part in any of the Nama revolts over the past decade and were too poor to warrant an expensive, new garrison to ward off the few cattle raiders that roamed the outskirt farms of the region. Conrad suspected that Baumhauer's real motive was to undermine any political influence Beaunard might gain for Leutwein in the central region.

The principal danger in the area was that Baumhauer would now be able to cause trouble with the tribes: the Schutztruppe could conduct raids away from Leutwein's direct oversight. Beaunard might be able to keep an eye on the Major, but any real action to block the Schutztruppe's actions would come several days too late.

The Major and Leutwein's personal war was again coming to a head. Once more, it appeared that Baumhauer had gained the upper hand.

Conrad and Sybille avoided the town's few cramped hotels for the evening. Instead, they made their way through the mass of travelers and walked the six long miles to a small village that Sybille said was called Witvlei. Although the rains had not yet begun, the sky was thick with moisture. Conrad's light khaki shirt clung to his chest by the time they arrived at the home of Anna, one of Sybille's friends.

Sybille had told Conrad little about her plans for their journey, but Conrad had gleaned that Anna was Herero, and that she lived in Witvlei with her brother's family.

Witvlei, Sybille told him as they trudged along a worn, dirt path that led out of Okahandja, was a small village to the northeast, one in a long chain of Herero settlements in the colony's central region. Even so, Conrad was still surprised at how few people he saw after they had left the bustling town for the muted browns of dry farmsteads and parched earth.

The sun had nearly set by the time they walked into Witvlei and reached Anna's home. The compound was simple, a series of mud-walled huts with thatched roofs, all lying within the boundary of a thin, wooden fence. In the center stood the largest hut, built for Anna's brother and his wife. A ring of smaller structures lined the rest of the compound: homes for Anna, her brother's children, aunts, uncles and a vast collection of other relatives. There was a small pen at one end of the fence where several chickens pecked absently at the dirt. A lone goat bleated loudly when it saw Conrad enter the compound.

Anna, a stout, solid-looking woman, ran towards them squealing with girlish delight when she poked her head out of her doorway and saw Sybille. Then, Anna's family seemed to emerge from all sides at once. A vortex of screaming, half-naked children and shouting adults swarmed Sybille in an instant. Amid all the delighted laughter and questions raining down on Sybille, Conrad hung awkwardly apart from the celebration, understanding absolutely nothing of what was being said.

At one point, he saw Anna pointing at him. He thought he heard Sybille, who shook her head in obvious denial. For a moment, he felt relieved, if not a little curious to know what Anna had asked and a little disappointed that whatever it was, Sybille had quickly dismissed it.

But for the most part, he simply waited, a well-dressed, perspiring white man, an unlikely guest in this rural African village.

Anna's brother, Nokokure, called Noko, plainly did not care for Conrad. But apart from an initial cold glance and a greeting that was more grunt than salutation, Noko was a gracious host.

"You take my bed. As guest," Noko said curtly in rough German over a loud supper of mashed yams and a stringy meat soup Conrad was told was guinea fowl. "Tomorrow, we go. See Maharero."

Conrad had politely tried to refuse Noko's offer. He insisted that he would be fine sleeping on a pallet on the floor, but Noko would not hear of it. Guest laws were guest laws. Even though Noko gave Conrad the feeling that he might like to run him through with one of the feathered hunting spears that hung on the wall of the hut, Conrad was his guest and a visiting dignitary at that. In his chief's absence, Noko would show Conrad the highest respect while he was under his roof and then escort him personally to Maharero.

After that, well, Conrad tried not to think about it.

The bed consisted of a worn animal hide stretched tight across several iron springs and a small wooden headboard. The springs dug uncomfortably into his back. Conrad wondered how tough his large, muscular host must be to be able to sleep through the night on such a thing. Somewhere out in the night, he heard the high-pitched yipping of a jackal, no doubt scavenging for scraps near the family's compound.

As he lay sleepless beneath the scratchy blanket Noko's wife had lent him, he heard Noko and his wife speaking in hushed tones in the main room where they were sharing their children's pallet. Conrad could not make out many of the words, but he caught *Omundoitji*, "the German," clearly enough. He also heard several words that sounded far from hospitable.

His ears pricked up when he heard Sybille's name and *Omundoitji,* "German," again very soon after it. Noko's wife seemed to be saying the words *kora*, "tell," and "Maharero," with a slight inflection that made Conrad think she was asking a question.

Noko stayed silent a long time. Conrad held his breath, trying not to move a muscle for fear of missing even one of his whispers. At last, his response came. A plain *"Ayee."* No.

He added something like *omatoororero*, "a choice," then Sybille's name. And after a long pause, he added, *yari oujova we*, "she made a stupid choice." Noko and his wife's snores soon sounded lightly from the other room, but Conrad lay awake in the darkness for hours, his heart pounding in his ears.

*

Hochfeld's wooden palisade was almost invisible among the added swell of thousands of Herero from at least three dozen clans camped outside Maharero's village.

As Anna and Noko explained to Conrad over the two-day trek from Witvlei further north to the Herero village of Hochfeld, a great gathering of the Herero chiefs had been called a month earlier. All but the very old and the sick had come from all corners of the colony to attend the council.

Sybille had known nothing of the gathering, having been in Windhoek when the chieftains had called for an assembly, so Anna and Noko had waited for her before journeying to Hochfeld themselves. Samuel Maharero had had no way to contact his daughter ahead of the council and had sent a message to Noko, asking him to wait for her arrival, knowing that Sybille always stayed a night or two with Anna on her yearly trips back home.

Conrad was evidently an unwelcome surprise insofar as Noko was concerned. Still, Conrad could not fully understand why his presence so unnerved Anna's brother.

The trek to Hochfeld was not overly grueling, though it was certainly hot, as the rough road beneath them seemed to absorb every ounce of heat from the sun. When at last they stopped for the night on the first day, thirsty and footsore, Conrad realized there were no tents. They were meant to sleep on pallets in the open brush.

Along with their small party trotted three of the ugliest dogs Conrad had ever seen, each an odd mixture of black faces and mangy, tanned fur that looked like the color of kicked-up dust. When they stopped just before twilight, while Anna, Sybille and Noko's wife looked after the children, Conrad saw Noko stroking one of his dogs tenderly.

"Interesting pups you have there, Noko," Conrad said in an effort to make conversation.

Ko snorted and gave Conrad a derisive smile.

"No *ozombona*," he said, looking out into the dry brush. "Not puppies. They watch. *Ongwe*. Leopards. They come at night. Try and steal you away."

Noko laughed loudly and walked away.

"Are there really leopards out here on this road?" Conrad whispered to Sybille, barely managing to hide the discomfort in his voice.

"Yes," Sybille replied casually. "But Noko's dogs are very skilled. He just wants to frighten you."

"Well, he's managed that well enough," Conrad muttered under his breath.

From the other side of the camp, Noko's wife walked toward them as though she did not like the idea of Sybille being left alone with an *Omundoitji*. Before the woman came within earshot, Conrad turned toward Sybille again.

"Sybille," he said quietly. "Do you know anything about this gathering? Do you know what it's about?"

Sybille gave him a direct look.

"No," she said briskly, though something in her gaze told Conrad that that was not entirely true.

"What can you tell me about your father? What kind of man is he?"

But before Sybille could answer, Noko's wife beckoned her away to help finish setting up the camp.

Conrad did not sleep at all that night.

Yet it was not merely the fear of a leopard or a pack of roving hyenas slipping in and out of the firelight's shadows that kept Conrad awake. Now, he was sure that the Herero chiefs were gathering in response to the execution of the Grootfontein boys. Every time Conrad tried to close his eyes, he saw the limp bodies of the five boys swinging on the hangman's block.

How am I possibly supposed to fix this, he asked himself as he lay shivering on the cold ground.

By the time they approached Hochfeld near noon the next day, Conrad was exhausted. His limbs ached, and his head was pounding. But as they reached the top of the small hill overlooking the village, his fatigue evaporated instantly. Across the sagebrush plain below lay acres of tattered tents and wooden shelters, and thousands of Herero.

It took their small party nearly half an hour to reach the original outskirts of Hochfeld. The further Noko and Anna led them through the mass of Herero, the more uneasy and anxious Conrad became.

Unlike on the train to Okahandja, where he had been merely one more in an array of unusual fellow travelers, in Hochfeld Conrad stood out more than if he had announced his arrival by firing a pistol round into the air.

As they made their way through the city of tents and into the village, nearly every face turned to meet them.

Conrad was not sure what exactly he'd been expecting, but Sybille and Noko's family were greeted without much ceremony. There were no loud whoops for joy and no frenzied embraces. Most people they passed merely nodded to Sybille and Noko as though they had been gone a few hours rather than a few months.

For Conrad, it was different. He was not another accepted oddity as he had been on the train. Here, he was an obvious stranger. Foreign, dirty, and unwelcome. Several times, as they worked their way slowly through the press of people, younger men armed with large sticks jumped out from behind a hut or a wall to shout angry threats at Conrad. They spat at Conrad, and one of them shouted at him with tears in his eyes.

"*Omuzepe!*" the man cried. Murderer.

Each time, Noko would push his large frame into their path and shout something equally unpleasant back at them. Most of the young men wore the traditional loincloths, their bare chests and naked arms shaking with every curse and insult.

But none dared to get too close to Noko or his dogs, and so each small gang would eventually give way and let them pass. But even as Noko rescued him again and again, Conrad could feel the young men's unmistakable hatred boring into the back of his head.

Several times, he thought he saw Albert Witbooi in the crowds. Conrad had to fight the urge not to rub his shoulder in reflexive memory.

He wanted fiercely to reach out and take Sybille's hand for comfort. But he held back of course, knowing that such an action would only make things all the worse.

Conrad found himself cursing Leutwein. Why had the man sent his aide to such a large gathering to...what, to tell them all to just let bygones be bygones?

He was quite sure now that, given the chance, most of the men and women in this village would tear him apart.

However, Conrad quickly realized Leutwein could not have known the full extent of the Herero gathering. This was no meeting of a few Herero chiefs as Leutwein had described. This was a congregation of thousands, many thousands of angry Herero. And Conrad was terrified. He had come to negotiate with a single man, only to discover a mob of angry natives between himself and the man's front door.

Leutwein must have thought there was still time before relations between the Germans and the Herero reached this point. He had sent Conrad to Hochfeld in good faith to try and persuade Maharero not to convene such an assembly. But Leutwein had badly miscalculated. The Herero had acted. They had followed their chieftains' summons to Hochfeld.

Conrad shuddered. Not only had Leutwein misgauged how long before the Herero might organize, but Baumhauer's Schutztruppe had completely missed the movement of *thousands* of people across the colony. The Major's petty war with Leutwein had distracted the colony's entire security force. Now, Conrad, a mere commissioner's aide, was walking into the beginnings of a revolt. And his only hope of protection sat oblivious in their expensive new fort, two days away to the south.

Out of the corner of his eye, Conrad saw an elderly man with long, etched wrinkles in his brow. The man was polishing the barrel of an ancient musket that looked even older than he was. He looked up, and his glare told Conrad the man had not brought his gun to hunt with.

Conrad quickened his pace and began to recite to himself every psalm he could remember. Whatever Leutwein had originally expected in Hochfeld, it was clear that things had escalated far beyond anything Conrad had anticipated.

Gott behüte mich, Conrad whispered over and over as Noko steered their small group through the throngs of Herero around them. God help me.

CHAPTER 7

NOVEMBER-DECEMBER 1903

Conrad didn't know what he had been expecting Samuel Maharero to look like. He'd heard little about the man until a few days ago. Though thankfully, he hadn't heard anything half as terrifying about Maharero as the infamous tales the Germans told about Hendrik Witbooi and his Nama raiders.

What he did know from his short time in Windhoek was that the Germans had helped Samuel Maharero unite the Herero tribes under his leadership in 1890. The then-Commissioner, Heinrich Göring, had offered Maharero the protection of the German colonial forces against a ceaseless barrage of cattle raids from Hendrik Witbooi's Nama clan. Maharero had accepted the agreement, ceding various lands to the colonists in exchange for German protection against the Witboois. That deal had been made nearly fifteen years ago when Maharero had been little more than lord of a small region of the vast, ungoverned hinterlands. Now, however, Maharero was the leading representative of the Herero people, who outnumbered the Germans by more than ten to one.

But that was only history. All Conrad knew about the man, from Leutwein and from the small bits and pieces he understood of Noko and his wife's conversations, was that Maharero was a strong ruler whose patience was wearing thin.

The Herero did not have a king. They were governed by a collection of chiefs who seemed to change whom they traded with, fought against and made peace with on their own personal whims. Conrad had seen the decorations and trimmings of at least a hundred different chieftains as Noko led him through the crowds surrounding Hochfeld. Maharero was only one of the many chieftains. But it was clear to Conrad as he moved through the pitched camps and temporary shelters towards the center of the village that as Maharero went, the rest of the Herero would follow.

Although Samuel Maharero did not have the muscular frame of a particularly strong man, his height set him nearly a full head above most. His beard was rough and woolly, and he bore the same small cap of short-cropped hair on his head as Sybille.

Samuel had attended a Lutheran missionary school as a boy, where, it was said, his teachers had found trying to teach him "an exhausting and impossible experience." After his father had died in 1890, Maharero inherited the chiefdom. He was then in his early thirties. Previous German officials who had met him said he drank too much and had a fierce temper. He swore openly and freely. He had taken to wearing a sword while he held court in the evenings, and it was said that the local missionaries from Okahandja were so afraid of his unpredictable, drunken tantrums that they slept in shifts during the night whenever they passed through his lands.

When Noko had told him to wait outside a simple bungalow with a dried-grass roof in the middle of the town, Conrad expected to be greeted at any moment by an African war god, adorned in tattoos and animal skins with a piece of animal bone pierced through his nose.

Yet the man who stepped outside his home wore a freshly pressed cream suit and polished leather shoes of the same buff color. He smiled widely and shook Conrad's hand with a charming politeness that stunned Conrad more than if the man had shouted at him and slashed at him with a gnarled club.

"*Willkommen* to our village, Herr Huber," Maharero said in flawless German. "I trust you had a pleasant journey?"

Maharero's voice was deep, and he spoke with a venerable smoothness, even though he didn't look a day over forty.

"Thank you, Your…" Conrad started, pausing midway through addressing Maharero.

How in the world did you address a Herero chieftain?

"Thank you, sir," Conrad recovered as he returned Maharero's handshake without thinking. "A bit different than I'm used to, but it's beautiful countryside. Especially once the sun starts to set."

Conrad knew he was smiling like an idiot, and he felt utterly foolish talking about the weather with the man he was supposed to talk politics with. He didn't dare chance a look at Sybille for guidance for fear his face might give him away. A sizeable crowd had followed Noko's small party to Maharero's home. Standing before their chieftain, Conrad felt all their eyes boring into his back.

Much to his relief, Maharero smiled and offered a cordial chuckle in response.

"It's not so bad after your thirtieth or fortieth wet season," Maharero laughed. "Stay here long enough in the rains, and they'll have you begging for the hot sun of the dry season. But, Herr Huber, I've kept you waiting in the heat long enough. I invite you to please join me in my home for some refreshment."

"Thank you … er, sir," Conrad replied, grateful to escape both the sun and the growing number of Herero onlookers.

Maharero's house was as simple on the inside as it had looked on the outside. The walls were thick and stout, and Conrad saw the grass from the roof prod Maharero's hair as he welcomed them inside. There was a table with some stools in the main room, as well as a small cooking fire and a threadbare rug stretched out in the middle of the dirt floor. The only decoration was a modest assortment of wooden carvings that sat in the hut's small windows like a row of loyal pets.

Noko and his family took their leave to set up their own campsite, leaving Conrad alone with Sybille and her father. Without saying a word, Sybille rolled up the sleeves of her dress, kissed her father's cheek and went to tend the embers in the cooking fire as casually as though she did it every day.

As Sybille built up the fire, Maharero removed his impossibly clean jacket and hung it carefully on a small nail that protruded from a nearby side beam. He picked up a gourd on the lone table and filled it with a red, sweet-smelling liquor.

"Have you ever tasted *ombike* before, Herr Huber?" he asked Conrad in a friendly tone as he poured.

"Yes, once," Conrad replied, grateful for the welcome shade indoors. "A friend of mine suggested I try a cup from a group of rather...*mischievous* Ovambo in Windhoek to immerse myself in their customs. I'm afraid it was far stronger than I was expecting. It nearly knocked me off my feet, I coughed so hard."

From the corner of his eye, Conrad saw Sybille's mouth curl into a sly smile. Petyr had doubled over in laughter the day that he and Conrad went to the Windhoek market together, just as Conrad was still getting accustomed to life in Southwest Africa.

Petyr had impishly insisted on Conrad trying the Ovambo's bush liquor, and he had ushered him to a notorious brewer's stall. Conrad had paid the man and taken a good-humored swallow from the offered cup. The liquor had burned his throat as if he'd swallowed a gulp of antiseptic, and he had spluttered and wheezed in the middle of the town square. This drew a chorus of laughter from the old Ovambo brewers and several disapproving stares from some nearby white storeowners and shoppers. Conrad had no doubt the whole Residence staff had heard about the incident from Petyr.

Maharero laughed, a deep, throaty sound that drove the tension from the small room, as he handed Conrad a wooden cup of the sweet-smelling liquor.

"Ah! The *Onngadjera* Ovambo claim another victim. Do not worry, Herr Huber. I am too old for such pranks now."

Conrad took the cup with a nod of thanks. He felt Sybille watching him from behind her father's back.

"I'm relieved to hear it," Conrad said, taking a small, tentative sip from his cup.

The ombike was cool and tart, and while it was still considerably stronger than what Conrad might have considered refreshing, he at least managed to stay standing upright.

"Please call me Conrad, sir," he added, trying his best to seem at ease.

Maharero picked up a second cup from the table that appeared to be filled with cold milk, and Conrad recalled from somewhere in his brain that most Herero abstained from liquor and preferred the taste of fresh milk from their herds. Conrad marked that down as another thing he'd been wrong about. Maharero drank deeply from his own cup and smiled.

"Very well, Conrad. Please call me Samuel," he said, motioning his guest to sit.

Conrad nodded, unsure of what else to say. He had never seen Leutwein speak with a chieftain in his own home before. They had always come to the Residence with a specific problem or a request. And they were almost always older chieftains Leutwein had known for years. Younger upstarts rarely came to the capital. When they did, they said little and deferred to their elders.

According to Leutwein's meticulous records, Maharero had been to Windhoek to see Leutwein, but that had been some ten years ago. He'd come as part of a large coalition of Herero who wanted to protest the expansion of German farmlands in the central region. All the talking had been done by a more senior chieftain, though Maharero had made a great show of unrolling his copy of the 1890 treaty and pointing accusingly at Heinrich Göring's signature on the document. The whole event had been greatly embarrassing to a freshly arrived Leutwein, and he had granted the coalition's request and revoked the illegal land sale. Leutwein had even made a point of shaking Maharero's hand and thanking him for upholding the Kaiser's law.

But although he'd corresponded with Maharero through Sybille over the years, Leutwein had not seen Maharero personally since. Now he seemed to have transformed from a young upstart who frightened missionaries into perhaps the most influential native in the DSWA. And Conrad had no idea how he was even supposed to begin to talk to him.

Maharero's manners were superb. He sat on his wooden stool as confidently as if they were in one of the poshest drawing rooms in Europe. Yet the man's confidence and meticulous clothing unsettled Conrad even more. Maharero smiled pleasantly as he sipped his milk and smoothed out the edges of his shirt cuffs, while Conrad remained silent, feeling embarrassed in his wrinkled and sweat-stained khaki.

Through the afternoon shade, Conrad's eyes were just able to make out a small wooden zebra on the corner of the table between them. Maharero caught his eye and reached across the table. He picked up the carving as gently as though it were a living thing.

"Wood carving is a hobby of mine," he said as he passed the zebra to Conrad. "It helps to clear my mind."

Conrad took the offered zebra from Maharero, his hand brushing the Herero chieftain's in passing. Maharero's fingers were long and narrow, giving them an almost spidery look, despite their immense size. Nearly every inch of them was rough and callused, the mark of a man who'd spent the better part of his life toiling in the ground.

"I always save the last hour of sunlight for myself," Maharero continued. "I find I carve best when the sun is setting. Something about the last warmth of the day makes me enjoy the cutting even more. That one I finished yesterday and gave it a short painting with pitch for the stripes this morning."

Conrad turned the zebra over carefully in his hand. It had been masterfully crafted. Each painstaking knife stroke in the soft, pulpy wood had been made with clear purpose. He ran his fingers over the zebra's mane, a curved ridge of wood where Maharero had taken special care to bring out the animal's natural skittish appearance. Even the painting, a few simple strokes of blackish brown, had been done so carefully that Conrad got the impression the small statue might come to life and run from his hand at any moment.

"It's quite lovely, sir...er, Samuel," Conrad said, handing the carving back to Maharero. "I truly envy your skill. The only things I've ever carved were railroad ties back home in Germany."

"You flatter me, Conrad," Maharero laughed, obviously pleased as he pushed the carving back into Conrad's hands. "Please keep it if you like. I've already far too many of these things cluttering up my windows. Besides, I'm sure there's some young lady back home in Germany who'd love an *exotic* present, hmm?"

Conrad felt himself tense. Maharero continued to smile guilelessly, but Conrad's ears were suddenly pulsing with the sound of his own heart thumping.

Had Maharero also guessed what Noko and his wife suspected? No, surely he hadn't given Maharero any reason to suspect that he and Sybille…

Out of the corner of his eye, Conrad saw Sybille casually glance his way over the fire, raising a furtive eyebrow in equal, apprehensive questioning.

"Thank you, Samuel," Conrad said, accepting the zebra with a tone of soft reverence. "As a matter of fact, there is someone back home I'd love to give this to."

Behind her father's broad back, Sybille narrowed her gaze at him in disbelief.

"My cousin, Frieda," Conrad added after a pause. "She's been badgering me in her letters for months for something from Africa to show around to all her friends. I'm sure within a month or two you'll be the talk of all of Hamburg."

Maharero laughed and raised his cup in toast. Conrad joined him, catching Sybille's silent scoff as she stood up from the fire and moved quietly out the back entrance of the hut.

Before Conrad could wonder where she was going, Maharero pushed his cup aside and folded his arms across his chest.

"She's gone for more firewood," Maharero said, following Conrad's eyes. "And while she is out, perhaps we might talk plainly?"

Conrad nodded nervously.

A large stack of firewood sat unused by the cooking fire. Maharero must have given Sybille some signal to leave the two of them alone, but Conrad accepted the excuse. He didn't really have much choice.

Maharero let out a deep sigh, his eyes briefly falling to the floor before he spoke again.

"Things in Windhoek must truly be bad if Leutwein could not come himself," he said evenly.

It was a statement rather than a question, one that Conrad had been dreading ever since he'd left Windhoek. Maharero was a widely respected man among the Herero. a chieftain by birth and renowned king in all but name.

Conrad was merely the aide to the colony's German Commissioner.

Oh well, Conrad thought as he set his cup aside. There's no reason to lie to the man when he obviously knows he's been insulted.

"Commissioner Leutwein is..." Conrad said, trying to choose the most diplomatic word he could think of. "His position is very...*difficult* at the moment."

Maharero frowned at this.

"*Difficult*," he repeated, his face donning a sudden and frightening scowl. "We are all in a *difficult* position. All the Herero are in a *difficult* position. The only difference is that we pay with our land, our loved ones and our lives, while the Commissioner only fears a smaller pension and the snow back home should he be recalled!"

Maharero checked his temper after a moment and exhaled slowly as if in a practiced motion to calm himself. Conrad, cursing himself for his evidently poor word choice, opened his mouth to try and smooth things over before Maharero gestured to stop him.

"My apologies, Conrad," he said. "I did not invite you into my home to shout at you. I know the Commissioner is a more moderate man than he used to be, but to me and many people here he will always be the man who built those cruel prison camps."

Conrad found himself speechless. While Leutwein had tried to undo his failed labor camp experiments, that clearly did not matter to Maharero. Even though still popular with the local tribes near Windhoek, Conrad was beginning to grasp how little influence the Commissioner's name carried outside the colony's main cities.

This was not going well, Conrad thought. And he had barely begun to speak yet.

If Maharero already distrusted Leutwein, then how could Conrad possibly expect him to listen to what the Commissioner proposed?

Suddenly Conrad recalled the day of the hanging. Berriz had held onto a stoic, detached façade, looking every bit like a martyr. But his two youngest brothers had been terrified and wept loudly when the hangman had put the nooses around their necks. *Mein Gott*! The youngest couldn't have been more than eight or nine years old. Conrad had seen their bodies hanging limp before the crowd of native prisoners pressed up against rusted barbed wire.

He felt the familiar painful tightening in his chest.

"I am sorry," he finally said, the force of his words surprising both Maharero and himself. "Those camps should not exist. I truly wish they did not."

Maharero said nothing, and Conrad continued, without knowing what exactly he intended to say.

"Those boys did not deserve to be hanged. They were…criminals, yes…but they were also children. I wish I could give them back to their families, but I can't."

Conrad paused a moment, his voice trembling slightly.

"They're gone. Nothing can change that, and nothing I promise can bring them back. But I'd like to do everything I can to make sure that their lives were not lost for nothing."

Maharero's eyes widened slightly as Conrad spoke, as though he were either taken aback by Conrad's words or merely skeptical.

"So would I, sir," Maharero said after a beat.

For a few moments, neither man spoke. Maharero seemed to be focused somewhere far away. Conrad felt his thoughts drifting back to the hangman's block and the sea of solemn faces looking out from behind the wire. Outside Maharero's hut, Conrad could hear children playing in the village streets. Their laughter rang in his ears like the eager calls of the black buzzards that loitered contentedly beside the Windhoek camps.

Maharero cleared his throat, bringing Conrad back to the task at hand.

"I will be honest with you," he said, "because I believe that today you have been honest with me. The Herero want war. It is not just because of the Grootfontein boys. German farmers continue to encroach on our lands. The agreements that our chieftains sign with your government are never enforced. Our people are being rounded up like cattle at the slightest infraction and thrown into prison camps hundreds of miles from home.

"But what I want to know is *why*? Why does Leutwein hate us so?"

"He doesn't!" Conrad almost shouted in response.

Conrad had spoken more loudly than he'd meant to, and Maharero raised an eyebrow.

"Sorry," Conrad said gently. "What I mean is that Leutwein has been trying to honor the Kaiser's agreements and has been running himself into the grave trying to keep the peace."

Even as Conrad spoke, he could see the Commissioner in his office, slumped over a pile of accusing telegrams and detailed railroad maps, utterly exhausted.

"But there is a divide between the Commissioner and the Schutztruppe," Conrad continued. "The security forces' commander, Major Baumhauer…"

"I know about the Major," Maharero interrupted. "He is an evil man. But does your King not control his own soldiers?"

Maharero leaned forward on his stool as he spoke.

"Does your Kaiser not command the loyalty of his people?"

Conrad felt himself shrinking slightly as Maharero leaned towards him. It was more the force of Maharero's words than his intimidating physical stature pushing him backward. Nothing Maharero said about the state of the colony's affairs was wrong. Conrad was embarrassed at how paltry his explanations sounded against the full weight of the Herero's grievances.

But still, he had to say something.

"The Kaiser has the loyalty of every German citizen," Conrad offered up meekly. "But the Kaiser's interests in Southwest Africa are…mixed. The Commissioner and the Major have very different views of the colony and… unfortunately, the Kaiser's advisors in Berlin are beginning to side with Major Baumhauer, who has a brother in the Kaiser's inner circle."

Conrad's words hung in the air between the two men. All the politics, chaos and terrors of the past month summed up in two plain and inadequate sentences. Conrad picked up his cup of ombike just for something to do. Maharero leaned back on his stool, silent for several minutes.

A bird could be heard somewhere outside the bungalow. Its high notes rose and fell in a ridiculous pattern that immediately reminded Conrad of Beaunard. Though Petyr had told Conrad once about these birds, he could not

THE SANDS SHALL WITNESS

recall their name. He concentrated on the bird's tune, determined not to stare mutely at Maharero and make himself seem an even greater fool.

What was that damn bird's name?

Back in Windhoek, the moment you left the city, you could hear these African birds calling to one another like the constant bugle of the bush. Conrad couldn't see the bird outside Maharero's window, but he could picture her easily. She had a small body the color of worn sand and long, black and gray wings.

Not two weeks ago, Conrad had watched Petyr snatch one right out of the air at a local spot where the ridges surrounding Windhoek created a peaceful swimming hole.

"How on earth did you manage to catch such a small thing, Petyr?" Conrad remembered asking as he sat on a rock at the water's edge, waiting for his shirt to dry.

"Oh, it's easy," Petyr said with an older child's bravado, relishing Conrad's praise. "Once you know their song, you can call them right to you."

"Er, their song?" Conrad asked, still in disbelief that Petyr had simply snatched the bird right out of the air in front of him.

Petyr pursed his lips and whistled, mimicking the rise and fall of the calls of the other birds nearby. The bird in the boy's hand craned its neck up at Petyr, utterly confused as to whether Petyr was a friend or a predator. Petyr laughed and un-cupped his hands, letting the little brown bird fly away in a hurry.

"If you listen closely, you can hear them talking," Petyr added, plopping down on the warm rock next to Conrad.

No one else had come to the swimming hole that day, so Petyr jumped into the water with Conrad. Conrad enjoyed these moments when Petyr would forget his station and act like a young boy. He reminded Conrad of his cousins back home and he smiled now, recalling how Petyr had stretched himself out on a warm rock like a lithe house cat.

"Talking?" Conrad had asked, playing along. "And whatever are they saying?"

Petyr smiled and pointed at two nearby trees.

"Well, that tree on the right is where all the lady birds sit, and they are all telling the male birds in the left tree to, '*Work, Har-der! Work, Har-der!*'"

Petyr mimicked the female's call with a nagging expression on his face.

"And then the males call back to the lady birds," he said, shifting his face to a look of relaxed defiance. "They shout, '*No! Drink, La-ger! Drink, La-ger!*'"

They had both laughed and stayed another hour or so before gathering their clothes and heading back to Schwerinsburg. Conrad had gone straight to Leutwein's library after supper that night and dug out a thin, crumpled book from one of the bookshelves entitled *Birds, Mammals, and Fauna of Southwest Africa.*

The book had supposedly been inspired by the sketches the great Portuguese explorer Bartolomeu Dias had made of the creatures he had encountered around the southern tip of Africa. It had only taken Conrad a few moments to find the small gray bird with a distinct black ring around its...

The ring-necked dove!

Conrad all but shouted the bird's name out loud, rousing Maharero from his thoughts and bringing Conrad uncomfortably back to his current task.

"This is what I have feared," Maharero finally said, his face a mixture of anger and muted despair. "Leutwein is one thing. There are some among us who consider him a devil, yet there are others who think he can be reasoned with. But the Major...the Major is an *evil* man."

Maharero paused a moment, trying to gauge from Conrad's reaction whether he should continue. Conrad tried to keep his expression neutral but found himself reflexively nodding assent to Maharero's depiction of the Major.

"I know what his men tried to do," Maharero added quietly. "And I know *you* stopped them. That makes you a good man."

Conrad felt his face flush in embarrassment. There wasn't really any social protocol for accepting a father's thanks for saving his daughter from being raped.

Sybille had tried to keep word of the attack from spreading beyond

Windhoek. But evidently, her father had found out. Though, he hadn't said anything when they had arrived as far as Conrad could discern.

Conrad merely nodded again, dreading whatever else Maharero might have heard.

Maharero seemed to deem Conrad's silence appropriate and continued after a long sigh.

"I do not like violence, Conrad. I beg you to please believe me when I say that. But in three days' time, the Herero chieftains will all speak and say whether they believe we should join together and go to war with the Germans. I am a chief, and I will also be expected to speak. And right now, I do not know what other choice we have. We may all die, but I think I would rather die fighting on my feet than starving in a labor camp."

Maharero took up his cup. He made no move to drink from it but stared intently into the before looking back at Conrad with an air of resignation.

"Has Sybille ever told you anything about her mother?" he asked.

Conrad didn't think Maharero could have said anything more unexpected. One moment they were discussing the Herero going to war with Germany, and now he was asking if Conrad knew anything about his wife?

If Maharero was trying to keep Conrad off balance, he was doing an excellent job of it.

"She has never mentioned her mother," Conrad replied, trying not to seem too taken aback.

"No, I don't suppose she would," Maharero said, rising from his stool.

Maharero's cup wasn't half empty, but he refilled it anyway.

"It might shock you to know," he said, hesitating a moment more before continuing. "That her mother was German."

Conrad felt his jaw drop open. Sybille's eyes were unusual, even amidst the colony's mosaic of racial colors, and he'd never met another African with blue eyes. He had suspected that Sybille must have a white ancestor somewhere in her family tree. But it had never occurred to him that it might be her mother, married to a Herero chieftain.

Too dumbfounded to offer any intelligible comment, Conrad merely sat upright on his stool gawking as the chieftain, who had remained standing, went on.

"She had been a farmer's wife back in Germany. I've long since forgotten the name of the village, somewhere in the southern part of your country, I think. Her parents had wanted her to marry an unpleasant, older banker, but she had her heart set on a young, penniless farmer's boy. They ran away together and, though poor, they somehow made it to Berlin where they learned your Kaiser was granting large tracts of land to Germans who would come settle in Southwest Africa."

Conrad knew what Maharero was referring to. There had been a similar advertisement in the Hamburg newspaper on the day Conrad sailed for Africa.

"They leapt at the chance for a new start," Maharero went on. "But sadly, they arrived here in the dry season and could make nothing grow on the land the old Commissioner gave them. Other German farmers here had already claimed the fertile lands along the banks of the Hoanib River—your colony's boundary. They sold new arrivals a desolate patch of land deep in our territory, but Wilma and her husband went eagerly, not understanding that they had been deceived.

"I do not know what was wrong with her husband's heart, but one day as they were toiling in the earth, tending their meager harvest, it stopped beating. Wilma was widowed and left all alone in the bush."

Maharero's voice seemed to grow slightly faint as he spoke, as if it could hardly bear to say more. At some point, he abandoned his drink and now shifted his hands in and out of his pockets as though he had no idea what to do with them.

"She had no money for the return passage to Germany and no friends or family to sustain her," he continued.

"At that time, my father, who was chieftain before me, thought surely one of the other German farmers would buy her land or marry her out of pity. But all the white men knew that her land was no good for planting, and most were already married with families they had brought along.

"When she began to starve, my father could not bear to watch her suffering in the dirt. My father was a great man. He always tried to see the best in even the most wicked people. But he was getting old and could not travel so far in a day and so he sent me to help her. Her farm was only a few hours journey from our village, and I knew some German from when I attended the Rhenish missionary school in Okahandja as a boy.

"I patched her roof, helped her scrounge a meager wheat crop at the very edge of her land where there was a small patch of passable soil, and brought her guinea fowl or a small pig whenever my family could spare one. Every few weeks, I would come to help her, mending a fence, showing her where to gather nettles and bristles that could help sustain her when her food ran low, or helping her to draw water from the base of a quiver tree.

"Throughout the dry season I helped her, hoping that one day she would have the money to return home and leave me in peace.

"But when the rains came, and her small stack of wheat was sold, she stayed. I could not understand why at first. Then I realized that she loved me and that I loved her, too. And so, we got married."

Conrad did not know what was more unbelievable: that Sybille herself was half-German or that the most influential Herero chieftain, who was considering leading his people to war against Germany, had a German wife.

Maharero seemed to sense Conrad's disbelief.

"It was different twenty years ago," he said with a mild shrug. "The Germans either kept to their own lands or stayed in their towns. A few farmers were close to our lands, but they were isolated and did not seem to care one way or the other. My father and more than a few of our elders questioned the wisdom of marrying Wilma when I announced my intentions, but in the end, my father decided that such a union would help our people's relations with your colonial government. We got married, and Sybille was born soon after, followed soon after by her three brothers."

Brothers? Conrad asked himself. Sybille had never mentioned that she had siblings. How many more revelations was he going to hear from Maharero today?

"Is Wilma here now?" Conrad asked and immediately regretted doing so.

Maharero's shoulders slumped, and he sighed heavily as he eased his weight back onto his stool.

"For a few years, things were not so bad," he said, his voice low and halting. "Then more and more of your people came here. They began to steal more of our lands and those of the Nama. There were clashes between your soldiers and the local men. Usually, they were only fistfights that could be resolved by your commanders and our chiefs. But as time went on, the clashes became more frequent and more deadly. Men died on both sides until one day, several Nama chiefs banded together and rose up against your government.

"Hendrik Witbooi is a formidable man. He always has been. Our people despise him now, and even my father hated him once his people began to steal our cattle. But back then, many young Herero men wanted to join him when he launched a war—his *first* rebellion—against your people. I was such a man."

Maharero reached for his cup and took a large swallow of milk. Despite the shade, Conrad saw a single bead of sweat run down Maharero's face.

"Wilma begged me not to go," he said after a breath, his voice cracking as though the memory pained him to recall. "She never said a word to me about fighting her people. I don't think she cared in those days that she was a German. But she *was* scared. Scared that I wouldn't come back…and that she'd be left all alone again.

"My father urged our people to be patient. He thought that things would settle down soon and that the new German Commissioner, Theodor Leutwein, in the new capital city, would offer to negotiate with Witbooi and not rush into a war with the Nama. In the end, I relented.

"But whatever Leutwein might've done, Hendrik forced his hand when he attacked your garrison at Hornkranz in 1893. Everything changed then. Witbooi was defeated, but he won concessions from Leutwein and got a steady commission for himself and his men as mercenaries. The Nama rebellion had ended, but now people saw that the Germans could be bloodied, and that war might be profitable, even in defeat."

Conrad sat transfixed on his stool. Some part of him must have registered that Maharero was talking about his own people, but he forgot his station for a moment or two, lost in the stories of the African chieftain in the crisp, cream suit.

"It was two years before we got another chance to go to war. A German trader was found dead in the Khauas' lands. Leutwein sent a demand to all the local chiefs that the murderer be turned over to the Schutztruppe.

"The German man was a well-hated drunkard and a crook, and so the murderer's chief, a man called Andreas Lambert, refused to turn the guilty man over. The Khaua rallied around their chief and dared the colonial government to come and fight them. Once again, many of us wanted to go and fight. And this time, I did not listen to my father or to Wilma.

"I knew Lambert. He had attended the same German school that I had, and everyone knew he was a practical man. He would not challenge the colonial forces unless he was confident of negotiating with them.

"A dozen of us stole away in the night and took our villages' small cache of old hunting rifles with us. We ran for days with the guns slung over our shoulders, willing our feet to go faster so we could join the Khaua and kill some German soldiers."

Conrad flinched and felt a small shiver run down his spine. Maharero seemed not to notice.

"After a week of running, we arrived at Lambert's village. However, all we found were embers and a few carcasses that the hyenas had not yet picked clean.

"Leutwein was in another…*difficult*…position back home and did not want to be labeled as a pacifist by his critics. So, he decided to make an example of Lambert and the Khaua. With the Schutztruppe, Leutwein smashed the Khaua's uprising and led Lambert away in chains. The Germans took twelve thousand cattle and every weapon the remaining Khaua had. Lambert and the other chiefs were led away to Leutwein's camps, and without a chief to protect them, the Khaua faded away to disease, raiding, and starvation.

"It was not until last year that we learned that Lambert was shot by the Schutztruppe shortly after he arrived in the camp."

Maharero took another large swallow of his drink. A few droplets hung from his thick beard and threatened to spill onto his suit. Just before they fell, Maharero wiped them away with his long hands.

"I know violence, Conrad," he said quietly. "I know the costs of rushing off to war before you are ready.

"We didn't know there were any Germans left near the village to see us. We tried to bury the bodies of the Khaua we found, but a group of Schutztruppe scouts saw the guns on our backs and took off after us. They had horses, but we knew the terrain, and after two days, I thought they'd given up and gone home.

"We were cautious and took three more days to avoid the other villages so we did not lead the scouts to them. I led the men with me to Wilma's farm, thinking that I could shelter the others for a few days more to ensure that the soldiers had really gone.

"We knew something was wrong the moment we saw the cabin early on the morning of the third day. The goat that my father had given us as a wedding gift was not baying to be milked as she always did in the morning. Sybille was not outside helping her mother tend to the small wheat field, and there was no sign anywhere of my young sons. I did not want to go into the house, but I also knew that I could not make one of the other men go for me.

"Wilma lay dead just inside the door, the wound still warm where the bullet had torn through her chest. There were horse tracks everywhere around the house, and anything of worth was either stolen or shattered on the floor. Our goat had been butchered and hastily cooked and eaten at my own table, just a few feet from where Wilma's body lay. One of my other men found Sybille and her brothers huddled together in a patch of tall sagebrush, too shaken and terrified to protest being picked up.

"My wife's body was still warm, and I knew the Schutztruppe must still be nearby. I grabbed my children and didn't stop running until I reached my father's village. Sybille did not speak for several days, but eventually she told me that when the Germans had come, Wilma had told her to take her brothers and to sneak out the back and hide until she came to fetch her. Etuna was only two, and Sybille had to clamp her hand over his mouth for hours to keep him from crying out. She'd seen the Germans ride in and watched them shoot her mother right in the doorway.

"Wilma had been toiling for years in the sun and dust, and her skin had grown tanned and dark. We scarcely ever traded with the Germans in Okahandja, and that morning Wilma had been wearing a gray cloth dress she'd spun herself with a scarf wrapped around her head to help keep the sun off her face. I've no doubt the Schutztruppe assumed she was an African and simply killed her without thinking …with poor Sybille watching from beneath the sage. She was twelve years old."

Conrad felt as though he'd been slapped. He wanted to disbelieve what Maharero said, but the truth of the Herero chieftain's words was etched in the pain on his face.

When Sybille was twelve? *Verdammt nochmal*! Of course, she hated Germans! And to think she was now working as Leutwein's maid. And had then nearly been raped by troops in the same uniforms as those who had shot her mother?

Dear God. And then Conrad had kissed her! What must she have thought of him at that moment? What did she think of him now? He was a German. And were that not enough, he was currently sitting across from her father, trying to convince a pained, terribly wronged man not to fight back despite all the evil things that had been done to his family.

Verdammt didn't even begin to describe this situation.

"I'm sorry," Conrad said softly because there was nothing else to say.

Maharero nodded slightly, a practiced reflex to others' sympathy.

Conrad opened his mouth but closed it again as quickly. He had no grounds to tell this man not to fight, and that realization made him feel hopeless.

To tell Maharero that the Kaiser was considering sending the army to pacify the colony would be treason, but if the Herero decided to fight and Leutwein lost control of the colony…there was no telling what might happen to the Herero, or to Sybille.

"Samuel," Conrad tested, unsure after such a terrible story if Maharero would still be willing to listen to him. "I don't have any words to make such terrible things right. But the colony is very near to tearing itself apart. And perhaps…rightly so."

Conrad did not know where his words were coming from, but he made no effort to stop them. Perhaps he was giving away too much. So be it. He wasn't going to sit there and let an entire people march to their deaths without at least trying to convince them not to.

"But war will not gain the Herero anything," Conrad continued. "European powers are still jostling amongst themselves for control over Africa. The Kaiser is a proud man. A *very* proud man. He won't let Germany lose control of a colony while the other European states look on. If you go to war, Leutwein will likely be sacked and replaced with someone far less likely to offer you a compromise of any kind. The Nama won concessions last time; that's true. But this time, if war comes, there won't be any concessions to be had, only defeat."

Conrad was shaking inside now. He could feel his lungs constricting on the edge of an attack. He had no idea how to make Maharero understand him or if Maharero were even listening at all. He tried to concentrate on the big man's gaze, but he couldn't keep his mind from drifting back to the image of a young Sybille, her hand clamped over her brother's mouth to prevent his screaming and being discovered by German troops.

Those same troops that existed to protect Conrad from Sybille's people. Conrad shivered.

"Please," Conrad said, his voice almost a whisper. "Consider what happened to Andreas Lambert."

Maharero gave Conrad a hard look, and Conrad was afraid he'd gone too far. Maharero scratched his chin, where the tiny milk droplets hung precariously from his beard and made a noncommittal sound from the back of his throat.

"I thank you for your honesty, Conrad," he said as he stood up, his voice neutral. "I will think upon what you have said. But I would also ask a favor of you if I may?"

"Of course," Conrad said as he stood as well, trying as he had when he was a boy to lock away his array of emotions into compartments he could try to address methodically later.

"I would ask that you leave us in the morning," Maharero said. "Whatever decision is made over the next few days, it would be better for all if you were not present. There are those here who would not take kindly to the thought that I'd been swayed by a German, and there are more than a few here that will be angry I've housed you and not killed you when I had the chance. It would be best for both of us if your time here is brief."

Conrad tensed as he recalled the gangs of young men that had harassed him as he made his way through Hochfeld. He hastily nodded agreement. The warning was clear enough. Maharero might be able to protect Conrad tonight, but once the chieftains began their meeting, he should be far away from the angry young men and their knives.

"Of course," Conrad said again as he shook Maharero's offered hand, knowing at once that he had failed.

*

Twilight was Conrad's favorite time of day in Africa. The heat had dissipated enough for him to enjoy sitting outside, and today there was a slight, pleasant breeze that carried the sweet anticipation of rain. The train depot at Okahandja was mostly empty at this hour, and it had been no trouble to acquire a first-class ticket for the evening train to Windhoek. His back aching from sleeping on Noko's mangled mattress the previous night, he was unabashedly looking forward to the soft leather seats of the train car.

He had plenty to think about as he sat sipping absently at a pint of lager he'd purchased at the small depot's café. But out of all of it, he chose to think about Sybille and the night before he had left her village.

His afternoon conversation with Maharero was already blurred in Conrad's memory. Maharero had shaken Conrad's hand, and then the two men had stood there awkwardly for a bit longer, having nothing else to say. Sybille had returned at some point, but Conrad did not see any firewood. Maharero was speaking to her in Herero as she busied herself about the bungalow. He thought he caught the names of several important chieftains and quickly understood that Maharero had sent her to take stock of what the other prominent chieftains were saying.

Conrad had felt the familiar clawing begin to rise in his throat as it tightened and had stepped outside to get some air. He didn't offer an excuse for leaving; instead, he slipped covertly out the doorway while Sybille and her father talked and found himself once more in the unforgiving heat of the southern African sun. Nonetheless, without Noko to steer him through the overcrowded village and the menacing gangs of young men, Conrad was terrified to leave Maharero's compound.

Mercifully, the compound boasted a large flame thorn tree with long, overhanging branches. Conrad crawled underneath a small gap in the thick branches.

He gazed up absently at the tree's deep-red seed pods that hung in abundance above him like some tantalizing, bitter fruit. The flame thorn's branches were so thick it looked more like a giant fern sprouting from the earth than a tree. Conrad supposed if anyone were to walk by his hiding spot, they might mistake him for a long-limbed honey badger burrowing into its den.

Conrad had no idea how long he had sat staring up into the branches of the strange tree, and he couldn't pull himself together enough to really care. He didn't want to think about war or Leutwein or Maharero.

Instead, he just wanted to stare up at the flame thorn's pods, listening to the echoed calls of the ring-necked doves above and block out the memory of the faces in the Windhoek camps or the thought of Wilma's body lying dead in her doorway that hot morning as her children cowered, traumatized beneath a nearby bush.

Before the sun had completely set, Sybille squeezed through the gaps in the branches and sat beside him. For a while, she said nothing. She simply sat beside him patiently, sharing the warmth of her nearby body as the temperature began to fall.

"I'm so sorry," Conrad whispered after a time. "I didn't know how much you had suffered. And then when I kissed you at the party…you must think me a monster."

He heard rather than felt Sybille place her hand lightly on his shoulder.

"Do *you* think you are a monster?" she asked him as she leaned in closer to him.

"How can I not be?" Conrad nearly whimpered back. "Everything that's happened…"

"Do you think that *you* are a monster?" Sybille repeated more firmly this time.

Conrad couldn't bear to look at her, couldn't bear to turn and face her after everything he now knew his countrymen had done.

"I…" he started before she cut him off.

"You are *not* a monster, Conrad," she said, pulling his face across to her so that he was forced to look into her eyes. "You are a sweet man. You have done nothing to harm me or my family."

"But," Conrad said feebly, trying to push aside his competing emotions. "But I'm German…"

Sybille pushed aside one of the flame thorn's branches where it had fallen near her face, ignoring the sharp barbs on its stem. She took Conrad's face in both hands and shook him slightly to ensure he was listening to her.

"Yes, you are a German. But you are not a monster," she said, her voice raising slightly with emphasis. "You might come from a land of monsters, but *you* are not one."

He smiled slightly at that, and she smiled back at him.

"I hate Germans, Conrad," she said. "But not because of where they were born. My mother came from Germany, and she always told us it was a beautiful place. I suppose it must be. I know that Leutwein did not kill my mother or even give the order to the men who did. Leutwein is no saint, but I do not hate him. I hate Beaunard because he treats me worse than Leutwein's dogs. I hate the Schutztruppe who tried to rape me. I hate the men like Monsieur Perrot who push our people underground by the hundreds to mine some silly rocks. And I hate Major Baumhauer for everything he has done to drive us to war."

Conrad could feel her hands tighten slightly where she still held his face, as though the mere mention of all they'd encountered together caused her body to tense. She seemed to notice this herself and took her hands gently from his face.

"But I do not hate you, Conrad."

She was beautiful against the twilight sky. Her face hung inches from Conrad's, her azure eyes locking onto his own as if trying to force both fear and guilt from his heart.

Those were her mother's eyes, Conrad thought. The last remaining evidence of the difficult life of a German girl who'd chosen love over family and searched for a new beginning in the wilds of Africa.

Taking both of Conrad's hands in her own, Sybille kissed him softly beneath the sanctuary of the flame thorn. A few stray tears escaped Conrad's eyes. A jackal called out for its mate nearby, but Conrad scarcely heard it. His heart was too full to embrace anything other than the softness of Sybille's lips on his own.

At last, they broke apart, and Sybille lay her head on Conrad's shoulders.

"I do not hate you, Conrad," she said again.

Conrad sighed a moment and then lay his head on top of Sybille's.

"I do not hate you either," he echoed.

They sat in silence for a long while, watching the last light of day slip beneath the sounds of the congregated village and the smoke of a thousand cooking fires. A sense of peace wafted over Conrad as they sat with their bodies pressed closely together. A peace that he knew he would never be a part of.

"This is what you feared, isn't it?" Conrad asked Sybille. "This is what you warned me about the night of !Gai!ga's party."

Sybille was silent a moment, her eyes glimmering like sapphires in the final rays of the sunset.

"Perhaps," she said solemnly. "But my father has heard what you had to say, and it's nice sitting underneath this tree with you. That's enough for now."

*

Conrad spent that night on a worn pallet on the floor of Maharero's small hut. Guest laws were one thing, but it would have caused a violent uproar in Hochfeld if word had spread that a white man had taken Samuel Maharero's bed and forced the chief to sleep on his own floor. In any case, Conrad slept poorly but found the pallet to be at least marginally better than the dirt itself.

He departed just before sunrise as Maharero had requested, with a grumpy Noko in tow. The latter had been loath to miss the assembly, but if Maharero wished him to escort Conrad back to Okahandja, then there was nothing more to be said about it.

Noko insisted they leave before the sun was up to avoid running into more of the young gangs from the previous day. Having witnessed Noko bully the younger men away, Conrad had no desire to test whether the large man could fight off a truly determined gang by himself...or to see if he would even bother to.

Maharero had risen early as well to bid Conrad farewell. Conrad hadn't dared try to wish Sybille a private goodbye with both Noko and her father so near. He returned to Maharero's hut from the flame thorn red-faced and guilty; it was a miracle Maharero hadn't noticed as they ate the evening meal side by side.

In fact, Conrad had almost missed Sybille completely. She was nowhere to be found inside Maharero's compound when Conrad rose in the morning, and she still had not appeared when Noko came to fetch him.

Then, as Conrad shook Maharero's hand in the doorway, she suddenly emerged from the bungalow with a small strand of black lace.

"Give me the zebra," she'd said without explanation.

Conrad fished it gingerly out of his pocket. Sybille took it from him and tied the strand of lace into a tiny bow around the zebra's neck.

"Now it looks like a proper present for Frieda," she'd said, handing it back to Conrad with a proud smile.

Her hand lingered an extra moment or two on Conrad's. Sybille glanced at her father from the corner of her eye, but Maharero didn't seem to notice his daughter's small flirtation.

Conrad had no idea where Sybille had procured the lace. It was Belgian, he thought. Still soft and silky despite its age, as if it had come from some lady's fine dress. The little zebra looked wonderfully elegant now: he could just hear Frieda's squeals of delight when she received his package fresh off the next steamer back home.

Conrad almost kissed her, but he caught himself as he noticed Maharero and Noko looking back at them, Noko's ragged pack of dogs all lying impatiently on the dusty road nearby. Conrad told Sybille goodbye and that he would see her in Windhoek after the rains, trying to suppress the hope in his voice. Then he turned away and followed Noko through the sleeping village.

This will all blow over, he'd tried to tell himself mile after mile. There won't be a war. Sybille will be back at Schwerinsburg in a few short months.

He and Noko barely spoke five words to one another on the journey back to Okahandja. But despite his grudging mood during their travel, Noko delivered Conrad to the train depot on time.

When Conrad held out his hand out in thanks, Noko had glared fiercely at Conrad for several moments as if trying to figure out if Conrad was insulting him. At last, when it was clear no one else was looking, he quickly shook Conrad's hand, then disappeared with his dogs into the town's late afternoon crowds.

Conrad had originally planned to spend a day or two visiting with Beaunard on his way back to Windhoek, but too much was happening too quickly for him to dally.

He'd paid a young Ovambo boy hanging around the depot to go to the Mayor's Residence and inform Beaunard that urgent matters had recalled him to Windhoek faster than he'd expected. Conrad wasn't sure the boy had understood the message or if he would even attempt to deliver it to Beaunard, but with the Major and the Schutztruppe patrolling Okahandja like a swarm of restless bees, Conrad didn't dare try to send Beaunard a written note.

The last thing Conrad needed was Sören Baumhauer intercepting his message and marching murderously on the Hochfeld assembly before

Leutwein even knew that the Herero had gathered there.

His train arrived in Okahandja on time, a surprise given the still-heavy traffic of late migrants trying to beat the rains home to their villages. No sooner had he gotten himself situated in the train car than the sky unleashed a brilliant, angry flash of lightning and a sudden torrent of pent-up rain.

The long-promised droplets pounded against the metal roof with a loud *thunp-thump* that echoed powerfully throughout the whole train. Sybille had warned him that the first rain of the season was almost always violent. She was right; any visions he'd had of people dancing in the streets as the first raindrops fell, vanished almost instantly. Germans and natives alike who were still stuck on the platform broke into a run and pushed past the lone ticket officer into the small, crowded station depot. Piles of luggage lay abandoned on the platform, soaked beyond recognition in minutes.

The train was mostly empty for the return leg to Windhoek. Only three men and a woman passenger sat in first class with Conrad. The man sitting across from him flipped casually through a copy of the *Windhoek Press*, the colony's main newspaper.

"Anything of interest?" Conrad asked politely.

He didn't particularly want to talk to anyone, but the thought of sitting in silence all the way back to Windhoek and trying to figure out what he was going to tell Leutwein was enough to make him more socially inclined.

"Same old news," the man responded dryly. "France has decided to split French Equatorial Africa into three new colonies, and the British are going ahead with their march into Tibet. Apart from that, the Danish Royal Family is in Berlin visiting the Kaiser."

Conrad nodded, barely attending to what the man was saying but glad for the conversation, nonetheless.

"There was one interesting mention on the front page about a Nama man the Schutztruppe arrested several weeks ago in Swakopmund for attempting to set fire to one of the Kolonialgesellschaft's ships. Apparently, the rest of this gang of would-be arsonists escaped across the foothills, but the troopers managed to capture an older man in town who couldn't run away. It's a bit of a scandal, so I'm told, because the Hottentot they arrested used to be an attendant for this very railway."

For a few hours, Conrad chatted amiably with the man, discussing the continued difficulties of Hamburg's *Fußball* team. Conrad had nearly gotten a hold of his nerves when the woman behind them screamed.

She had peeled back the drapes from her window and was transfixed in horror at the display before her.

"*Mein Gott!*" she cried, grabbing the rest of the car's attention with her terrified scream. God forbid!

They were near the outskirts of Windhoek, and all at once Conrad felt the train grinding quickly to a halt. The rain continued to fall with purpose; only a few moments ago, it had been impossible to see anything through the thick, wet night. Yet all of a sudden, three blinding lights cut through the darkness and lit up a terrifying display just a few hundred meters in front of the train.

The searchlights of the Windhoek Iron Palace hovered separately in the air for a moment, then all combined their focus at once on the edge of the barbed wire fence near the railroad. From somewhere in the camp a siren wailed. Conrad could hear the frantic, threatening shouts of the Schutztruppe guards calling to one another through the blackness.

Perhaps ten yards from the train track, the rain had washed away a small bank of earth under the wire, creating a running flow of mud and silt only a few inches tall. Now, bathed in the disorienting beams of the searchlight towers, Conrad and the other passengers could see what had caused the woman to scream.

A dozen mud-covered natives stood outside the fence, pulling another of their fellow prisoners out from under the wire.

As their train skidded to a stop, Conrad saw the escaped prisoners yank the last of their comrades through the gap. When the last man was free, all but two of the escapees dashed across the track, disappearing behind the train without a sound. The last two men made to flee over the track as well. Then someone within the fence cried out, making the two free prisoners turn around. It was an old man, hobbling as fast as he could with a small girl slung over his shoulders.

One of the two men seemed to decide that the old man and the girl were not worth the risk, and he, too, fled over the tracks and into the darkness. The old man cried out again while the last remaining prisoner ran back for the small hole in the fence.

The last prisoner was massive, and although his view was partially obscured by the rain-soaked window, Conrad thought there was something familiar about the man's bulk. He suddenly remembered the Black porter that Erik had brought into Conrad's cabin to unload his luggage from the *Calypso*. He had been the largest man Conrad had ever seen, and he had given most of the money Conrad had paid him at the train station to a little girl. What had the man's name been? Christoph?

The prisoner had to fall to his knees to grab the screaming child as the old man shoved her under the wire. The large man clutched the child tightly to his chest as he bent back down to pull the wire up for the old man. But before the old man could crawl through, the crack of a rifle split the night, and the old man fell forward, his limp body catching on the wire.

The lady in Conrad's car fainted. Her husband and one of the other men began to fan her frantically. The large prisoner gripped the little girl closely as the sound of German voices grew louder. He sprinted away from the fence and crossed in front of the stopped train after the other fugitives.

Conrad could hear the cracks of more rifle shots and the soft whistling of bullets as they thumped harmlessly into the soft muck around the train. Several Schutztruppe guards cursed nearby as they realized that the train blocked their shots at the fleeing prisoners. The train conductor had obviously panicked at the display, and Conrad could already feel the grating pull as the steam engine ground itself to a halt right in front of the troops' line of fire.

Within minutes, the Schutztruppe were swarming around the stopped train, searching for escaped prisoners who might have jumped on board. Sometime later, the guard captain of the prison camp came through their car to ask if all the passengers were all right, but Conrad barely noticed.

Just next to Conrad's window, bathed now in the camp's searchlights, the old man's body hung limp and tattered across the barbed wire, his white hair almost invisible beneath a layer of blood and grime.

It was Mikal, the kind train attendant who had shaken him awake and brought him red bush tea his first morning in the colony. Now, amid the nervous chatter of other passengers and as the lightning flashed around them, the eyes of Mikal, the old valet who had saved the little girl, stared lifelessly up at Conrad. And as another crash of thunder shook the train car, Conrad turned away and vomited onto the train's leather upholstery.

CHAPTER 8

JANUARY 1904

Conrad gripped the latest of Beaunard's telegrams tightly, his knuckles shaking the folded paper. For a week, there had been no news from Beaunard, and now a backlog of his daily reports had arrived all at once in a dramatic escalation.

The heavy rains in Okahandja had dislodged the telegraph wire near the Mayor's Residence, and it had taken the better part of a week to have it repaired. The Schutztruppe garrison's own wire had been nonoperational for months. As to why Beaunard did not simply send a man in person on the evening train each day, Conrad could only guess. Perhaps Beaunard did not have a man he could trust to deliver the message.

But whatever the reason, a small pile of a week's worth of alarming telegrams had been waiting for Conrad when he'd gone to the Windhoek station that morning.

He'd read each of the messages a half-dozen times already. Erwin, frowning across from him in the kitchen, preemptively added an extra dollop of sugar to Leutwein's morning oatmeal.

Things haven't fallen apart, Conrad tried to convince himself. They just haven't.

Unable to believe what he was seeing, Conrad made himself read each of Beaunard's telegrams one more time.

January 4th, 1904
Theodor, Stop.
Major has issued illegal land grants. Stop.
Three German farmers with political connections. Stop.
Farmers moved into Hottentot territory with military escort. Stop.
Request you come at once. Stop.
Beaunard

January 5th, 1904
Theodor, Stop.
Confronted Major. Stop.
Land grants approved by Berlin Office. Stop.
Farmers have signed papers from new Colonial Minister. Stop.
Dietrich Baumhauer. Stop.
Request you come at once. Stop.
Beaunard

January 6th, 1904
Theodor, Stop.
Received reports that farmers began clearing land today. Stop.
Mob of Hottentots confronted troops. Stop.
Warning shots fired and crowd dispersed. No bloodshed. Stop.
Major has left town to lead farmers' security. Stop.
Request you come immediately. Stop.
Beaunard

January 7th, 1904
Theodor, Stop.
Farmers razed grasslands near village, Witvlei. Stop.
Hottentot man attacked a soldier, shot dead. Stop.
Man's dogs attacked soldiers, two dead soldiers, one severely injured.
Stop.
Major ordered garrison mobilized, marching on village. Stop.
Request immediate aid. Stop.
Beaunard

Conrad could see that the telegraph operator in Windhoek had struggled to record the messages in rapid succession, but Conrad was just able to decipher the man's hasty handwriting.

Noko was dead. Lots of the Herero kept dogs, and so many at Hochfeld had been ready to fight Germany only a mere month ago. Yet somehow, Conrad felt sure it was Noko who had been killed.

He paused a moment. There was no love lost between him and Noko; the latter had been emphatic in driving that point across to Conrad on several occasions. Yet it was impossible to think about Ko without picturing the man's wife and small horde of children. Conrad suddenly realized he'd never learned the name of Noko's wife, though he could see her strained, tired face in his mind now, convulsed with grief.

Poor woman, he thought. And poor Anna too.

He wondered for the fifth time if Sybille had learned what had happened yet. Did Maharero know? Did the Herero know that Sören Baumhauer had mustered Okahandja's garrison to march on Witvlei?

There had been no activity from Hochfeld since Conrad's return a few weeks ago. The Christmas holiday had passed with no word of any violence from the colony's central regions. If Maharero had heard about the prisoner escape from the Iron Palace and the subsequent public execution of the one escapee the Schutztruppe had managed to catch, he was keeping quiet about it.

145

Conrad had no idea what decision Maharero had made, but the last month of relative quiet had given him hope that Maharero had listened to him and chosen peace.

But now, it looked like Maharero's own man had been killed. Thanks to whatever petty political scheme Dietrich Baumhauer had formulated, Maharero might now change his mind.

Damn Dietrich and all his fellow war hawks.

Leutwein had signed an agreement with a group of Herero chieftains three years ago, promising to hold back German cultivation east of Okahandja. Whatever Dietrich had been thinking in issuing these land grants, they were illegal according to the treaty. The newly appointed Colonial Minister was breaking German law!

Scheisse, Conrad swore to himself.

He knew it was pointless to protest the grants now. They would have been approved months ago. Small favors like this were handed out to loyal patrons all the time. Circumventing an inconvenient agreement with the Herero could be done without a second thought thousands of miles away in Berlin. It was possible the Kaiser himself had signed the grants, unaware that he was violating his own government's treaties as he did so.

Regardless of how it had been allowed to happen, Dietrich's paper pushing had become his brother's marching orders.

Conrad's throat clenched in anger as he read on.

January 8th, 1904
Theodor, Stop.
Major has taken nearly all of garrison. Stop.
Token force left in town, 25 troops. Stop.
Native populace has shrunk overnight. Stop.
German population uneasy. Stop.
Request reinforcements for town garrison. Stop.
Beaunard

January 10th, 1904
Theodor, Stop.
No word from Major. Stop.
Troop force gone two days with no word. Stop.
Local populace all but gone this morning. Stop.
Fear something has happened. Stop.
Request immediate reinforcements. Stop.
Beaunard

Beaunard had to be exaggerating. The man was clearly just nervous. It was a little less than two days' journey to the village of Witvlei from Okahandja. The Major had likely not even reached Witvlei before Beaunard had sent this last telegram.

There was no reason to suspect that there would be anything for the Major to report on. And besides, Baumhauer and Beaunard were not on particularly friendly terms.

Yet something was clearly amiss around Okahandja, making Beaunard uncharacteristically anxious.

Curse this stupid rain, Conrad thought for the dozenth time.

When the colony wasn't a scorching desert, it was subject to sporadic rainstorms that did little for the heat, serving only to water the lions and paralyze the government's limited infrastructure. It was no wonder so many of the tribes across the colony's bone-dry plains and shifting sands referred to the place as the "land that God made in anger."

God only knew why Beaunard had even bothered to send the full weeks' worth of missed telegrams. Most likely, the telegraph officer in Okahandja was either young or inexperienced and had not wanted to be reprimanded for not sufficiently informing the Commissioner's Office of ongoing events. Conrad could easily imagine the young man dashing to his post once he'd heard the wire had been fixed early this morning, tapping away at the knob of the straight key like mad, trying to relay a week's worth of messages to his counterpart in the capital.

Regardless, the telegrams were worrying. Could Beaunard be correct in saying that nearly all the natives in Okahandja had left the town in the middle of the night unnoticed? Without enough troops to patrol, Conrad supposed such a thing was possible. Yet the natives in Okahandja had lived in a primarily German town for over a decade and had endured the added daily tax of Major Baumhauer and the new Schutztruppe's headquarters without serious protest.

Why, then, should nearly five hundred natives suddenly decide to leave now?

Whatever the reason, Beaunard's last telegram was the most unsettling of all of them. It had been dated by the Windhoek station operator as having been received late the previous night, and its frantic tone was chilling.

January 11th, 1904
Theodor, Stop.
Something terrible has happened. Stop.
Still no word, no natives left in town. Stop.
Can sense something coming in the air. Stop.
Garrison too small to hold town. Stop.
Request permission to evacuate the town to Windhoek. Stop.
Please Theodor. Stop.

There was no signature from the Windhoek operator as to who had sent the last telegram, but Conrad knew that it must've come from Beaunard himself.

The last line was truly troubling. Beaunard was a man wedded to etiquette, but this latest telegram abandoned the formalities of his office as though he were trying desperately to stress his urgency to his friend.

Evacuate the town?

Either Beaunard had grown paranoid working so close to Baumhauer…or Maharero's decision had not been as ambiguous as Conrad had hoped.

Conrad looked up at Erwin, and Erwin nodded silently, both men agreeing that Leutwein's strict diet should be ignored today to soften the blow of this morning's news. As Erwin left the kitchen to fetch a few eggs to fry, Conrad drummed his fingers on his knee, trying to ignore the thought of Leutwein having a heart attack while reading Beaunard's messages. Leutwein had just about fainted from distress when Conrad had returned a month before and had told him about the Herero's assembly.

It had been the second most horrible moment in Conrad's short career. It was embarrassing to have to relay to Leutwein that the Commissioner had been so badly mistaken in predicting the Herero's resolve, but the look Leutwein had given Conrad as his words sunk in was worse. Conrad had shivered watching Leutwein's features react to the news. The Commissioner simply stared, unfocused, at nothing in particular. It reminded Conrad of the forlorn, despairing gazes of the prison inmates the day Berriz and the other Groontfontein boys were hanged.

It was the gaze of a man devoid of hope.

And that was to say nothing of the public indignation that had come in the wake of the prisoner escape the same night. Leutwein had received several petitions from the passengers on the train who with Conrad had also witnessed the escape from the Iron Palace, demanding that the Commissioner restore order to the colony by any means necessary. And there had been yet more outcry in the colony when the Schutztruppe had rooted out another of the escaped men who'd been hiding with family in the city. The soldiers had gunned him down in the public square as he tried to flee across Kaiserstrasse, sending the flocks of white shoppers into a panic.

Of the dozen or so prisoners who had crawled under the wire that night, only two had been caught. The colony was on edge. The white population was growing restive as false rumors of vicious gangs of escaped, savage men circling the capital spread among DSWA's social circles. And in a vicious paradox, the German colonial citizenry heaped blame on Leutwein for the bloody displays of force in public places, then protested in outrage that Leutwein was not doing enough to quell disobedience among the natives.

Men and women alike whispered their concerns at the backs of parlors, or they shouted red-faced, drunken protests in bars that the colony was in a terrible state. The one thing that both groups agreed on was that it was all Leutwein's fault.

Not only the colony's politics but the harsh, searing climate of Southwest Africa, never for the faint of heart, seemed bent on killing Leutwein, sapping both his physical strength and sense of purpose.

Things had remained quiet through the holidays, and Conrad had allowed himself to hope the Commissioner might improve. The Colonial Office had been mercifully silent the past few weeks, but even this current respite did not seem to spare Leutwein: his health continued to deteriorate.

Though he still worked ceaselessly throughout the day, Leutwein rose later and later each morning. Mayor Grober had declined to call on Leutwein for two weeks, pretexting a flare-up of gout that no one at the Residence believed. If Conrad had had to write down a list of Leutwein's friends at that moment, he would've been hard-pressed to come up with more than three or four names.

Conrad let the Commissioner sleep a bit longer, knowing he would have to rouse Leutwein soon, regardless of how badly the man needed his rest. None of the telegrams from Beaunard were dated for this morning, so perhaps the hysteria surrounding Baumhauer's march on Witvlei had already abated….

Conrad hoped that Beaunard had not been so panicked as to have already evacuated Okahandja, only to have the Major return hours later to a deserted town. There were quite a few prominent Kolonialgesellschaft officials living in Okahandja, and a fiasco like that would surely be reported angrily to the Colonial Office and get both Beaunard and Leutwein sacked.

Conrad was about to read over the telegrams yet again when Leutwein surprised him by walking into the kitchen with hardly a sound.

The Commissioner looked dismal. The heavy bags under his eyes had darkened overnight, and his new gray suit was unfashionably wrinkled. Heavy rains added thick humidity to the stifling heat, making it nearly impossible to keep formal wear in any sort of presentable fashion. Paula, one of the dry-season maids, had gone home to her village near Walvis Bay for the rainy season, and when her usual replacement hadn't shown up on the first of the year, Leutwein had resigned himself to wearing puckered suits.

"Good morning, sir," Conrad said, standing as Leutwein walked into the room.

"Good morning, Conrad," Leutwein replied, giving Conrad a worn half-smile that showed he thought it was anything but. "I saw Erwin out the window on his way to the hen house as I came down the stairs. How bad is the news today, then?"

The man was still sharp, Conrad thought. No matter how tired he was, at least his mind was still intact.

As if summoned by name, Erwin returned to the kitchen and cracked three large eggs into a pan. Without a word, Erwin scooped a large serving of oatmeal into a bowl and placed it before Leutwein, along with a generous pot of steaming coffee. Conrad could smell the brown sugar chunks, clumped together in the humid air, but he had little appetite this morning. Not knowing how to even begin to describe Beaunard's messages, he merely handed Leutwein the stack of telegrams.

"The telegraph wire near Okahandja has been repaired, sir," Conrad said plainly.

There, he thought. At least start with a *little* good news.

"These all arrived at our station late last night. They're a copy of all the correspondence from the Mayor's Office that we did not receive last week."

Leutwein did not touch the oatmeal or the coffee but took the stack of telegrams from Conrad and began reading quickly. After the first two telegrams, Leutwein's complexion lost its color. He had entered the room with a knit brow and a strained smile, but as the Commissioner read on, he grew increasingly dejected.

"This came in last night, you said?" Leutwein asked, his sunken eyes tearing themselves away from the paper to look at Conrad briefly.

"Yes, sir, last night," Conrad replied.

Leutwein burned through the pile of messages until he came to the last one. The one that Beaunard had sent himself the night before. For a moment, Leutwein appeared petrified, his gaze frozen at the bottom of the telegram.

Conrad cleared his throat. Startled, Leutwein leapt from his chair, suddenly filled with crazed purpose.

"Damn Sören Baumhauer to the depths of Hell!" Leutwein shouted as he rushed from the kitchen. "How could he leave an entire town defenseless?"

Conrad followed Leutwein, taking the stairs three at a time to keep up with the Commissioner as he stormed through the Residence towards his office. He had not seen Leutwein move so quickly in weeks.

Conrad reached the Commissioner's office, out of breath with the effort, and found Leutwein hunched over his desk. He was writing so furiously that Conrad wondered if the parchment might catch fire from the friction.

This wasn't like Leutwein at all, Conrad thought as he stood nervously in the office doorway.

Even after years of duress, Leutwein had always remained composed, and Conrad had never seen him act without reason. Yet now Conrad could not see why Leutwein was so incensed. Surely, Beaunard's telegrams were a tad far-fetched, weren't they?

Baumhauer hadn't even been gone five days. You couldn't simply *sense* that something terrible was going to happen…could you?

Evidently, Leutwein trusted that Beaunard could.

The Commissioner tore off the message he had been writing and slapped it into Conrad's hand hurriedly before turning back to begin a second order.

"I'm calling up the Windhoek garrison to mobilize," he explained to Conrad, not looking up from what he was doing. "Take that to Captain Jund and tell him I want two companies ready to ride to Okahandja by noon. I'll draft an emergency order to seize the train there this evening and put Jund's men on it."

"Sir," Conrad prodded hesitantly. "Is all that really necessary? The Major has only been gone for…"

Leutwein rounded on him.

"I trust *Beaunard's* judgment of the situation, Conrad," Leutwein snapped at him. "If he is requesting permission to evacuate the town, then this is something serious. Get Captain Jund mobilized immediately, and I'll meet you at the telegraph station. And you can tell that imbecile of a captain that if he refuses a direct order from me again, I'll be happy to shoot him right in his fat face!"

Realizing that he'd been dismissed, Conrad left Leutwein's office with a growing sense of dread.

As he hurried down the stairwell, he heard a heavy fist slam onto the Commissioner's desk in anger, followed by the sound of even more furious scribblings.

Nein, Conrad thought as he flew past a quizzical-looking Erwin to fetch his coat and find Petyr. There was no way that Beaunard was correct. It wouldn't, couldn't, come to war.

It simply wouldn't.

As his lungs began to constrict in the hot morning sunshine, he found himself counting as his feet hit the cobbled pavestones of the Residence's drive. *Eins...Zwei...Drei...*

*

The telegraph station in Windhoek looked less like the colony's main communications headquarters than a repurposed toolshed, which, in fact, it more or less was. When the old station had burned to the ground the previous year in an unfortunate accident involving leaking lamp oil and one too many graveyard shifts from the station foreman, Leutwein had leased the shed from the owner of a prominent warehouse in Windhoek as a temporary measure.

There were blueprints in Leutwein's office for a replacement, an expanded telegraph station attached to the train depot. Somehow, unlike Major Baumhauer's new central garrison, the funding for such a project had been "unfortunately tied up" in the bureaucratic slog of the Colonial Office for over a year.

Luckily, the shed could just barely accommodate two station officers and their equipment and was situated high enough near the surrounding ridge as to minimize any interference with its transmissions from the rocky terrain. However, none of the temporary station's advantages did anything to shield its exposed position from the heat or the overwhelming claustrophobia inside its walls.

Conrad was already more than a little nauseated from dealing with Captain Jund when he arrived at the telegraph station. One of Major Baumhauer's close aides, Jund was as thick as he was tall and scarcely did anything without the Major's direct orders. Personally, Conrad thought the man was a lout. Jund had dark, round eyes and a plain, doughy face. Coupled with two prominent and protruding front teeth, the man looked like a plump gopher in uniform, which had earned him the title of the "Gopher Captain" among the other Schutztruppe officers.

It was obvious to everyone, except Captain Jund, that he had only risen through the ranks through Baumhauer's favor.

While Baumhauer had moved himself and most of his staff to Okahandja, he had left his loyal lug behind as commander of Windhoek's now shrunken garrison. And Jund had unfortunately taken to his new command with vigor; his newly inflated sense of self-worth made the man even more intolerable. He kept Conrad waiting at the fort's barracks for over half an hour, despite Conrad's repeated insistence to Jund's aide that he was under strict and urgent orders from the Commissioner.

It had taken another quarter of an hour for Conrad to impress upon Jund that, regardless of how he felt about Leutwein personally, if Major Baumahuer were indeed in danger, then it was Jund's duty to rescue his commanding officer.

Once converted to the cause, Jund proved to be as tactless in executing his duty as Conrad had feared. Instead of quietly mustering the two companies that Leutwein had requested, he had ordered the fort's siren to sound for a full emergency muster. Its wailing echo had rebounded off the surrounding ridge and rang out clear across every street in Windhoek.

Within minutes the whole capital was in a wild panic. A flood of terrified Germans dropped their midday purchases and fled from the storefronts in the main square toward the protection of Alte Feste. The past few weeks of gossip about the prison break and the fearful rumors of marauding native war bands lying in wait out in the bush had driven all of Windhoek to the point of hysteria. As the fort sirens wailed over the city, every German was convinced that Windhoek was under attack.

The crowds clogged the entrance to the fort in their mad dash, and Conrad and Petyr were nearly trampled as they tried to break out through the chaos. No doubt it would take hours to reassure and calm the civilians before Jund could even begin to organize his men to move to Okahandja.

This had already become an embarrassing disaster. And once Leutwein delivered his notice of the colonial government's seizure of one of the railway's primary steam engines later that morning, Conrad knew the telegraph station would be flooded with a series of outraged telegrams from the railroad's main headquarters in Walvis Bay.

Conrad felt sure that even if they managed to survive the mayhem of today, the whole lot of them were likely to be sacked. All because of Beaunard's alarmist telegram.

He arrived at the telegraph station a good hour after the Commissioner to find Leutwein red-faced and bellowing at the young officer in his commander's parade voice.

"I don't care if there's no return answer, Lieutenant Wedekind! Send the message again!"

"But sir…" the young officer tried. "If there's no response on the wire, then no one at the other end can retrieve the message, sir."

"If you have to send that message a hundred times until someone responds, then you'll tap it out until your fingers fall off, Lieutenant! Am I clear?"

"Y-Yes, sir!" Wedekind responded with a shaking salute.

Leutwein grabbed his hat and coat from the station's small table and tore off in a hurry, pausing long enough to instruct Conrad to wait until they received a response from Okahandja.

In the Commissioner's steaming wake, Wedekind scurried to the back half of the shed where he and the other station operators kept the telegraph. A tattered cloth curtain separated the telegraph from the rest of the shed to prevent the delicate machine from being damaged by the wind and sand on the frequent occasions when the door was blown in. It was a poor precaution to Conrad's mind, but given how often the night officers at the station fell asleep during their shift, he supposed it was better than nothing.

While Wedekind resigned himself to fretfully tapping out Leutwein's message once again on the telegraph's well-worn knob, the other telegraph officer on duty looked up at Conrad fearfully.

Conrad immediately recognized the wan complexion and riot of carrot-colored, curly hair. The young man's name was Gert Fromm.

Most of the telegraph "officers" were incredibly young. They were recruited Schutztruppe either too weak for the long horseback patrols across the hinterlands or those who had fallen afoul of their commanding officers and been placed at the telegraph station as punishment.

Conrad had met Gert in town a few times. He was the son of one of the Major's aides who lived with his mother in Windhoek. Gert was still too young for serious fighting, so he'd been left behind when his father had relocated to Okahandja with Baumhauer and given a commission manning the telegraph station. Conrad had never met the boy's father, but he recognized the disappointment etched in the boy's face that he'd been left behind to rot in Windhoek's sweltering telegraph office.

At least, that's how Gert must have been feeling until this morning. Now the boy sat fidgeting at the cramped table, his voice cracking as he spoke to Conrad.

"Do you think something bad really has happened to Major Baumhauer, Herr Huber?" Gert asked hesitantly. "I've never seen the Commissioner so shaken up before."

Conrad felt bad for Gert, and he felt even worse that he did not have an answer for him.

"I'm not sure, Gert," he admitted with a sigh. "It's not like the Commissioner to overreact, but the Major has only been out in the bush a few days."

Gert nodded in eager agreement. Wedekind returned from behind the curtain a moment later.

"There wasn't a response, Herr Huber," he reported dutifully.

Seeing the troubled look on Gert's face, he continued.

"But it might easily be the rains again. They've gotten far more of it up there than they were expecting this year. Or the wire might be damaged again. Or a baby baboon might've climbed up on one of the poles and chewed through the wire. That happened three times last year. Had to drive the whole troop of them off with dynamite before we could repair it."

Gert smiled, slightly cheered at the thought that the entire day's angst might be the sole responsibility of a tiny monkey.

"Should I keep trying the message, sir?" Lieutenant Wedekind asked him.

It took Conrad a moment to realize that he was, effectively, in charge. Both Wedekind and Gert were younger than Conrad, and by virtue of being the Commissioner's only active aide, Conrad outranked them both.

"Best keep trying," Conrad replied, though he knew Wedekind was unlikely to get a response.

If the wire had indeed been damaged again, it would be days, not hours, before it could be repaired. And that was assuming that the Okahandja station was even aware that their wire was damaged. The operator there had likely just been relieved and as a result, it would take the new officer a while to realize that incoming transmissions were not coming through. Then there would be the even longer exercise of tracking down the damaged wire over a wide stretch of rough terrain and then the even lengthier process of having an engineer repair it.

It seemed foolish to have the two boys repeatedly send a message in the vain hope that the wire would be repaired today, but Conrad had heard the demand in Leutwein's voice and didn't see any good coming from contradicting him at this moment.

Wedekind sighed in resignation and disappeared once more behind the curtain.

"Petyr," Conrad called out the door of the shed to where the young boy sat absently kicking rocks.

Hearing Conrad's voice, Petyr rushed right over. The day's earlier trials and subsequent disasters in dealing with Captain Jund were more than enough to rattle Petyr, though he did an admirable job of trying to seem unfazed.

"I need you to stay here and let me know immediately if Lieutenant Wedekind manages to get a response from Okahandja."

Petyr's eyes grew wide for a moment. The boy peered around Conrad, staring pointedly at Gert's blue-gray uniform. Clearly, Petyr was afraid to stay at the station with two Schutztruppe boys without Conrad. Still, he said nothing as Conrad ducked back inside the shed.

"I'm leaving Petyr here as my messenger," he told Gert. "He can bring me any messages that you're able to receive."

Gert looked at Petyr, his face unreadable. But after a short pause, he stood and gave Conrad a curt salute.

Lieber Gott, Conrad prayed. Don't make me regret this.

He didn't want to leave Petyr alone, but he didn't have much choice. If Leutwein intended to commandeer a train in his current agitated state, as he'd already said that he did, then Conrad would be of far greater use in restraining the Commissioner and mollifying the conductor than in waiting for a telegram that would almost certainly never arrive.

"If anything happens, come and find me," Conrad said to Petyr. "I'll either be at the Residence or the train depot."

"Okay," Petyr managed to say.

For a second, Conrad hesitated. He couldn't leave the poor boy here if he was terrified, could he?

Older boys were scarcely known for their acceptance and fair treatment of younger boys. Conrad remembered that well enough from several fights he'd managed to get in back home in Aschaffenburg. To say nothing about what boy soldiers might do to a native boy if left to their own devices.

Well, he didn't really have a choice, did he? If something truly were happening in Okahandja, then all the Commissioner's Office staff must be on duty, and that included Petyr.

Conrad gave Petyr a small squeeze on the shoulder and then began back down the steep trail towards the city to try and keep Leutwein from doing something he'd regret.

*

Conrad arrived a few moments too late to save Leutwein the black eye. He'd run into the station nearly out of breath to find Leutwein and a particularly burly train conductor exchanging heated words. Conrad didn't quite catch all of what the two were shouting. He heard Leutwein yell something rather unsettling about the conductor's genitals and a goat, then watched helplessly as the Commissioner took a strong right hook to the face.

It had taken far more breath than Conrad had had to pacify the conductor and assuage the flustered railroad company representative for the Windhoek station, who had quickly joined the commotion. Now there would certainly be a barrage of irate telegrams from the railroad's main office in the morning. Conrad couldn't think about that now.

He managed to get Leutwein back to Schwerinsburg with the aid of his coachman and somehow convince Leutwein that he needed to rest an hour or so if he were, in fact, going to join Captain Jund's expedition. Leutwein was not acting like himself. Conrad felt an immense relief to have the Commissioner back at the Residence where he could not blindly sever any more important connections.

Erwin had brought the Commissioner a wet cloth to press against his face, which Leutwein had accepted with muted embarrassment. Now, he and Conrad sat in silence in the library, lost in their respective thoughts.

The dark green drapes were gathering dust in Sybille's absence. For the first time today, Conrad allowed thoughts of Sybille to enter his mind. No matter where Baumhauer was, Sybille should be safe in Hochfeld. It was two days' journey ride from Witvlei to Hochfeld. There, she was surrounded by thousands of her people. Surely, if nothing else, she would be safe there.

The drapes had been closed during the last storm and were still closed. Conrad pulled them open now, receiving a soft shower of dust as the old, green velvet gave way to the fading evening light.

Yes, Conrad told himself once more. Sybille would be safe.

Captain Jund's reinforcements were supposed to be ready to depart in little less than an hour. Conrad thought about running to retrieve Petyr, who hadn't returned before Leutwein left with Jund's two companies. As he moved to leave the room, Leutwein stopped him.

"Did you hear something?" he said, letting the compress fall from his face onto the floor.

It was the first thing the Commissioner had said since Conrad had brought him back from the train station. At first, Conrad heard nothing. But then, he heard the faint, growing sound of a horse steadily pounding down the northern road. And then he heard the shouting. He couldn't tell who it was, the horse's rider or one of Leutwein's remaining staff, but whoever it was, they were clearly in distress.

Leutwein rose from his armchair and staggered out onto the porch. Conrad followed closely behind. Gustavus and Ivan barked wildly from somewhere within the compound, and all the household staff rushed from the various buildings of Schwerinsburg in a confused scramble as if the whole compound had suddenly caught fire.

"Conrad, shut those dogs up right now!" Leutwein snapped over his shoulder as he tried to hurry toward the main gate.

Before Conrad could respond, Gustavus and Ivan came charging around the side of the Residence, teeth bared and all the fur on their ridged backs standing straight up. As the mystery horse tore through the gate, Conrad had to dive off the porch to keep the dogs from attacking it. Neither dog ever wore a collar, so Conrad was forced to grab both Gustavus and Ivan by the scruffs of their thick necks. Each dog weighed over forty kilos, and neither's efforts were daunted in the slightest by Conrad's grip on their necks.

Erwin, who had come running out of the kitchen's back door, saw Conrad struggling and grabbed hold of Gustavus as he was about to twist out of Conrad's grasp.

The coachman quickly went to take the man's horse, but he had to run and catch the rider himself as he nearly fell from the saddle. The rider's Schutztruppe uniform was almost unrecognizable beneath a thick coat of dust and sweat. His jacket was missing its left sleeve, and his horse looked as though it, too, might collapse from exhaustion at any moment.

Conrad didn't know how the man managed to keep from sliding off his horse, but as Leutwein approached, the rider forced a bleeding arm into a weak salute.

"Corporal Knef reporting, Commissioner," he said, his voice choked with dust. "The Major is dead, sir. An army…of Hottentots ambushed us near Witvlei…only a few of us managed to get away. There was no time…to evacuate Okahandja. The savages burned the whole city…to the ground and killed over a hundred Germans…women and children too, sir. Lieutenant Protz…is leading a group of refugees here…he sent me ahead to report."

Leutwein's face turned a ghostly white. All the native staff immediately fell silent, looking with fearful eyes between the terrifying sight of the bloody Corporal Knef and the stricken Commissioner. Gustavus and Ivan continued to bark, both of them growing more frantic as a deathly silence descended on the crowd.

Conrad looked at Leutwein and saw at once that the Commissioner was losing command of himself.

"And Mayor Hertzog?" Leutwein asked, ashen.

Corporal Knef took several heaving breaths before responding, still struggling to stay upright in the saddle.

"The Mayor is dead too, sir," he gasped. "I saw him take a bullet through the neck…in the main square. He was trying to find someone…someone to surrender the city to…and some old Hottentot just shot him…point blank… with a musket."

Knef suddenly leaned over his horse's side and began coughing violently. One of Leutwein's house staff hurried back toward the main house to draw the man some water from the Residence's well. When the corporal's fit subsided, he turned back to Leutwein and steadied himself with one hand on his horse's neck.

"What are your orders for Lieutenant Protz, sir?" Knef asked.

Leutwein stumbled backward as though he, too, had been shot. He spun, almost in a drunken daze, and nearly collided with one of the grooms. His mouth was open, as if he were screaming. But the only sound he made was a whimpering that might come from a whipped puppy.

"*Sir*," Corporal Knef repeated urgently. "What are your orders?"

The Commissioner looked at Knef, but his mouth opened and closed wordlessly. Then, all at once, he collapsed into a heap and began to sob uncontrollably.

Several of the staff exchanged anxious glances. No one moved for a breath, and even the dogs finally fell silent. Erwin slowly released his grip on Gustavus and approached Leutwein. Gently, Erwin was able to pull the Commissioner to his feet and help him back toward the main house. But Leutwein's sobs were growing hysterical now, and Schwerinsburg's garden echoed with the Commissioner's pitiful cries.

"I should have helped them!" Leutwein screamed. "*Gott*, I should have helped them!"

Gustavus followed his master slowly, then paused on the porch where he lay down, confused and frightened. Ivan began pulling against Conrad again, this time back towards the Residence as he began to whine after Leutwein as well.

As Conrad struggled against the big dog's pull, he swore to himself. He fought with Ivan a moment longer then finally gave up and let the dog lope into the house. He took a moment to catch his breath, his head spinning too much to notice that everyone in the courtyard was suddenly looking at him.

"Sir," Knef said to him with another pained salute. "What are *your* orders?"

CHAPTER 9

JUNE 1904

Walvis Bay looked very different from when Conrad had first arrived there a year ago. It was still crowded with jostling hordes of people, but instead of the wild cacophony of Africans that had greeted him near the docks before, the city was now crawling with rank upon rank of soldiers of the Imperial German Army. Adorned in their fresh field uniforms with blue piping and white buttons, Conrad thought the mass of German regulars looked almost hilariously out of place amongst the backdrop of the burnt orange dunes, like a brand-new tin of toy soldiers dumped unceremoniously into a sandbox.

The Berlin Colonial Office had obtained permission from the English government to land an advance portion of the German division at Walvis Bay. The other half of the Imperial army would land at Swakopmund over the next few days, but at least three infantry regiments, the high-ranking officers of the division, and nearly all the artillery batteries had come ashore this morning at Walvis Bay.

I wonder what Herr Kleinschmidt had to give the British to secure this deal? Conrad fanned himself in the paltry shade of an awning outside a small bar near the main docks, diligently guarding the Commissioner's luggage and watching a nearby gun crew supervise the unloading of their field piece over the side of a repurposed ocean liner.

Probably either some exuberant sum or control over a few of the uninhabited rocky outcrops that passed for islands along the coast of Kamerun, he thought.

Leutwein had been sacked.

The Major's death had set now-Colonial Minister Dietrich Baumhauer on the warpath. From the telegram Conrad had received from Herr Kleinschmidt regarding the emergency hearing that had been held in Berlin to determine Leutwein's future status as Commissioner of the DSWA, Dietrich had screamed at the committee until he turned purple. He swore that their defense of the incompetent Leutwein had cost him his brother. He had then dissolved into a frenzied mix of shouting and sobbing and had pounded his fists on the committee table until he had had to be removed from the meeting.

Regardless of Dietrich's connections in the Kaiser's inner circle and his distraught display before the committee, the loss of Okahandja and the failure to prevent an open war with the Herero were too damning for the Kaiser to ignore. He recalled Leutwein to Berlin.

Leutwein had read a prepared face-saving statement in Windhoek's main square three days ago, telling the pitifully small crowd that he was resigning of his own volition to address his failing health. But anyone with half a mind already knew that Leutwein had been sacked.

Conrad had seen no sign of his former boss since Leutwein had muttered something about needing a drink after they had arrived in Walvis Bay that afternoon. He had disappeared into the first bar they'd come across near the docks, leaving Conrad outside to mind his luggage.

Conrad's own steamer trunk lay in the dilapidated pile of assorted baggage, and he glanced ruefully at its chipped paint amidst the orderly mayhem of the dockside storefronts. While there'd been no official word from Berlin that Conrad, too, had been sacked, he hardly expected Leutwein's replacement to want any member of Leutwein's culpable staff to join his own. He was already dreading the thought of turning up on his uncle's doorstep in Hamburg after less than a year and having to explain to his family how things had gone so badly for him in the colony.

But Conrad still had one final task to perform for the colonial government. He pushed aside his humiliation and scanned the bustling dockyard for the General's entourage.

Conrad had heard a great deal about the man the Kaiser had appointed as Leutwein's successor. Everything, in fact, except where he might be at this particular moment. He had received a curt army telegram at his hotel that morning, instructing him to meet one of the General's aides at one o'clock to help facilitate a discreet meeting between the two commissioners before an official ceremony later that evening. But it was now nearly half-past three, and he hadn't received any word on what was detaining the man he was supposed to meet.

Conrad took a deep breath and let it out slowly after a long pause. He was angry. But he wasn't sure who he was angry with: Baumhauer for causing this mess; Leutwein for crumbling under the pressure; Sybille's father, Maharero, for starting a war he could not possibly win or control; this new General's aide for keeping him waiting in the sweltering city streets, or himself for having ever stepped onto the decks of the *Calypso*.

In the end, all the players had done what they thought was best. It was hard to fault anyone for doing that, Conrad supposed, perhaps even someone as unpleasant and bellicose as Major Baumhauer. Yet now Leutwein's worst fears had unfolded like the curtain call of a dismal play. And he and Conrad could only watch as the new uniformed actors bowed eagerly before a humorless audience.

*

The past six months had been a grueling farce.

Conrad had thought he, too, would faint when Corporal Knef had looked at him that evening in the garden, wounded and panting, asking for orders. The Commissioner's Office had always held the final authority over Schutztruppe officers, at least in theory, and with Leutwein indisposed, Conrad had suddenly been thrust forward as the next-in-line for command by virtue of being the only other colonial officer in the colony.

A small part of him thought it must all be some great, elaborate joke organized by Major Baumhauer to make Beaunard and Leutwein look foolish. But Conrad could see the desperate certainty etched in Knef's pained face and the blood flowing from shallow wounds and staining his coat. He, at least, was not joking.

"Er..." Conrad stammered. "How far away is Lieutenant Protz now, Corporal?"

"About five or six hours, sir," Knef responded, clearly just glad at that moment that Conrad had not also dissolved into hysterics. "They'll be slow coming. They've got children with them."

"*Gottverdammt*," Conrad swore under his breath.

He couldn't see how this situation could possibly get any worse.

What would Leutwein do now if he had his wits about him? For that matter, what would Baumhauer do? Just then, Conrad wasn't too picky about whose actions he copied as long as he could think of something that wouldn't get anyone else killed today.

"All right," he finally said, trying to muster as much confidence in his voice as he could. "Tell Protz to make it here as soon as he can. We've got two of Captain Jund's companies nearly ready to march. I'll tell them to hurry the train along behind you to pick up the survivors."

Conrad had no idea if what he said made any tactical sense.

Just protect people, he thought to himself. That can't be too poor a decision, can it?

It must have made some sense, for Knef replied with as sharp a salute as he could manage and slid off his spent horse. One of Leutwein's grooms had brought out a fresh horse, and Corporal Knef swung himself into the new saddle with his good arm. He spun his new horse around and shot back out the main gate, galloping up the northern road back into the bush to deliver Conrad's orders to Lieutenant Protz.

Conrad didn't recall much about the next hour. He knew that he'd dispatched one of the grooms to retrieve Petyr from the telegraph station, and then he had run like a madman to the train station to convey his improvised orders to Captain Jund.

He had expected to need a good deal of shouting and threats to get Jund to move his men without the Commissioner, but once the gopher captain learned that Baumhauer was dead, it proved easy to order Jund around. The simple man was plainly alarmed, and Conrad was too, for that matter. And after only a brief hesitation, Jund had himself saluted Conrad and ordered his men onto the train to find Protz and the refugees.

Apparently in the thick of war, some rivalries vanished like smoke.

At some point after that, one of the remaining officers suggested mobilizing the rest of the Windhoek garrison to prepare Alte Feste for whatever might happen next. Corporal Knef had not said that any of the Herero were chasing Lieutenant Protz, but Conrad had had enough surprises for one day. He helped the remaining Schutztruppe to gather food and clothing for the incoming flux of refugees, and then he'd returned to the Residence, exhausted and uneasy.

The main house was eerily silent when he arrived. For a moment, Conrad remembered the horrible story he'd once heard from a Schutztruppe guard about men being stolen away in the night from their homes by packs of ravenous hyenas.

No, Conrad told himself. Don't be ridiculous.

Nevertheless, he found himself standing just inside the doorway, craning his ears to see if he could hear any sound of a hyena's maniacal laughter. He'd heard hyenas on his first night in the bush with Noko, and remembering their high-pitched cackling made him suddenly wish he knew where Gustavus and Ivan were.

A small clattering of pots and pans came from the kitchen.

Well, that was fine then, Conrad told himself, his breathing easing slightly. Hyenas weren't in the habit of using cutlery.

He cracked open the kitchen door and was relieved to find Erwin washing a pile of dishes.

"Long day," Conrad said, pushing the door fully open.

Erwin grunted and continued to scrub the pot in his hand. For a good while, neither of them spoke. Conrad knew he should sleep; the next few nights were going to be anything but restful, but he didn't want to be alone. Even Erwin's gruff silence was better than returning to his dark bungalow to face the harsh realities that dawn would bring.

After a while, Erwin decided the pot he was washing was clean and surprised Conrad by speaking to him.

"You know, Leutwein is a dead man," Erwin said plainly.

Conrad looked at Erwin, stupefied.

"Has something else happened?" he managed after a moment.

Erwin shook his head.

"No. But he a dead man anyway. All those people dead and his little Afrikaner friend too…men don't come back from that kind of grief."

Conrad stared at Erwin for a moment.

"What do you mean?" he asked finally said. "Are you saying that that episode in the garden is permanent? Are you saying he's snapped?"

Erwin paused for a while as he scrolled through his mind to find enough German words to describe what he meant. Then he shrugged his shoulders and picked up another pot to scrub.

"He just be dead," Erwin said again. "No more life to live in him."

Conrad tried for several minutes to think of a rebuttal. But the longer he sat and watched Erwin wash dishes, the more he realized that he was right. Leutwein might live another twenty or thirty years if his health recovered back home in Germany. But the spirit that had driven his ambitions in Africa was gone now. The Commissioner's iron resolve had finally broken, and the last of his old Prussian fire lay in ashes strewn across the Residence's garden.

Before today, Conrad had been hopeful that there would be a way to avoid war with the Herero. But it was too late now. Beaunard and Baumhauer were both dead, Leutwein had cracked, and Germany was now in open war against the Herero.

The faint sound of muffled sobs echoed down the stairwell from Leutwein's bedroom, and Erwin shook his head at Conrad.

"He going to be up there a while," Erwin said as he scraped the last bit of uneaten food off the next pot. "You better get used to giving orders."

And Conrad had been giving orders, unofficially, for months now.

Leutwein spent the weeks after the attack floating around the Residence like a wraith, eating little and staring out the sunroom window for hours at something only he could see.

Eventually, with Erwin and some of the other house staff's help, Conrad was able to force Leutwein into a suit each morning and push him through his daily briefings with Captain Jund, the now acting-commander of the Schutztruppe. Leutwein rarely spoke as Jund explained scouting reports and the progress of hastily erected fortifications, adding only the occasional "fine" before excusing himself early.

Captain Jund, in turn, spent most of his time trying to control the shaking in his hands as he thought about the prospect of actually fighting the Herero. The gopher captain reminded Conrad of a schoolyard bully who'd finally been called out to a real fight but was too terrified of the assembled crowd to throw a punch. For all his browbeating, Conrad thought, Jund would probably be next to useless if he ever had to command men under fire.

When Leutwein cared enough to offer up an order of his own, it was generally to defer to Jund's judgment of the situation. Yet Jund was little more than a dithering shell without Baumhauer. The gopher captain would end most meetings by staring pleadingly at Conrad as though he were a lost dog waiting desperately for his master's orders.

In the end, it was Lieutenant Protz who proved to be the most competent commander in the colony. Somehow, he had managed to rendezvous with Captain Jund in the wilderness, guide the German refugees to the railway, turn the lumbering steam engine around at the nearest wye, and then report to Conrad at the Residence to assist in organizing Windhoek's defenses.

A seasoned man in his late thirties with fading blond hair and the tough, tanned skin of a professional frontiersman, Protz was a practical soldier. He was quick to recommend to Jund and Conrad that fortifying the colony's major towns and waiting for reinforcements from Germany was a far better course of action than trying to chase a much larger native force through the bush.

Protz's rearguard had been attacked by a group of Herero warriors while escorting the Okahandja refugees to Windhoek and had only survived thanks to their quick-loading, modern rifles. Protz had nearly taken a spear thrust to the thigh when three dozen Herero had simply materialized out of a gully that he'd ridden right over.

The landscape in the colony was harsh, and the Herero knew it far more intimately than the Schutztruppe. Best to withdraw to defensible positions, protect the railways, and wait for reinforcements, Protz explained to Conrad. To wade blindly into the desert and hinterlands was to invite being picked off piecemeal by the Herero.

It was clear that the man was by far the most sensible commander left in the DSWA, and Conrad took a liking to Protz right away. However, despite his fear of facing the wild Herero army, Jund clung stubbornly to his status and refused to accept a strategy suggested by anyone he outranked.

Evidently, not *all* rivalries died in war.

The gopher captain masked his feelings in their emergency meetings at Schwerinsburg, only showing his fear when he'd dismissed the other officers and was alone with Conrad. Whenever Protz tried to make a suggestion during a briefing, Jund would puff out his thick, round frame and make loud scoffing noises as Protz spoke, as though he were an impatient schoolmaster forced to endure a slow pupil's answer.

It was a small miracle that Conrad had held theatric rank over Jund. Otherwise, they might all have perished. Before each meeting, Protz would pull Conrad aside to advise him on what suggestions to make to Jund. Jund would then accept Protz's proposals once everyone else had left, and then Jund would take what he assumed were Conrad's recommendations to Leutwein, which the Commissioner would blindly approve. Completing the farce, Leutwein usually could not even be bothered to sign his name to orders, so Conrad would have to forge the Commissioner's signature.

Meanwhile, in Berlin, the Kaiser wasted no time dealing with Leutwein. Within thirty-six hours of the loss of Okahandja, the Colonial Office committee had met, and the Kaiser had called for Leutwein's resignation. Petyr had brought the official telegram to Conrad first thing in the morning, sporting a swollen lip and several bruises along his arms. Conrad had read the telegram, feeling wretched as Petyr slinked away, dispirited and exhausted, towards the staff quarters. Evidently it *had* been unwise to leave Petyr alone with Gert and Wedekind If he ever found himself alone with those two again...

The telegram also informed the Commissioner's Office that the Kaiser was mobilizing 11,000 Imperial soldiers who would be dispatched to the colony in six months' time under the command of the new Commissioner. Even though barely 3,000 German citizens were living in the entire DSWA, it was clear that the Kaiser did not intend to take the Herero uprising lightly. German blood had been shed. Now the Kaiser would dispatch a proper army to avenge the insult.

At first, six months had seemed to Conrad like an eternity to have to hold out against the Herero. But there was very little fighting after Witvlei and Okahandja. Major Baumhauer had taken nearly 200 men with him to Witvlei, which had been more than a quarter of the entire Schutztruppe's strength. Conrad didn't know exactly how many men were in the Herero army. Still, if only half of those he had seen at Hochfeld had decided to join in the fighting, then the colonial security forces were severely outnumbered.

Outnumbered perhaps, but not outgunned.

Most of the Schutztruppe were armed with German-made Mauser Gewehr 98 rifles, and both the Tsumeb and Windhoek garrisons boasted Maxim automatic machine guns that Baumhauer had meticulously kept in working order. The Herero had no such firepower. Most of the men Conrad had seen in Hochfeld possessed only spears, machetes, and a few outdated firearms.

There had been a brief assault on Tsumeb by a few hundred Herero warriors shortly after the massacre at Okahandja, but one sweep from the garrison's Maxim gun had felled thirty of the attackers and broken the Herero's half-hearted effort.

The largest "battle," if it could even be called that, had occurred inside Windhoek itself. It had started in the labor camps. Lieutenant Protz had pronounced his suspicions of Hendrik Witbooi and his Nama auxiliaries to

Conrad shortly after Okahandja. The man had led a revolt against German rule once already, Protz had argued. Although the Herero and the Nama distrusted one another, who was to say Witbooi would not join the Herero if he thought there might be something in it for him?

Protz had wanted Witbooi and his men disbanded and to order them to turn their weapons over to the garrison at Alte Feste immediately. Conrad had been sorely tempted to push Captain Jund into ordering them to do just that. He, for one, would certainly sleep better knowing Albert Witbooi no longer carried a rifle. But Conrad and the other Schutztruppe officers had dithered. In their minds, Witbooi was a nasty Hottentot, but his men added another forty guns to Windhoek's defenses, and as much as the garrison might loathe Witbooi, they were hesitant to give up his protection.

Yet in the end, Protz's suspicions had proven correct.

Conrad still did not understand how he had done it, but somehow Hendrik Witbooi and his men had pilfered several officers' pistols from Alte Feste and smuggled them into the Iron Palace at night. Commonly referred to as "broomhandles" by the officers because of their notched wooden grips, Mauser C96s were the most powerful machine pistols in Europe. Officers in the Schutztruppe had been issued them as state-of-the-art replacements for their outdated *Reichsrevolvers*, a final parting gift from Sören Baumhauer.

The C96 was favored by German field officers in Europe, and several who were veterans of the Boxer campaign in China told the younger men how their Chinese allies had balked at the German's *hézipào*, or "box cannons." The Schutztruppe men even boasted that one could tear a hole in an elephant from a hundred yards.

Yet without the pistol's wooden shoulder stock, the gun could often prove somewhat clumsy and difficult to aim. An inexperienced marksman could easily empty his entire magazine and be spun in a full circle by the recoil. One young lieutenant had even joked that you were far more likely to kill a man by hitting him with an actual broom handle than you were by shooting at him with the C96.

But whether it had been a fluke of the wind or a masterful stroke of luck, one of the prisoners in the Iron Palace had managed to aim the smuggled pistol at a camp guard and hit him squarely in the chest. The gunshot had echoed like a cannon across the city suburbs, and the guard had collapsed off his post, his dead body landing with a sickening *thump* on the hard mud of the prison camp.

After the first shot rang out, all hell broke loose in the camp. Already on edge, the other guards had wasted no time in firing on the densely packed camp, not caring where they aimed or who they shot. Prisoners trampled one another trying to get out of the way, but there was nowhere to flee within the barbwire fence posts. A few more peppered rounds had shot out from the mass of prisoners, but they flew wide of the enraged guards.

Within minutes, more than seventy prisoners had been shot dead, and dozens more lay wounded and dying beneath of the mass of frightened bodies.

Conrad wasn't sure if Witbooi had tried to incite a revolt in the camps or if he simply wanted a distraction, but half an hour after the shooting had stopped, Lieutenant Protz arrived at the Residence to inform Conrad that all the Nama auxiliaries were gone. They'd been seen riding out of the city, heading southward toward Namaland. One of the city's grain stores was burning, and there had been a brief skirmish as Albert Witbooi attacked one of the smaller prison camps outside Windhoek and tried to liberate the prisoners. Three more Schutztruppe guards and two of Witbooi's men had been killed.

Conrad had suppressed a groan and shook his head in disbelief. Witbooi had not gone north to join Maharero but had fled south back into his native Namaland. Anyone could guess that the old guerrilla would inevitably raise more men to join his band of raiders. Now the Germans would be forced to deal with two rebellions at once.

Perhaps that had been Maharero's aim all along, Conrad thought as he tried to listen to the rest of Protz's report. Maharero didn't need more men to swell his ranks. He needed a way to stretch the heavily armed German forces thin, and with the help of the Herero's greatest rival, he'd achieved it in a masterful stroke.

It was several days before a young officer had taken it upon himself to raid

Witbooi's home in Windhoek. Inside, the Schutztruppe found little of value, but one man had brought Conrad a series of letters he'd found half-hidden behind a desk. There were dozens of letters, dating back months before Conrad had even arrived in Southwest Africa. And they were all addressed to Hendrik Witbooi from Samuel Maharero.

Conrad read every letter. It was clear from Maharero's terse words that he did not like Witbooi. In fact, Conrad doubted from the guarded way Maharero wrote that he trusted Witbooi at all. It seemed not even a common enemy was going to erase the long-standing animosity between Herero and Nama.

But Maharero must've struck a nerve with Witbooi in his last letter, dated a few days before the assault on Okahandja. At the bottom of the letter, Maharero had ended with:

…Though we may never share a people or a country, I say this to you, brother. If we are to die, then let us die fighting.

-S. Maharero.

Conrad had folded Maharero's letters away and put them in his steamer trunk. He couldn't say why he'd decided to keep them, but perhaps, if nothing else, someone in the new administration might use them to figure out a clue to the Hereros' or Namas' strategy.

After Witbooi's desertion, Maharero and Witbooi held an advantage in the countryside, but the short-lived firefights outside Tsumeb and Windhoek set off a wave of reciprocal violence from the Schutztruppe garrisons greater than Conrad had seen before.

Fearful men are hateful men, Conrad's father had preached to his congregation on several occasions. And in the months that followed the outbreak of the failed prison revolt, Conrad saw just how correct Ekkehardt Huber had been.

The camp guards had been relatively uninterested in the prisoners. Most guards regarded the prisoners as dumb savages rather than as the "dangerous political dissidents" they were technically classified as by the Colonial Office. But now, after a successful escape and the failed uprisings that had killed four of their own, the Schutztruppe became vindictive.

Corporal Knef, who was serving as the foreman for the construction of trenches around Windoek while his arm healed, had begun taking chained groups of prisoners outside the city to dig the new fortifications. Conrad knew that Knef and his men were beating the prisoners. He could also hear the occasional muffled rifle shot from the camps as he lay sleepless in his bungalow late at night. There were nearly five thousand Herero, Ovambo, Nama, Kavango, and Zwartbooi men, women, and children in Windhoek's labor camps. And until the German army arrived, they were the only thing the Schutztruppe could retaliate against.

Conrad also knew that some of the guards had begun to carry a fiendish whip called a sjambok on their belts. Lieutenant Protz had brought him one that he'd confiscated from one of his men. It was a simple, wicked thing, a leather rod and throngs made from the hide of a hippopotamus. It made an evil whistling sound when swung, and the tough hide could break a prisoner's skin with minimal force.

Protz had asked what Conrad wanted done about them. Conrad could not tell whether Protz was personally opposed to their use or whether he thought it was his duty to inform Conrad of their existence.

Conrad considered telling Protz to issue a ban on using them, but he decided against it. The Schutztruppe were out of control, and there was nothing Conrad could do to stop them. He could try to ban the men from using the weapons, but most would likely ignore his orders, and the few that did obey would find new ways to abuse the prisoners. The only thing Conrad would achieve by banning the whips would be to erode whatever authority he had. He'd be no better off than Leutwein had been, only with a full-scale rebellion to fight.

The planting season was what saved the Germans more than anything else. Though the women did most of the actual planting in the villages, among the Herero the rainy season was a time to replenish and renew one's household, and each man in a home had a part to play.

Men abandoned the Herero army daily. Some left with their chieftains when they pronounced it time to go home for the harvest, but according to the Schutztruppe scouts that trailed Maharero's force like a pack of wounded wolves, most left the Herero camp in ones and twos. It was as though each man in Maharero's army decided when he'd had enough of sleeping on the hard ground and playing at war and when he wanted to go home to his wife and his crops. And as the early fighting petered out and the long summer ground to a standstill, that is just what the Herero did.

Maharero's army was a little more than a mob, and like a mob it ebbed and flowed from the field when the men's temperatures cooled and their wives needed them at home.

Few Herero commanders had known how to or had bothered to sever telegraph wires or destroy railroad ties before their men began to disperse. And so, Conrad, Jund, and Protz had been able to communicate with most of the other major towns throughout the colony and determine, at least minimally, how many Herero rebels were where. Apart from the desultory attack on Tsumeb, the Herero did not seem to be in any hurry to attack fortified towns, and their army had melted away until the planting was done.

*

Now, standing on the bustling street corner of Walvis Bay, Conrad found himself thinking about Maharero. He did it often these days – if nothing else to keep himself from thinking about Sybille.

Conrad's formal sacking would send him back to Berlin tonight, and it was foolish to imagine he would ever see her again. He prayed constantly that she was safe, but always his prayers led to daydreaming and thoughts of her soft skin and knowing eyes. Still, he knew it did him no good to think of her.

So, he thought about Maharero instead.

Maharero would not kill children. Conrad had only known the man over the course of a day, but he was willing to bet anything the man had not ordered his men to kill German children. There were many among the Schutztruppe officers who assumed that he had. They believed that Maharero must've savagely ordered the women and children in Okahandja killed to strike fear into the rest of the German colonists.

It didn't really matter, though, Conrad thought. Those women and children were dead, the colony was at war, and now the German army had arrived to restore order.

Down by the docks, the gunner crew had finally succeeded in lowering the cumbersome field piece off the ship, a feat met with equal parts of cheering and cursing from everyone involved.

Conrad was suddenly shaken from his thoughts by a nearby shout.

"Connie!"

Before Conrad could even turn around, he found himself in a vice-grip embrace, staring down into his cousin Georg's plump, smiling face.

"Georg?" he gaped. "What on earth are you doing here?"

"Saving your ass!" Georg replied, breaking their embrace so that he could look up at Conrad. "*Mein Gott*! When we heard what happened…and no word from you in months…Aunt Georgina's nearly driven herself mad with worry. I had Father pull every string I could think of to make sure my battery was assigned to the division. *Gott sei Dank*! You're alive!"

Georg grasped Conrad in another embrace, and Conrad felt himself slump with relief. Georg was here! If affable, easygoing Georg was here, then surely everything would be all right.

Conrad felt a slight pang of guilt for not having thought to write to his mother to tell her he was all right. He wasn't sure how, but it seemed he'd mostly forgotten about her these past five months. He had forgotten about nearly everything of his life back in Germany while trying to navigate the influx of scattered reports concerning Herero movements and the idiocy of the current colonial command structure. It seemed like just yesterday that Corporal Knef had ridden half-dead through the gates of Schwerinsburg with that fateful message.

Conrad now felt his mother's absence wash over him like a rogue wave. Perhaps returning home to Germany would not be all bad. He could scarcely believe that the stress of the colony had made him forget about his own mother! It was no wonder Leutwein had collapsed under the strains of running it.

Conrad realized that he hadn't said anything for several moments and that Georg was staring at him expectantly.

"Thank goodness you're here, Georg," he said after a moment. "Everything in the colony has fallen to pieces. I doubt there will be time for me to tell you everything that's happened before I leave tonight."

Georg raised an eyebrow as he caught sight of the small pile of Conrad's baggage amidst the general clutter of Leutwein's.

"Are you planning on taking a holiday while we're at war, Conrad?" Georg asked with a laugh.

"Er...no," Conrad said, his face flushing red as the familiar embarrassment washed over him again.

"I'm sure to be sacked along with Commissioner Leutwein," he said sheepishly. "And I plan to catch the next boat back to Germany today rather than wait a few more weeks until the final paperwork is done."

Georg stared at Conrad a moment and then nearly fell over with laughter.

"Sacked?!" he gasped through several attempts to catch his breath. "Oh, Connie. You're not sacked! You've been promoted, *Dummkopf!*"

Conrad was not sure he'd heard his cousin correctly.

"Promoted?" Conrad asked, stupefied. "Me?"

"Of course!" Georg answered, giving Conrad a hard, jovial punch in the shoulder. "You have more experience in this colony than anyone in that stuffy Colonial Office. Save perhaps that fool Janson, but you can be sure Herr Kleinschmidt wasn't going to let that lazy slug weasel himself back into this post.

"It's all been arranged, Connie. You're the Colonial Office's new Chief Expert of Southwest Africa."

Georg produced a travel-worn envelope from his coat pocket and handed it to Conrad. Inside was a letter from Herr Kleinschmidt congratulating him, a series of various documents from various other Colonial Office officials outlining his new assignment, and a commission statement signed by Kaiser Wilhelm himself!

Conrad could hardly breathe.

"Father and Mother send their congratulations, of course," Georg added. "And I've got a whole suitcase of letters for you from Aunt Georgina and Frieda back at my barracks. Right now, however, I've come to fetch you to introduce you to the colony's new Commissioner, General Lothar von Trotha. You are to serve on his staff."

Conrad's head had already been spinning amidst the heat and noise of the city, but Georg's arrival and astonishing news nearly knocked him over the curb. Through the muffled sounds of the portside shops and warehouses, he hardly noticed the other soldiers who bobbed, weaved and cursed as they tried to maneuver past Leutwein's pile of luggage.

Chief Expert, he thought to himself. He wasn't sure whether he was exuberant or terrified. He had been sure he was about to be sacked. Instead, he'd been promoted by a few tired bureaucrats who simply assumed that he had learned enough by now to be useful.

The boy who'd been splitting rails outside Aschaffenburg a year ago to keep his mother fed was now the most senior diplomat in a colony larger than France. He had a signed commission from the Kaiser! And with the income from this position, and perhaps even more lucrative ones when he rotated back home, Conrad might never need worry about employment again.

He was staying then. The reality of that was paralyzing. All throughout the heavily guarded train ride to Walvis Bay, Conrad had looked out the window and thought of the colony's woes as a jagged wound. But thankfully, he admitted to himself, one that would now be someone else's job to sew up. He was little more than a stretcher-bearer. He'd done what he could to stop the bleeding, but he had always assumed someone else would come along behind him and do the real surgical work.

But now, he was formally charged with saving the Kaiser's colony with a skillset that senior Imperial officials were wagering he possessed.

Competing thoughts swirled through his mind, but all he could manage at the moment was to force himself through polite conversation with his cousin.

"Did you say you came with your whole battery, Georg?" Conrad asked as his gaze returned to the cargo ship being unloaded in front of him.

Georg broke into another huge grin.

"I did indeed!"

He took Conrad by the arm and called to a man in the crowd behind him to mind the pile of baggage. Then Georg led Conrad down onto the nearby dock and motioned to the latest field piece the sailors and gun crew had just unloaded.

"She's a Krupp 7.5mm field piece, the very latest model in the army," Georg said proudly. "She's one of mine. Begging for her first taste of a real battle. She's going to help us, what is it the Americans say, 'Put those Negroes in their place?'"

Conrad had seen photographs of artillery pieces before, but he had never seen one up close before. The brass barrel of the Krupp 7.5 mm was enormous, and the base of the thing looked as though you'd need a team of ten horses just to move it. It sat atop massive wooden wheels, and the entire dock groaned as the sailors maneuvered it onto the landing.

This was a *field* piece? How in the world did Georg intend to move this thing over sand dunes?

"She's got a mean recoil when she's angry," Georg continued. "But she's never failed me yet in our drills! It's why I named her *Frieda*!"

Georg paused to laugh at his own joke, and Conrad smiled politely.

"You can imagine how well that went over with my sister when I wrote home about it. Oh! That reminds me, Connie."

Georg suddenly kissed Conrad's cheek in a grandiose display, provoking a chorus of laughter from the sailors and his gun crew.

"Frieda told me to give you that when I found you. That little zebra is the talk of every social party in Hamburg! Whose idea was it to add that little black lace bow? That was absolutely brilliant."

*

Leutwein's farewell ceremony was graciously short. Conrad had feared a long, drawn-out affair where Leutwein would be paraded onto a stage while the new Commissioner offered a maudlin retelling of Leutwein's former military exploits and accomplishments in the colony. It would have been a face-saving act that Conrad didn't think Leutwein could survive. The man didn't currently possess the stamina to stand in one place for very long, and Conrad wasn't sure he'd last long at all today with as much as he'd had to drink that afternoon.

Leutwein had shown up to the home of the British Cape Colony attaché disheveled and drunk. The British administrator for Walvis Bay, a dreary Englishman named Harold Sutton, rolled his eyes when he greeted Leutwein at his door and summoned a valet to make him somewhat more presentable.

Mr. Sutton's home was among the few brick structures that dotted the main square of the British port city and boasted a modest enclosed garden that Mr. Sutton had graciously donated to welcome the new German colonial government. Light refreshments were served, but it was clear that neither Mr. Sutton nor the new Commissioner wished for the transfer to be a lengthy event.

General Lothar von Trotha was a striking man. A career Prussian officer before unification, the General had dark, almost black eyes that gave his oval face a slightly owlish appearance. He had a crisp, wide mustache, turned upward in the latest fashion. He wore cavalry boots and spurs, though Conrad had not seen the man arrive on a horse, and his parade helmet, which prominently displayed the Imperial eagle and plume. He stood in the center of the garden in deep discussion with a collection of equally decorated *Oberste*.

They'd been at the reception only a few minutes before Georg reappeared at Conrad's shoulder, two glasses of Mr. Sutton's champagne resting mischievously in his hands. He handed one to Conrad and then took a hearty sip of his own. Conrad accepted the glass with thanks. It was remarkably good. Conrad held his mouth on the rim of the glass an extra moment to savor the feel of the soft bubbles on his cracked lips.

Several rose bushes bordered Mr. Sutton's well-furnished veranda, and dense hedges sheltered the garden from the hectic port streets and offered moderate relief from the afternoon heat. Conrad couldn't help but be impressed that the Englishman managed to keep his garden so green.

"I will say this about the English," Georg said. "They certainly appreciate the finer things in life."

Conrad nodded admiringly, giving his surroundings one more appreciative glance. He had thought Leutwein's garden with its modest fountain and chokecherry flowers a regular oasis in the middle of Windhoek, but Mr. Sutton's small, well-tended rose garden put Schwerinsburg to shame.

The brisk departure of one of von Trotha's aides from the General's circle pulled Conrad's focus back to the new Commissioner.

"I've never seen a man with so many medals," he said quietly to Georg as he reexamined von Trotha's impressive wardrobe.

Georg turned his attention from admiring the decorations in Mr. Sutton's foyer back to the General's assembly.

"Ah, yes," Georg answered. "But every one of them is well-deserved! You'd be hard-pressed to find a more decorated officer even amongst a group of French marshals."

Georg laughed heartily before taking another generous gulp of champagne.

"Simply put, he's the most famous general in all Europe. From a wealthy, noble family in Saxony, he joined the Prussian military some forty years ago, according to Father. The man's beaten the Austrians at Königgrätz, the French at Sedan, put down savage uprisings from Bagamoyo to Zanzibar, and he even led one of the joint European forces that crushed the opium rebellion in China a few years back.

"Father heard from Herr Kleinschmidt that the Kaiser personally asked von Trotha to manage the colony. It's a real stroke of luck for my battery that he's our commander. The man has an appreciation for artillery and is rumored to have a fondness for promoting young, *competent* officers. I might even be a major by the time I return, eh?"

Conrad continued to look at von Trotha, scarcely aware that he would make a rather rude first impression if the General caught him staring. But von Trotha was still surrounded by his staff and was paying no attention to Mr. Sutton's strained hospitality. The General seemed to have already assumed command of the colony, as several aides came and went intermittently, carrying von Trotha's orders to the officers overseeing the rest of his division's landing.

As he watched the new Commissioner, Conrad thought von Trotha bore the look of a man so suited to military command that it was impossible to imagine how he might look out of uniform.

After a few minutes of idle conversation with a few of Mr. Sutton's deputies, who had never seen so much excitement in their small outpost of a colony, Conrad felt a tap at his shoulder. Mr. Sutton's valet now reappeared at his side with a somewhat more presentable, sober-looking Leutwein in tow.

Conrad excused himself from the group and walked over to meet Leutwein on the veranda.

"Are you all right, sir?" Conrad asked Leutwein.

Leutwein ignored him. Conrad guessed that someone had told Leutwein of his promotion. The now ex-Commissioner might feel betrayed by Conrad remaining on von Trotha's staff, or perhaps Leutwein was still too drunk to have heard him.

Most likely, Conrad thought to himself, he just didn't care anymore.

But before Conrad could say anything else, one of von Trotha's staff directed the General's attention toward the veranda. Von Trotha nodded, dismissed another aide with his latest dispatch, and then crossed the small garden to meet Leutwein.

"Colonel Leutwein," von Trotha greeted him plainly. "I would like to offer you my congratulations on your retirement."

Von Trotha's accent was particularly thick, made even more jarring by a direct and deep voice. Conrad didn't think the General had meant his remark to be snide, but the General's assertive frame and Upper Saxon vowels gave his words a slight, mocking undertone. Leutwein seemed not to notice, however, and mechanically saluted von Trotha in response.

"Thank you, sir," he responded, just slightly slurring his words. "Congratulations on your appointment to the DSWA."

Conrad wondered if the two had ever crossed paths before. Certainly, they must've at least heard of one another. They had held similar stations around the same time. Whether they knew each other previously or not, their present meeting was awkward at best. Leutwein either had nothing to say to von Trotha or was still too inebriated to make the attempt, and von Trotha clearly did not have anything beyond pro forma courtesy to offer his predecessor.

Von Trotha had taken control of the colony the moment he had landed at

Walvis Bay. Anyone looking between the General and Leutwein could tell as much. Leutwein was the broken, once-loved man that the Kaiser had shipped out without assistance and depended on for too many years. Lothar von Trotha was a new man, fresh off the steamer with a dazzling display of firepower and with the energy and purpose that Leutwein had been bled dry of.

The two stood in awkward silence for a moment or two longer before von Trotha made to leave. Leutwein stopped him, however, much to Conrad and the General's surprise, and produced a sealed letter from his coat pocket.

"I've compiled a list for you, General," Leutwein said, his voice even and controlled for the first time in months. "It's a collection of all the names of prominent Herero and Nama chiefs that I have had correspondence with in the past and what each man is likely to consider most important to their villages. I hope it will be of some use in negotiating the rebels' eventual surrender."

Conrad was astonished. He didn't know when Leutwein had compiled such a list. But it was evident that Leutwein had pulled himself together in the dockside bar long enough to put a considerable amount of effort into this last gesture.

Von Trotha, however, did not share Conrad's enthusiastic surprise.

"Colonel," the General responded, his disdain obvious despite his accent. "It is that kind of attitude that got over a hundred Germans killed at Okahandja."

The General took the letter from Leutwein's hand coldly, then tore it in two.

"I will not negotiate with Hottentots," von Trotha said firmly.

For a moment, Conrad thought Leutwein might say something in protest. But after only a breath or two, whatever he had been about to say died in his throat.

"You are my new Chief Expert of this colony, are you not?" von Trotha asked, suddenly turning his attention to Conrad.

"Er...yes, sir," Conrad answered. "I am. My name is Conrad Huber, sir."

"Good," the General said with a curt nod. "I see your cousin managed to track you down amongst this port's sweltering crowds. Skirt-chaser that one, but a fine officer, I believe. Good eye for artillery placement. Tell me, Herr Huber, those dunes near the city shift a fair amount, do they not? I can't imagine our field pieces will be able to get over them."

It took Conrad a few seconds to realize that von Trotha had asked him a question.

Leutwein excused himself from the General's company without a word and retreated into the shade of Mr. Sutton's home, ignoring or not seeing Conrad's attempts to catch his eye.

Conrad suddenly realized that he had made no arrangements to transport Leutwein's dogs to Germany. In the rush to coordinate an armed Schutztruppe escort for their train ride to Walvis Bay, the two lion dogs had completely slipped Conrad's mind. He was sure they had not slipped Erwin's mind, which would explain the look of utter contempt Erwin had borne when Conrad had left him in charge of the Residence on the morning of his and Leutwein's departure.

"The dunes do shift, sir," Conrad finally replied when Leutwein had disappeared, and it was clear that von Trotha expected an answer. "I saw one of Georg's field pieces on the docks this afternoon, and something that heavy would sink right into the sand and drag a full team of horses down with it."

The General nodded. That had been the answer he was expecting.

Conrad stole a quick glance over his shoulder to see if he could still spot Leutwein. The man had disappeared. If Conrad had to guess, he likely wouldn't see Leutwein again before he boarded the *Oldenburg* this evening and sailed for Hamburg.

Verdammt, Conrad swore to himself.

No ship captain was going to take two dogs of that size on board their ship without Leutwein, to say nothing of being able to transport Gustavus and Ivan out of Windhoek. Conrad swore again, suddenly realizing he had just become the de facto and very reluctant owner of two lion dogs.

Georg caught his eye from the corner of the garden and gave him an encouraging wave. Mr. Sutton's daughter Olivia had finally made an appearance at her father's reception, and Conrad watched his cousin detach himself from the English officials and head straight for her.

"Won't be able to march the army together then," von Trotha said aloud, continuing his train of thought. "I understand the Hottentot army does not stay in their mud-hut strongholds long?"

"Er...no, sir," Conrad replied, trying not to watch Georg's animated flirtation with Mr. Sutton's daughter. "Lieutenant Protz of the Schutztruppe led a scouting party out three weeks ago and reported that the Herero force is done with their harvests and has begun reassembling further north, presumably to try and attack Tsumeb again."

Von Trotha nodded. This had all been in the last dispatch that Conrad had forwarded to the Schutztruppe outpost in Swakopmund, and the General should have received it without issue. Nevertheless, given the traumatic state of communications over the past few months, it was nice to see that von Trotha appeared to have received Conrad's dispatch and read it.

"And has Tsumeb been attacked yet?" Von Trotha asked, lowering his voice for the sake of privacy in the crowded garden.

"Not yet, sir," Conrad replied, wondering just how flirtatious Olivia planned on being with her father watching like a hawk from the veranda. "We believe the Herero intend to take Tsumeb and then burn the Kolonialgesellschaft's mining operation, where many of their people were previously employed.

"Many of the Herero chiefs see Tsumeb as the real heart of the colony, and Lieutenant Protz believes that the Herero want to destroy the mines in the hopes of forcing the Kaiser to sue for peace."

Von Trotha seemed to scoff, but he motioned for Conrad to continue.

"The Herero chiefs have been stuck for the past few months," Conrad went on. "Most of their army went home to tend their fields and so they could not seriously threaten any of our larger towns. Even now that the Herero warriors are returning, Alte Feste is too well-fortified for them to attack Windhoek, and the Nama tribes in the south are too disorganized and too distrustful of the Herero to offer any real threat of coordinated action.

"It takes the Herero a long time to do anything, particularly to move en masse. The Herero move with their families, even when going to war. Schutztruppe scouts from Tsumeb engaged a Herero scouting party a week ago, but it was small. Far smaller than when the Herero tried to attack Tsumeb earlier this year. The leader of our scouting team believes that the Herero do still intend to attack Tsumeb and are assembling their entire force to do so. If that is true, then it will take them quite a while to gather that many warriors. Months perhaps."

As he finished, Conrad's thoughts were drawn to something he'd been considering since he'd received the most recent reports of the Herero's movement. If the Herero were now moving together, did that mean that Sybille was moving with them?

Most likely, yes. If Maharero was indeed the commander of the Herero, then Sybille would travel with her father.

Conrad stifled a groan as von Trotha continued to question him.

"Do we know where their *leader* has based himself?" Von Trotha asked with the faintest hint of excitement.

Conrad paused another moment. He thought about Maharero standing in the doorway of his bungalow in his cream, pressed suit. He had liked the man a great deal, despite the circumstances that had led him there. Maharero had been kind to him, and Conrad thought he had seemed an honorable and reasonable man. An honorable and reasonable man that von Trotha intended to fight, and, if the General's previous comments were to be taken seriously, a man he intended to crush.

It's come to war, Conrad told himself reluctantly as he remembered his new commission, signed by his sovereign. Maharero was now the enemy. As was Sybille, as far as the Kaiser and von Trotha were concerned.

"The Tsumeb scouts say the party they encountered fled to the southwest," Conrad answered. "In the direction of the Waterberg Plateau."

Von Trotha reached inside the jacket of his uniform and produced a small map of the DSWA.

Conrad was astonished. He'd never seen such a small and detailed map of the colony before. The Schutztruppe had to rely on clumsy, incomplete field maps to navigate through the bush, but von Trotha's map was compact and included far more detailed topography of the colony than Conrad had ever seen in Leutwein's office. Von Trotha must have had it made in Germany before he set sail.

"Show me," von Trotha said, taking over the railing of Mr. Sutton's porch as a few flustered English guests scurried out of the way.

Conrad stared at the map, scouring the detailed parchment furtively to get his bearings. He couldn't quite say why, but he found the General's energy contagious. Von Trotha was a sharp and direct man, and for the first time in months, Conrad found himself swept up in the excitement of someone else's plans. It was exhilarating not to be drowning under the pressure of having to make his own frantic decisions. Von Trotha knew precisely what he was doing, and how he wanted it done.

A small part of Conrad remained hesitant as he poured over the map. Had von Trotha really meant what he'd said about not negotiating with the Herero?

Probably not, Conrad concluded after a moment. Military men were famous for bravado statements. The quicker the war was over, the better off the Kaiser's and Germany's reputations would be.

"Just about here," Conrad said, pointing to a mountainous ridge near the upper mid-section of the map. "Waterberg means the 'Water Mountain' in Afrikaans. It's not a particularly fertile place, ironically, but it's the only area between Hochfeld and Tsumeb that *could* sustain thousands of people, at least for a time."

Von Trotha studied the spot on the map that Conrad had pointed to for a moment, his face only inches from it.

"If they are moving to attack Tsumeb, then they'll need water," the General said out loud, his mind calculating something Conrad couldn't see. "And food. Do the Hottentots still move with their cattle?"

Conrad was again surprised. He'd tried to include everything he knew about the Herero's customs in his reports to Berlin, but he hadn't truly expected anyone to read them thoroughly. Von Trotha, however, seemed to have read every word.

"Yes, sir," he replied. "They do when they move in large groups. A small group of warriors wouldn't, but if they are assembling all their men and their families together, then they will have to bring their livestock with them as well."

Von Trotha nodded again, the specific details of a plan formulating in his mind.

Beyond a row of short rose bushes, Conrad saw Georg, true to form, steal a quick kiss from Olivia while Mr. Sutton turned away for a moment to speak to one of his guests.

"Our rail lines run just past here, yes?" von Trotha said, pulling Conrad's focus back down to the map. "It can't be more than a hundred kilometers from Waterberg. If we can't move our artillery over the dunes, we could move them by rail, surely?"

Conrad thought about that, a small shiver of unexpected adrenaline running through him.

Von Trotha's continued focus was thrilling. Conrad forgot his cousin's antics in the garden below him, selfishly reveling in the engagement and attention of the most famous general in Europe. After all, if the German army could move an entire artillery battery within striking distance of the Herero, perhaps there wouldn't even be a battle! No commander would be foolish enough to attack modern artillery head-on.

"It's possible, sir," Conrad said, his mind now rapidly envisioning an end to the revolt without any more bloodshed. "Most of the Kolonialgesellschaft's flat cars are in the railyard in Tsumeb, but they keep a few older ones in Swakopmund in case of breakdowns. I doubt one of those old cars could support more than one cannon at a time, though."

"Hmm," von Trotha said, taking a brief pause to consider that. "I'll issue a military order to seize the flat cars. I doubt the Kolonialgesellschaft will protest their being used for their own rescue."

Conrad was not sure if the General had made a joke or not, but he offered a polite chuckle anyway.

"You've done well, Herr Huber," the General said. "You were right to hold up and wait for reinforcements. It will be refreshing to have a young man with your sense on my staff."

Conrad found himself beaming.

"The Schutztruppe will have to be incorporated into the main army as well," von Trotha continued. "Captain Jund is their senior officer, if I remember correctly from your latest report? I'll have a transmission sent to tell him to rally his men and to prepare to escort the artillery cars between Windhoek and Walvis Bay. Our main force will march to Windhoek and then cut up toward Waterberg once the artillery is gathered. We will need a staunch railman to oversee the transport, someone who won't be afraid of a fight if the trains are attacked. Do you know anyone who might be a sufficient overseer, Herr Huber?"

This was going to work, Conrad thought.

Von Trotha's plan would move an entire German division and artillery battery right in front of Maharero. There was no way that the Herero could hope to best a fresh and prepared European army. Maharero would have no choice but to surrender, the Herero revolt would be over, and the Nama rebellion would fizzle out shortly afterward. And, in time, things would resume some sense of normalcy. Von Trotha was a stalwart military man. He wouldn't let the Schutztruppe continue the sjambok whippings, and he certainly wouldn't allow his men to execute prisoners of war.

The General was a smart man. He would fix the colony.

For the first time in months, Conrad felt the weight of decision-making lift from his shoulders, and he nearly sighed from the relief. Georg was here, Sybille would be fine, and the war would be over quickly.

"Yes sir," Conrad answered, remembering the burly conductor who'd given Leutwein a black eye. "I think I know the perfect man for the job."

CHAPTER 10

AUGUST 1904

When the bugle sounded in the pre-dawn blackness, Conrad had already been awake for hours. He supposed he must have slept at some point, but he couldn't remember either falling asleep or waking up on his cot. Perhaps he had been staring at the roof of his small canvas tent since he returned from the officers' meeting late last night.

Had that really been only a few hours ago?

Mein Gott, Conrad whispered to himself in the darkness. Is this what all men feel like before battle?

Outside the thin flaps of his tent, Conrad could hear the German army slowly waking and beginning their sluggish pre-muster activities. There wasn't any need to keep quiet after all. Von Trotha was hardly concerned with maintaining the element of surprise.

Like clockwork, a minute after the bugle call had faded away, Conrad heard the familiar steps of his newly appointed attaché, Private Dieter Raske, followed by his cheerful knocking on Conrad's canvas tent.

"*Guten Morgen*, Herr Huber," Dieter called from outside the tent. "It eez almost de call to muster. Officer meeting in ten minutes. Woot you like a cup of coffee? Two sugars dis time, ja?"

Dieter's father was Belgian, Conrad thought. Or was his mother Danish?

He was too groggy to remember, despite being awake for so long, and he couldn't focus on much of anything.

The air was thinner on the plateau, but somehow, he felt that the pain in his chest was more than his usual shortness of breath. He was anxious and muddled all at once, and his throat felt dry, as though his esophagus might have scabbed over during the night.

Dieter's high-pitched accent reminded Conrad of Beaunard, as it had every morning for the past few weeks. Conrad shook himself awake and swung his long legs out of the short, cramped cot. Coffee sounded heavenly.

"*Guten Morgen*, Dieter," Conrad replied through the tent's canvas. "Coffee would be wonderful, *danke*."

Conrad heard Dieter leave to fetch the coffee and quickly set about dressing himself for war. Since he was not a formal commander in the army, he'd not been given an officer's saber, but even surveyors and cooks were expected to be armed in the field. Conrad had been issued a new Luger P08 semi-automated pistol, and it sat, oiled and polished, in its holster by his bed. He'd practice fired a few rounds in Windhoek at the quartermaster's insistence, and the short-barreled Luger had surprised Conrad with its accuracy. The holster's belt hung a bit loose on his reed-like frame, but the quartermaster had already turned away to the next man.

Von Trotha had been very generous to his new Chief Expert. Although his station entitled Conrad to his own tent, von Trotha had also ensured that Conrad received his own horse, a crisp, royal blue officer's uniform, and a retinue of five attachés to assist him with anything he might need to help the army prepare for battle.

Conrad had avoided wearing the uniform for as long as he could. It seemed like a farce to Conrad that he should even possess one. He had tried to politely refuse it, saying that he had no military training at all, but von Trotha would not hear of it.

"Nonsense," von Trotha said. "You ran this colony for six months. You've done more to earn that coat than most of the officers in Europe. Besides, men respect men in uniform. Particularly when your uniform is nicer than theirs."

Conrad didn't know whether he believed the General or not, but it was made quite clear that as a member of von Trotha's staff, he was expected to wear the uniform, regardless of his own opinion.

It had been more difficult than Conrad had anticipated to learn how to manage all the buttons of the jacket in the dark, but after a few dozen times, he was able to dress himself passably. The coat was also heavier than Conrad had expected. It boasted silver epaulets on the shoulders, though Conrad had no idea what rank they bestowed upon him, and he was far too embarrassed to ask. He supposed he held the dubious equivalent authority of a captain since Georg's uniform matched his own.

Just as Conrad was buttoning up his coat, Gustavus poked his large head through the tent flap behind him. Von Trotha had been generous in that regard as well. The German army normally forbade its men and officers from traveling with personal pets, but von Trotha had felt compelled to make an exception in this case. He had found the lion dogs fascinating during the army's brief stint in Windhoek, and he had insisted upon bringing the two of them along. Much to Erwin's relief and Conrad's chagrin.

The enlisted men loved Gustavus and Ivan and made a point to slip them food and pat their heads whenever they got the chance. Ivan was presumably off somewhere, taking advantage of the morning cooking fires and making his usual rounds to beg for scraps.

"All right, all right," Conrad said, ducking his head to keep from knocking off his helmet as he peeled back the tent flap. "I'm coming, *mein Hund.*

Conrad couldn't say he was any fonder of Leutwein's two pets than he'd been before the army had set out for Waterberg. But the pair did give him an elevated status in the eyes of the enlisted men, and with the dogs, he wasn't worried about a hyena sneaking into his tent in the middle of the night.

The sky was beginning to brighten. The first cracks of light yawned softly across the Waterberg plateau, casting a muted purple glow over the rows of army tents and waking soldiers.

Things happened slowly in Africa, until they didn't.

The sun was rising lazily now, but by the time Conrad reached von Trotha's command tent, it would already be reaching halfway up in the sky.

"Today eez a goot day for a battle, I sink," Dieter said as he met Conrad outside the tent with a steaming cup of the army's rationed coffee. "Will we see de lions today, Herr Huber? Some of de men haf heard rumors from de Schutztruppe dat de Africans haf lions as pets."

Conrad took a small sip of coffee and stifled the desire to spit it back into the cup. As usual, the coffee was horrible and did not live up the expectations Conrad confected while lying sleepless throughout the night. The army drank coffee that had been harvested from German East Africa: it was a bitter brew von Trotha had acquired a taste for in Ruanda-Urundi. Most of the non-colonial officers could barely stomach it. Weeks at sea coming around the Cape of Good Hope and prolonged storage did little to improve the taste.

"*Danke*, Dieter," he replied, gritting his teeth against the harsh bitterness, despite the extra sugar. "No lions today, I'm afraid. They don't like noise, and they tend to stay far away from the railroads. And you can report to Private Roth and the others that the Herero are terrified of lions. Only an idiot would try and keep one as a pet."

Dieter frowned, obviously disappointed. Conrad made a mental note to have another talk with Private Roth about spreading any more dangerous rumors about the Herero's customs. If nothing else, Conrad's new role had made his word law among the enlisted men when it came to matters of Africa. He fielded an average of a hundred questions a day from privates and colonels alike, and Roth's wild imagination was certainly not helping to lessen the demand.

A small part of him had been surprised and more than a little pleased at how often he'd been able to offer at least part of an answer.

Noko had taught Conrad that bit about lions hating noise. He clanged two pots together religiously all around their campsites before going to sleep each night. And even within the confines of Hochfeld, he'd seen nearly every family perform this same ritual. Most families knew at least one distant relative who they claimed had been eaten or mauled by a lion. All Herero held a fearful respect for lions. It was utterly ridiculous to think the Herero would come anywhere near one if they could help it.

Sometimes, though, Conrad had had to improvise so as not to seem ignorant about something an officer assumed he should know. He didn't know anything about when rhinos actually mated, but when Colonel Voigt had confronted him about the lack of available rhinos for him to hunt as the army wound its way northward, Conrad had hurried informed Voigt that the rhinos were in the peak of their mating season and, perhaps a bit cheekily, had added that they were rather shy about it.

The colonel had reddened, embarrassed, and nodded appreciatively before slipping back into a cluster of his own officers.

Dieter waited patiently while Conrad sipped his coffee. The ten minutes in between the morning muster and the first officer's meeting were the only non-chaotic minutes of the day while traveling with the army. Conrad did his best to enjoy this rare sanctuary and Dieter's tactful companionship.

Von Trotha's strategy had worked flawlessly. At times it had seemed impossible, but the General's careful maneuvering had succeeded in placing an entire division and fifteen Krupp 7.5mm cannons between the Herero and Tsumeb.

Moving the artillery 400 kilometers between Walvis Bay and Windhoek had taken weeks. In the end, Georg and the other artillery captains had deemed only two of the Kolonialgesellschaft's flat cars to be in good enough repair to bear the weight of the field pieces. That meant that as the main force began its march, only two cannons were able to travel from Walvis Bay to Windhoek at a time.

Yet when the first two cannons had been loaded, they proved so heavy that the steam engine transporting them had burned through its coal supply a hundred kilometers from Windhoek. The transport had come to an abrupt, screeching halt, leaving the two gun crews stranded in the middle of the bush, terrified that the Nama would attack them at any moment.

But von Trotha hadn't allowed the army to be troubled. He sent a company of dragoons back along the tracks to defend the stranded men, then dispatched a second company to bring up enough coal from the capital to allow the train to limp into Windhoek. A group of Nama rebels had indeed been preparing to attack the gunners, but just before their attack, the dragoons had arrived and ridden down nearly all the Nama ambushers.

The train carrying the first of the Krupp guns arrived in Windhoek the next day, under the escort of both dragoon companies, who were flush with the excitement of having routed their first Africans.

However, the excitement of the army's first strategic victory was short-lived. As soon as the division arrived in Windhoek, the men found that the capital had nearly run out of coal. The few trees that once dotted Kaiserstrasse had been sacrificed for charcoal months ago; most German citizens and natives alike had resorted to burning garbage with palm oil.

Most of the coal in the DSWA came from southern coastal areas. The growing number of Nama villages that joined Hendrik Witbooi's revolt in the south made it nearly impossible for the Kolonialgesellschaft or the Schutztruppe to transport coal safely to the capital.

Von Trotha was not troubled. He simply dispatched one of his favorite officers, a notoriously brutal man named Colonel Abt, and several dragoon companies to burn Witbooi out of hiding. If there were no Nama villages left around the southern coalfields to hide in, von Trotha told his staff, then the Nama rebels would have nowhere to stage an ambush along the German supply lines.

In the interim, however, von Trotha instructed his staffers remaining in Walvis Bay to purchase coal on credit from the English. The English colonial government imported its coal from the Cape Colony. They would likely charge the division a fortune, Conrad warned, but von Trotha did not seem bothered by cost. He'd been brought to Africa for victory, he said, not penny-pinching.

Weeks later, all the artillery pieces had finally made their way to Windhoek, and enough coal had been brought up from Walvis Bay for the capital to relight its cooking fires, albeit only once a day, and for the army to transport the troops and the cannons on to Waterberg, nearly another 300 kilometers northeast of Windhoek. Conrad had been impressed when the last cannon had steamed into Windhoek, but with each passing day, he began to doubt that von Trotha's strategy would work. The Herero might move slowly, but word would eventually reach Maharero, if it hadn't already, that von Trotha had arrived in Southwest Africa and that he'd moved a fearsome fighting force to Windhoek. Conrad couldn't imagine the Herero would wait for the Germans to march right in front of them.

And, in fact, they hadn't. Once the main army left Windhoek, after only a brief respite, the Herero had tried to retreat from Waterberg. Conrad doubted Maharero knew of von Trotha's reputation as a famous general, but he had no doubt that Maharero knew more about fighting than Conrad did. The Waterberg plateau was high in altitude, but it was mostly flat with little cover and no natural defenses, save for the mountain itself. And even Conrad could see it was not a good place for the Herero to fight.

But von Trotha had anticipated that.

"What do the Hottentots think of horses?" he asked Conrad one morning during their brief stint at Schwerinsburg.

The General was sitting behind Leutwein's old desk, affectionately patting Gustavus as the big dog rested his head in von Trotha's lap. It was strange to see von Trotha in the Commissioner's Office. Conrad had worked exclusively with Leutwein for over a year, a fading authority in an increasingly empty house. Now von Trotha had cleared away all Leutwein's old papers and maps and sat behind an orderly, sparse desk, calmly petting Leutwein's dog while aides and officers scurried around the Residence like a legion of mice.

"Horses, sir?" Conrad asked uncomprehendingly.

It was the first day he had been instructed to don his new uniform, and his coat and collar hung embarrassingly askew on his lanky frame.

"Yes, horses," Von Trotha replied somewhat impatiently. "You have perhaps heard of them, Herr Huber? What do Hottentots think of them? Are they frightened of them?"

The General stared out of the office window into the courtyard below. After a moment, Conrad realized he was watching one of the grooms, Lucas, struggling to bring one of the General's horses under control. Lucas was a poor horseman and, ironically, terrified of horses. Two other grooms ran out to help him unsaddle the bad-tempered war horse as the General watched.

Conrad pondered von Trotha's question. He knew of several natives in Windhoek terrified of horses. Nor had he seen a single horse on his journey to Hochfeld, but that didn't mean much. Sybille had managed herself on horseback far better than Conrad had on their failed excursion to Grootfontein.

"No more than most people, sir," Conrad answered after a pause. "Many of the Herero near Okahandja will have seen the Schutztruppe mounted on small patrols before, but I can't really say what their warriors will think of them."

Von Trotha continued to scratch Gustavus with one hand while he drummed lightly on the desk with the other.

"I'll bet the swine will panic," the General said plainly and then nodded towards the door as a dismissal.

And von Trotha had been right.

When they encountered von Trotha's vanguard of saber-brandishing dragoons, the Herero warriors panicked and fled right back into the path of their wives, children and cattle at Waterberg. Companies of dragoons and hussars encircled the plateau, harassing the Herero at every turn, pushing every warrior they could find back toward the mountain while the main German army set up position.

The last cannon had arrived the day before. Now, after months of careful preparation and precision, the German army was ready to fight. Maharero was trapped.

*

Ivan appeared next to Conrad just as he finished the last of his foul coffee.

"Done making your morning rounds and come to beg for *my* scraps, huh?" Conrad said as the big dog rubbed its massive head against his knee.

Ivan looked at Conrad, twisting his impressive jowls into a pitiful pout, and whimpered like a puppy. Conrad nodded to Dieter, who stood by with two extra slabs of bacon. As Gustavus and Ivan devoured the treats, Conrad stood to brush the dust off his uniform.

"Do you want me to tie 'sem up here in camp during de fighting?" Dieter asked, running an affectionate hand over Ivan's head.

Conrad's hands began to shake. He had managed to stave off his worry about the approaching battle for a few minutes as he swallowed the bitter coffee. But Dieter's innocent question quickly brought back the harsh reality of the day. He was tempted to have Dieter tie the two dogs to his tent, but it took little imagination to envision Gustavus and Ivan ripping his tent out of the ground in excitement and barreling after the army with all of Conrad's personal effects scattering behind them.

"Better not," Conrad said, adjusting his heavy officer's helmet. "They'll do more harm here by themselves than the Herero ever could. I expect they'll mind themselves if it comes to a fight."

Dieter nodded and saluted as Conrad left to make his way to von Trotha's command tent.

If it comes to a fight, Conrad repeated to himself. *If.*

Von Trotha had encircled the Herero and, despite the difficulties of doing so, had positioned all fifteen of his cannons directly in front of the rebels. It was a remarkable feat.

Conrad had heard his Uncle Johannes once describe war as almost entirely a game of chess, where the actual hand-to-hand fighting was merely a formality. Conrad wasn't sure he believed that, but in this case, he hoped that his uncle was correct. Von Trotha had clearly outmaneuvered Maharero and placed him in check. Colonel Abt's forces had already engaged and routed several Nama militias in the south and driven Witbooi's renegades from the coalfields. The Herero could expect no rescue from the Nama.

Surely Maharero could see this and would not try to fight. He would have to make peace, and the General could hardly refuse an offer of surrender.

All around him, the army was mobilizing. Half-eaten meals were abandoned, and rifles were checked and re-checked as the men scrambled to fall in line with their units. The day's battle lines were forming, but with any luck, they would not be needed.

As he approached von Trotha's command tent, a lone thought snaked its way into Conrad's mind, one that he'd been fervently trying to ignore ever since he'd arrived at Waterberg. Von Trotha had encircled all the Herero at Waterberg…including Sybille. Conrad knew she would have accompanied her father here, like all the other Herero families. Maharero couldn't have talked his daughter out of accompanying him even if he'd wanted to.

If it *did* come to a fight today, would Sybille be safe?

Conrad adjusted his helmet, which despite von Trotha's standard for precision was a bit too large for him, and quickened his pace. When he reached the General's tent, he nearly plowed right into Georg, who grabbed him by the shoulders to avoid being trampled.

"Whoa! *Guten Tag* to you as well, Connie," Georg laughed. "Still asleep this morning, eh? Sorry we had to interrupt your beauty sleep, but we had to rally a bit earlier this morning to attack the Hottentots."

"Attack?" Conrad asked, straightening himself and trying to hide his rising dread from Georg. "Is von Trotha not going to offer terms?"

Georg gave a small snort of laughter.

"If he was, he isn't going to now," Georg said. "I guess you haven't heard what happened last night?"

Conrad shook his head, and as he did so, the loose helmet slipped down over his eyes.

"The Herero tried to sneak through Colonel Voigt's lines last night," Georg explained. "Some of his pickets were butchered. The General was apoplectic this morning when the new pickets found them. They were torn to shreds, Conrad. One was even missing his head, poor bastard. Damn savages will get what's coming to them if I have anything to say about it."

Conrad felt as though Georg had punched him in the gut. Von Trotha was not a man who was going to overlook six dead German soldiers. There really *would* be a fight now.

He pushed the helmet back on top of his and felt his fingers trembling as he tried to tighten it again.

Georg noticed Conrad's obvious distress.

"Which one of those demon mongrels of yours is the one that beat Colonel

Hummel's horse in a race yesterday?" Georg asked with a smile, trying to shift the subject. "The next time you let one of those hellhounds loose, let me know, eh? I'd have loved to have put a few marks on him."

"Oh," Conrad said, feeling all at once drained and dizzy. "That was Ivan. Some of the men thought it would be funny to set Ivan off on Hummel's horse while I wasn't looking. He caught the horse in a few strides but didn't want anything to do with the horse's hoofs, so he just started running alongside it. Lucky for me that Colonel Hummel thought it was 'great sport.'"

Von Trotha suddenly emerged from his flock of staffers, ending their discussion. Two intelligence officers Conrad had never seen before had produced a crude map of the area surrounding Waterberg and stretched it across a large table in front of von Trotha's command tent.

The map highlighted the German positions reasonably well, but it was clear the two army surveyors had merely guessed at where Herero forces might be. Nearly fifty or so officers were pressed tightly around the table. The sun had not yet fully crested the horizon, but even under a canvas awning, Conrad found the heat from the other men suffocating. In an hour or so, the sun would be unbearable.

Conrad stood next to Georg, banished with the rest of the lower-ranking officers to the edge of the briefing.

"*Guten Morgen*, men," von Trotha said, addressing the crowd that fell silent as he took his place at the head of the table. "Today, we will strike down these savages and restore the honor of the Kaiser and of the Empire."

There was a general murmur of approval among the crowd of officers, and several of the older men nodded solemnly in agreement.

"The enemy have *keine Ehre*," von Trotha continued, speaking slowly so that the men furthest from him could understand his heavy Saxon accent. "By now, I am sure you all will have heard the news. The bodies of several men from Colonel Voigt's picket line were found mutilated this morning. There's not much left of the brave men who watched over our sleep last night, but what little does remain of them has been torn to pieces, covered in teeth marks."

Conrad felt his morning coffee turn in his stomach. Several of the men beside him whispered quick, muffled prayers, and he saw a few others cross themselves. Conrad knew that the Herero weren't cannibals, but the rest of the German army did not.

Had the six men been patrolling together or separately? Conrad wondered sickly.

Surely a leopard wouldn't attack a cluster of six armed scouts? One or two, maybe, if it were desperate enough, but not six grown men together. Conrad was reasonably sure that he was correct about the lions too. Even a whole pride of them wouldn't come anywhere near an army camp, even at night. That left only one horrifying alternative, which sent a cold shiver down Conrad's spine despite the heat.

Hyenas.

They hunted in packs that could range from four or five to several dozen, and in the dark…yes, Conrad thought. A pack could easily have surprised six tired, bored guards.

Conrad cleared his throat to suggest as much to the General, but von Trotha continued before he could interject.

"The Hottentots are savage and cowardly dogs," the General said, his voice building like a terrific thunderclap as he spoke. "Murderous, villainous cannibals that must be put down!"

Many of the other officers responded with animated shouts of agreement. Von Trotha nodded and tapped the table in front of him with his riding crop, drawing all eyes to the infantry figurines that were positioned precisely on the General's map.

"Colonel Voigt's wing will engage the savages from the east while Colonel Hummel's and Colonel Burgstaller's forces block off their retreat from the west and south. *Meine Herren*, today we will crush these swine and avenge the innocent Germans they have slaughtered!"

A second round of cheers rang out. Conrad was surprised to see Georg stomping his feet and whistling loudly with some of the other young captains.

Amongst the rancor in their own camp, Conrad imagined the similar cheers and shouts from the Herero camp on the other side of the plateau. The Herero must be preparing for a fight as well, Conrad knew, and he could not tear his mind away from wondering what Sybille was doing at this very moment.

He tried to speak again, but no one was paying him any attention. The General soon disappeared back into the crowd of officers.

Nothing Conrad could do would stop the fighting now.

Lieber Gott, Conrad prayed beneath the roars of excitement from the German officers. Just let it be over quickly.

*

Conrad's mood improved somewhat when he was assigned to assist Colonel Hummel's column for the duration of the battle.

Originally the commanding officer of a decorated rifle company in the Prussian army, Hummel was a wiry man who had developed a reputation within the army as a tenacious skirmisher but a dismal assault planner. Hummel was a defensive mastermind who had won his spurs with von Trotha in China. Every enlisted man knew that Hummel was cool under fire and would only surrender a position when his men had run out of ammunition. But it was also widely rumored that Hummel did not possess the military savvy to plan a main assault.

A few veterans of the Boxer campaign informed Conrad as they rode to their positions that Colonel Hummel was a peculiar man with nerves of steel but a nervous stomach.

"He's like a mountain," one of the older lieutenants said to Conrad and Georg as they moved into position. "Give him a line in the ground to hold, and not even a hurricane could push him off it. But ask him to move the line forward a yard…and it's as if he can't make up his mind which foot to put forward.

Conrad had only spoken to Hummel briefly during the army's march north. He was a round-faced man in his early fifties with a clipped gray beard. Drawing more than a few words out of him at a time was nearly impossible. Compared to von Trotha's pageantry, Hummel was a reserved man who never seemed to do much of anything he hadn't thought through completely. If others among the General's staff were bolder, Hummel was the most calculating officer in von Trotha's circle.

Colonel Voigt, on the other hand, was von Trotha's favorite officer. The second-most decorated officer with the division after von Trotha himself, he had been charged with attacking the bulk of the Herero forces from the east.

Voigt was a blond and barrel-chested man who looked like a bear crammed into a soldier's jacket. He held his powerful frame rigidly upright as if constantly standing at attention, and the taut threads of his coat suggested a swell of raw strength that might burst forth at any minute. Conrad thought the man looked like a Viking chieftain.

What limited crags and thicket Waterberg had to offer were far closer to Voigt's line than the German army to the west. If the Herero were determined to fight, then that would be the most natural place to try and form a defense.

Voigt, as the main driver of the assault, would push the Herero southward back through the plateau's few gullies to where the young Colonel Burgstaller, the third arm of von Trotha's plan, would be waiting with a small force to make a second attack from the south.

Unsurprisingly, Colonel Hummel had already dug in along the western end of the plateau when Conrad and the other officers arrived. Hummel's men had dug a series of red-dirt trenches that stretched halfway across the plain. Georg's battery had also been assigned to Hummel's line along with two others. It took Georg and the other two captains only a quarter of an hour to deploy their cannons along the trenches.

Von Trotha had charged Hummel with blocking the Herero from retreating westward. This likely meant that his men would be left out of the heavy fighting. In the center of Hummel's line opposite a vast, flat track of the Waterberg plateau, Georg's battery had positioned their guns to form a sharp, narrow wedge. No one really expected the Herero to attack Hummel by crossing the open plateau, but if they were foolish enough to try, then von Trotha would let them smash themselves against Hummel's well-placed defenses.

But as Georg explained to Conrad, as he cursed his battery's luck, it seemed for all intents and purposes that Hummel's men were going to be sidelined from battle. So confident was the German army in what they assumed the Herero would do that von Trotha had assigned several non-fighting specialists to Hummel's line for their safety, including Conrad.

Maharero will surrender to Voigt or Burgstaller, Conrad said to himself after wiping his brow for the third time and stuffing his handkerchief roughly back into a pocket. And then this can all be over.

It was half past ten. The men of Hummel's line were hot and bored. The distant sounds of battle on the far side of Waterberg had subsided. Only a few echoes of cannon fire drifted over Colonel Hummel's lines, and it seemed clear to everyone that Colonel Voigt had routed the Herero even sooner than had been anticipated.

Conrad's hopes rose that the silence meant that Maharero had already surrendered.

Hummel's officers were growing tired standing at the ready for half the morning in the blazing heat. Soon the welcome call to stand at ease came down the lines.

Several of the officers walked out in front of the now-relaxed German lines, kicking at the baked earth and looking for buffalo horns and chipped antlers among the dirt.

Strolling beyond the lines, Georg stifled a yawn beside him and flicked away the remnants of a nara peel from his uniform. Conrad's cousin had been thrilled at the prospect of eating the spiked, green melons when he'd first landed at Walvis Bay and seen the strange fruit in a market stand. Now, after only a few short weeks, he was hopelessly addicted to them.

Conrad had avoided eating the exotic fruit at all costs after Petyr had made him try one back in Windhoek. The orange flesh of the fruit was buried beneath the sticky, sharp spikes, and it was so sweet it that it gave him painful headaches and stomach cramps. But Georg possessed an even more insatiable sweet tooth than young Petyr, and he usually ate one or two whole nara himself by the end of the day.

"Bit of an unfortunate assignment," Georg grumbled, biting off a piece of melon peel as he spoke. "Those damn Hottentots won't come within a thousand kilometers of Hummel's line if they know what's good for them."

The nara peel's smell was vile, though, of course, it didn't seem to bother Georg. Conrad nearly gagged on the aroma that reminded him of the foul coffee he had drunk that morning.

"Ah well," Georg sighed just out of hearing range of another group of officers. "I'm sure there will be glory enough to go around for everyone once Voigt's through. Would have loved to have seen my guns in action, though. Seems a shame to have lugged the ladies all the way from Hamburg and not invite them to the dance, eh?"

Georg, as always, found his own joke hilarious and cast a raised eyebrow at Conrad when he said nothing.

"Connie?" Georg asked, ripping off another mouthful of melon skin. "Are you *gut*?"

"Fine," Conrad tersely replied as he watched Dieter throw a stick behind the lines for Gustavus to chase. "Just a bit nauseous. It's either the damn poison this army calls coffee or that disgusting melon of yours. You know that most natives don't eat the skin, right?"

Georg smiled at that and beamed proudly as he ripped off another sticky bite and patted his uniformed paunch.

"It's all right, Connie," he said, giving Conrad's shoulder a light squeeze. "You've just got a case of the jitters. We all get them. My gunner Harald back there pissed himself the first time someone fired a live round at him. Mind you, he'd had three or four pints beforehand for courage, but still…hard to live that down in the barracks."

Conrad gave Georg a small smile, but his cousin had done little to ease the knots in his gut. Georg dropped his hand from Conrad's shoulder and gave him a comforting look.

"It'll be fine, Connie," Georg said. "There's no safer place in the army than with my battery. Not even a group of dumb Africans would be stupid enough to charge an artillery line."

Georg gestured out towards the plateau with a small scoff.

"Besides," he said with a short laugh as he chewed another bite of nara. "There's no one around for..."

Just then, a rifle round cracked right over Georg's head.

Georg sprung around like a cat and dove to the ground, pulling Conrad down with him. Two more shots rang out, and Conrad saw the dust fly from the ground a few yards from his face as it was peppered with bullets.

From somewhere behind them, Conrad could hear Colonel Hummel's voice furiously barking orders and the frantic sounds of the other officers breaking back toward the lines in a mad dash. A German sergeant collapsed to the dust near them, the outline of his neck disappearing in a sudden flash of red.

Conrad could hear shouting near him. Sharp howls and war cries growing closer and closer from somewhere he couldn't see. He fumbled at his side for his Luger, but his hand came up empty. Conrad's holster was gone. The damn thing must've slipped off his hip when Georg had thrown him to the ground.

Conrad knew he should move, but he couldn't. His heart was thumping too loudly in his ears, and he clung violently to the ground as though it might somehow save him from dying. More rifle shots fired above his head, but Conrad couldn't tell what direction they came from.

Another round thudded into the dirt, this time just an inch or two from his face. He wanted to vomit. The Herero shouting was getting louder now. *Gott,* they were right on top of him!

He felt someone tugging at his jacket and a new wave of terror pulsed through him.

Mein Gott! Conrad screamed in his head. I've been captured.

Then over the chaos, Conrad heard Georg yelling in his ear. He felt his cousin pulling him backward through the now non-stop, whizzing storm of bullets.

"Move, Connie!" Georg yelled as he pulled Conrad to his feet. "Stay low and get back to the battery!"

Conrad somehow stumbled to his feet and started to run blindly. Where were the German lines?

A round cut past Conrad's ear and slammed into Georg's left shoulder.

Georg gave a sharp yelp of pain but managed to keep his footing.

"Go!" Georg shouted at Conrad as he drew his Mauser officer's pistol from his belt and emptied several shots in the direction of the Herero shouting.

Conrad continued to stumble as Georg grabbed him by the arm and pushed him toward the German lines. They both ran, half-crouched against the ground. A round of shots hit the dirt directly behind them, and Conrad felt something pierce his leg.

A blinding, hot stab of pain tore through him. His leg seemed on fire. He staggered, but somehow Georg caught him and pulled him forward towards the batteries.

"Medic!" Georg shouted as he dragged them both toward the trenches of the German lines.

Georg's arm was now bleeding profusely, but he ignored it. Conrad couldn't run anymore; his leg had begun to convulse beneath him, and with every step he took, he felt as though something important was tearing inside him.

"Prime cannons!" Georg yelled to his men as he continued to drag Conrad toward his battery.

Someone scrambled over the defenses and came running to take Conrad from Georg. Conrad's head was spinning too fast to see who it was. Dieter? Or was it Private Roth? He felt his good leg buckle, but the man's strong arms grabbed him and held him upright.

"Aim!" Georg bellowed as he helped the man pull Conrad over the barricade and took up his position with the battery.

A third man ran to Conrad's side and quickly knelt beside him. The man wore a medic's uniform and began hurriedly wrapping several layers of gauze around Conrad's thigh. The man was speaking to him, clearly trying to get Conrad to do something, but Conrad couldn't understand him over all the gunfire.

All at once the heat in his leg began to disappear and was replaced with a piercing chill. Conrad started to panic again as the medic shouted at the other man to lower Conrad to the ground. He was in a desert, with the sun blazing down on him. Why was he suddenly so cold?

"Fire!" Georg roared nearby.

The battery erupted beside them in a thunderous boom as Georg's field pieces recoiled in a thick cloud of gray smoke. The cannons were already hot from the morning sun, and several lifted off their mounts as they sprung backward on the hard ground.

Through the smoke, it looked for a moment that Georg's battery had missed their first shots. But then a wave of pained screams rolled over the Herero charge. Conrad ignored the medic's determined shouting and craned his head back to look over the barricade out at the plateau.

The Herero were everywhere. It was as though they had sprung from the ground, hundreds of Herero warriors charging the German line, yelling, screaming and shouting in terrifying war cries. Some stopped to fire their weapons as they ran, but most just charged onwards, waving their rusted rifles and machetes over their heads as they came. Conrad couldn't tell how many of them Georg's cannons had slain, but the Herero continued toward them like an unstoppable surge.

"Serve your vents!" Georg shouted above the Herero cries. "Load shrapnel shot!"

A stray round thudded harmlessly into the dirt near Georg's foot, but he ignored it. His gun crew moved feverishly, loading the shot and powder so quickly that Conrad could not tell which man was doing what. From somewhere nearby, a Maxim gun crew had managed to finally unjam their weapon, and they began firing it into the rush of Herero warriors. The methodic *bratatat bratatat bratatat* of the Maxim gun rang in his ears as it hummed over the loud echo of the artillery.

Scheisse, Conrad wanted to scream at them. Were they firing it right over his head?

Many of the Herero were falling now. But their charge continued as thousands of angry warriors clawed their way defiantly across the dry plateau.

The Herero were so close now that Conrad could make out the features of the men in the front of the mob. Their faces were rimmed with sweat and dirt, and every one of them was shouting in anger, torment or fear.

"Prime cannons!" Georg yelled.

One of the gunmen near Georg, Harald, gave a soft grunt and collapsed, his body spinning backward from the impact of a bullet. Without hesitating, Georg ran forward and took the fallen man's place, snatching up Harald's rammer and jamming the shot into the barrel with his good arm. Dozens of shots whizzed passed him as he and the gun crew heaved the heavy pieces back into position.

The Herero were almost upon them now.

"Aim!" Georg shouted, pushing against the cannon barrel with his good shoulder.

Conrad could see all the Herero faces clearly now. Distressed and vengeful eyes glared at him as the attack pressed closer. Conrad wanted to run again, but the medic was holding him fast to the ground.

Amidst the threatening swell of dark faces, Conrad's eyes fell on a thin man who stood a head taller than most of the other warriors around him. The man had a rutty beard and a small cap of wooly hair on his head. He ran in the very front of the men, leading them forward as he waved a curved sword above his head, charging defiant and unafraid.

The man seemed familiar, and Conrad tried to place his face as the numbing cold in his leg spread over his body.

Then, suddenly, Conrad remembered the man.

Maharero? Conrad thought.

"Fire!" Georg roared.

If possible, the thunder of the second artillery salvo was even louder than the first, and Conrad felt the blaring sequence of each cannon firing in precise rhythm with its neighbor.

Boom. Boom. Boom.

The ear-splitting explosions shook the ground, and all around him, Conrad saw soldiers trembling from the vibrations. He heard the sharp recoil of the cannons and then the sickly, whistling sound of thousands of hot shrapnel shards tearing through the smoke-thick air.

The medic was running his hand over Conrad's leg now while two other men continued to hold him firmly against the dirt. Conrad knew he should feel pain, but he couldn't. His whole body had gone numb; he felt only a terrifying chill clutching at his chest.

For a moment, everything was still. A new cloud of gray smoke rolled over the German lines, obscuring the view of the plateau before them.

Conrad heard a muffled thumping as the shards found their targets and hot metal tore through flesh. And all at once the Herero charge stopped.

Then, there was nothing but screaming. Terrible shrieks and wails drifted over the battlefield, the Herero's cries sounded so churned and gutted by pain that he couldn't understand them. New volleys of rifle fire cracked eagerly from the German lines, and a second Maxim gun sputtered to life from somewhere down the line.

"Cavalry!" Conrad heard an officer's voice call over the chaos. "Run the bastards down, men!"

Georg broke the Herero charge, Conrad thought wearily as the cold clawed intently at his chest. They'll probably give him a medal for this.

Conrad heard hundreds of sabers sliding free of their scabbards somewhere in the distance and felt the ground shake again under him as a company of hussars thundered into the mass of wounded Herero.

The medic was shouting at him again, but Conrad couldn't hear anything the man said. He was suddenly very thirsty and felt an alluring urge to close his eyes for a moment.

Someone else was calling his name now.

Georg?

The new voice was saying something important, something he ardently wanted Conrad to understand.

"…going to be okay, Connie," Georg said as he suddenly appeared and pressed his hand into Conrad's. "You hear me? You're not allowed to…Aunt Georgia will…you're going to be okay…"

Conrad blinked, not grasping Georg's words. He looked up and saw Georg's shoulder still bleeding freely, his army coat stained a deep red from the wound.

"You should see someone about your arm," Conrad managed to tell him.

And then he passed out.

CHAPTER 11

AUGUST 1904

Conrad woke up in Georg's tent three days later.

Before Conrad had fully opened his eyes, Georg appeared beside him and held a canteen to his lips. He wanted to vomit, but Georg held him upright until the bout of nausea subsided.

Conrad drank greedily from the canteen until he began coughing, spraying the warm water along Georg's arm.

"Jesus, Connie," Georg swore with a laugh. "Not so fast. I just managed to get this uniform clean. Take it easy, eh?"

Conrad tried to steady himself upright, but a blinding pain shot up his leg and forced him back onto Georg's cot.

"What did I just say?" Georg said, this time more serious. "Take it slow, Connie. You're not going anywhere on that leg for at least a few weeks. That medic, Borchard, said that bullet nearly tore through an important artery. I forget what he called it exactly, but he said you're lucky to be alive, his fine work notwithstanding. But if it makes you feel any better, Dieter's been insisting to the whole division that he shot the bastard who hit you."

A soft whine came from beside the cot, and Conrad slowly turned his head to see Ivan and Gustavus both staring at him, their enormous frames bent and cramped inside the tent, their heads cocked in questioning sympathy. Ivan laid his head on the edge of Conrad's blanket and licked his knuckle.

"Didn't know I meant that much to you," Conrad said softly to him.

He placed his hand on Ivan's massive head and rubbed one of dog's ears weakly. He'd never touched one of their ears before and was surprised at how soft they felt.

"Colonel Hummel wants to commission these two beasts as sergeants," Georg chuckled, bringing up a small stool so he could sit beside the cot. "They went completely berserk when you got hit. I've never seen a pair of dogs countercharge an oncoming enemy horde, and I doubt those Hottentots had ever seen it either.

"Completely fearless, these two. Went right through the cannon smoke and chased down the savages for you. Rumor has it von Trotha's going to petition the Kaiser to start a breeding program for the military back in Germany. Wouldn't be surprised if he tries to buy them off you. They deserve to spend the rest of their days humping and sleeping if you ask me. Damn loyal pups. They haven't left your side since Borchard and I carried you here."

Conrad reached his other hand carefully across his body and laid it on Gustavus' head. He tried not to picture either of them "running down" the Herero. That was too nauseating to even consider, and his head was spinning far too much already. Instead, he concentrated on petting the great dogs, rubbing their velvet ears until the second wave of nausea subsided.

Conrad turned to look at Georg for the first time and was thoroughly impressed. For a man who had been shot in battle only a few days prior, Georg looked remarkably cheerful. His arm and shoulder were encased in a firmly pinned sling but hung around his neck was a lavish medal with a blue and yellow ribbon that supported a golden, crowned cross.

Georg caught Conrad's stare and beamed back at him gallantly.

"Commander's Cross, Second Class of the Military Order of St. Henry," he recited proudly. "A personal decoration from the General on behalf of the Herzog of Saxony. I'm to be promoted to major once Berlin confirms the appointment."

"Congratulations," Conrad offered meekly. "I suspect Uncle Johannes will probably faint from excitement when he hears the news."

"Got a telegram off to Herr Kleinschmidt this morning!" Georg laughed. "Apparently, one *can* use official Colonial Office connections for personal correspondence when one is given an award like this. The thing is preposterously heavy, though. I wonder how von Trotha manages to keep himself upright in his full parade uniform."

Conrad wondered how Georg had received his medal so quickly. Did von Trotha carry a chest of various medals around in his personal luggage in the event one of his men did something heroic?

"I take it the fighting's over?" Conrad asked, battling another bout of nausea as he spoke.

"For my batteries, it is," Georg said, easing himself onto the stool across from Conrad. "Don't know how the bastards surprised us, but they surprised Colonel Burgstaller as well. I knew that man was too young to have such an important commission.

"The Hottentot's leader threw most of his force at Hummel and Burgstaller, not at Voigt as we expected. He feigned Voigt with only a few hundred men and drew the General's best man far away from the rest of the fighting."

For a moment, Georg sounded almost impressed. But then, as if catching himself, he quickly shifted his tone.

"We completely routed their forces along Hummel's lines, but Burgstaller got bogged down in some gullies those shit-eating mapmakers overlooked. It looks like a large number of the Hottentot families and cattle slipped right between Voigt and Burgstaller while we were busy killing the men."

Georg paused a moment to adjust his sling more comfortably across his lap.

"Don't know how many of them escaped, but not near enough to trouble the colony seriously again. We're done here, I suspect, though I'd love nothing more than to run those filthy savages down once and for all. More than likely, we'll be headed south to capture this Witbooi turncoat if I had to wager a guess, and we'll leave the mop-up job here to a few light companies."

Conrad sighed, releasing a breath he didn't know he'd been holding in.

The fighting was over, and if most of the Herero families had escaped… then perhaps Sybille had escaped too. The loss of life was terrible, truly terrible, but if most of the Herero families had escaped and the division's blood had cooled, then the war was all but done. The Herero would have no choice but to surrender. Many of their chiefs would doubtless be imprisoned or hanged, but in time, peace would return to the colony.

And Conrad could see Sybille again.

Thinking of Sybille gave him a warm glow in his chest. It would take time, but eventually, she might return to Schwerinsburg.

Suddenly Conrad recalled something from the battle. A tall, thin man leading the Herero charge. Conrad had recognized the man. And then there'd been the booming roar of the field guns, and the man had vanished into the eclipsing smoke.

"Er, Georg," Conrad asked after a moment, his voice cracking from the dryness in his throat. "Does anyone know what happened to Samuel Maharero?"

"Who?" Georg asked as he reached for a half-eaten nara he'd left on the stool beside the canteen.

"Samuel Maharero," Conrad repeated weakly. "The leader of the Herero."

"Oh," Georg replied between mouthfuls. "That's the Hottentot King that Leutwein sent you to treat with, right? The one you mentioned in your last report to the General. We don't know. All the Hottentots look the same. That last artillery barrage took down over half of their front line. There's not much of anything left of their bodies now."

Conrad couldn't help but notice the twinge of pride in Georg's voice.

"By the way, Connie, what is a jackal anyway? Whatever they are, they've been making a hell of a loud racket these past few nights. Haven't been able to sleep at all with them running around out there on the battlefield."

Just then, Dieter poked his head in through the tent flap. Before he could speak, Ivan and Gustavus tackled the private to the ground in eager anticipation, nearly upending Conrad's cot in the process.

Conrad swore loudly as his leg was jostled in the melee. Georg barely managed to stifle a laugh before coming over to help him.

"*Guten Nachmittag*, Major Huber," Dieter said, trying his best to salute Georg through the slobbery barrage.

Ivan succeeded in prying out whatever scrap of food Dieter had secreted in his pocket while Gustavus sniffed curiously at Dieter's overturned helmet.

"De General iz about to speak. Woot you like a hand with mofing, Herr Huber?"

"*Danke*, Dieter," Georg said with an amiable smile. "But I don't think Connie's feeling up to it. He only just woke up."

Conrad gritted his teeth and slowly propped himself up on his pillow.

"What's going on?" he asked groggily, unable to focus on anything Georg had just told him.

"Von Trotha's called the division together for an address to the troops this evening," Georg explained. "Most likely it's to congratulate the men on our victory. It'll be a boring peacock speech, but a necessary one to keep the enlisted men's spirits up in this heat. Nothing to worry about missing."

"I want to go," Conrad said plainly after a moment.

He wasn't particularly interested in listening to von Trotha's speech, but he knew that he didn't want to continue to lie on the suffocating cot.

Sybille was likely free, Maharero was likely dead, Georg had been promoted, and von Trotha was giving a speech. Of everything that he had been told since waking up, listening to a simple speech seemed the most digestible at the moment. He could worry about the rest when he wasn't smothered beneath hot blankets with a spinning head and a parched throat.

"I've been asleep for three days, and it's hotter in this tent than it is outside," Conrad said as level-headedly as he could manage. "I'll come with you."

Georg looked as though he was about to protest, but after a moment, he shrugged his shoulders and took pity on Conrad's sweating face. In all the excitement that was surely swirling around the camp about his cousin's medal,

Conrad couldn't imagine that Georg found tending to his injured family member very entertaining.

"Alright, Connie. Alright," Georg said, popping the last of the nara into his mouth. "Dieter, go and find Private Roth to help me carry the colony's Chief Expert to the gathering. And see if you can't find us a spot in the shade!"

*

An hour later, the center of the division's camp was packed as soldiers jockeyed for a place close to von Trotha's tent. The men had fought and won a battle, but that had been three days ago, and now they were clamoring for something else to do. The few spurts of shade from solitary camel thorn trees had long since been occupied, but when a cluster of officers near the front of the crowd saw Georg walking towards them, they hastily made room for both him and Conrad.

It had taken more than half an hour for Conrad to hobble towards von Trotha's tent, even with Dieter and Roth bearing most of his weight. One of the officers produced a stool from somewhere, and Conrad sank onto it gratefully, his back resting against the knobbed tree trunk. The sun was beginning to set, and between the relief of the shade and a fresh canteen of water, Conrad managed to make himself decently comfortable.

Their spot was just to the side of a small platform that had been erected in front of the General's tent for von Trotha to address the troops. Yet as they settled into their allotted slivers of shade, all the nearby men's attention switched to Georg.

Georg's heroics in the battle had made him a celebrity among enlisted men and officers alike. He was a man who'd been shot but had not fallen. He'd not only managed to kill his attacker and rescue his cousin from the midst of the enemy, but he'd then taken up the post of one of his fallen men and fired the key artillery salvos that had broken the middle of the Herero charge.

Sergeants, lieutenants, and captains all congratulated Georg on his promotion, and Colonel Voigt even appeared for a few moments to shake Georg's plump hand and to let him know that he'd already requested the

General transfer Georg to his command as soon as his arm healed. Everyone wanted to share a drink with Georg when the division passed back through Windhoek, and despite his nausea and the overhanging gloom of uncertainly he felt for Sybille and Maharero, Conrad couldn't help feeling proud of Georg.

It was an odd and disconcerting feeling.

Suddenly, von Trotha himself appeared amongst the officers to shake Georg's hand.

"You wear the metal well, Major Huber," he said with convivial straightness. "How's the arm?"

"Nothing that will slow me down, sir," Georg replied, beaming. "Though I suspect the barmaids in Windheok will be mortified to learn I'm confined to this sling. I'm left-handed, you know!"

That brought a chorus of laughter from several of the General's retainers, and von Trotha himself even offered up a small smile.

"Herr Huber," von Trotha said as he spotted Conrad sitting on the outskirt of the group. "You've rejoined the world of the living, then. For a while there, I'd thought my Chief Expert had left us all alone in this rugged wasteland."

Conrad was not sure if the General was having fun with him or not. The General rarely made jests, and when he did, they were almost always hackneyed.

"Still alive, sir," Conrad replied as he tried painfully to rise and greet the General.

Conrad stumbled, and von Trotha waved him down as Dieter bent to help steady him.

"No need for that," the General said dismissively. "Just glad to see you among us again. Your assistance was quite invaluable in orchestrating this maneuver, Herr Huber. I've said as much to Berlin in my reports. Herr Kleinschmidt will be proud to know that *one* of his men is serving the Empire well. I'm sure he'll be pleased to recommend you to a more comfortable post when you rotate home next May."

Von Trotha turned to leave but then paused to look behind him.

"Exceptional dogs you have there, Herr Huber.

Conrad looked behind him to see Ivan and Gustavus trotting towards him.

Their new tie ropes were trailing uselessly in the dirt behind them, along with the torn edges of Conrad's tent. Dieter looked guilty, and Conrad tensed as the two dogs trotted straight up to him.

"Exemplary in every way," the General continued. "I don't suppose you'd consider parting with one of them, Herr Huber?"

As the dogs padded towards them, Ivan pushed a path through the crowd of officers, and Gustavus came and sat beside Conrad, staring at him as though he were indignant at being left behind.

Conrad stared back at Leutwein's dog and thought about what Georg had said about them running Herero men down on the battlefield. For a moment, he was sorely tempted to let the General take them both.

Then Gustavus licked Conrad's hand and plopped his big head into Conrad's lap while Ivan curled himself into a large ball beside the stool.

Before Conrad could respond, von Trotha scratched Gustavus' ear and said, "They don't seem to think they're for sale."

The General nodded to Conrad and Georg as he regathered his staff and headed toward the crude stage.

Georg gave Conrad a wink before being re-absorbed into the fold of admiring officers.

"Looks like you'll be promoted in no time, too, Connie," Georg whispered to him.

Dieter bent down to ask Conrad if he was alright. Conrad considered telling Dieter to take the dogs back to his tent, but a bout of nausea hit him, and he nodded his head weakly. Dieter gave Conrad a short salute and then left with Private Roth to find a spot of their own among the enlisted men.

Conrad tried to push Gustavus' head off his knee, but Gustavus' seemed to have fallen asleep, and Conrad gave up and lay his head back against the tree trunk to rest.

It took von Trotha several minutes to navigate his way through the men and onto the wooden platform. The General wore his full parade dress with a decorative saber that hung gloriously at his side, and his signature cavalry spurs that clicked loudly as his heavy boots pounded against the dry wood.

A resounding cheer rose from the division as von Trotha took his place on the stage. The General waited patiently until the noise had subsided.

"*Meine Herren*," he finally said. "Gentlemen. We have won a proud victory for the Empire and the Kaiser over a horde of godless savages."

Several whoops and cheers sounded throughout the division once more, and von Trotha paused again until the men's voices began to ebb.

"We have defeated the enemy in battle," he said emphatically. "But our task is not yet done."

Conrad's ears pricked up from his sickly doze.

"The Hottentots are a dangerous race of sub-human animals," von Trotha continued. "They have stained the honor of the Kaiser, murdered His subjects, butchered good men and consumed their flesh! These are not the mollified Negroes of the Americas. These are evil and godless cannibals who cannot be tamed!"

This was not what Conrad had been expecting von Trotha to say. Several of the officers nearby looked surprised as well. Was the division not returning to Windhoek, then?

"They're fucking swine!" Conrad heard someone shout in reply from just in front of him.

He was shocked. It was Georg.

"They should be shot! Every last one of them!"

The other officers under the tree all shouted in agreement, and their calls were quickly picked up by the surrounding enlisted men. Conrad didn't know how many of their fellow soldiers had died in the fighting. He knew it was far fewer than the number of Herero, but it never took much to make soldiers despise their enemy. From the few weeks he'd spent traveling with the army, Conrad had learned quickly that even soldiers that hated one another were brothers when the shooting started. And even the loss of a few was unforgivable.

A new wave of nausea hit Conrad, and he fought to suppress it as von Trotha continued.

"We cannot allow monsters such as these to exist in the Kaiser's realm. And we cannot allow them to threaten the safety of civilized people in the colonies!

Our scouts report that what is left of the Hottentot horde is running westward toward the desert. They think that they can run and hide from German might and that we will let them stay and fester like an open wound within our borders…."

The division was growing increasingly agitated as von Trotha's theatrics whipped them into a frenzy, and the air became rife with hot-blooded shouts of protest.

Conrad's mind was swirling through confusion and pain. The Herero were defeated; why fight them again?

He should say something.

He tried to stand, but Gustavus' head was too heavy to move, and he couldn't put any weight on his leg. None of the other officers were looking at him to offer help; they were too transfixed by von Trotha's words.

"But we shall not allow their disease to spread any further!" von Trotha shouted, his well-manicured face sunburned and straining in the heat. "We shall drive their rabble from our lands and destroy them with bullets and bayonets! We will poison every watering hole, burn every fruit-bearing bush, and slaughter every last one of their livestock that carries their madness with it. We will raze every village, pull down every hut and salt the very ground they walk upon. We will hunt them down until the very last one is destroyed and the Kaiser's people are safe once more!"

The division erupted in frenzied applause. Von Trotha, exhausted, saluted the men, which caused an even louder roar of approval as the General retired from the stage and departed with his flock of colonels.

No, Conrad shouted to himself as he tried to shake the clouds from his head. No, the General couldn't do this!

Conrad had to say something. He had to talk to von Trotha and convince him to…to reconsider. Conrad's head throbbed from the heat and the howling of the men beside him. They were going after the Herero. After Sybille. He had to stop them!

Conrad grabbed hold of a knot in the tree trunk and tried to pull himself to his feet, ignoring the blinding pain that shot through his leg. Gustavus woke with a start and began to bark in concern.

Somehow, Conrad had to make von Trotha listen to him. The fighting was done; the Herero were no longer a threat. They couldn't kill them all! That was madness! He had to try and stop them.

Conrad tried to take a step forward from the tree, but a new round of hot pain tore through his leg, and he felt his legs buckle beneath him as something in his leg reopened once again.

He cried out, and Georg turned his head at the sound.

"Connie!" Georg shouted, turning to run towards Conrad. "Jesus, what are you thinking?"

Conrad's head hit the ground hard near the tree. He was vaguely aware of blood running down his face from where he'd smacked his head against a twisted root. His vision was whirling, and he could scarcely hear anything over the roaring of the division. But he had to tell Georg to help him. Von Trotha couldn't do this. He simply couldn't.

Conrad opened his mouth to speak, but he vomited and then passed out again.

CHAPTER 12

SEPTEMBER-OCTOBER 1904

It took a month of recovery in Windhoek before the army physicians deemed Conrad well enough to venture beyond the confines of the Residence. A week after collapsing at von Trotha's speech, Conrad woke up in his small bungalow at Schwerinsburg to see Erwin's scowling face staring down at him. Erwin sat beside Conrad on the bed, dabbing at his fevered forehead with a damp rag, while Petyr stared wide-eyed from the corner of the room.

"Wasn't sure you gunna make it," Erwin said matter-of-factly. "You looked dead when soldiers bring you back."

Erwin nodded slightly to himself, as though privately deciding whether he was glad that Conrad had not died, and stood to fetch a nearby pitcher of water.

As soon as Erwin had stood, Petyr raced to Conrad's bed and flung his arms around Conrad's neck. The boy's knee collided painfully with Conrad's bandaged leg, and Conrad groaned loudly. He hadn't fully come around yet but hugged Petyr back with as much strength as much as he could manage.

Erwin pried the boy off Conrad and held the pitcher out for Conrad to drink from. Conrad tried to thank Erwin, but his words sounded garbled and slow, and Erwin ignored him.

Erwin told Petyr to run and tell Major Huber at Alte Feste that Conrad was awake. When Petyr did not leave immediately, Erwin scowled and pushed the boy away from the bed. Petyr looked hesitantly at Conrad for a moment, torn between his current fear of Erwin and his dread of another trip up to the city's fortress. Erwin growled something at Petyr in Ovambo that Conrad didn't understand, and Petyr disappeared quickly out the door as the flimsy hinges slammed back on the doorframe with a loud *whack*.

Erwin took the pitcher from Conrad and laid a fresh, wet rag over his forehead. The rag wasn't cold, but the dampness still brought a wave of sudden relief. Conrad felt sleep washing over him again, but as Erwin turned to leave, Conrad called out to him.

"Sybille?" Conrad croaked out feverishly.

Conrad didn't know what Erwin thought of him beyond the forced courtesy of his station. Erwin usually said very little, and when he did speak, he always acted as though he were having to explain something that Conrad ought to have already known. He didn't think Erwin hated him, but that wasn't saying much.

But regardless of what Erwin thought about *him* beneath his silent civility, Conrad knew that Erwin cared for Sybille. Erwin had always pretended that he hadn't seen Conrad and Sybille together on the few occasions he'd stumbled upon one of their discreet rendezvous, and everyone could see that Erwin doted on Sybille like she was his own daughter.

It didn't matter if Erwin liked him; it only mattered that he cared for Sybille too.

Erwin turned his head back to Conrad and shot him a look that Conrad couldn't read. It might have been pity, or it might have been disgust. But whatever it was, it vanished quickly as Erwin strode out of the bungalow.

"Don't know," he called evenly over his shoulder as the door slammed shut behind him.

*

When he'd recovered enough to be permitted to walk more than a few yards at a time, Conrad tried hopelessly to look for Sybille. The medics had permitted him to exercise his leg as he saw fit, but Conrad quickly discovered that he couldn't walk more than three paces or so without the assistance of a cane. And on the rare occasions he had enough strength to walk down the long hill from Schwerinsburg and into town, Dieter or Private Roth always had to accompany him.

He was never alone for very long, and he had no idea where to look.

To make his search even more difficult, von Trotha had decided to return to Windhoek early, leaving Colonel Voigt in charge of mopping up the remainder of the Herero campaign. The General had been patient while Conrad had recovered, but when Conrad was cleared to begin walking again, von Trotha recalled him eagerly back to active duty.

On his return to the capital, the General informed Conrad that the division's main resources would shift over the coming months from eradicating the remaining Herero in the north to dealing with Hendrik Witbooi and his Nama guerillas in the south. After their folly at Waterberg, von Trotha was fully disillusioned with the division's surveyors, and therefore he insisted that Conrad be present in every strategic meeting as the division's only reliable source of information.

The General wanted to know everything about the villages and landscapes in the south, most of which Conrad had never seen. Conrad spent his days pouring over Leutwein's old records, trying to determine which Kavango villages might be sympathetic enough to the Nama's cause to hide Witbooi's warriors, or how long it would take a troop of infantry to march between Bethanie and Grunau.

Whenever Conrad did manage to find time to search for Sybille, his only means were to examine the field reports that Colonel Voigt sent to von Trotha, which Conrad found as distressing as they were unhelpful. The reports came daily, but they were brief and served only to heighten Conrad's own fears of the terrible fates that might've befallen Sybille.

From: Colonel Voigt's Field Command Headquarters, Tsumeb
To: Division Office of General Lothar von Trotha, Schwerinsburg,
Windhoek
September 16th, 1904
Hussar company engaged Hottentot band sixty kilometers north of
Gobabis. Stop.
All killed, no German causalities. Stop.

From: Colonel Voigt's Field Command Headquarters, Tsumeb
To: Division Office of General Lothar von Trotha, Schwerinsburg,
Windhoek
September 17th, 1904
Two additional wells poisoned south of Grootfontein. Stop.
Dragoon company discovered two female natives half-eaten in
bush. Stop.
Hyena or large cat likely cause of death. Stop.

From: Colonel Voigt's Field Command Headquarters, Tsumeb
To: Division Office of General Lothar von Trotha, Schwerinsburg,
Windhoek
September 18th, 1904
Light infantry patrol discovered sixteen dead Hottentot in bush.
Stop.
Appeared to be digging for water. Stop.
Four men, eight women, four children. Well poisoning effective. Stop.

Dozens of similar reports arrived daily for von Trotha from several of his senior field officers. Conrad caught short glimpses of them in the mornings before one of the General's secretaries came to collect them from Conrad's desk. And after von Trotha had retired for the evening, Conrad would sneak into the General's office just to read them all a second or third time, desperately searching for some detail he might've missed.

There was danger in doing this. If anyone saw him sneaking in and out of von Trotha's office, he would, at the very least, be questioned as to what he was doing. As the colony's Chief Expert, Conrad could have simply asked one of the General's aides for a copy of Colonel Voigt's reports. But he did not want anyone to know that he was reviewing the General's records for fear that someone would eventually ask him why he was doing it.

Pouring over the reports well into the night was a miserable business. Conrad had only spent a handful of nights in the bush himself, but he remembered how shockingly cold and frightening it was. He still remembered the image of Noko's dogs, whimpering sentinels lying at the edge of the fire, alone against the unseen terrors of the pitch-black, feral night.

And while he sat in the General's office pouring over stacks of reports, Sybille was out in the bush somewhere, alone in the wilds with no dogs to protect her from prowling leopards or other far darker evils.

Colonel Voigt's latest telegram had shaken Conrad worse than usual.

Mein Gott, he groaned after reading it again.

A family. With children. All of whom had died from thirst while trying to dig for water.

This wasn't war. This was cruel and pointless slaughter.

At some point every night, Conrad's eyes would always fail him, and he would be forced to limp back to his bungalow and slip into a dreamless, exhausted sleep until he managed to rise again a few hours later.

The early mornings were when the Schutztruppe patrols usually returned with their new arrests, and Conrad made sure that he was always at the gates of the Iron Palace by five each morning to scan the faces of the new prisoners the division brought in. He had to be. It wasn't as though the prison guards bothered to keep an active inmate list, and if Conrad missed Sybille on the day she was led through the gates, he might never find her amongst the swelling mass of frightened prisoners.

Von Trotha had enacted a series of new crackdowns on the camps that made Major Baumhauer's reign as warden seem tame. Using the Witboois' orchestrated prison revolt as evidence, the General had successfully petitioned the Kaiser for permission to construct a series of new prison camps along the southern coast.

Having dangerous prisoners so near the colonial capital was unwise, von Trotha argued, and building new prison camps in lands recently retaken from the Nama would make a powerful show of strength to any other tribes thinking of assisting the Witbooi renegades.

In addition to building his new string of camps along the coastline, von Trotha had ordered the Schutztruppe to double their patrols in the rest of the colony. This, in turn, had increased the number of arrests three-fold. And the resulting lack of space in the crowded Windhoek camps had spurred von Trotha to organize his latest project: a mass movement of native prisoners from the old camps near the capital to the new ones in the south.

The citizens of Windhoek were pleased, Mayor Grober was ecstatic, and the natives were utterly terrified.

When word of the General's plan spread, several Damara chieftains in the hinterlands surrounding the capital came to Windhoek to protest the plan almost overnight. The Damara had remained peaceful subjects of the German colonial government, yet nearly every one of their villages had at least one prisoner in the camps, and the chieftains pled with von Trotha not to take their people so far away from their loved ones.

Unlike Leutwein, who had dealt with formal protests decently enough in his later years and had thrown an elaborate birthday party for !Gai!ga, von Trotha had no patience for what he had deemed "an appalling display of the savages' disobedience." He'd had the entire Damara delegation arrested, including !Gai!ga, and sent a company of riflemen to root out any further dissidents in the neighboring villages.

Conrad had tried to remind the General that the Damara had always cooperated with the colonial government. He'd even dared, in one of his braver moments, to suggest to the General that such harsh treatment of a friendly tribe's leaders might push other peaceful tribes like the Ovambo and Zwartboois into rebellion.

But von Trotha would not be persuaded to release the chieftains.

He'd had his hands tied by Leutwein's like in the Colonial Office when he'd been deployed in Ruanda-Urundi. Soft men who thought they could tame the savagery of Africa with pretty words and promises to pagan chiefs whose grandfathers had sold their own people into slavery for a pound of sugar and a rusted musket. Now that von Trotha had broken the Herero rebellion, he was determined to rip out all roots of dissent among the natives by any means necessary.

"No," von Trotha told Conrad sternly when he'd tried to plead for the Damara's release a second time. "I will not make the same mistakes that Leutwein made. You were taught by a poor teacher, Herr Huber, so I don't blame you for your lack of foresight. But it's important that you understand the realities of Africa. Call them negroes, Hottentots, whatever you like. The Black man is of an inferior, brutish race, and the only thing he respects is strength.

"The Damara do not have the same rights we do in Europe. God has ordained them as our subordinates, and I must make an example of any who dare to think they can challenge the Natural Law. The rifle will bring Africa to heel. Not the misguided bleating of politicians and clerics."

Conrad had been thunderstruck. How could he have misread von Trotha's aims so badly? All he could manage was a short salute to the General as he limped out of the Commissioner's office, heartbroken. If he had sheltered any remaining hope that von Trotha might be convinced to reverse his brutal tactics, it had died as soon as the door to the General's office closed behind him.

He had been an utter fool to think that the Herero's defeat would allow things to go back to the way they were. With von Trotha in command, there was no place for any Africans in Southwest Africa.

News of the army's raid on Damara villages spread quickly, and as hundreds of young Damara men were rounded up and thrown into the camps, the rest of the colony's northern tribes fell into fearful compliance with the new government.

Thousands of natives were moved in the General's first wave of relocation, and Conrad did not want to think about how many of them had likely died before they even reached the southern camps.

Von Trotha learned of the prison guards' sjamboks and the natives' corresponding fear of them, and had insisted that all Schutztruppe guards carry them to dissuade any thoughts of rebellion among the prisoners while they were being transported. The General had even taken to wearing a sjambok himself, saying to his officers on several occasions that he felt safer walking among natives carrying the whip than his revolver.

The army had requisitioned boxcars from the Kolonialgesellschaft to transport the prisoners to the south, and Conrad could not help shivering each time he passed the train depot. The memory of Berriz and the other boys from Grootfontein crammed into rusted, sweltering boxcars on the long journey from Grootfontein was still fresh in his mind. Conrad did not even know if any of the remaining boys from Berriz's gang were still alive.

Trains seemed to leave every week from Windhoek's Iron Palace. The camp guards drove the prisoners chosen for transport into the cars as Conrad had heard that American cowboys did with their cattle. He'd seen the camp guards separating out prisoners for transport in the early darkness, sjamboks rising and falling with a ghostly whistling amongst the crowds of terrified prisoners.

Conrad tried to scan the horde of faces for any sign of Sybille, but there were always too many faces, all running into the hot iron cars, cutting themselves on loose shards of its jagged metal to avoid the guards' whips.

The new commander of the Schutztruppe was in charge of determining which prisoners to keep incarcerated in Windhoek and which should be deemed too dangerous to be kept close to Windhoek and sent to the southern camps. And therein lay Conrad's additional source of gloom and his reason for dutifully reporting to Alte Feste each afternoon to have lunch with the new commander of the colonial security troopers.

Georg.

While Conrad was recovering, Georg had been busy. Following the Battle of Waterberg, and once the army medic had assured him that Conrad would indeed recover from his second collapse, Georg had resumed active duty.

Berlin had confirmed his promotion to major, but Georg's own injury had prevented him from either joining Colonel Voigt's northern forces or being deployed to the new southern campaigns to pick off Witbooi's guerillas. Von Trotha quickly realized that Captain Jund was ill-suited to remain the senior commander of the Schutztruppe a minute longer than absolutely necessary, and he had leaped at the idea of installing Georg, at least temporarily, as the new Commanding Officer of the Colonial Schutztruppe.

Georg, in turn, had taken to his new role with zeal.

His first action had come in early September when Colonel Burgstaller's men razed Hochfeld. Most of the Herero had followed Maharero to Waterberg, and Burgstaller's men had found only a few dozen Herero who'd been either too old or too sick to join Maharero. But von Trotha wanted to make a statement by burning Maharero's home village to the ground.

Unsure what to do with the young and elderly Herero he'd captured, Burgstaller eventually decided to march his prisoners to Windhoek. The colonel had sent word of his intention back to Windhoek, and Georg had ridden out with a small company of Schutztruppe to collect the prisoners from Burgstaller's escort.

Neither company expected trouble along the road. After all, the Herero had been routed, and von Trotha had stripped the tribes surrounding Windhoek of most of their fighting men.

However, !Gai!ga's oldest son, !Notago, was determined to avenge his father's and the other chieftains' imprisonment. A prominent warrior among his father's Arodaman clan, !Notago had quarreled with his father when !Gai!ga had refused to join the Herero uprising, and they'd fought again publicly when horrific reports of the aftermath of Waterberg reached Damara lands.

But !Gai!ga would not be swayed by his son. The Damara clans had been supporters of the German colonists for years, and the old man saw no good coming from trying to resist von Trotha's army now. !Gai!ga would be patient and seek an audience with the new Commissioner when he and the other chieftains were in Windhoek.

!Gai!ga was arrested in the capital three days later.

!Notago had been angry at von Trotha's treatment of the fleeing Herero, but when his father was taken prisoner, he flew into a blind rage. Without consulting any of the remaining chiefs, he'd gathered a force of some hundred and fifty Arodaman men who had managed to escape the army's raids on their villages.

He led his men northward towards the burned remains of Hochfeld and stalked Colonel Burgstaller's dragoon company as it led the Herero prisoners away from the main force. !Notago was determined to rescue the Herero and send a message of defiance to von Trotha.

!Notago was unlucky. In his eagerness, he sprung his ambush against the heavily armed dragoons just as Georg had arrived with his mounted Schutztruppe. The Arodaman, armed mostly with spears and bows and arrows, were all slaughtered within minutes.

Only two Germans had been killed in the fighting, along with twelve Herero prisoners who had been killed in the crossfire.

Georg had been livid. He had only lost two men, yet the fact that !Notago's warriors had been bold enough to stage an ambush on German soldiers so close to the capital was an affront to his new authority that Georg's pride could not ignore.

He raided several Arodaman villages the next day with a much larger force and arrested over a hundred natives. There had been a skirmish of some sort in one of the larger villages, although no one seemed to know who had started it. When the smoke had cleared, the fighting had left !Gai!ga's youngest son, Charles, dead. !Gai!ga's elderly wife and the rest of his remaining relatives had all been arrested. Georg did not even bother bringing the survivors to Windhoek. He had them immediately ferried to one of the new southern camps.

After that, none of the other surrounding Damara clans had dared to defy either von Trotha's orders or Georg's men. !Gai!ga's brother, Iazrus, had written to von Trotha asking if he might be allowed to know where his brother and his family had been taken, but so far as Conrad knew, no one from the General's staff had even bothered to hand the General the letter.

The Schutztruppe carried out their new spree of arrests across the colony's northern and central regions, ignoring clan and tribal distinctions. Georg's men did not care whether a Damara was an Audaman or a Tsoaxudaman, or whether a woman looked more like an Ovambo than a Herero. Georg had fully committed himself to ensuring that the German forces were not surprised again, and that the Empire's colonists were made safe. Arrests occurred daily, and German authority in the northern half of the colony became absolute.

Von Trotha was pleased, and it was even rumored in the streets of Windhoek that the Herzog of Saxony had referred Georg's name to the Kaiser, who was considering inducting Georg into the Order of the Black Eagle, the Hohenzollern family's highest honor.

"I very much doubt it's true," Georg said to Conrad over lunch one afternoon in mid-October. "Von Trotha himself hasn't even received an invitation to join the Black Eagles. It's a decoration reserved for princes and politicians. The last man Father remembers receiving it was Bismarck himself!"

They were having lunch in Georg's office at Alte Feste today, Georg being too busy that afternoon to justify the long walk into town to his favorite restaurant on Kaiserstrasse. As a result, their lunch consisted of what a thin-framed private had been able to requisition from the barrack's kitchen: a few hard bread rolls, a thick wedge of sharp cheese, and much to Conrad's dismay, two ripe nara. Georg had tucked in hungrily, but Conrad ate little.

Conrad felt sick sitting in the stuffy barracks office, and it was more than the overpowering stench of Georg's fruit or the constant throbbing in his leg.

Conrad was being smothered by guilt. No matter which way he turned, he felt as though he were suffocating, buried beneath an inescapable bog of horrible and hopeless thoughts. He'd failed Maharero by not convincing him that war with Germany would only bring ruin. He'd failed Leutwein as well, letting the man self-implode into bitterness and despair. And worst of all, he'd failed Sybille.

He hadn't been able to warn her or protect her. Conrad knew that she was probably dead. He'd stayed up far too many nights reading the reports from Colonel Voigt's staffers to think otherwise.

Last night he'd finally been caught snooping around the General's office. It was the pretty Ovambo maid, Ndahepuluka, Conrad thought her name was. Ndahepuluka was tall and slender, and when she moved, she always seemed to sway her hips just a little more than she really needed to. It was like watching a reed bend back and forth hypnotically in the wind.

She watched Conrad root around von Trotha's desk for a while, until Conrad looked up and caught her staring at him. For a moment, Conrad stood frozen behind von Trotha's desk, afraid Ndahepuluka would speak and alert the whole Residence to what he was doing.

Instead, she gave him an amused smile and took a step inside the doorway. She was dressed in a thin nightdress, and when he met her eye, she let her dress fall open slightly to reveal one of her brown, bell-shaped breasts. She gave him an appraising look and took a second step toward him.

The candle in his hand was burning low. In the flickering light of the hallway, Ndahepuluka's warm body seemed to glow like mana.

But in front of her inviting stare lay piles of fresh field reports, each one a few paltry lines of an endless, terrible tapestry.

Sybille was the woman Conrad loved. She was the one he wanted to embrace and kiss, to take him away from this nightmare. And if there was any chance of salvation, he knew it lay not in Ndahepuluka's bed, but in the horrific fantasies of Colonel Voigt's descriptions.

He smiled sadly at Ndahepuluka and shook his head. She shrugged as though she did not care much either way and continued silently down the hall toward von Trotha's bedroom.

When Conrad was alone again in the silence, he had read on, the words from the field reports sketching nightmarish scenes in his mind.

Woman's corpse found in tree half-eaten by leopard. Stop.

That could've been Sybille.

Three women found dead with bloated bellies. Unknown cause. Stop.

One of them might be Sybille.

Five women shot while fleeing hussar patrol. Stop.

Any one of those five dead women could be Sybille.

Conrad's hopeless search was driving him mad. And each day that passed, he knew he could've done something more.

Sybille, and God knew how many others like her, were out in the bush and the desert dying. The weight of that knowledge was crushing him, and he was bearing it alone. Von Trotha had not listened to him, and Conrad understood he could never speak to Georg about any of this.

Georg had cheered louder than the rest during von Trotha's speech and had now inherited Baumhauer's command, conducting more raids and making more arrests than the old, terrible Major ever had. And what was even more troubling to Conrad…Georg seemed to enjoy it.

The Schutztruppe post had brought something out in Georg. It was something that Conrad wondered if he would have ever seen in his cousin if they hadn't come to Africa. It was darker than the normal social elitism found in the German upper classes back home. It was a fiendish trait, a determined enmity that fed upon itself, yet which nearly all the colonists in Windhoek seemed to find commendable, even honorable.

There was Georg, the civilized bastion of the law, bringing a long overdue social order to this remote part of the Empire. Men bought him drinks, and pretty women flocked to him as they had in Hamburg. Yet to Conrad, his affable cousin seemed more brutish and more consumed every day.

What would Georg say if he discovered that the reason Conrad continued to have lunch with him every day was the hope that Georg might let slip some faint detail about a woman he'd arrested or assaulted? That the real reason why Conrad was working himself into an early grave was to find a Hottentot woman?

The fact that he was not only using Georg but also hiding this personal treachery from him, gave Conrad a near-permanent glumness that he couldn't disguise. Georg had noticed it on more than one occasion but had mistaken it for pain or fatigue.

"I'm telling you, Connie," he said as the private came in to clear away their dishes. "You need to put in for a holiday. Von Trotha will give it to you if you ask. *Mein Gott*, you haven't had a day off in well over a year. Apart from being shot, that is, but I'm not sure that really counts as a holiday, even by the army's standards, eh?"

Conrad managed a weak smile. He had barely touched any of the food and took a short sip of water to soothe his headache as Georg continued.

"Certainly doesn't in my book anyway. Von Trotha won't move against the Nama for a few more weeks; take some time away to rest, Connie. No one's ever going to screw you with those bags under your eyes and a face longer than a horse's."

"You're one to talk," Conrad replied, shifting the subject with a practiced effort. "Your clerk told me this morning that you're here well past the time he leaves every evening. Surely a future Black Eagle can afford to take a few nights off?"

Georg shook his head as he brushed a few lingering crumbs off his desk.

"Couldn't do it," he said with a mild sigh. "I've missed my weekly card game with some of the other officers three weeks in a row now. And that's not likely to change so long as von Trotha keeps me chained to the colonial guard. There's always something that keeps me occupied. At least I'm able to ride again. If my arm hadn't healed, I think I'd have gone insane. No idea how in the world you've managed not to crack with your leg slowing you down."

The conversation lulled for a moment, and Conrad decided to chance asking Georg about his patrols again.

"Have you made any more arrests since Sunday?" he asked casually.

Conrad had had a painful flareup in his leg and hadn't been able to make the trek up to Alte Feste for the past two days. His physicians had forced him to wait out the pain lying flat on his back in bed, and Conrad had nearly lost his mind staring at the dry ceiling beams. Those two lost days had haunted him all morning, his mind feverishly exploring every possibility that Sybille had somehow been arrested, imprisoned, and executed all while he'd been holed up, helpless, just a few meters away.

"Not lately, no," Georg said as he started to leaf back through a stack of requisition orders on his desk. The desk was a large, bulky piece of furniture that had previously belonged to Major Baumhauer. Georg's short stature kept him constantly bent over the edge as he searched through thick stacks of army papers.

"It's been pretty quiet for a week or so. Apart from the five, *Kavango* I think you called them, that Protz's men brought in last week, the only other troublemaker we've had to deal with was some lunatic witchdoctor we arrested in town. Half the inmates in the Iron Palace are scared shitless of him. Damn African kept speaking in tongues the whole time I questioned him, so I just threw him back in with the rest of the lot. At least his presence helps keep order."

Georg swore softly as he finally found whatever document he'd been searching for on his desk.

"Damn it, I don't see how I'm going to make my card game tonight either. I've got to get through all these requisition requests sorted out before the morning muster. Blasted wind and sand. I've never seen equipment wear out so fast in my life."

Georg must've glimpsed something in Conrad's face, for he paused in his paper shuffling and looked up at him.

"Are you alright, Connie?" he asked.

"Fine," Conrad replied hurriedly, as he reached for his nearby cane to help him to his feet. "I'd better get going. Von Trotha will be expecting me back soon for a briefing at two o'clock. Thank you again for lunch."

"Would you like for me to have someone fetch that boy of yours to help you home?" Georg asked.

Georg's tone made Conrad pause mid-rise. He knew that his cousin was trying to be kind. Just the latest in a long string of kindnesses Georg had showered him with. Georg had asked the question innocently, but behind his caring tone lay a festering disdain that made Conrad uneasy.

Conrad shook his head. He knew that even for him, Petyr wouldn't come within a thousand yards of Alte Feste for fear of being beaten by the younger guards while he waited for Conrad at the gate.

"I can manage," Conrad replied as he finally got to his feet.

Georg mistook Conrad's shortness for disappointment and stood up as well.

"You know, Connie," he said warmly. "All this paperwork probably won't mind sitting another day. There's nothing pressing that I've seen so far, and Sergeant Koch likely won't cable my requests to Berlin till we can flush him out of the bar. How about I leave all of this for tomorrow morning, and you and I join the other officers for cards tonight? What do you say?

"I could use a party, and most of these provincials are terrible poker players. All the better for us, eh? Protz is also usually good for a bottle or two of something good. He's got a brother in the distilling business back home."

Conrad managed to give Georg another weak smile before collecting his hat at the door.

"Sure," he said meekly. "That sounds wonderful."

They agreed to meet for dinner at six o'clock in the Main Square beforehand, and Georg returned to the pile of paper on his desk.

It usually took Conrad a little over an hour to hobble home from the fortress if he took the longer, flatter route down Kaiserstrasse. But he had lingered with Georg too long this afternoon and so forced himself to take the quicker, hillier side streets. Conrad had only walked for a few minutes after making his way down from the fort, but already his shirt and coat were soaked with sweat, and he was forced to stop and rest.

Conrad had always had trouble catching his breath back in Germany, and the day's heat was only making things worse. His sweat stung him painfully along the holes in his leg as he eased himself down onto the stoop of a small tailor's shop. The shop owner had not yet returned from his own luncheon, and the afternoon shoppers had not begun their daily fluttering along this particular street.

Conrad could hear the not-too-distant bustling of the main square crowds, but the backstreet where he currently sat was all but deserted. There were not too many shops along this street to begin with, which was partly why he had chosen it. No crowds meant that he could make his way along the streets at a reasonable pace and not have to worry about being jostled or bumped by careless pedestrians.

He checked his pocket watch. It was half past one. He could afford to rest a bit along the way and still make it back to Schwerinsberg by two o'clock.

Conrad didn't see the blow that struck him hard across the face. The force of it toppled him, and he cried out as his wounded leg twisted and buckled under his weight. A second blow hit him in the back, and he crumpled to the ground.

For a few seconds, Conrad could see nothing beyond the whirling street corner above him. When his vision finally cleared, he found himself on his back staring into the murderous gaze of Albert Witbooi.

If possible, Albert looked even more terrifying than the last time Conrad had seen him. Months of fighting in the bush had left Albert's clothing little more than rags that hung over his powerful frame like strangling vines. His eyes were bloodshot, and he reeked sweetly of ombike. His infamous rifle was slung menacingly over his shoulder, and a long, jagged knife hung readily from his belt.

"You killed her," Albert growled at him, swaying heavily as he fumbled at his belt for his knife. "You killed her same as if you shot her yourself. She's dead in the bush, and you and your German *doos* friends put her there."

Albert wasn't shouting. His words were slurred, but there was no mistaking the venom and hatred in them. He finally managed to grab the hilt of his knife and as he stared down murderously at his prey, Conrad saw that there were tears in his eyes.

"I'm gunna kill you, German," Albert said again, his voice chillingly even, despite his drunkenness. "I'm gunna kill you...for her."

For a moment, Conrad's fear was replaced with paralyzing shock. Dead? Sybille was...*dead*?

Albert yanked the knife free from his belt and took a step toward Conrad's slumped form. Conrad knew he was trapped, but he still tried frantically to get to his feet. Albert stomped down heavily on Conrad's wounded leg, pinning him firmly to the ground. Conrad screamed in pain.

It was no use. No one was around to help him. Even if someone in the square heard his screams, he'd be dead long before they could reach him, and Albert would have melted away into the city outskirts. Conrad knew he was dead.

And if Sybille was too, what did it even matter? Conrad didn't know how Albert could have possibly found her, but it was all too easy to believe that he was right.

Perhaps Sybille had headed southward, trying to reach Windhoek, but had been killed along the way. Maybe Albert had deserted the Nama rebels when he heard what had happened at Waterberg and gone out looking for her. He might've even found her body in the bush somehow, collapsed against a flame thorn or strewn helplessly across the orange sands.

And what had Conrad done? Rested in a soft bed and read through a few papers trying to find some hopeless, buried clue.

Albert was a brutal man, but he'd been strong enough to search the bush for her. In the end, both of them had failed Sybille, but that hardly seemed to matter now. She was dead, and soon, Conrad would be too. At least the pain in his leg would be gone.

Suddenly a gunshot pierced the air of the side streets, and Conrad heard Albert give a muffled grunt of surprise. Albert dropped his knife, which landed with a soft *thump* in the dirt beside Conrad. The Nama guerilla kept his feet, too drunk to understand what had happened to him. Two more shots rang out, slamming into Albert's broad back and ripping a single, large hole in his chest.

Albert made an angry, gurgling noise and tried to reach down for Conrad. Albert's blood splashed Conrad's army coat as the strength was sapped from his legs and he fell backward onto his knees. A fourth shot struck him between the shoulder blades, and Conrad heard footsteps running toward them.

For a moment, Conrad thought that Albert might get back up. He glared down at Conrad with a look of such utter hatred that Conrad feared Albert would will himself back to his feet. But Albert coughed once, and his mouth began to fill with blood. His eyes glazed over as his large body crumpled and then collapsed into the dirt. Albert twitched once and then went limp, his vacant, teary eyes still open inches from Conrad's own face.

Conrad's heart was still racing in terror as Georg knelt beside him, smoking pistol in hand.

"Jesus, Connie, are you alright?" he asked, as he inspected Conrad for injury and ignored Albert's pooling blood beside them. "That fucking ape nearly got you. I'm so sorry, Connie…I don't know how that animal got hold of a rifle, but I promise you, the whole lot of his kind will pay for this. I'll make them pay!"

*

Once Georg had escorted Conrad back to Schwerinsburg and had the division's surgeon reexamine Conrad's leg, it had taken Conrad another hour to persuade Georg that he was alright. Georg's blood was still up, but reason eventually took hold of him, and he left to explain to von Trotha why a dozen citizens had swarmed to Alte Feste in the middle of the day to report hearing gunshots fired in a back-alley street.

Conrad knew he'd been very lucky. He was only alive because his cousin had decided that he'd sent Conrad off in a bad state. Georg had decided to try and catch up with him to walk him home, and Georg's kindness had saved Conrad's life.

It had taken Georg a few minutes to realize that Conrad had not taken the main road and after cutting up several side streets, Georg had emerged just in time to see Albert Witbooi attack him. Georg had run to Conrad's rescue as fast as he could, firing his pistol at Albert as he ran.

"Good thing you didn't have a broomhandle, Major Huber," Lieutenant Protz said as Georg retold the story to the other officers over cards later that night. "If you hadn't had that fancy Luger, you'd most likely have shot Herr Huber before the Witbooi bastard got to him."

Conrad had told Georg who Albert was to spare his cousin's reputation from von Trotha's wrath. An armed Hottentot evading Georg's patrols and assaulting a German citizen in the colony's capital would have been an inexcusable fault on Georg's command and could have easily gotten his cousin sent back to the rear ranks.

However, the killing of a high-profile insurgent was a different matter. When von Trotha learned that Georg had killed Hendrik Witbooi's adopted son, the General seemed to excuse the matter of Albert's presence in Windhoek entirely.

The more the General learned about the incident, the more he saw that Albert had been no ordinary Hottentot, but a savage, cunning warrior who was the son of the colony's last remaining rebel. Georg had bested him, and that made Georg an even greater hero than before. Conrad would not be surprised if Georg received another medal within the week.

After he'd made his report to the General, Georg had eventually left Conrad alone to rest. But he returned to the Residence later that evening with a coach he'd rented from Mayor Grober, at no small expense Conrad was sure, to bring Conrad to Alte Feste to join in the officers' card game. Conrad had not really wanted to go, but there was very little point in saying so. Besides the money Georg had already spent on such a luxury, Conrad had done nothing but lie in his bed for hours, numb.

The Residence made him think of Sybille. She was gone and he had failed her. Nothing really mattered anymore, and in a daze Conrad had allowed Georg to fling open his screen door, fetch his cane, and help him up into the coach.

The Schutztruppe officers truly were terrible poker players. Conrad himself barely understood much more than the fundamentals of the game, but his own initial stack of marks had grown considerably while he'd half-heartedly managed to collect a few sets of threes and a flush. American poker was not Georg's strong suit either, though between several helpings of Protz's liquor and several crude jokes from Colonel Knef, he seemed to be having a marvelous time.

"You doing all right then, Herr Huber?" Captain Jund asked Conrad after a few hands.

The rest of the officers were all howling at Colonel Knef's impersonation of a famous prostitute in Walvis Bay, known to the brothel's patrons as "Fat Black

242

Mary." Captain Jund, who usually did not understand a good deal of Knef's jokes, had chosen to sit beside Conrad at the card table.

"I get by," Conrad replied, forcing a smile in return for Jund's attempt. "Most days are not nearly so exciting as today. Are you glad to be back in Windhoek, Captain?"

Georg had reassigned Jund from active patrol duty the week before. Conrad didn't have the slightest idea what his cousin had Jund doing now, but he couldn't envision Georg granting the gopher captain a very important post.

"Yes, I am," Jund said blankly.

Conrad didn't know if Jund was attempting to mask some unhappiness or if the Captain really did not have anything else to say on the matter. Jund was clearly not as drunk as the rest of the officers and for a moment, Conrad almost felt a soft pang of pity for Baumhauer's old lackey.

On paper, Captain Jund was one of the most senior men in the room. But that fact was lost on everyone else. Georg had invited some fellow officers from the division to join their game, and these men had readily mingled with Protz and Knef, who Captain Jund outranked, but most avoided Jund himself. So Jund was consigned to keeping Conrad company, which was proving to be a difficult task for them both.

"The depot's not so bad," Jund said quietly to Conrad after some time. "Lots of people to talk to there, and the work's not so hard."

Ah, Conrad thought to himself. Georg had delegated his predecessor to run the Windhoek train station's customs office. It was not a prestigious post, but Jund's recent experience in transporting the army's artillery by railroad was at least an understandable reason to dispatch him to the depot office. It was a demotion to be sure, but not an unreasonably humiliating one.

"Connie," Georg called loudly from across the table. "It's your bid, if we're not keeping you from something?"

Conrad apologized and tossed in a few minor chips, not even bothering to look at his cards this time around. He thought he had a pair of sixes, but he honestly couldn't remember when he'd even picked up his hand.

It was Jund's turn next. The man looked at his cards for several minutes, receiving several impatient jeers from the other men as he did so, before he finally folded. Captain Jund's original pile of chips had been hemorrhaging heavily throughout the game, and Conrad supposed that Jund was simply trying to avoid losing any more money than he already had.

Conrad had glimpsed some of Jund's cards and watched as Jund folded with two queens and three nines. He wondered fleetingly through his own gloom if Jund even knew how to play poker.

The rest of the hands passed without too much excitement. After a while, one of the invited division officers produced a cabinet box of cigars, which were distributed eagerly among the card table. Such a delicacy was a rare treat for the provincial officers, and it did not take long for Georg's office to be filled with the warm, aromatic smoke that even Conrad found comforting, despite his asthma.

"Damn shame you couldn't have shot King Witbooi himself, Huber," one of the division officers said after a long puff. "The General's deploying our battalion down south soon to help chase the monkey king, and I'll be sweating my ass off trouncing through sagebrush for the next few months."

Georg took a few puffs on his own cigar with a wide grin.

"Yes, it will be a real shame not to have you around, Ulrich," Georg said. "You're almost as bad at this game as Jund over there. I could afford to retire in a month if you stayed put!"

That got a round of laughs from everyone, even Jund, though Conrad did not think the man understood that he'd been insulted too.

"He's right," said another of the division officers seated across from Conrad as he refilled his glass. "Our battalion hasn't seen any action since we rounded up that group of Hottentot women in the desert a few weeks back."

The smoke from Conrad's cigar stuck in his throat, sending him into a wild coughing fit that took several moments to subside. Jund struck him hard on the back, which sent a spasm of pain down Conrad's side and did little to help his coughing.

"You alright, Herr Huber?" the officer who'd provided the cigars asked. "Not your first smoke, is it?"

The man had a soft, mild voice and wore a uniform with cornflower blue shoulder boards and silver epaulets that matched Conrad's own. He was a captain then, in one of Colonel Voigt's dragoon companies, Conrad thought. He recognized the man's face and seemed to remember meeting him briefly on the train deployment to Waterberg. He had also been one of the young officers near Georg who had cheered so thunderously during von Trotha's speech. Conrad thought the man's name was Tobias, but he couldn't recall for certain.

"Fine, fine," he said, recovering himself somewhat. "Just got a little smoke down the wrong pipe. *Danke.*"

"Connie's always had weak lungs," Georg laughed at the other end of the table. "His father made him sweep the floors of the chapel one too many times. I swear he's had a decade of pew dust stuck in his throat for as long as I can remember!"

All the other officers laughed, and Conrad smiled politely. When the laughter died down somewhat, Conrad turned back to Tobias.

He hesitated a moment and grabbed one of the near-empty liquor bottles to cover up the sudden shaking in his hands. He poured a little more of the dark liquor into his already full glass.

It was foolish to raise his hopes. Albert had told him that Sybille was dead. But Conrad was drunk and dizzy from the smoke, and Captain Tobias had offered him a chance to believe that she was still alive, if only for a few more minutes.

"You were saying something about a group of native women in the desert, Captain?" Conrad asked as casually as he could manage. "Were they fleeing Herero, do you think?"

"I think so," Tobias said, paying more attention to the cards in his hand than to Conrad's question. "Can't tell the damn difference, but they were a good way out east when we caught 'em."

Conrad pretended to contemplate his own cards for a time, maneuvering a two pair to the middle of his hand to feign interest in the game. The other end of the table had resumed their own conversation, and Conrad took a chance to press Tobias further.

"What did you do with these women?" Conrad asked. "Did you…kill them?"

Once the words had left his mouth, Conrad immediately regretted them. With a simple offhand comment, Tobias had brought Sybille back to life. Yet now Conrad's owns words were endangering her life all over again. His stomach lurched forward as Tobias scratched his chin and took a few, long puffs on his cigar as he thoughtfully fingered two chips. Until he spoke, Sybille might just be alive! But once he did, Conrad's question exposed her to death or far worse fates.

Conrad's voice had cracked slightly when he'd spoken, and he feared he might've betrayed himself. He was more animated now than he'd been in weeks. From across the table Georg raised a curious eyebrow at him, but Tobias and the other officers did not seem to notice the sudden change in him.

"Not that bunch," Tobias said, stoically deciding to toss both chips into the pot. "All intact for the most part, so Colonel Voigt sent 'em down to Shark Island."

Tobias sipped his drink before chuckling and nudging Ulrich in the ribcage.

"Oddest Negress I ever saw in that group," he said with a smile. "She must've been over two meters tall at least, with eyes like ice shards. And I'll remember her forever too, because the bitch nearly gutted Ulrich with a knife she had up her sleeve when the idiot thought he'd hump her before we handed her over to Voigt! Go on, Ulrich! Show us the scar!"

Ulrich feigned reluctance for a moment, and then laughed along with the others as he rolled up his shirt to reveal a nasty looking, half-healed cut along his stomach.

"Never seen a Negress with blue eyes before," Ulrich said with a wicked grin. "Thought I'd *introduce* myself…"

"She gashed him with the knife when he had his trousers half-off!" Tobias roared.

That brought a chorus of even wilder laughter from the rest of the officers. All the men demanded to see Ulrich's scar up-close, and the Captain complied eagerly as though it were a badge of honor.

Conrad felt his ears begin to steam, but he managed to restrain himself and hold his seat. The blue-eyed Herero woman *had* to be Sybille, and if she was still alive then Conrad would not do her any good by launching himself across the card table and trying to throttle Tobias and Ulrich. The two division captains had seen her, and if Conrad had any hope of reaching Sybille, then he had to keep his head.

"Shark Island?" Conrad asked when most of the laughter had died down. "That's one I haven't heard of before. Is that what they're calling the new camp outside of Mariental?"

"Nah," replied Ulrich, rolling his shirt back down gingerly over the scar. "Mariental wasn't open yet when we brought that bunch in. Shark Island's down further south outside of Lüderitz. It's where Voigt's been sending all his troublemakers as of late. I struck that Negress bitch across the face with the butt of my pistol and sent her down to there to rot."

Georg let out an entertaining snarl from the other end of the table. He stood to wave his rear end seductively at Ulrich as though he were an enormous ape. The other men howled with laughter as Ulrich drunkenly stumbled around the room after Georg, who kept calling to Ulrich in garbled grunts. All the officers cheered the two men on, but Conrad barely heard them. He felt a few tears roll down his face.

Sybille was alive!

The rest of the evening passed in a sluggish haze. The card game went on well into the night, and Conrad feared that it would continue well into the next morning. At some point after midnight, Protz's liquor supply at last ran dry, and as the other officers teetered out of Georg's office, Conrad was forced to stay behind while Georg mustered enough sobriety to send for the coachman to ferry Conrad back to Schwerinsburg.

Whoever Georg had sent to fetch the coachman did not appear to be in any kind of a hurry, and for a while Conrad was left to sit in the smoky fog of the office alone and wonder if Georg had fallen asleep in his desk chair.

After several minutes of staring into the dark, Georg finally stirred himself and turned to speak to Conrad.

"You alright, Connie?" he asked, sounding groggy but more clearheaded than Conrad had expected. "Apart from being nearly murdered today, I mean?"

Georg paused a moment, and then laughed stutteringly at his own joke.

"But seriously," Georg asked again once he'd regained himself somewhat. "Are you alright? You seemed…distant tonight. Except when you were talking with Ulrich and Tobias, come to think of it."

Conrad felt a thrill of fear rise up in his chest. Had he been more obvious in his questioning than he'd thought? Was Georg just drunk or was he suspicious?

"I'm alright," Conrad replied, trying to think of something to say despite the alcohol and tobacco mangling his thoughts. "I was thinking about what you said this afternoon. I think I might put in for a holiday. Ulrich and Tobias suggested I go to Lüderitz to see the seals. They're supposed to be calving soon, and I've got an acquaintance in Lüderitz that I met on the passage from Germany I've been meaning to visit."

"Good for you, Connie!" Georg bellowed drunkenly from his chair. "You *deserve* a holiday. I knew tonight would be good for you!"

Georg then promptly fell over and began to snore as soon as his head hit his desk. Conrad knew that his cousin would somehow force himself awake in a few hours and scrub himself spotless. Georg never seemed to get hangovers, or if he did, he simply ignored them.

It was another half an hour before one of the Schutztruppe grooms returned with the bleary-eyed coachman Georg had rented, but Conrad didn't care. Sitting alone in the dark, with the glow of Protz's spirits keeping him warm, Conrad felt more alive than he had in months.

The blue-eyed Herero that Ulrich and Tobias had captured had to be Sybille. It *had* to be. And now, at last, Conrad knew where to find her.

CHAPTER 13

NOVEMBER 1904

Lüderitz was a charming, sleepy port that looked as though it had been built by fairies. The colorful town was perched on top of long shelves of rock that stretched along the coast of a glove-shaped bay. Nestled between the scorching Namib Desert on one side and the wind-swept southern coast on the other, the town's box-shaped houses stood pleasantly oblivious to the elements, dotting the stony hills in extravagant hues of pink, green, yellow and blue.

German traders had constructed Lüderitz around an old missionary outpost, hoping that they might establish a port city to compete with the British Cape Colony. But the Europeans had misjudged the power of the unpredictable winds that swept the shallow bay at whim, churning violent waves that made their port unnavigable to all but a small, brave fleet of seal hunters and fishermen.

A humble Lutheran church overlooked the odd town from a high rock, its tall wooden frame casting a shepherding gaze over the paintbox town below. Behind the churchyard, the crag descended precariously to a saw-toothed beach, home to thousands of fur seals.

The seals were a pleasant addition to the town in the afternoons when they lay, leathery and lazy, sunning their great, brown bellies on the beaches. Yet in the mornings, their barking caused such an overpowering commotion that the town's minister was often forced to postpone Sunday services until the majority of the seals had slid back into the ocean for their daily hunt.

This hilarity was only topped in the evenings when several turned-around seals mistook the town's wharf for their beach and wobbled confusedly down Lüderitz's residential streets, popping their whiskered faces into storefront and café windows.

It was an unusual town, but a charming one. And it seemed an odd choice for a prison camp.

The people Conrad met as he stepped off the early-morning train were friendly and relaxed. It was as if the Nama insurgency that gripped the rest of the south in a panic and had paralyzed the colony's coal supply did not exist here. Nearly everyone in Lüderitz was German, though Conrad did hear a few snippets of Afrikaans and English as he walked along the docks. He'd seen almost no natives since he'd arrived, only a handful of Kavango fishermen who kept their heads down, staring at their nets as he passed.

As Georg had predicted, von Trotha had approved Conrad's request for a holiday without any trouble, and Conrad had been granted a full week's leave.

It had taken three of those days for Conrad to make the necessary travel arrangements and form his cover story. As far as von Trotha and his staff at Schwerinsburg knew, Conrad was traveling to Lüderitz to visit Dr. Eugen Fischer, the immaculately dressed professor from the University of Freiburg Conrad had met the year before aboard the *Calypso*. Though Fischer himself knew nothing of this arrangement.

Conrad had been tempted to telegraph Fischer and ask to stay with the man for a night or two. It would have been nice, soothing even, to pretend for a time that nothing had changed since he had first stepped off the deck of the *Calypso*. Yet Conrad had come to Lüderitz on a mission, and he could not afford to stray now, no matter how inviting Fischer's company seemed.

As he strolled down Lüderitz's main *platz*, Conrad thought it would probably be better if he avoided Fischer altogether. It would be difficult to detach himself from the man if they happened to run into one another, and Conrad did not want to jeopardize his mission. He had fooled Georg and the General as to why he had come south, but Conrad was not so sure he could fool the doctor.

An hour later, as Conrad paced along the deck of the small ferry that ran between Lüderitz and the island, he saw several large black and gray fins glide menacingly through the rough waves. Shark Island was nothing if not aptly named.

Once, a colossal shadow rose up without warning just inches beside the boat, scattering the school of smaller sharks like rats. Conrad pushed back from the ferry's flimsy railing as a lone white fin broke through the surf. The shadow beneath the great fin was nearly seven meters long, and it rocked the bow as it propelled itself effortlessly through the rough water.

"Great White," a weathered English deckhand told Conrad gruffly as he passed by, crossing himself as he did so. "Devil's fish is what they are. Swallow a man whole when they get big enough and rip one apart when they ain't."

The shark stayed with the ferry a moment longer before slipping silently beneath the waves where its shadowy outline disappeared as quickly as it had surfaced.

"How many of those things are down there?" Conrad asked the man over the roar of the wind.

Conrad's heart was pounding in his ears as he imagined himself tossed overboard by a cruel wave, not knowing how many of those monsters were gliding, unseen and hungry, toward him.

"Dunno," the deckhand responded. "That's the scary part, in'it? Usually, the bigger ones like that stick to the mainland beaches to gobble up the seals. Lots of littler ones in the shallows, though. Lots of Zambis near the island that wait for the swimmers."

Conrad was not sure he'd heard the man correctly. Surely no one swam in these waters? The current was rough enough, and the wind was so sharp, Conrad thought the water must be freezing. But before Conrad could ask the man what he'd meant, he'd scurried away.

When the ferry finally reached the wooden wharf on the island, Conrad practically flung himself onto it. He could not see much further below than the surface of the dark blue waters everyone assured him were shallow. When the other passengers had disembarked, he nearly ran across the gangplank for fear of being devoured by whatever a "Zambi" was.

The island itself was small. Only about a hundred acres altogether, it rose out of the water like a misshapen turtle's shell. The rocky ground was permanently damp from sea spray, and it stuck to Conrad's leather shoes in large, sodden clumps.

After the terror of the ferry crossing, Conrad was surprised to see a colony of small penguins waddling carelessly near the docks. Several German families were clustered around the end of the dock, their children giggling wildly as they ran down the beach, mimicking the penguins' bizarre walk. Conrad saw a vendor doling out chucks of stale bread, and a few of the families stopped to purchase scraps to feed the birds. Many families had brought picnics, and no one seemed the least bit perturbed by the presence of so many sharks lurking just a few meters offshore.

What an odd place, Conrad thought.

The presence of the German families gave Conrad hope. If people brought their children to Shark Island to play with penguins and stroll along the beaches, how terrible could a prison camp here be?

Conrad waved farewell to the ferry captain. The same captain made the trip back and forth between the mainland several times a day and assured Conrad it would be no trouble to get back to Lüderitz in the evening. It was only mid-morning, and he'd be ferrying families back and forth to the penguin beaches until at least half-past four.

Plenty of time, Conrad thought. Now, I just need to find the camp.

Conrad could see the extent of the island's coast in either direction, but he saw no trace of a camp containing Herero prisoners. Perhaps he'd come to the wrong island. He looked back out at the surrounding sea; there was no other land mass in any direction. This had to be the right place.

He turned back to families on the beach.

At the end of the dock, Conrad could see the small penguins running eagerly towards a cluster of German children, their flippers flapping comically behind them. One of the bolder penguins reached the children first and snatched a piece of bread out of a young boy's hand. The child squealed in delight.

Conrad was watching the little boy and the penguins as he walked toward the beach, and without paying attention to where he was going, he collided with another man heading the opposite way. Both men staggered backward, and Conrad dropped his cane. Conrad lost his footing, and the other man reached out to steady him. As Conrad recovered himself, he looked up to apologize and found himself staring into the smartly trimmed beard of Dr. Fischer.

"Conrad!" Fischer exclaimed. "What a delight to see you again! What in God's name are you doing all the way out here? I was beginning to think the Colonial Office was averse to their employees taking holidays!"

Dr. Fischer had kept up his acquaintanceship with Conrad for the past year, sending him a telegram at Christmas and writing a few short letters once or twice a month inquiring after his health and happiness. He'd also reextended Conrad several invitations to come and stay with him in Lüderitz. Conrad had still been dealing with the aftermath of the Grootfontein railroad bombing when Dr. Fischer had first invited him. Their correspondence had fallen off completely during the Herero and Nama insurgency.

"Dr. Fischer!" Conrad replied with nervous surprise.

Conrad was wearing his division uniform and was immediately glad that he'd chosen to do so. He'd been fabricating his story to tell the Shark Island camp guards for days, but in the shock of running into Dr. Fischer, it had taken Conrad a moment to remember it.

"It's great to see you as well, Doctor," he managed to say. "I'm here on official business for General von Trotha. He's asked me to inspect the new southern camps, make sure they're secure before the division shifts its focus toward quelling the Nama. Can't have any more prison riots like the one the Witboois started in Windhoek. I'm here to inspect the Shark Island camp, but it looks as though I've come to the wrong island."

Fischer smiled pleasantly as he straightened his black suit jacket and picked up Conrad's cane off the dock.

"The General's got a sound mind," Fischer said as he handed Conrad back his cane. "I'm sure he'll make a fine Commissioner once this mess with the natives is sorted out. Some nasty fighting further inland, I hear, but we've been spared it in Lüderitz, praise God."

Dr. Fischer gave Conrad a brief once-over and a fond nod as he noticed the silver epaulets on Conrad's shoulders.

"I see they've put you in uniform, Conrad," he said with admiration in his voice. "You must've been promoted. Congratulations! I assure you, you've come to the right place. The camp's not far; it's just over the ridge there. I'm returning there in a few minutes, if you care to join me? I just have to pick up a parcel I asked the ferry captain to fetch in town for me. Do you mind a steep climb? I'd heard you were wounded at Waterberg…"

Conrad waited while Fischer collected his package from the ferryman, followed the wiry doctor off the dock, and up a winding dirt path away from the beach.

The trek to the island ridge was indeed steep, but Fischer walked at an accommodating pace. They made polite small talk as they climbed up the well-cleared trail, leaving the picnicking families behind them. The wind grew stronger the higher they climbed, and Conrad felt as though he needed to shout at Fischer even though the man was right beside him.

"What brings you to the Shark Island prison, Dr. Fischer?" Conrad asked over the continuous howling. "Are you a friend of the guard captain?"

"Captain Abel and I have developed a professional courtesy, I suppose you might say," Fischer replied, holding his hat firmly against his head as they climbed. "But I'm on Shark Island conducting my research. I believe Dr. Mollison and I are on the verge of proving our theories. It's been a very long expedition, but once I get back to the university…ah, here we are!"

The trail fell away without warning as Conrad crested the ridge. Below them lay an exposed beach alcove, devoid of any of the protective rock outcroppings scattered along the tourist beaches near the pier.

Amidst the wind and heavy swells below stood a few Schutztruppe guard houses dotting the beach like miniature dunes. From where he stood, Conrad could also just make out clusters of pitiful, broken shelters of torn canvas and driftwood strewn haphazardly along the sand. Marking the entrance to the camp was an iron gate already beginning to rust under the strain of the damp air. Long rows of barbed wire stretched out from the gate, encircling the camp like the boundaries of a half-washed-away sandcastle.

The officer in charge of the camp met them at the gate as they came down the ridge. Captain Lars Abel was a young, mean-looking man whose freckled face was half concealed beneath a tangled, ginger beard. His uniform was clean, though it was noticeably wrinkled and off-color from long patrols in the thick salt air.

The captain bore the aggrieved complexion of a young man who had joined the colonial forces seeking adventure but who, through some twist of fate or failed rivalry, had been deposited in a far-off outpost and long since forgotten.

Captain Abel greeted Dr. Fischer warmly but cast a wary gaze at Conrad's uniform. Abel was about as thin as Conrad but stood nearly a foot shorter. The small man stuck out his chest and looked as though he intended to make a show of questioning Conrad, much like a dachshund might have asked a Doberman what business it had on the dachshund's porch.

Conrad noticed a sjambok looped loosely through Abel's belt and cast a brief glance at its worn leather handle. It seemed evident that the captain used the whip often.

"Herr Conrad Huber," Conrad introduced himself before Abel could speak. "Chief Expert of the Imperial Colony of German Southwest Africa, and personal aide to Commissioner-General Lothar von Trotha."

Conrad knew he must sound pompous to Dr. Fischer and the small cluster of men at the gate, but he didn't care. He'd come all this way to search for Sybille, and he was not going to be impeded by the likes of Captain Abel.

Conrad's pomp had its intended effect. Captain Abel's attitude shifted immediately. Mention of the famous von Trotha had garnered Conrad instant authority over Abel, and the guard captain shook his hand eagerly, thrilled beyond disguise to have a representative of the General come to see him.

"Of course, of course!" Abel said, pumping Conrad's arm vigorously. "How can I be of service, Herr Huber? Has Lüderitz fallen under siege?"

Conrad could see the desire in Abel's eyes. Clearly, the man would not have minded if Lüderitz was on fire. Anything to get him out of his current miserable post.

Conrad had counted on having to deal with his sudden and unexpected presence at the camp, and he had his speech for Captain Abel well-prepared. But Dr. Fischer's presence made him nervous. Von Trotha knew nothing of Conrad's visit to Shark Island, and Conrad thought that a Schutztruppe officer in a remote, southern camp would not stop to question his story. Dr. Fischer was another matter, however, and Conrad was now gambling that the professor would not find anything suspicious in Conrad's sudden appearance and dubious authority.

"Lüderitz is sound, Captain," Conrad replied, assuming an impatient air. "I am here on orders from General von Trotha to inspect the Schutztruppe's management of the new southern camps. I'm to evaluate them and their commanding officers for a report back to the General."

Captain Abel's eyes went wide, just as Conrad had hoped they would. Von Trotha was notorious for rooting out officers who did not meet his high standards, but he was also known for rewarding skill and initiative when he saw it. Georg was a perfect example of how quickly von Trotha's favorites could climb. Abel must've known this too, for all at once he became flushed with a desire to impress Conrad.

"My pleasure, Herr Huber," Captain Abel said, motioning for two other guards to open the gate. "Welcome to Shark Island. I'm sure your trip was exhausting, bouncing around on that old ferry. I've been telling her captain for months now to scuttle her and buy something more suitable to transport all those families in.

"Will you allow me to offer you some refreshments in my office before you begin your inspection? Afterward, it would be my pleasure to personally give you a tour of the grounds. Dr. Fischer, would you care to join us? I'm sure Herr Huber would be interested to hear about your research and the Schutztruppe's small contributions to your efforts."

"I'd be delighted," Fischer said, ignoring Abel's obvious plea for an endorsement. "Do you have a preference in refreshment, Conrad? It's not Schwerinsburg, but you'd be surprised what Abel keeps secreted away on this island."

Conrad followed Dr. Fischer and Captain Abel into the camp, craning his neck to try and catch a glimpse of the prisoners. The strength to restrain himself was ebbing. Sybille was here. She *had* to be. He wanted to shout out her name and run along the beach, calling for her.

"I'm on duty unfortunately," Conrad replied a bit tartly. "Redbush tea, please."

The sand grew soft without warning and Conrad nearly lost his footing as he took his first step inside the camp. He steadied himself with his cane and began to limp along the beach as the gate swung shut behind him.

*

The camp had seemed small from the top of the ridge. However, once he was inside, Conrad realized that the alcove beach was much larger than he'd first thought. And it was crammed beyond imagination with well over a thousand Herero.

After enduring half an hour of aimless prattle from Captain Abel about everything from whether Conrad had gotten a chance yet to try the roasted gemsbok served in town at Café Wilhelm to avid calls for a description of what had happened at the Battle of Waterberg, Conrad was at last given a tour of the Shark Island camp.

He had never been *inside* a camp before. He had peered in through the barbed wire of the Iron Palace in Windhoek enough times that he had thought he had some idea of what to expect.

But Shark Island was different. Conrad had been expecting the squalor and the long, pained stares of native faces. But as he strolled the spray-churned beach alongside Captain Abel, his gut twisted with every step as they passed into a landscape of utter horror.

Shark Island was not a prison camp. It was a death camp.

The Herero had lived their entire lives in the arid hinterlands and vast plateaus of the colony. Shark Island was a wave-beaten bastille, crudely maintained and exposed to constant bone-chilling gales. What little shelter the Herero had managed to construct for themselves lay ramshackle across the oozing muck as though each of them was the sole survivor of some great and terrible shipwreck.

The Herero themselves were rotting. Unseasoned against the conditions on the island, each bowed, shrunken face that Conrad searched was fetid and pale. The bodies of all the men, women, and children were rancid as though their flesh had been drowned in the sea and then been draped carelessly back over their bones, ready to fall lifelessly away at any moment. Cuts did not heal in the damp, and Conrad saw hands, feet, backs, and shoulders covered in festering sores.

As Captain Abel led them along the camp's outer fence toward the water, the Herero shrunk away in lethargic panic. Some, having nowhere to escape to, crumpled over in heaps and began whimpering with their arms wrapped protectively over their faces, cowering like beaten animals.

The Herero were little more than hollowed shells. They seemed like people who had been human once but whose minds had now dissolved into feral submission under the unbearable strain of constant abuse. There were well over a thousand Herero pressed into the confines of Shark Island, and Conrad had only seen a handful of Schutztruppe guards since he'd arrived. There could not have been more than thirty in the entire camp. If the Herero simply swarmed their captors, the guards would be torn to shreds in minutes. Yet every native scurried away from the young Captain Abel, shoving friend, family, and child alike out of their way.

Abel strode at ease amongst the Herero masses like the unchallenged tyrant of the island. He seemed to guess Conrad's thoughts and spoke proudly as he pulled his sjambok from his belt and brandished it casually before a group of Herero who had not been able to flee fast enough.

"Rest assured, Herr Huber," Captain Abel said as the remaining Herero cowered before him. "You're perfectly safe here. Shark Island may be a small garrison, but we know how to keep these Hottentots under control. A credit, which I'm sure will be mentioned in your findings, Dr. Fischer?"

"Indeed, Captain," Fischer replied, somewhat put out by Abel's continued badgering. "I will make sure you and your men's contributions are properly credited in any of our future publications."

The two men spoke so plainly, with the group of broken Herero shivering beneath them, that Conrad could only stare at them in blind shock.

Dr. Fischer mistook Conrad's stare for a sign of interest in his research.

"You see, Conrad," Dr. Fischer began, oblivious to the prostrated Herero just two steps away. "I've been studying the merits of subhuman races as they might pertain to the advancement of more civilized peoples. The natives of this colony possess a few remarkable traits. Primitive strength and endurance mostly, yet remarkable traits all the same.

"Dr. Mollison and I set out on this expedition to test whether some of these traits might be transferrable through controlled interbreeding. A few of my colleagues back at the Institute have postulated that primitive races are only primitive because of their isolation, but I believe that I'm on the cusp of proving that savages like the Herero are *genetically* limited in their ability to become civilized.

"Therefore, they must belong to a class of subhuman, much like the natives of the Americas and Australia. But if there were a way to isolate traits and pass along only the desired ones to civilized offspring, can you imagine what a boon that would be for Germany? A society of superhumans could be achievable within a generation!"

Dr. Fischer grew excited as he spoke but maintained a polite civility that was nearly drowned out by the roar of the crashing surf.

"I came to Southwest Africa because there were plenty of specimens to study: the *mischling* offspring of German soldiers and indigenous women. I had hoped that there would be evidence to support that a superior seed might overcome a savage womb yet allow the offspring to retain its primitive desirables.

"But, alas, the mixed offspring I've observed throughout the colony are unruly and dense, as savage and primordial as the dams. There's more research to be done on the subject, of course, but I believe I'm prepared to recommend against mixed-race coupling. No matter the sire, the offspring is always more savage than not."

Fischer paused a moment to check the time on his watch as though waiting for some important news.

"However, Dr. Mollison and I have had a marvelous breakthrough in our secondary research," Fischer continued. "Have you ever heard of Sir Francis Galton's work on the subhuman races?"

Conrad could only shake his head numbly, his eyes fixed on the cowering Herero, who had still not dared to move.

"He's an insufferable Englishman, to be sure," Fischer went on. "And his lectures leave a great deal to be desired. But he's one of my colleagues back at the University, and he's all but proven the existence of inferior races through statistical metrics. Bone length, circumference of the head, and the like. It's all still in development, but Sir Galton and I believe we could soon use forensics to document potential intelligence in newborns. Imagine knowing the extent of your child's potential and limitations on the day he was born?"

In front of them, one of the Herero made an involuntary whimpering noise against the sting of the wind, and Captain Able turned on a dime and kicked the man hard in the ribs.

The man was so thin that Conrad was sure the blow must've shattered his ribcage. The other Herero didn't make a sound as the Captain drew his sjambok from his belt and thrashed it menacingly.

Abel barked at the group and held their terrified gaze a moment longer before returning his weapon to his belt. Then he turned back to Dr. Fischer, and the two of them continued to chat about Fischer's research. Conrad did not hear a word they said.

The other Herero, mere scarecrows themselves, tried half-heartedly to lift the fallen man, but they were so weak that they could not move him an inch. Abel suddenly turned back around as though he had been expecting this, and the other Herero abandoned the fallen man and scattered along the beach.

"Insects," he said disdainfully as he stepped over the fallen Herero man and beckoned for Conrad and Dr. Fischer to follow him.

Conrad could not be sure, but he thought the Herero man had stopped breathing.

Conrad's head was spinning. He felt as though he were observing everything through a thick pane of glass. He stood frozen in place, the gruesome images of the camp passing through the frame, reflected in a contorted, distant display that he could not escape.

He had seen men beaten. He had witnessed Herero being shot at and mowed down by cannons and Maxim guns at Waterberg. That was a kind of violence he could understand. It was a war, after all. He'd survived the horrors of the battlefield and had read so many morbid reports—had so many nightmares and dark thoughts—that he had thought himself hardened.

Yet what he saw as he followed Captain Abel along the western fence line of the camp went beyond the savagery of soldiers, beyond what he could even remotely understand.

The Herero moved, if they could move, like phantoms, drained of all meaningful signs of life, but anchored miserably to Shark Island by their bodies' stubborn will to survive. A small child lay whimpering near the fence, its back slashed into a bloodied mess, with no one daring to venture out to comfort it. The child's face was bruised and cut so horribly that Conrad could not tell if he or she still possessed a nose.

Nearby, a laughing guard tossed the remnants of his lunch to a cluster of starving men. They did not move to snatch it up as Conrad expected but stood staring at the sand-covered morsels, each of them too afraid of the guard's whip to risk claiming them.

Sören Baumhauer had been malicious, even cruel, but the late Major's wrath seemed a distant blessing to the Herero now. Conrad saw everything in front of him, but he could not believe that any of it was real.

It would have been so much better, Conrad thought in detached shock, if Colonel Voigt had ordered them all shot.

Captain Abel continued to speak, too preoccupied with his lengthy explanations to notice that Conrad could no longer hear him.

"The boats arrive on our dock here in the cove, so as not to interfere with the regular ferry traffic for the rest of the island. Depending on the influx of Hottentots from the north, I usually send a hundred and twenty to a hundred and fifty of the stronger ones back to the mainland every week to dig out the track for the new railroad to Aus. I could send more to expedite the construction, but we have not been able to locate a large enough boat to carry any more in the hold.

"Another hundred or so go to help upkeep the Lüderitz harbor from time to time. The foremen have to use explosives occasionally, so I rarely get more than half my numbers back. I don't suppose you might know if General von Trotha might be persuaded to part with a cargo vessel or two once the Nama campaign has ended, Herr Huber? I've heard he has license from Berlin to rent such resources from Walvis Bay and the British Cape Colony. There are more profits to be had for the colony if I could send more of the Negroes to the railroad. Their overseers pay much more than the odd-job sewing or textile contracts that sometimes float in."

The three of them reached the end of the western fence where the wire gave way to an impenetrable wall of rock, a high cliff that rose like a guard tower before them. The sand beneath Conrad's feet softened even further, and his soft shoes sank deeply into the low-tide muck. From where they stood, Conrad could see the other end of the cove, flanked by another equally imposing bluff. The rock was far too steep to climb, and it descended so slowly into the ocean that its formidable precipice stretched several meters out into the dark blue water.

"There's no fence along the beach," Conrad noted absently.

It was a statement rather than a question, a simple utterance to ground himself in something other than the decay and dread engulfing him.

"Indeed," Captain Abel said, leaping at another chance to explain the camp's design. "A schematic of my own design, Herr Huber. The cliffs are too steep to climb, and they seal off the edges of the cove quite nicely. No prisoner can get around them without swimming at least four hundred meters out to sea, and from there, the only other beach is on the far side of the island. We could put up a fence, but exposing it to the elements would be a costly waste. It would likely rust in days. Besides, the Zambis are the best guards in my unit, and I don't have to pay them a thing!"

Abel laughed at his own joke, and Dr. Fischer chuckled politely as though he'd heard the jest a dozen times before. Conrad recalled the English hand's words about Zambis waiting for swimmers, but he did not fully grasp Abel's joke until he caught sight of a stout, dark fin cutting across the water just beyond the end of the cliffs. The fin was much shorter than the great whites he'd seen on the ferry; he could just barely see its outline cresting over the top of the waves. Yet it moved more swiftly, swimming back and forth across the mouth of the cove as though it were pacing in angry anticipation.

"Every new lot I get in always has a few who think they can make it back to the main shoreline," Abel explained to Conrad. "Sometimes it takes only a few days, sometimes it takes a week or more, but sooner or later, one of them always swims. Keeps my men entertained to place bets on which of the new ones will be the one to try it. Haven't had a swimmer in about six days now, so we're due. I bet that poor Zambi out there is starving."

Conrad could see the African coast that lay enticingly beyond the circling shark fin. He could only imagine how much closer the mainland beaches must seem after days of brutality, hunger and fear.

The shark at the edge of the cove was doing nothing to conceal itself. Its confidence in the appearance of another meal was absolute.

Conrad wondered if the swimmers simply stopped seeing the fin in their desperation or if they welcomed it as a merciful end to the torments they'd endured. The Herero came from the inland plains. Conrad could not imagine any of them being strong enough swimmers to reach the coast. They would either drown trying or fall prey to one of the sleek creatures lying in wait beneath the waves.

At some point, Conrad felt his feet shuffling away from the water's edge. He was flanked on either side by the doctor and the Captain, giving vague, lifeless answers to questions he did not hear. The two men guided him across the beach, taking turns regaling Conrad with their work, Abel asking him every minute or so if he thought von Trotha could be persuaded to send him more resources.

As they walked back toward the center of the camp, a white man's huddled frame emerged from one of the guard houses.

"Dr. Mollison!" Fischer hailed as they walked toward the Schutztruppe bunker. "Conrad, may I have the pleasure of finally introducing you to Dr. Theodor Mollison? He was too seasick to bother with decent manners on the *Calypso*, but I think you'll find his mood has improved after a year on dry land."

Theodor Mollison was a thin, balding man who would've been considered quite ugly, save that he hid his appearance behind a broad smile and an eager gait.

"Delighted to finally meet you, Herr Huber," Mollison said as he took Conrad's hand from his side and shook it warmly.

Despite the chill of the winds, Mollison was sweating heavily, and he dabbed at his face with a handkerchief as he spoke.

"You've picked the perfect day for your visit," Mollison continued. "Our specimens are finally ready to travel."

"Really?" Dr. Fischer asked readily. "I thought they were still a few days away from your estimates?"

"Hard to gauge anything with all the salt in the air," Mollison responded, equally excited. "But as of this morning, I believe we're finally gotten a batch to stick. We can arrange transportation in Lüderitz this evening. Come and see for yourselves, Gentlemen!"

Mollison led them inside the barracks with Captain Abel trailing behind, explaining as they ducked inside how he had graciously converted the building —at his own expense—to accommodate the needs of the doctors' research.

The interior of the barracks had been stripped of all its furnishings, save for a single worktable and two writing desks that Conrad presumed belonged to Fischer and Mollison. It was sweltering inside the building. Compared to the raw chill of wind and brine outside, the heat trapped inside the small billet was dizzying. There was a strong odor swirling amidst the heat. It was a strange mix of putrid chemicals and the savory aroma of roasting meat.

Conrad followed Mollison and the others into the center of the barracks, which until recently had served as the sleeping quarters for roughly half of the Schutztruppe garrison. Abel likely now had his men doubled up in the remaining billet to provide the doctors their working space.

When he rounded the corner of the room, Conrad felt his cloudy paralysis clear instantly. It was replaced with a surge of fresh revulsion that sent shivers of terror up his spine. He dropped his cane, which fell onto the concrete floor with a sickening clang.

The twelve women gathered around the boiling cauldrons did not flinch at the sound. If they had heard the noise at all, Conrad doubted that they would have possessed the energy to turn their heads to look at him. The women were little more than skeletons, each tending to a vat of boiling chemicals. And floating in each woman's cauldron were the embalmed remains of one of their fellow prisoners.

"Sir Galton collected specimens from Egypt to the Congo, but I'd wager his collection doesn't have any subjects as fascinating as these," Mollison boasted, retrieving Conrad's fallen cane from the floor and pressing it happily into Conrad's hand. "Come and take a closer look, Herr Huber."

At Mollison's instruction, one of the Herero women picked up a large wooden ladle and scooped out one of the floating body parts in a hypnotic swoop. She selected a large, swollen head and balanced the weight of the ladle on the rim of the cauldron so that the specimen rested right in front of Dr. Mollison.

Conrad felt bile rising in his throat. The urge to vomit was overwhelming.

The head's flesh was charred and flaky, but it still bore the pained complexion of the dead Herero man's face. Its eyes had been sewn shut, but the head's mouth hung slightly open, twisted in a permanent, starving grimace.

Conrad was suddenly seized with panic. He looked into the faces of each of the Herero women, praying that Sybille was not solidifying in the bottom of one of Mollison's cauldrons.

None of them were Sybille, and Conrad felt his resolve waver. Tears began to well up in his eyes. What kind of monsters were the men standing next to him?

Mein Gott, Conrad heard himself crying in his mind. Did the women tending the cauldrons know the person whose head they were displaying for Dr. Mollison? What if it was one of their husbands? What if it was one of their children?

Conrad wanted to run, but Captain Abel was slouched in the doorway, blocking his escape. German children were waddling around with penguins mere yards from where Herero children were being subjected to indescribable terrors.

Conrad felt the urge to pray, but it dissolved before he could mutter a single word. It would not have made any difference, he thought. God was not on Shark Island.

"Is that B26, Theodor?" Fischer asked as he took out his glasses and examined the preserved head. "My word, I didn't remember it being *that* large."

"I know," replied Mollison with great excitement. "I thought the very same. We'll have to re-measure once it's dry but look at the pronouncement of the forehead! It slides right into the scalp at such a flat angle. This one must've possessed scarcely any intelligence at all. Likely a field laborer of some sort, just as we theorized! I'll inquire in town tonight about getting some containers made to transport everything back to the University."

Conrad felt his charade crumbling as he turned on his heel and nearly bowled over Captain Abel, who had to straighten himself hastily as Conrad strode out the door.

"I've seen enough" was all Conrad managed to say.

Conrad wanted to leave Shark Island immediately. He picked up his pace, trying to hobble through the soft sand fast enough so that Captain Abel could not catch up to him. But Abel easily overtook him and, not understanding what had caused Conrad's sudden displeasure, was trying ardently to worm himself back into Conrad's good graces.

"Are you sure you have to leave now, Herr Huber? The ferry will not return for another hour. Perhaps I might show you our plans for the rail extension to Aus? The work is most impressive. I'm sure that Herr Hertzog would have been pleased, God rest his soul."

At the mention of Beaunard's name, Conrad's disgust turned into rapid fury. Hot tears were running freely down his face. He spun around, intent on eviscerating Captain Abel with his bare hands, when he saw her.

For a moment, Conrad did not think it was her. Her face was drawn and sunken, pulling her once-lighted eyes deep underneath its faded gloom. What remained of her clothes hung feebly from her gaunt frame, exposing a series of deep bruises along her spindly limbs and thighs.

She was toiling in a group of prisoners over a large chunk of driftwood that Abel was no doubt trying to collect and sell as kindling in Lüderitz. She cut at the wood with a small piece of iron, the pulpy wood catching the dulled shard with every stroke and slowing her progress. Her palms were bloody, the shard slicing her spongy flesh as she worked.

A group of Schutztruppe stood idly nearby, overseeing the pointless task and occasionally intervening to whip those who did not cut fast enough.

Sybille lifted her head and stiffened when she saw Conrad. Her eyes met his, and she mewed in terror as though she thought he was a ghost. She wavered slightly, the red-stained iron falling from her hand.

She began to cry.

Sybille tried to stand, but her legs buckled, and she collapsed into the sand. Two guards started toward her, annoyed at the pitiful sounds she made, and raised their sjamboks threateningly over their heads.

Conrad saw them move toward Sybille and strode forward like an enraged bull, waving his cane at them as though it were a sword.

"*Stopp!*" he roared, too distraught to give a damn about his actions. "Back away from her this instant, you fucking *Drecksau!*"

The two Schutztruppe were large men, but they froze where they were, caught completely off-guard by the limping man in a division uniform who had appeared out of nowhere to brandish his cane at them. Captain Abel stood stunned as well. He gaped dumbfounded as though Conrad had suddenly grown horns.

Conrad reached Sybille and fell to his knees as he took off his coat and draped it over her shrunken shoulders. Sybille was sobbing uncontrollably now, clutching at Conrad's chest with her butchered hands. Conrad's leg screamed as he bent it underneath him, but he ignored it as he gathered Sybille to him. She was so frail she felt like a child in his arms. Her breathing between sobs was frantic and forced, and her skin felt like ice under his touch.

She could not have been on Shark Island long, but already she was so close to death.

"Herr Huber!" Captain Able shouted, having finally overcome his shock and followed Conrad to where he sat holding Sybille. "What is the meaning of this?"

The two Schutztruppe guards still stood stupefied as though Conrad were some vengeful apparition that might turn upon them again if they made any sudden movements.

Conrad did not answer Abel at first. He sat in the wet sand, cradling Sybille's shattered body to his chest and hating Captain Abel, Dr. Fischer, and Dr. Mollison with every pained breath he took. Around him, the other Herero continued laboring unfazed, immune to his presence amongst them and Sybille's miserable sobs.

Conrad counted to calm himself, his rhythm in time with the raspy gasps of Sybille's weeping.

Eins...zwei...drei...

At last Conrad stood, finding his feet in the soft ground. Sybille's crying grew even more hysterical as he broke away from her, as though she thought that he might dissolve like a vision, abandoning her once again to her fate.

Conrad fought every pulsing nerve in his body not to pummel Abel. If he'd had a gun, Conrad knew he would have murdered the guard captain and his two men without hesitation. But that was not what Sybille needed right now. She was alive, but barely. She did not need *his* vengeance now; she needed his help. So, with as much strength and guile as he could muster, Conrad wiped away his tears, forced a charming smile onto his face, and clasped Abel in a jubilant embrace.

"You've found her, Captain!" Conrad cried gleefully. "Well done! Von Trotha will be thrilled."

Whatever Captain Abel had been expecting Conrad to say, he had clearly not expected to be congratulated. Abel's ginger hair highlighted the confused flush in his cheeks. Conrad had seemed impatient and distant when he'd first arrived at the camp, and then he'd gone from dour to crazed in a sudden flash. It was bizarre behavior for a general's aide, but Conrad's burst of praise was enough to excite Abel, even if it confused him.

"Er, thank you, sir," Captain Abel replied, accepting Conrad's praise with skeptical eagerness. "This Negress is…important to the General?"

"Indeed she is!" Conrad said, acting as if he were suddenly indifferent to Sybille's wailing and reaching for him. "This Negress is the daughter-in-law of the rebel leader, Hendrik Witbooi. You've captured the Princess of the Nama, Captain!"

Conrad knew he was playing a dangerous game. He'd concocted a lie to get him inside the camp, but now that he'd found Sybille, extracting her from Shark Island was going to be an entirely different challenge.

Sybille looked nothing like the rest of the few Nama prisoners that Conrad had glimpsed scattered throughout the camp. She was nearly a foot taller than most of them and several shades lighter. And although Hendrik liked to fancy himself as the "King of the Nama," in truth, the Nama had no king. Albert Witbooi was not even Hendrik's real son, and Sybille had wanted nothing to do with Albert. Anyone who knew anything about the Witboois or the Nama would've been able to see through his lie in an instant.

To complicate matters, Sybille's eyes made her instantly recognizable. Every division soldier and Schutztruppe guard from Tsumeb to Lüderitz would remember her face if they'd seen her before. She'd stabbed Ulrich when she'd been captured, and if that story had reached Abel, Conrad's bluff would fall apart at once.

If Abel knew that Sybille had been captured in the northern desert instead of near the southern coast, he would surely stop to ask what Princess Witbooi had been doing nearly a thousand kilometers from home. Conrad had no idea if Georg kept records on the prisoners he sent to the south, but a Herero woman with blue eyes who'd stabbed a division captain was far too interesting not to have been noticed.

Too much hinged upon Abel overlooking what was right in front of him.

"Finding her will end this wretched war with the Nama, Captain," Conrad continued before Abel could respond. "Von Trotha asked me to keep an eye out in case one of our patrols happened to get lucky and stumble upon whichever one of these twine and mud villages that wretched ape, Witbooi, had his family stashed away in. I used to see her skulking around the capital with Witbooi's gang of villains. Terrible band of savages; Leutwein should have hanged them all when he'd had the chance, if you ask me."

Conrad watched Abel's face as he spoke, trying to gauge how many of his lies the young captain believed.

"I once had the unfortunate experience of meeting this one's husband, Albert, in Windhoek," Conrad continued. "A savage if ever I saw one. He nearly beat me to death in the capital. Twice. But he's dead now, thank God and the General, and this one could be the lure von Trotha needs to force the Nama apes to finally come out of the bush."

Conrad didn't know if Sybille could hear his words through her panic, but he prayed that she could not.

"The Princess of the Nama?" Abel asked slowly as though he did not believe Conrad.

"Indeed," Conrad replied with a mocking grin. "She's royalty. My apologies for shouting at your men and causing such a stir, but von Trotha can't have Witbooi's daughter branded across the face. Don't know if the beasts would recognize her otherwise!"

Conrad forced himself to laugh at his jest. The two other Schutztruppe guards laughed as well as they looped their sjamboks back through their belts. It seemed *they* believed him at least. Abel looked Sybille over for a long moment, and then he turned back to Conrad.

"Wouldn't it save the General trouble if I had her hanged in Lüderitz?" the

Captain asked plainly.

Conrad watched Abel's face as the Captain worked through all that Conrad had just told him. Conrad didn't need Abel to understand the imaginary strategy of von Trotha's that he had fabricated. He merely needed Abel to see enough value for himself in allowing Conrad to take Sybille out of the camp.

"The General and *me*," Conrad replied with feigned exasperation. "I'll have to transport the bitch back to Windhoek tonight, I suppose. Then von Trotha will probably put me right back on the next train to continue the tour. But he'll want to know who it was who captured her for him, of course, so perhaps, with any luck, I'll be returning to Lüderitz at the end of my tour with a commendation for you, Captain. I swear the General's keeping a chest of them under his bed the way he hands them out in Windhoek."

Abel's jaw clenched.

Conrad suddenly worried that he'd gone too far. He had shown up at Abel's camp unannounced, flustered, without official orders, and was now saying that he intended to leave with one of the prisoners he claimed was a princess von Trotha wanted to use as a chess piece in the war with the Nama. If Conrad were in Abel's position, he couldn't see how he'd believe half of the things he'd said.

The wind had picked up once more, but Conrad could still feel nervous drops of sweat pooling under his arms and on his neck.

Abel still seemed to ponder Conrad's words for a moment, and then he broke out into another fawning smile.

"You flatter me, Herr Huber!" the Captain said graciously. "I would be humbled by any recognition you'd consider mentioning to the General. Shall I organize an escort for the prisoner back to the capital?"

Conrad felt his fear slowly begin to fade.

"No need," Conrad replied swiftly. "I'll arrange my own affairs at the train station this evening. The conductor who runs this link and I are... well acquainted. He'll be more than capable of finding a place for her with the luggage, I assume, while I try this gemsbok you recommended in town. Besides, I doubt this one's going to make much fuss anymore."

Abel nodded along with Conrad's every word, already envisioning himself being presented with one of von Trotha's vibrant medals.

"Of course, of course," Abel said eagerly. "Would you like me to arrange for the princess to be brought ashore by one of my contractors? I can't imagine the picnicking families would find her presence suitable on the ferry."

"It's quite alright," Conrad assured Abel, not willing to leave Sybille in the man's care for another moment. "I saw several children scuttling around with the penguins. I doubt their parents will be able to separate them from their games for a long while still. I'd like to have this one secured in town as soon as possible anyway. I still have a few things to attend to in Lüderitz. I'd be grateful, Captain, if you could spare two of your men to carry her. I'm somewhat inhibited by this cane, and I doubt the wretched girl can walk."

Abel agreed and, with a quick bark, motioned for the two guards who'd been about to whip Sybille to fetch her off the ground. They lifted her up with little effort. She was still sobbing uncontrollably, too dizzied to know who had picked her up and where they were carrying her.

"Thank you, Captain," Conrad said warmly. "Would you mind explaining to Dr. Fischer and Dr. Mollison the reason for my hasty departure? I would hate for them to think I'd been unappreciative of their showing me their research."

After a few more perfunctory words with Captain Abel and a promise to buy him a drink the next time they met, Conrad followed the two Schutztruppe men out of the gray, rusted camp. Captain Abel stood waving after Conrad as the small group climbed up the steep slope and began their long descent back toward the tourist docks.

It was only after the gates of the Shark Island camp had swung shut below them that Conrad wondered seriously if they had been the gates of Hell.

CHAPTER 14

DECEMBER 1904

Throughout the night on the train to Windhoek, Conrad checked Sybille's pulse repeatedly for fear she had died in her sleep. Her breathing was so shallow that he couldn't hear it over the soft *click-clack* of the railroad car wheels. He sat beside her, glancing down every few seconds to watch the subtle rise and fall of her midriff to reassure himself that she was still alive.

It had not been difficult for Conrad to secure a private car. The conductor, the same brute who had clobbered Leutwein and who had been requisitioned by von Trotha to move the division's artillery to Waterberg, had been easily bribed with a few marks. The traffic in the Lüderitz station was minimal in the middle of the afternoon, and with a few more marks, Conrad was able to persuade the Schutztruppe station agent on duty to let Sybille and he occupy his office until their train left that evening.

The man had ignored Sybille's condition as Captain Abel's men laid her on the floor of his office, and had flashed Conrad a wicked, knowing grin as he pocketed the money and left.

After several attempts, Conrad had been able to convince two passing Kavango women to help him. The women were hurrying home from the market with their unsold bundles of fish strapped across their backs, and Conrad did not speak a word of Kavango. When Conrad finally persuaded them to peek inside the custom agent's office, their eyes immediately fell on Sybille, lying unconscious on the wooden floor, half-concealed beneath Conrad's jacket. The older of the two women had made a disgusted noise and hurried out, but she returned to the station minutes later with reinforcements.

The two Kavango women had enlisted three others to help them, and Conrad feared that their clustering outside the small office would attract attention. But the station remained empty as the women worked, and they all kept their voices low.

Two of the women managed to wash the salt and grime out of Sybille's wounds and bandaged her hands with strips of cloth while the other three women cut away her remaining rags and forced an old but clean dress over her. Sybille lay still as a statue as the women tended to her, whimpering softly whenever one of the women ran her hands over some part of her body. She did not reach for any of the food that the Kavango women offered her.

Several times Conrad thought he saw the women throw accusing glances at him, but when they had finished, they left without a word. Conrad offered the last woman several marks, which she accepted with a stare of practiced coolness. Evidently, Sybille was not the first woman she'd been called upon to tend to.

When the conductor returned to collect them several hours later, Conrad took Sybille in his arms and carried her onboard. He shouldn't have been able to manage her with his leg; he was alarmed to find just how easy she was to carry. The conductor had secured them a third-class car, and Conrad lay Sybille down carefully on one of the wooden benches. He slipped the conductor another handful of marks for his silence and then closed the door. He sat beside Sybille as the train began to pull away from the terrible fairy town, and she soon fell asleep as the train rocked her shattered body.

Once they were safely onboard, Conrad's own eyes sagged with fatigue. More than once, he caught himself drifting off to sleep, and he would bolt upright, terrified that he might collapse from exhaustion instead of watching over Sybille.

In the end, Conrad's thoughts were what kept him awake. The night air was still and dry, and from the light of the stars passing through the open railroad car windows, Conrad watched Sybille sleep and tried to keep the darkest of his thoughts at bay.

What had happened after Conrad had left Hochfeld that morning? Had Sybille been at Waterberg? How had she been captured? How long had she been rotting on Shark Island? Had any of the guards…touched her?

Conrad shook that last thought from his mind. He promised himself that he would never ask Sybille that question. Whatever had happened to her, she had endured enough already.

For the eighth time, Conrad placed the back of his hand lightly on Sybille's forehead. She did not seem to have a fever, but her face felt chilled, despite the heat of the car, and that worried him more.

As he removed his hand, Sybille's eyes opened hesitantly. She was still mostly asleep, but she managed to look up at Conrad through her dazed fog. Her hair had grown much longer since Conrad had last seen her, and it hung in long, matted coils by her face, hiding most of the cuts along her cheeks. Sybille fixed her pale, hollow gaze on him and managed to speak in a raspy, croaking voice.

"Are you a ghost?" she asked him.

"No," Conrad replied as gently as he might have to a child. "I'm not a ghost."

Sybille started to mouth something else, but she collapsed back into a limp sleep before Conrad could understand what she'd said. Twice more throughout the night she opened her eyes, but she did not speak to him again. The second time Conrad managed to get her to drink a few strained gulps of water.

When the train began to slow on its approach into Windhoek several hours later, the reality of the situation began to set in on Conrad. He had no idea what he would do with Sybille. She was in dire condition, and he was bringing her right into the center of von Trotha's division and Georg's Schutztruppe.

The sun had not yet risen, but Conrad could already see the faint outlines of the Windhoek camps through the dim, pre-dawn light. If someone found Sybille in the capital, she'd be cast right back into one of them, and Conrad wouldn't be able to intervene a second time.

He pushed that thought out of his mind as he gently shook Sybille awake. He would not let that happen. He simply would not.

Sybille opened her eyes cautiously as though expecting to find herself back on the wind-torn beach. She said nothing as Conrad gathered her up in his arms and swung her across his shoulder as delicately as he could. The faintest idea of a plan traced its way through Conrad's mind. It was a frail scheme that he did not trust in the slightest, but he could not think of any better ideas.

As the train pulled into the Windhoek station, Conrad pushed open the door at the back of their train car open before the train had fully stopped. He abandoned his cane in the car and leapt onto the opposite platform with Sybille over his shoulder. His leg threatened to buckle underneath him as he lost his footing on the platform, but he stumbled forward stubbornly, knowing he only had a few seconds to do what he intended.

Mercifully, the conductor had given them one of the rearmost cars. The Windhoek station was deserted this early in the morning, and Conrad muttered a quick prayer of thanks that Captain Jund was not a punctual man.

Their train had pulled into one of the furthest tracks from the main entrance, next to a row of the Schutztruppe's boxcars that Georg stored at the station's railyard when they were not in use. Conrad did not know how many people were in the last two cars behind them, but he limped quickly past them, praying that no one would bother to look out the back windows as they gathered up their belongings.

Conrad turned the corner at the end of the platform and nearly dove behind the far side of the nearest boxcar. He leaned heavily against the sharp metal, his chest heaving wildly as he heard the doors of their train open and the rest of the passengers begin to disembark.

If he'd been a few steps slower, he wouldn't have made it. He stood unmoving for several minutes, ignoring the ache in his back and the shooting jabs of pain in his leg, for fear that someone might've seen him leap from the train and decide to follow him.

After five minutes, when no one had peered around the boxcars and the sleepy chatter of the Lüderitz passengers had risen enough to muffle his steps, Conrad crept furtively along the line of cars. He found what he was looking for, a boxcar whose door had been left slightly ajar by a lazy attendant. As tenderly as he could manage, Conrad lay Sybille down inside the car and then climbed in himself.

The boxcar was completely dark inside. A heavy odor hung in the air, the lingering smell of terrified sweat and other bodily fluids.

The little air that drifted in through the holes in the metal was stale and thick. Conrad felt miserable kneeling inside the car, but he knew it would become a literal oven once the sun began to rise. He had to be quick. Sybille would not last long in the boxcar in her condition. She would suffocate in the stagnant heat if he could not find her help soon.

He did not know if Sybille could hear him or whether she'd be able to understand his half-hatched plan. Most of all, he hoped that she did not recognize where she was.

"Sybille?" he whispered to her limp form, barely visible right in front of him. "Sybille…can you hear me?"

She did not respond. Conrad prayed that she was simply too weak and had not died in his arms as he'd lifted her into the boxcar. He'd felt her breathing then, but now he could not see her, and the nearby shuffling of the train passengers drowned out any faint sound she might have made.

"Sybille, I have to leave you to go and get help," Conrad whispered, hating the truth of his words as he said them. "I can't carry you through town, and if anybody sees you, they'll either kill you or send you back to the camps. I'm going to go and get help, but I have to leave you here to do it."

Conrad hadn't noticed that he'd started to cry. He was so exhausted, and the layers of dust and grime from the boxcar stung his eyes. Sybille was very near death. She was so delirious from abuse and sorrow, and Conrad could not believe he was about to abandon her, even if he was trying to save her life.

"I have to go now, Sybille," he said again. "I have to go, but I'll come right back as fast as I can."

A few breaths passed before Sybille responded in a voice that was so soft and strained that Conrad almost didn't hear it.

"Okay," she said.

Conrad took another look at her shadowed outline. As he began to scramble his way back out of the boxcar, he suddenly realized that Sybille must've endured hours of agonizing transport, crammed into a boxcar with dozens of other terrified Herero. Perhaps this very one. For a second, he lost his nerve, unwilling to leave Sybille alone in case she woke up and discovered where she was.

But he had to leave to try and save her. So without allowing himself a final look at her, he hurried out of the boxcar and crept back down onto the platform. He examined the rusted orange door of the car until he found its identification number. The chipped white paint was barely visible through the peeking sunlight.

SA-120.

He burned the letters and numbers into his memory and then hurried along the platform as fast as he could. The loss of his cane slowed him, but Conrad hobbled along the line of boxcars, rejoining the tail-end of the departing passengers from the main platform. No one had seen where he'd come from. Most of the few other passengers were still drowsy from the long train ride, and Conrad melted unnoticed into the rear of the small crowd.

Sybille was safe for the moment, but she'd have to be moved quickly. But *where*?

Conrad could not bring Sybille back to Schwerinsburg. That was von Trotha's den now, constantly crawling with division and Schutztruppe officers. Even if some of the staff agreed to hide her, he could not be sure that one would not turn her over to von Trotha. None of the remaining staff there were Herero, and they might fear the soldier's wrath enough to betray Sybille, even knowing what would happen to her.

No, Conrad thought. I have to get Sybille somewhere where *I* can hide her.

He almost made it out of the train station without incident, but as soon as he stepped out of the entrance to the depot, Captain Jund hailed him from across the street. Conrad tried to pretend that he hadn't seen the man, but Jund had already crossed halfway to him before he could escape.

"*Hallo*, Herr Huber," Jund said plainly, extending his hand in greeting.

Conrad shook the Captain's hand, hoping his sudden dread was not plastered across his face. What if Jund decided to inspect the boxcars today? Was that something he'd do out of boredom or assertive purpose? Or worse. What if Georg was planning to send a load of prisoners from the Windhoek camps south today and had ordered Jund to prepare the boxcars?

"*Guten morgen*, Captain," Conrad replied.

"You don't look very rested, Herr Huber," Jund said rather bluntly. "Back too early from your holiday?"

Conrad forced a sad smile, hoping Jund would not seek to prolong this conversation much longer.

"Yes," Conrad replied shortly. "The General decided he wanted me back, so I had to cut my trip a few days short."

Conrad was still wearing his uniform from the day before, which was crumpled and filthy from the trials of Shark Island. He looked as though he'd slept in a gutter, and if Conrad had run into any other officer, they might have pressed him as to why he looked so wretched. But for once, Jund's simplicity proved a blessing. The gopher captain shrugged sympathetically, gave Conrad a friendly nod, and then continued into the train station.

As Jund disappeared, Conrad let out a short sigh of relief. The sun was beginning to rise over Windhoek; he did not have much time. Gripping himself against the throbbing in his leg, he began to hobble toward Kaiserstrasse in search of Petyr.

*

Erwin carried Sybille into the small, rented flat later that night. He'd waited until the cover of darkness before picking his way silently through the alleys of the capital. He met Conrad at the back of the apartment building on

Lüderitzstrasse and quickly slipped inside the building with Sybille in his arms as Conrad ushered him up the back stairwell. Petyr fell in behind them as they climbed the creaking stairs to the third floor.

The keys rattled uncooperatively in Conrad's shaking hands, and he could feel Erwin and Petyr's angst as though it were a living, squirming thing behind him, crawling up his back and begging him to hurry. Someone might see them at any moment. All it would take was the elderly night watchman strolling along the corridor on his evening rounds or one of the other tenants deciding to poke their head out of their door to catch a glimpse of their new neighbor. If that happened, they would all be finished.

Conrad would be sacked and sent home, but Erwin and Petyr would either be hanged or sent south to one of the camps. They'd risked their lives to help, and it was a miracle that they had all made it this far.

At last, Conrad forced his key into the flimsy lock and ushered everyone inside before closing the door and latching the lock behind them.

Erwin took Sybille into the bedroom and lay her gently on the mattress. Both he and Petyr were panting heavily, and Conrad could see the heavy droplets of sweat sliding down their faces even in the dark.

When Erwin returned a few minutes later, all three stood silently clustered in the middle of the flat. Sybille lay unconscious in the other room, but Erwin thought she had merely passed out from exhaustion again and would recover somewhat once she rested. In a moment, Conrad would find some bandages and change Sybille's dressings, but he paused for a few breaths, savoring the silence beyond the door that yielded no raised alarms or sounds of pursuit.

Conrad saw the edges of Erwin's mouth curl into a small half-smile of satisfaction. They had made it. Sybille was safe.

Conrad had found Petyr almost immediately at the Residence and had quickly steered him out of earshot of one of the passing Damara maids. Petyr had nearly fainted when Conrad told him about Sybille's condition and where he had stashed her. Conrad had been sorry to involve Petyr in this, but he needed someone he could trust, and Sybille did not have time for Conrad to be concerned about Petyr's innocence.

Much to the boy's credit, Petyr had snapped out of his shock when Conrad told him what he needed him to do and had sped away toward the train depot, looking both determined and terrified. Conrad didn't know how Petyr had done it, but somehow the boy had snuck his way into the station, found Sybille and kept her alive.

Conrad had dispatched him with some old towels he'd pilfered from the Residence's laundry and a canteen of water, and Petyr had not faltered. He'd found the right car and kept Sybille as cool as he could while he himself roasted in the furnace-like heat, unable to make a sound for fear of discovery.

It had taken Conrad far longer to find Erwin than he had expected. He managed to avoid notice at Schwerinsburg for a quarter of an hour, but then he was intercepted by two division aides, who were surprised to see him and stopped to chat. As soon as Conrad was able to politely detach himself from the two aides, he ran into a quartermaster waiting to speak to von Trotha, who also seemed determined to detain him with idle conversation.

As Conrad dodged through the crowded hallways, he felt himself inventing a new story at almost every turn.

The trip had been splendid, but the weather had been foul. His friend had fallen ill so he'd decided to cancel his trip. He'd spent most the day at the beach, and he'd gotten to pet a penguin.

The diversion of obligated pleasantries had cost him nearly half an hour, and Conrad grew increasingly fearful that he would bump into von Trotha and have to explain his sudden reappearance to the General himself. Thankfully one of the aides eventually informed him that von Trotha was at a luncheon at Mayor Grober's home and was not expected back for another hour at least.

When Conrad finally found Erwin, reluctantly doling out meat scraps for Ivan and Gustavus in their new kennel by the stables, he nearly hugged the man from relief. Erwin had not even blinked as Conrad explained his insane plan to the cook. He had merely nodded in agreement and called to an Ovambo groom to take over feeding the dogs for him before he set out for the train station after Petyr.

Erwin had been unfazed when Conrad had asked him to risk his life for

Sybille, and Conrad felt a strong pull of attachment to the dour man as he watched him hurry away through the courtyard.

Somehow Erwin, too, had snuck into the station and, even more miraculously, had managed to smuggle Sybille and Petyr out beyond the railyard. The railyard opened out onto a series of small sagebrush-covered hills, where Erwin and Petyr had secreted themselves with Sybille until nightfall. The rains had returned, but the day remained unpleasantly hot, and as Conrad hurried through the streets of Windhoek, he muttered constant prayers that the three of them would be alright.

When night had fallen, Erwin had gathered Sybille in his arms and crept back into the city. He had treated her wounds as best he could manage in the bush, and she had slept fitfully most of the day. She'd woken when Erwin had scooped her up into her arms, but whether out of fear or understanding, she made no sound as the three of them slinked down the hill into the city outskirts.

They had come close to being seen by a Schutztruppe patrol several times. Erwin was burdened with Sybille and the alleys Petyr led them down were crowded with trash and other obstacles. The streetlamps kept the main roads well lit, but Petyr's alleyways forced them to navigate the capital in near-total darkness. The Schutztruppe had managed to finally kill the leopard that had stalked the outskirts of the capital for more than a year, but that had not made navigating the deserted back alleys any less terrifying.

It had been slow going, but they had made it. And, at least for the moment, they were all safe.

The flat was bare, except for a few pieces of old furniture that the previous tenant had not bothered to take with him. Conrad had leased the apartment that afternoon. The landlord, a short, balding man, had raised an eyebrow when Conrad had expressed his desire to move in immediately, but the flat had been unoccupied for a month, and Conrad had enough cash on hand to pay the first month's rent upfront.

In the morning, Conrad would return to Schwerinsburg and inform the General of his desire to move out of the Residence. Many officers chose to live outside of barracks housing once they achieved a high enough station, and Conrad did not think von Trotha would object if he moved out of his ramshackle bungalow.

"She's alright, then?" Conrad asked Erwin, breaking the silence in the room.

"Think so," Erwin replied as he continued to try and catch his breath. "We kept her cool. Wounds will take a long time to heal, but she okay, I think. She sleep maybe three or four days."

Beside Erwin, Petyr still looked edgy. The adrenaline was slow to leave his small body, but he stayed silent as he looked over his shoulder back towards the bedroom every few seconds.

For the first time since he'd enlisted them in his scheme, Conrad recognized the second sacrifice he hadn't even been aware he'd asked Erwin and Petyr to make. Sybille, whom they both loved in their own way, was in bad shape. And they were now entrusting her safety to a German.

Petyr trusted him, but Conrad was not sure Erwin did. Once Erwin had found Sybille, he could have chosen to take her to a nearby village, or he could have fled Windhoek entirely and tried to take her up the northern coast somewhere away from the fighting. Conrad did not know where Erwin was from, but if he had a family somewhere, he might have tried to take Sybille to them or to anyone other than the thin, German man who still wore his army uniform.

But he hadn't. Erwin had brought Sybille to him.

As though sensing Conrad's thoughts, Erwin frowned, the muscles of his mouth firmly outlined despite the dark.

He had brought Sybille to Conrad and would leave her with him. He *had* to leave her with him. Erwin's presence in the kitchen would be missed at Schwerinsburg, and if he and Petyr did not return soon, they risked being spotted by the morning patrols of the other household staff.

Erwin's face hardened, imparting to Conrad an ultimatum that Maharero was not there to provide. Sybille was weak, vulnerable, and lovely.

"She care for you, Huber," Erwin stated with firm purpose.

Conrad was shocked for a moment. It was the first time that Erwin had ever spoken to him by name.

"She care for you," he repeated. "You care for her. Or I will kill you."

Conrad did not know what to say. He nodded meekly, which, after a moment, Erwin seemed to accept.

He went into the bedroom once more to make sure that Sybille was still asleep and then returned to the main room. After a slight hesitation, Erwin extended his hand to Conrad and stared at him with a stoic gaze that Conrad felt rather than saw in the darkness. Conrad shook Erwin's offered hand.

"Thank you," he said.

Erwin nodded again and grunted unhappily. He took Petyr's arm, leading the boy silently out the door and back out into the perilous, black night.

*

The next day Conrad returned to his post with minimal fuss. Von Trotha was glad to see Conrad home from leave, and he approved Conrad's request to move to the flat absently as he poured over a map of the northern Bushveld.

None of the General's staff suspected him of having done anything deceptive or treasonous, and slowly, Conrad settled back into his normal routine with unsettling ease. He departed the flat each morning for von Trotha's office, where he advised and helped plot the demise of the Nama insurgency.

After a week, Conrad put in a second request to von Trotha to allow Petyr to be dismissed from his footman duties in the afternoons. That was not unusual. Many foreign servicemen employed African staffers to do odd jobs for them on the side. And since Conrad was still hampered by his injury and Petyr was not an essential part of the Residence staff, Conrad's request was approved.

With Petyr assigned to Conrad's direction each afternoon, the boy was able to purchase food and medical supplies and to slip in and out of Conrad's apartment to tend to Sybille without harassment from the Schutztruppe or Conrad's landlord. A few of the division officers were skeptical of how Conrad could possibly trust an African coming and going from his flat, let alone with his money, but no one raised any serious objections.

Sybille healed slowly. Her hands continued to swell and ooze a thick, foul-smelling pus for the first few days, but gradually they began to scab over. She would have a long, ugly scar on both of her palms, though it appeared for the moment that she had not suffered any permanent nerve damage. She was able move each of her fingers, albeit with a great deal of pain and difficulty.

The gashes and bruises on her legs and thighs had begun to fade as well, and each day she seemed to recover a bit more energy. Her appetite was still poor, and she slept for the better part of the day, but she *was* improving.

The difficulty, however, occurred when Conrad returned home each evening.

Once Petyr departed each evening for the Residence, a reticent calm filled the flat. Sybille hardly spoke. She kept away from the small windows in the main sitting room and never ventured near of the door lest someone hear her footfall while Conrad was away. She did not want to know about the war, or at least she did not want to hear about it from Conrad. When she'd recovered enough, she helped Petyr prepare whatever evening meal the boy had purchased for them in town, but this, too, she did in silence.

The flat was a jail for Sybille. Conrad knew that. He might've saved her from Shark Island, but he had not been able to restore anything meaningful to her life. She was trapped in the flat, surrounded by a city of men who had exterminated her friends and family. Conrad was not her jailor, but he knew that Sybille must resent him all the same. When she'd told him that he was not a monster and kissed him beneath the flame thorn tree a year ago, she hadn't yet known what the Germans would do to her people or what they would do to her. She'd said she hated Germans then. What must she think of them now?

She'd cared for Conrad once, but no glimmer of affection could've survived Waterberg and everything that had come after.

They did not truly speak to one another until a few days before Christmas. Conrad hadn't even realized it was almost Christmas until Captain Ulrich had asked him over cards that evening what gift he intended to get his cousin.

"A few of us are pooling some marks together to get the Major something," Ulrich whispered to him across the table in Georg's office. "Have you already gotten him something, or do you want to go in with us?"

Conrad had stared at Ulrich dumbly until the date suddenly dawned on him.

"Er, I don't know," Conrad whispered back, feigning interest. "What were you thinking of doing?"

"Tobias has got a Belgian merchant in Walvis Bay who can get us a pair of elephant tusks. Cheap, off the books. Figured we'd splurge a little and get the Major something nice so he doesn't forget about us when we transfer to the fucking south next month. Can you help us out with a few marks? We'll put your name on it, too, of course."

Conrad chanced a look down at the far end of the table where Georg was laughing at something Corporal Knef had said. Conrad continued to attend Georg's weekly card games, partly because the other officers expected it of him and partly to ensure that his cousin did not drop by his apartment unexpectedly under the pretense of expanding Conrad's social life.

Georg had become a frightening stranger to Conrad. When they were younger, Georg and the rest of Uncle Johanne's family had always been a distant memory, completely separate from his own world. Yet now, as he looked furtively at Georg and his cousin shot him a friendly wink, Conrad realized that Georg was even more removed from him than when they were in Germany.

"Sure," Conrad whispered back casually to Ulrich, his gaze floating back to the cards he did not care about in his hand. "I'll bring you the money tomorrow."

They called it an early night when Protz's liquor supply began to run low, and several of the division officers began complaining of early muster duty the following morning. Conrad bid Georg and the others farewell and began his long descent from Alte Festa to Lüderitzstrasse.

The night air was thick from the overhanging musk of the recent rains, and it did little to improve Conrad's mood as he slowly made his way home. He hated playing cards with Georg and the other officers, but he told himself he did it to protect Sybille.

Conrad felt as though he, too, were imprisoned. He was not physically confined like Sybille, nor in nearly as much danger, but the streets and sounds of Windhoek weighed heavily upon him.

By his own choice, he was an actor now, a wretched thespian forced to inhabit a life he no longer viewed as his own. He was aiding a cause he did not believe in and playing cards and drinking liquor with the men who had tried to rape the tortured woman he was now secretly sheltering.

For a week or so, he had prayed every night for guidance. He'd prayed for some celestial lift in strength or courage, a sign that he was doing the right thing or, at the very least, that God understood he was acting with good intentions. But he'd stopped praying when there was no reply, and now he found himself trudging through a daily existence he no longer understood.

Conrad opened the back entrance to the apartment building and groaned slightly as he started to climb the steps. His own injury was healing, but the moisture in the air made his leg stiff, and the long climb to his apartment left him winded each time he made it.

When he reached his door, he opened the lock as quietly as he could manage, not wanting to frighten Sybille. He slept on a small sofa in the main room and tried to make no noise when he returned home after an evening playing cards. Sybille suffered from terrible nightmares most nights. On more than one occasion, she had been driven into hysterical panic when she heard him sneaking around the apartment, and Conrad had had to rush into her bedroom and clamp a heavy hand over her mouth so that his neighbors would not hear her screaming.

Yet tonight, Conrad was surprised to find Sybille awake when he slipped inside the apartment. She was sitting upright on the sofa with the lights on, staring at the doorway with muted purpose. She had clearly been waiting for him.

"I need to talk to you."

"Alright," Conrad replied quietly as he moved to join her.

He sat down in a chair opposite her and waited for her to speak again.

Conrad was prepared to sit in silence for a while. Sybille had tried to talk to him a few times before but had bolted from the room each time before she could speak. Most nights, Conrad felt as though he were living with a wounded deer and that if he clattered a pot too loudly or stood up from his chair too quickly, it was as if he'd fired a gun above her head. She would either retreat into the bedroom in hurried flight, or dissolve into tears where she stood.

Tonight, however, Sybille looked different.

She sat up on the sofa with her back straight and looked across at Conrad with a steadier gaze. Conrad could not say why, but something about Sybille this evening seemed...familiar.

She did not hold herself with the same poised assurance that she had once possessed, but there was something in the way she sat with her bandaged hands folded neatly in her lap that reminded Conrad of the intrinsic purpose with which Sybille had once moved.

When she looked at him, her eyes held an ember of their old, determined fire. Conrad could not help smiling slightly when her eyes met his. She was not the same; perhaps she never would be again. Yet as Conrad looked at her, waiting for her to speak, it was enough to know that some shadow of her dignity had survived Shark Island.

"Are you alright?" Sybille asked quietly, unsure why he was smiling.

"Fine, fine," Conrad said hurriedly, embarrassed. "How are you feeling today?"

Sybille waited a few moments before answering.

"I am feeling better...thank you," she replied.

Sybille was wearing a faded blue dress that hung like a tapestry over her tall, shrunken frame. It was one of the few dresses that Petyr had been able to smuggle out of the staff quarters at Schwerinsburg, and Conrad guessed that its owner would not notice its absence any time soon. The dress had at one time been a crisp shade of cerulean, but the color had long since faded with age, leaving a soft, blanched fabric that Conrad thought, fittingly, resembled a hospital gown.

"I never thanked you for saving me," Sybille said quietly after a while.

She opened her mouth again as if to say more but closed it when no other words came forth.

"It was nothing," Conrad said to fill the gap of silence. "I only wish I had found you sooner."

Conrad's words sounded hollow. He tried to think of something else to say, but nothing he could think of came close to bridging the distance between them. They were silent for several minutes, immobilized by the vast and horrible things they had experienced so differently. And after a while, Conrad saw tears forming in the corners of Sybille's eyes.

It was all too much for her, Conrad thought.

The pain of what she'd endured, the shame of what had been done to her, and a sense of all-consuming loss that Conrad would never be able to understand.

Conrad assumed his presence was only making things worse. Amongst all the torment that she experienced, Sybille had to suffer his presence as well. Whatever flicker of feeling she'd once had for him, his long, German face and his spotless division uniform had doubtlessly corrupted it. He'd kissed her eagerly a year ago; those memories of their snatched affections in the late afternoon shade around Schwerinsburg had surely turned to rot.

Sybille looked as though she were about to cry, and Conrad hurried to his feet, hoping that, as had worked so far, his leaving would help to calm her down.

A few stray tears rolled down her cheeks, but this time she stopped him mid-rise, wiping her face with her sleeve as she spoke.

"Please...stay," she said meekly.

Conrad nodded obediently and sank slowly back into his chair.

They were both silent again, but something in the room had changed. There was a glint of tenderness in Sybille's voice that had not been there before. Her request had been plain, but there was an honest need beneath it that softened the dark, oppressive air of the flat.

Part of Conrad still wondered if he should leave the room. Yet the longer they sat in silence together, the more distant the miseries that separated them seemed. It was...nice, almost, to sit with Sybille in the stillness and to know that each moment that ticked by, no matter how painful, was one that existed only between the two of them.

Conrad knew that he would have to say something soon, but he was scared of what awaited him on the other side of Sybille's stillness.

Conrad made to speak, but Sybille beat him to it.

"Do you know where my father is?" she asked tentatively.

Conrad felt his stomach twist into knots. Ever since he'd brought her back to Windhoek, he had been dreading this question.

"No," he said solemnly. "I'm sorry."

He wondered how much he ought to tell Sybille about what he knew. Whatever connection existed between them now, it was little more than a wisp, and Conrad was afraid that anything he said would snuff it out completely.

He'd lost Sybille once already. And now he clung selfishly to the ghost of her before him. He wondered fleetingly whether, if he never spoke again, he could preserve this version of her, the one perilous moment of intrigue she still bore for him.

No, he told himself reluctantly. Sybille deserved to know everything he knew. He owed her that much if nothing else.

"At Waterberg," Conrad started. "After I was wounded, the men that carried me to the German lines gave me to a medic just inside the defenses. I could not make out much of the fighting, but I remember seeing a man so much like your father in the front of the lines, waving the others forward with a sword in his hand."

Sybille leaned forward slightly on the sofa.

Conrad hesitated a moment, but Sybille's eyes begged him to go on.

"He led the Herero through the rifle fire and the first artillery round," Conrad continued. "But when the cannons fired a second round...he disappeared. Colonel Hummel's cavalry charged the remnants of the Herero line after that. I'm so sorry, Sybille, but I think that your father is dead. No one could have survived all of that."

Sybille said nothing, and Conrad thought that she would start to cry again.

But she surprised him.

She stood from the sofa and walked to one of the windows. There was little danger that she would be seen so late at night, and for a long time, Sybille simply leaned against the wooden windowpane and stared out into the darkness.

Conrad wondered again whether he should leave. Whatever Sybille was thinking now, it was probably best to leave her alone to grieve for her father.

Yet he still felt as though something were hanging between them, and he could not bear to leave it alone to disappear.

"That is what the other women said too," Sybille told him after a while, still staring absently out the window as she spoke. "They said that my father had been a hero in the front of the main charge. They said he was a good chieftain and I should be proud...but that he was dead now."

Conrad said nothing. There really was not anything he could say.

Sybille turned away from the window and returned to her seat on the sofa.

"My father was elected commander of the Herero army unanimously," Sybille told him quietly with a twinge of pride in her voice.

"He called on every chieftain to gather up their warriors and meet us at Witvlei. My father had heard that there were German farmers trying to claim land across the boundary he'd agreed to with the colonial government, and he planned to use this as a premise to launch an attack on Okahandja."

Conrad shook his head.

"And Major Baumhauer took his new garrison and marched right into the path of an army," Conrad whispered in amazement.

"They fought well, for what it matters," Sybille offered dryly. "But they were surrounded."

They were silent for a moment before Sybille turned from the window to look at Conrad.

"My father never meant to raze Okahandja, you know," she said quietly.

"Then why did he?" Conrad asked.

"Too many of our young men wanted blood," Sybille said evenly. "They were expecting to have to fight a German garrison, but when they attacked and found almost no resistance, their blood was up...and by the time my father managed to restore order, half the city was on fire.

"Father had wanted to shock the Germans into negotiating again by taking one of their capitals. He thought if he struck without warning and captured a

German garrison, Leutwein would rush to negotiate quickly without giving your Kaiser time to react. But when he saw the bodies of German women and children lying in the main square, he knew he'd failed. There was no hope for a small war now."

Conrad remembered the day Colonel Knef had ridden bleeding through the gates of Schwerinsburg to tell them that Okahandja had fallen. He could see the merit of Maharero's strategy, and thanks to the damaged telegraph wire, the Herero had succeeded in taking the small, skeleton garrison by surprise.

"Father was so angry that he wanted to kill the men who killed the women and children," Sybille continued.

"But he didn't?" Conrad guessed.

Sybille shook her head.

"He couldn't. Half of the ones who started the killing were the sons of chiefs. If Father had had them killed, he would've lost their father's men. And now he needed all the men he could get."

It was odd to talk about the past like this, Conrad thought. He remembered being filled with such panic when Colonel Knef had turned to him and asked for orders. He remembered being filled with despair when Leutwein had collapsed, and anger when he learned that Beaunard was dead.

He imagined Maharero, tall and powerful, bent in prayer in the husk of a burning city, willing his gamble would pay off. The Herero chieftain could not have known that Leutwein, whose restraint alone he thought would keep the destruction of a full-scale war at bay, already lay quivering in a shoddy heap—and that the wrath of Kaiser Wilhelm had already been unleashed by Conrad's own desperate telegram to Berlin.

But that was all a distant memory. He and Sybille spoke about the war as though they were both staring at one another through stained glass. Each helplessly trying to describe to the other the full picture that only they could see.

Sybille looked as though she'd guessed what he'd been remembering.

"I'm sorry about Beaunard," she said solemnly. "I didn't like him very much, but he was a friend of yours, and I'm sorry he's gone."

Conrad gave her a small smile.

"And I'm sorry about Noko," he said. "He didn't like me very much, but he was a good man."

Sybille gave him a soft, sad smile and turned to look back out the window. Conrad hurriedly changed the subject.

"So, what happened after Okahandja fell?" he asked her. "Why didn't Maharero attack another city?"

"Many people wanted him to," Sybille said as she gazed up out the window toward the faint outline of Alte Feste. "Many of them thought we'd never get a better chance to attack Windhoek and push the Germans into the sea. And when we heard a few days later that Leutwein had collapsed…"

"How did you…" Conrad started and then stopped as he saw Sybille's lips twitch and form the faint outlines of a coy smile.

"Petyr," he answered himself. "I should've guessed. I suppose he smuggled a good bit of intelligence to Maharero out of Windhoek at my expense."

Sybille turned back from the window.

"If it helps," she said, "Petyr is very fond of you."

Conrad thought about it for a moment and then shook his head with a short laugh.

"It helps," he said. "A little. But why didn't Maharero attack again?"

Sybille shrugged.

"I don't really know. The men *were* needed at home for planting, but I think every one of them would've stayed to fight if Father had asked them to. When Witbooi deserted your garrison, we all thought the war would be over within months. Maybe Father still held out hope that Leutwein would negotiate with him. Whatever the reason, he never told me."

Sybille fell quiet for a minute or so as if she were trying to guess why her father had not pressed his advantage. Then her shoulders slumped against the chipped window frame, and she continued.

"Your new general is a clever man," she said softly. "When Father heard that his army had landed in Walvis Bay, he regathered the Herero army and decided to attack Tsumeb. He thought if we could take your Kaiser's metals from him and then disappear back into the hinterlands, then your new general would be forced to negotiate. But you beat us to Tsumeb, and we became trapped on the plateau."

Conrad wondered if he should stop Sybille, but she carried on, her voice shaking a little as she did so.

"After the fighting at Waterberg, many families and their villages fled on their own. No one believed that my father and the other chieftains who had fought had survived. Only chieftains who had been too old to fight the Germans were left to try and lead their people off in different directions. It was terrifying. No one knew anything about where anyone else was or what had happened to all the warriors. Everybody was running, but nobody knew where they were trying to go."

Sybille paused as if she were reliving the fear she'd endured in the aftermath of the fighting. But she had said all she meant to say about the battle itself. Conrad did not push her.

"Anna and I were separated in the chaos," Sybille continued. "I don't know how it happened, but one moment she was running beside me, and the next moment she was gone. The other women with me did not let me stop to look for her. They pulled me along by the arms until I was too tired to resist. When we finally stopped running, I realized that I was surrounded by strangers. I recognized one woman who lived a day's walk from my father's village, but the rest I did not know.

"Our small group managed to hide in the hinterlands for a month. Not many people knew one another. After a while, we all realized that we would never be able to find enough food and water for all of us to stay hidden until the patrols gave up looking for us. A few of us volunteered to leave and try to find food or shelter with another village. Seven other women and I headed north to seek shelter in Grootfontein, but we were captured by a German patrol three days later."

Conrad started to apologize once more, but he stopped himself. Sybille did not want to hear that from him right now.

She did not mention Ulrich or how she'd stabbed him.

"Would you like some coffee?" Conrad asked her.

Sybille stared at him, surprised at the question, but then gave him a small, grateful smile.

"Yes, please," she replied.

Neither spoke as Conrad boiled the bitter army-rationed coffee he kept in the pantry. When he returned from the kitchen, they both sipped at the coffee in silence.

Conrad knew Sybille had much more she wanted to say, but he didn't know how hard to push her. They would need to combat more of the terrors that had made them strangers to one another, but for all Conrad knew it could be months or even years before Sybille told him everything that had happened to her.

Sybille fidgeted in her seat, and Conrad knew that she was once again on the verge of telling him what was really on her mind.

"I want to go and look for my father," she finally said, setting her cup down with some difficulty.

Sybille paused as though expecting Conrad to interrupt her. Conrad set his own cup aside. He might've guessed that was what Sybille was going to say, but that did not mean he knew how to respond.

"When I was in the camp..." Sybille began again.

Her lip quivered slightly as she spoke, but she forced herself to continue.

"When I was in the camp, one of the other prisoners said that their chieftain had been leading them to Bechuanaland when he was captured. They thought that the British could protect them from the Germans. If my father survived Waterberg, I'm sure that that is where he would have gone too."

Conrad considered that for a moment. Was Bechuanaland really a potential refuge for the surviving Herero?

Bechuanaland was a British Protectorate that bordered the DSWA's western boundary. It was ruled loosely by a collection of Tswana and Bangwato kings. The British had only recently declared the region a protectorate at the request of the elderly King Khama III, who wanted to ward off incursions into his kingdom from Ndebele desert tribesman to the west and the stubborn Boer settlers to the southeast.

If the Herero could reach Bechuanaland, Conrad thought, the protectorate likely would prove an effective haven. The British garrison in the capital, Gaborone, was probably sizeable, and the Governor-General of the British Cape Colony certainly considered Bechuanaland within his sphere of influence, if not yet an outright British colony. The German army could not pursue the Herero inside the British sphere without official permission from the British government, and if the Herero retreated far enough inside Bechuanaland's borders, no official actions would be possible without sparking an international incident.

The problem, however, was that the DSWA and Bechuanaland were separated by nearly a thousand kilometers of the Kalahari Desert.

Although not as barren as the infamous Sahara that divided the northern Arab states along the Mediterranean from the rest of Africa, the Kalahari was a sagebrush basin that was just as formidable an obstacle. Von Trotha had known this and had pushed the Herero into the bush as an assured means of extermination.

Conrad remembered the reports he'd scoured from Colonel Voigt's Field Office. Poisoned water wells and man-eating predators dotted the landscape, and he even recalled a few reports that suggested German patrols had encountered pockets of mindless San bushmen, who were more animal than man.

The Kalahari epitomized the wicked trickery of the African bush. The terrain seemed manageable at first, until its boundless emptiness began to close in around your mind. Those brave or foolish enough to cross it always lost their way in its vastness, never knowing how many unseen pairs of hungry eyes watched their struggle.

The Herero nation would have been swallowed by the Kalahari. Conrad had read hundreds of reports that told him so. There was simply no way that any of the Herero had made it to Bechuanaland. They had all been scattered to the wind. Those who had not been ridden down by German patrols had neither food nor water and could not hope to survive in the bush.

Conrad knew that Sybille was praying for a miracle, for any sign of hope that some part of her old world still survived. But it was impossible. Maharero was dead, and the Herero were gone.

"Sybille," Conrad said as gently as he could. "I know that you want to believe that Ma…that your father is still alive and that some of your people escaped von Trotha. I wish with all my heart that I could tell you that were so…but it's not. They're gone, Sybille. I'm so sorry, but they're gone."

Sybille did not meet Conrad's eye. She stared down at her coffee, which had grown cold.

"No," Sybille whispered. "They're not."

"Sybille…" Conrad tried again, soothingly.

"No!" Sybille shouted at him, her sudden flare of anger tearing through the flat and echoing across the walls.

Her bandaged hands threw her cup to the ground, and it shattered with a loud crash.

"They are not gone until I see for myself."

Conrad knew that Sybille's anger was not directed at him, but it stung him, nonetheless. Perhaps the whispering connection he'd felt between them earlier had not been real.

"You *have* seen it, Sybille," he said, foolishly trying to reason her out of her anger. "You've seen what the division did at Waterberg. You were there. Jesus, Sybille, you were in one of the camps. The Herero are gone."

"Stop saying that!" Sybille shouted back at him. "They're not gone!"

She was trembling now. She'd rushed to her feet in her anger, and the sudden movement had left her weak frame unbalanced. Conrad moved toward her to help steady her, but she shoved him away.

"Please, Sybille," Conrad pleaded. "Please calm down. What if one of the neighbors hears you?"

"They're not gone!" Sybille shouted again, ignoring him. "They're in Bechuanaland, and I'm going to find them!"

Sybille's anger was almost childlike in its ferocity, Conrad thought. She knew what she wanted was impossible, but she clung to her hope so fervently that she could not abandon her anger.

"Sybille, please be quiet. You can't go and look for them," he explained again. "You're still in terrible condition, and even if you weren't, you can't stick your head out the door, much less traverse the whole colony before you even reach the Kalahari."

"I don't care!" Sybille shouted at him.

"Sybille, please try to understand..." Conrad tried again.

"I don't care!" Sybille shouted again, tears running freely down her cheeks. "I'm going to find them."

"Sybille, if you get caught, you'll be sent right back to another camp," Conrad said, his own voice growing firmer and more frustrated as he stood in front of her. "Is that what you want? To be sent back to that hellhole or to be hanged at Alte Feste if one of the Schutztruppe men recognizes you? I'm trying to keep you safe, Sybille. You can't..."

"I don't care!" she shouted again.

"Well, you have to, damn it!" Conrad roared back at Sybille, his own emotions boiling over in a flash of anger that matched hers.

"Why?!" she screamed at him with the force of her pent-up fear and pain. "Why do I have to care?!"

"Because I love you!" Conrad thundered at her.

Conrad's words hung in the air around them like a thunderclap. Both fell silent, their anger still bristling like electricity in the air. Conrad's fury evaporated almost at once, leaving his face bright crimson. His body was shaking slightly from the shouting, and his glasses fell from his face and landed with a small *clink* on the floor beneath them.

Sybille's own anger receded more slowly, and she looked at Conrad with an unreadable face as though deciding whether to slap him or laugh.

Conrad had gotten to his feet and stepped directly in front of her as they'd fought, and Sybille had yet to concede any ground. She was so near to him that he thought he could hear her heartbeat in the hushed stillness. He wanted to look away from her, but for once, he held her gaze defiantly.

He'd already said it. There was no going back.

"Because I love you," Conrad repeated softly.

For another moment, Sybille remained frozen. Conrad feared that he'd lost her forever. She was wounded, a captive confined to his care, stripped of her family, her people, and her freedom, and he had chosen this moment to confess his feelings for her.

Perhaps he really *was* a monster, after all.

But before he could retreat or flee, Sybille leaned in to close the final gap between them and laid her lips gently on his.

"I love you too," she breathed, hunching slightly so she could burrow her head tentatively into his chest.

Conrad held her for a long time, savoring her warmth against him and the faint echo of her words. At some point, he felt himself press his lips against the top of Sybille's head and felt her bandaged hands begin to fumble with the heavy buttons of his military jacket.

It was not entirely graceful. Both of their bodies were broken, and it took Conrad a long time to force his wounded leg out of his trousers. He fumbled with the laces of her dress, and Sybille bumped his head with her elbow as she tried to help him. It was not the mad rush of anticipation that Georg had so often described to him.

It was something entirely different.

When at last he'd undone the final lace, Sybille stepped back to let her dress fall away from her shoulders.

Conrad did not know what to say. Standing before her in his own nakedness, he felt more scared than when he'd lain strewn, half-dead on the battlefield. He wondered for the first time in his life if he were attractive and was equally terrified of knowing the answer.

Sybille stood before him with her clothes pooled at her feet, her lithe arms hanging bashfully at her side. Her cuts and bruises had mostly healed, but she was still so thin that Conrad could almost count each rib as she breathed. Her small chest stooped a little as she looked at him, as though she were wondering the very same things as him.

"You're beautiful," Conrad said without thinking.

Sybille looked at him for a long moment, and then she snorted with laughter and pulled him to her.

Her small breasts were warm against his chest and Conrad lost himself in the exquisite pleasure of kissing her lips. Sybille leaned against him and gave a soft moan as she ran a bandaged hand through his hair. Conrad kissed her neck and ran his hands down the small of her back. Sybille moaned again and pulled his face his back to hers.

"I love you, Conrad," she said again, and Conrad saw that there were tears in her eyes.

She does love me, he thought to himself. And that thought filled him with such an overwhelming joy that he thought his heart would burst.

Conrad moved his hands further down Sybille to the small of her back, where he froze, unsure, and pulled his lips slightly away from Sybille's.

Sybille felt him stop and giggled softly in the dark of the apartment. It was a sound he'd never heard her make before; like hearing a mastiff sing.

"Sorry," he said, embarrassed. "I've never done this before."

"It's okay," Sybille said, kissing him gently on the mouth. "Neither have I."

Sybille wiggled herself against him until Conrad's hands cupped her butt. He gave her a tentative squeeze, and she laughed and kissed him again.

They made love on the sofa in the sitting room. They had to stop a few times to readjust themselves around their broken limbs, but they barely noticed.

Sybille gasped sharply as Conrad entered her, and he stopped, terrified that he'd hurt her.

"It's okay," she said, kissing him and pulling her back down on top her. "It's supposed to happen. Just go slowly."

Sybille urged him on, and Conrad kissed her neck again as they pressed close against one another, abandoning themselves to their newfound rhythm. All too soon Sybille gave a soft, surprised shudder and her mouth opened as if to scream. Conrad felt himself lose control as a hot, glorious sensation spread throughout his entire body. He gasped, breathless, as he came, and Sybille held him tightly against her body with her broken hands, unwilling to let him go.

They did not hear the footsteps coming down the corridor outside the flat, or remember that Conrad had forgotten to bolt the door behind him when he'd first come home.

"*Frohe Weihnachten!*" Georg bellowed as he let himself in, holding an expensive bottle of pear schnapps in each hand. "Merry Christmas!"

Conrad and Sybille froze, then turned to find Georg staring at them, dumbstruck. Georg stood in the doorway a moment. A look of wretched disbelief stretched itself across on his face.

"Conrad…" he shouted in disbelief. "A Negress?!"

CHAPTER 15

DECEMBER 1904

Conrad hurried down the hallway after Georg, trying desperately to shove his shattered leg back into his trousers. He heard Sybille locking the door behind him as he hobbled at a half-run, cursing every lingering second that it cost him as Georg flew down another flight of stairs ahead of him.

"Georg!" Conrad called down to him as he started down the main stairway, no longer caring if any of his neighbors heard him. "Georg, please wait!"

Georg ignored him and continued briskly down the last flight of stairs. Conrad swore again and staggered down the stairs as fast as he could manage. The building's lobby was empty when he reached the bottom, except for the elderly night watchman who sat gaping at Conrad from behind his small desk.

There was no sign of Georg.

Conrad stood petrified at the bottom of the stairs, leaning against the railing for support as he caught his breath.

Georg had seen Sybille. He'd seen the two of them…together. Georg had discovered Conrad's carefully constructed sanctuary, and Sybille was now in terrible danger.

Where had Georg gone? Conrad asked himself, his heart racing inside his chest. And what would he do?

"Excuse me, sir," the night watchman said hesitantly.

The small man peered at Conrad's flushed face with an odd look of lewd curiosity.

Conrad knew that he looked disheveled. His coat hung half-unbuttoned from his shoulder, and his chase after Georg had left him pink and breathless.

"The, er, gentleman who just departed left these for you, sir," the old man said, regathering himself. "He muttered something about them being a Christmas gift for you."

"Oh," Conrad said awkwardly as he tried to catch his breath. "Yes. Thank you."

He crossed the small lobby, picked up the two bottles from the night watchman's desk, and muttered another artless thanks. If his head were not already spinning, he might have laughed at just how badly he needed a drink right now. Conrad had no idea how Georg had acquired schnapps in an African colony at war, though he had no doubt it must've cost his cousin a small fortune.

Conrad stared out the main door, willing Georg to reappear. He would've preferred if his cousin had barged back into the lobby and eviscerated him on the spot. Conrad would have rather had Georg scream at him, hit him, and call him a fool. Anything was better than the uncertain quiet of the vacant lobby.

"Here," Conrad said as he handed both bottles back to the night watchman. "*Frohe Weihnachten.*"

The small man gaped at the bottles as Conrad began to limp back up the stairs, not believing his good fortune.

Almost belatedly, he called after Conrad.

"Th-thank you, sir! *Frohe Weihnachten!*"

As Conrad climbed the flights of stairs slowly back up to the apartment, he teetered between fear and despair. He hadn't caught Georg, and now Georg was out somewhere in Windhoek where Conrad would never be able to catch him. And he had seen Sybille!

After the first flight of stairs, Conrad forced himself to stop and consider what that really meant.

The Commander of the Schutztruppe had seen him locked in a lover's embrace with Sybille. That in and of itself was unfortunate but not immediately dangerous.

There were several establishments in Windhoek that provided Schutztruppe and division men far more passionate luxuries. Sex with a native was illegal for German colonists, but even if the crime might be looked down upon by the strictest inner circles of Windhoek society and the more prudish officers' wives, Conrad knew several officers who frequented Windhoek's Black brothels. Most Schutztruppe men considered it a sort of exotic rite of passage. If Conrad were truly lucky, Georg would think he'd found his cousin with a common whore and had rushed out for modesty's sake.

Yet something in the way that Georg had looked at him told Conrad that he would not be that lucky.

The real danger lay in Georg figuring out that Sybille was a Herero. But Conrad did not see how Georg could possibly know that. Apart from knowing to round up any dark-skinned people fleeing from Waterberg and to attack the villages their officers brought them to, Conrad did not believe that many German soldiers could tell exactly what a "Herero" looked like. Conrad himself still had trouble telling many of the smaller tribes apart from one another.

There might be older, seasoned Schutztruppe men who boasted that they could tell the difference, but Georg certainly was not one of them. It was not as if Sybille bore a mark or a tattoo that labeled her as a Herero. Georg would certainly remember her eyes, but Conrad could not do anything about that.

When Conrad reached his apartment, he unlocked the door quickly and hurried inside, thankful that none of his neighbors had ventured out into the hall to see what had caused the late-night commotion. He did not see Sybille as he slipped inside the door and guessed that she must have hidden in the bedroom. The night sky hung like a pair of thick, black curtains over the windows, obscuring all but the faintest glow from the streetlamps below.

It was probably somewhere close to midnight, Conrad thought to himself.

Nothing was going to happen before morning, at least.

Conrad stood just inside the door, utterly lost in an opposing swirl of terrifying and mollifying thoughts that led him nowhere. After some time, he heard Sybille's voice calling to him from behind the bedroom doorway.

"Conrad?" she whispered furtively into the main room.

"Yes," Conrad answered. "It's me."

"Is he here?" Sybille's voice asked hesitantly through the dark.

"No," Conrad replied. "He's gone."

There was a beat of silence, and then he heard the soft scratch of a match being struck and the hissing breath of a tiny flame. A small glow rose from inside the bedroom, and Sybille appeared slowly from behind the door, balancing a candlestick in her bandaged hands. The pale orange light shone eerily upon her. Her faded blue dress hung disheveled from her shoulders, making her look like a ghost in a hospital gown.

Conrad hurried to her and took the candle from her hands. He made to gather her up in his arms, but Sybille stopped him.

"Am I safe?" she asked him bluntly.

There was a real fear in her voice, though she was trying hard to mask it. Conrad felt the familiar pang of guilt. It was his cousin who had scared her so completely and who now held her life in his hands.

"I think so," Conrad said, placing the candle on the nearby counter. "Yes, I'm sure of it. You're still safe here. Georg won't know who you are or even that you're a Herero. And I think he'll be far too embarrassed to ask me."

A small glimmer of hope crossed Conrad's mind as he spoke. Could Georg's interruption actually help Sybille? If Georg knew that Conrad cared for her, perhaps that might afford Sybille some measure of protection. Perhaps she might be able to venture out of the apartment! It would be risky. She would have to avoid Alte Feste and Captain Ulrich's men, but with Petyr's help...it might be managed.

Sybille did not respond. After a moment, she folded her long frame back into Conrad's chest.

He wrapped his arms gently around her and tried to quiet everything else.

None of this was how he'd pictured it, but for the moment, he was holding the woman he loved, and that was all that mattered.

Georg had just been shocked and embarrassed. Sybille was safe for tonight, and they had time to figure everything out tomorrow.

A good while later, Sybille broke off the embrace, took Conrad's hand, and led him into the bedroom where they both collapsed into an exhausted heap.

*

Conrad slept horribly. His thoughts would drown themselves out for a few minutes, but soon an odd overhanging unease would grip at a corner of his mind, and he'd find himself awake again, unable to rest.

He'd felt this way the night before Waterberg when he'd lain restless in his tent, feeling his dread stalking him from just beyond his sight. He imagined that this was what prey felt like just before being run down. A gazelle never saw the leopard perched invisibly in the tree above, but it must surely sense a dooming change in the air.

Sybille slept fitfully as well, though Conrad did not think that she ever woke up. Conrad lay rigid beside her, afraid of frightening her in case she forgot in her dreams that he was there. He found her soft breathing soothing, and several times he'd felt his eyelids droop heavily as he listened to her and allowed himself to get lost in the rise and fall of her back.

Yet the foreboding he felt in the dark would not leave him, and each minute he spent alone in the blackness only stirred a desperate hunger within him not to face the shadows on his own. When he could no longer bear the pressing night, he chanced laying his hand gently on Sybille's hip. He needed to assure himself that she was still there and that he had not somehow imagined her.

Sybille did not stir, but in a drowsy motion pulled his arm across her sleeping form and tucked it between her breasts. She rolled her hips to meet his, and she curled her long limbs into the crooks of his legs.

Her body was warm, and Conrad clasped her as tightly as he dared. His fears would still not leave him, but holding Sybille, he felt he was at least anchored

306

to something real. As long as he held her, the trailing beasts in the dark could not consume him.

Sybille did not wake up until the sun had already half-risen outside the windows of the main room. Conrad would be late for von Trotha's morning briefing, but he could not bring himself to rise from the bed. He could've slipped his arm out of Sybille's grasp without waking her, but he'd stayed where he was, unwilling to relinquish the feel of her against him.

He kissed her cheek gently when she finally stirred, and then, at last, he forced himself into the washroom to dress for work.

Conrad had his coat half-buttoned when there came a heavy knock at the door.

"Herr Huber?" called a voice from out in the hall. "It's me, Corporal Knef. May I have a word with you, please? It's urgent."

Conrad did not move. There was nothing in Knef's voice that sounded threatening, but his presence at Conrad's door was troubling. Conrad was supposed to be at the Residence right now. Why would Knef have sought him out at home? He was not *that* late.

Sybille appeared from the washroom, and Conrad mouthed for her to stay still. He thought about gesturing for her to hide in the bedroom while he spoke to Knef, but something stopped him. The same gnawing shadow that had tormented him all night swelled inside him once more and choked off his response. Something was not right.

"Herr Huber?" Knef called again. "Herr Huber, are you home?"

Conrad decided not to answer. He hadn't turned on any lights inside the apartment, and so long as he did not make a sound, Knef would have no reason to suspect that Conrad was home. If anything, Knef would assume that he'd missed Conrad on his way back to the Residence.

After a few moments standing frozen in place, Conrad heard Knef's footsteps fade away down the hall. Conrad's sigh of relief surprised him. He hadn't noticed he'd been holding his breath.

Conrad did not fully understand why he had chosen to avoid Knef rather than talk to the man. They'd been playing cards together for months and had worked side by side holding the colony together before von Trotha had arrived. Perhaps he'd come to collect the money for Georg's Christmas present?

Yet as the last of Knef's footfalls sounded back down the corridor, Conrad began to worry once more that he had misjudged Georg's reaction.

Was Georg now searching for Sybille? Had he somehow discovered that she was a Herero? Had Knef been sent to question him and search his apartment?

Conrad suddenly decided that he would not go to Schwerinsburg today. That was risky if Knef was looking for him, but something in his gut told Conrad that he could not leave Sybille alone.

As the hours ticked by, Petyr did not appear at the apartment as he should have in the early afternoon. The boy's absence seemed to confirm Conrad's fears that something was amiss, although he did not know what it was.

Sybille sat on the sofa and fidgeted absently at a needlepoint set that Petyr had smuggled to her from her old room at Schwerinsburg. She could not grip the needle with any kind of dexterity and could only manage a few sloppy pulls of the thread before her hands began to throb.

Conrad sat in the small armchair opposite her and tried to distract himself with the only book he possessed, a copy of Bartholomeu Dias' *Birds, Mammals, and Fauna of Southwest Africa* that he'd borrowed from Leutwein nearly a year ago. Neither of them spoke as they waited anxiously for Petyr to come. Whatever was going on, surely Petyr would find a way to let them know what had happened.

When Petyr had not appeared by three o'clock, Conrad grew truly worried. He'd managed to fix Sybille and himself a meager lunch of hard bread and overripe fruit without too much noise, and they'd eaten in agitated silence, each only chewing a few muffled bites at a time. The food sat heavily in Conrad's stomach, and he dreaded the inevitable call to the washroom. It would be another noise, another chance for someone to hear them.

Perhaps he should have spoken to Knef that morning, but he was committed now. Until he knew what was happening outside the flat, Sybille wasn't safe. If someone should come looking for her, Conrad needed to be here to offer her at least a fleeting chance of protection.

The waiting was the worst part. Conrad had tried to read the same paragraph on Dias' theories about the grazing habits of the hippopotamus seven times before he found himself absently pacing around the small living room. He felt like a mouse hiding from a hungry cat. He couldn't look out of his windows or step within a shadow's distance of his front door.

Mist, he was even fearing using the toilet in his own washroom!

This is inhumane, Conrad thought to himself. How has Sybille managed to stay sane after all this time? She does this every day, and I doubt if I can take even one more minute of this.

Conrad could tell that Sybille was growing more anxious as well, but she hid it behind a practiced mask of deflection. He felt a sudden wave of affection wash over him, and he stopped his pacing to sit beside her.

Here I am, pacing like a loon, he thought. And yet she looks as comfortable as if she were sitting here by choice.

"I hope Petyr is alright," he whispered to her, breaking the silence.

Sybille didn't answer immediately. They hadn't spoken aloud since Knef had first knocked on the apartment door.

"I am sure he's fine," she whispered back after a moment.

Sybille continued to fuss numbly with her needlework, though it was clear that her mind was not on it. It was warm in the apartment, and Conrad longed to take off his heavy coat but could not bring himself to do so. In his mind, the uniform was the last safeguard he possessed for Sybille, and he could not bear to part with it.

Sitting next to Sybille, Conrad suddenly remembered that last night, she had told him that she loved him. And that then they had both lost their virginity. That seemed like a whole other lifetime now, and yet not even a single day had passed.

Conrad had no experience with what one was supposed to say to someone after they told you they loved you too, but he could not imagine a worse situation in which to discuss what had happened last night.

There was a gentle pleasantness that ebbed between them, despite the baking heat. It was the same sense of contentment that Conrad had felt that morning sitting next to her on the train to Tsumeb. The flat was stuffy and sour, but the closeness of Sybille's body to his own was refreshing. Conrad wondered hesitantly, amidst all the fears racing in his mind, if he ought to ask Sybille what they should do about last night.

Conrad had been so absorbed in his thoughts that he did not hear the cluster of heavy footsteps in the hall, and the sharp knock on his door nearly caused him to fall off the sofa.

"Herr Huber?" a firm voice asked. "This is Lieutenant Protz. Herr Huber, are you at home? It is urgent that I speak with you."

Sybille had been startled by the knock as well, and she dropped the needlepoint, which landed with a muted *thump* on the floor.

"What was that?" a second voice asked Protz on the other side of the door.

"What was what?" Protz responded, his voice somewhat muffled.

"I thought I heard something in there," the second voice replied.

Conrad could not be sure, but he thought he recognized Captain Tobias' mild-mannered voice.

There were other men with Tobias and Protz as well. No one else had spoken, but Conrad could feel their gathered presence just beyond the thin walls of the flat. First, it had just been Knef. Now Tobias and Protz had come, and they'd brought an escort.

A Schutztruppe officer *and* a division captain. If Conrad still had any doubts that something serious was going on, there could be no mistaking it now. He pressed his fingers to his lips and motioned for Sybille to stay seated.

"I didn't hear anything," Protz said. "We're wasting our time, Tobias. If Conrad's not dead in a ditch somewhere by now, he certainly isn't going to be holed up in his apartment."

"The Major won't like this," said Tobias. "We should search the apartment to make sure."

"It's locked," Protz said, agitated. "What do you suggest, Captain? That I break down the door in a respectable apartment complex in the middle of the day and announce to every resident that we're searching for a murderous native fugitive? I'm sure that won't send half of the city running for Alte Feste again.

You bust the door down if you want, but I'm not answering to the General when half the capital starts running around in a panic and jams up every road trying to force their way into the fort."

Conrad could almost hear Tobias frowning at Lieutenant Protz, not caring for the colonial man's curt rejection of his superior's suggestion.

What had Protz said? Did they really think that he was dead?

"Fine," Tobias replied. "What do you suggest we do, *Lieutenant*? We've already searched the city as quietly as we can. No one's seen him. The landlord downstairs says Conrad's always gone by the time he gets here in the mornings, and the night watchman's still too drunk to sit up straight, let alone remember if he saw Conrad last night or not."

"We'll double back through the outskirts and meet back at Alte Feste in an hour," Protz said decisively. "I've got men riding to the surrounding villages, but if he *has* been kidnapped, the Nama dogs wouldn't be foolish enough to take him along the main roads. You'd better hope he's still in the city somewhere, or we're not likely to find him at all."

"I still think we should search the place," Tobias said again as their voices began to move back down the hallway. "I'm not about to go back into the Major's office and tell him we lost his cousin. Even if he's a traitor, he's still…."

Conrad did not hear the rest of what the two men said as they hurried back down the hall. He sat immobilized by the single, damning word buzzing in his ears.

Traitor?

At best, it seemed that both the Schutztruppe and the division thought him kidnapped or dead. At worst, it sounded as though they thought he was a traitor on the run.

How in God's name had that happened so fast? What had Georg assumed from Conrad being with a native woman?

There would be time enough to worry about that later, Conrad told himself as he shook off his stunned disbelief. Right now, both he and Sybille were in a great deal of danger.

Georg had men searching the city and the surrounding villages for him.

Whatever the reason had caused this, the apartment was no longer safe. Soon enough, someone would come who was not going to be content to simply knock on the door. Sybille could not be here when that happened, and now, it seemed, neither could Conrad. The sanctuary he'd hastily constructed was crumbling, and unless they moved quickly, he and Sybille risked being trapped beneath its rubble.

When he was sure Protz and Tobias were gone, Conrad began to move purposefully around the apartment.

They would have to move at night, or they'd be seen for certain. They could hide underneath the back stairwell in the building's basement until then. Conrad had never seen a soul go down there.

Conrad quickly rummaged amongst his things until he found an old knapsack amongst a pile of boxes he'd never bothered to unpack when he'd moved from the Residence. Almost without thinking he began to stuff the sack full of a change of clothes for both of them.

He could hear Sybille in the kitchen gathering what food was left in the pantry into a small bag, and he heard her grab his canteen from where he'd hung it on the hat rack. He hadn't spoken a word to her, but she'd read his sense of alarm and busied herself right away.

They both worked fast, their heads spinning as they snatched whatever supplies they set their eyes on.

We'll stow away on the night train to Walvis Bay, Conrad thought as he opened the apartment door cautiously and ushered Sybille quickly onto the back stairwell.

His thoughts were racing now, trying to sketch the rough outline of a plan amidst his rising panic and fear of discovery. He didn't know how much time they had before the next officer came to call on him, and his legs carried him out the door before he even knew where they were going.

We'll take the back alleys to the boxcar yard and slip into a third-class car for Walvis Bay. No one rides third class at night, and once we're in Walvis Bay, I can book Sybille passage on a ship to Cape Colony at the British consulate. Then I can sell my pocket watch and book her a train ticket to Gaborone.

It was impossible to keep quiet as they hurried down the stairs toward the basement. Conrad could hear his heart's frantic thumping in his ears as he tried to urge Sybille faster down the flights of stairs. Someone might step out onto the staircase at any moment, and if they were seen, Conrad had no doubt that the Schutztruppe would hear about it.

Conrad was so focused on helping Sybille that he did not see Petyr rushing up the staircase toward them. Petyr bolted up the flight of stairs below them and slammed hard into Conrad's chest.

Petyr screamed in surprise, and Conrad just barely managed to clamp a hand over the boy's mouth to keep him from being heard. Petyr was wide-eyed, and his chest heaved as though he'd been running for his life. He twisted and squirmed under Conrad's grip like a fish caught in a net, not knowing who had grabbed him.

"It's okay, Petyr!" Conrad muttered as loudly as he dared. "It's okay, it's okay. It's Conrad!"

Petyr stared at him in horror as though he did not recognize him.

"It's okay! It's okay!" Conrad repeated. "*Eins...zwei...drei...*"

Petyr stopped struggling in Conrad's arms, and Conrad took his hand away from Petyr's mouth.

Vier...fünf...sechs, Petyr mouthed, though no sound came out of the trembling boy's throat.

Then suddenly, above them, they heard the doorway to the stairwell open and the creak of a heavy boot on the first stair.

Sybille wasted no time in snatching Petyr's hand and pulling him back down the way he'd come. Conrad followed closely behind them, preening his head back above them as they ran. Whoever was above them had surely heard them by now. Conrad started to panic.

When they reached the first floor, Sybille dragged Petyr with her down the final flight of stairs into the basement, and Conrad shoved the outside door open as hard as he could.

The flimsy, wicker door shot outward with a loud *whack,* and Conrad hurried down the basement stairs as the door ricocheted and slammed shut with a bang.

Conrad paused halfway down the last flight, frozen in flight until he heard one of his elderly neighbors curse under his breath.

"Damn soldiers," the gruff voice mumbled as the man opened the door gently and stepped out into the light of the street. "Breaking the damn door off looking for some dumb Negro."

Conrad waited for a minute or two until the old man's grumbling faded away down the street. Then, when he was sure that no one else was behind him, he hurried down the basement stairwell after Sybille.

*

The basement was little more than a half-floor chiseled out of the building's foundation. It consisted mostly of a small boiler room, which was almost never in use, and a few small closets that were available for residents to rent for storage. Conrad did not know many of his neighbors but judging from the few scattered pieces of decaying furniture that lay cluttered about the floor, he felt safe in his assumption that no one was likely to venture down here today.

And if they did, well, he would deal with that when it happened.

It was surprisingly cold. The basement was not large, but it had been dug deep. Almost no light filtered down from the ground floor entrance, and the walls were damp and half-covered in a pale, green mold.

Once the three of them had wedged themselves beneath the stairwell, Conrad noticed the blood on Petyr's face and arms. His right eye had nearly swelled shut, and he bore several deep cuts along his limbs. A nasty gash on his forehead was still trickling blood down his face, and the boy looked as though he might faint at any moment.

Conrad looked down at his own hands and realized that they were stained red from where he'd grabbed Petyr.

"Oh, Petyr," Sybille whimpered, gathering the boy as close to her as she could in the cramped space. "Oh, Petyr."

Conrad fumbled in his jacket pockets until he found his handkerchief. Sybille took it from him and began to dab at Petyr's wounds as best she could.

"What happened to you, Petyr?" Conrad asked tentatively after a moment.

Since he had practically forced the boy into helping him hide Sybille, Conrad wasn't sure he really wanted to know what had happened to Petyr. He didn't know if he could bear the additional strain on his conscience. But he had to find out what had had happened to give them away.

"What's going on out there?" Conrad added. "What's happened?"

Petyr took a few more frantic breaths, and then he told them.

The men had jumped him inside Leutwein's garden. He'd been carrying a pile of clean linens to one of the bungalows for Ndahepuluka, the pretty maid at Schwerinsburg who slept with German soldiers, and whom Petyr hated. Ndahepuluka did not feel like working this morning and had given Petyr her load of linens to carry. The laundry had been so tall that he hadn't seen them coming.

The men wore Schutztruppe uniforms. They had demanded to know where Conrad was. Petyr had not known why they would be looking for Conrad, but he had guessed immediately that something was wrong. When Petyr did not tell them, the men beat him. At first, just to make him talk.

Two harried division captains had walked out of the Residence and recognized Petyr. Petyr thought he recognized one of the men as Captain Ulrich, but he wasn't sure. They had wanted to know where Conrad was too.

Ulrich had been patient at first. He'd explained to Petyr that Conrad was a traitor now and that he and the other men needed to find him. He said there wouldn't be any more trouble for him if he told them where Conrad was. But when Petyr had remained silent, Ulrich had grown red in the face and had let the Schutztruppe men beat him again.

They'd screamed at him as they hit him and demanded that he give up Conrad.

He knew where Conrad was, didn't he? Where was the Nama princess? He knew where she was, too, didn't he? He was a fucking useless Hottentot. Nobody would miss him if they killed him, would they? And they would love to kill him. They were going to rip his arms off and leave him for the hyenas. They could write home to their girlfriends about how they'd speared a little native boy with their bayonets. Where was Conrad?

But Petyr had not told them anything. He'd cried and begged them to stop, but he did not tell them anything about Conrad or Sybille. When the Schutztruppe at last thought that they had either killed him or that he'd blacked out, they'd left, and Petyr had crawled underneath a nearby bush to hide.

He had hidden underneath the bush for an hour or more. He'd cried for a while, but his body hurt too much when he sobbed, so he'd forced himself stop. He didn't know where Erwin was, and he didn't think that any of the maids would help him.

He was too scared to leave the bush. After a while, two clerks from von Trotha's staff wandered into the garden. The men were relaxed and had taken a break from their morning work to smoke a cigarette outside. Neither of them saw Petyr hiding beneath the bush.

"...should have seen the General when he read the telegram," the first man said to the other. "I thought he was going to explode. Shouted himself hoarse about all the corruption Leutwein had allowed. Said he always knew Leutwein's boy was a blackie-lover. 'They're all blackie-lovers in that lot! Every last fucking one of them. Leave soft men in Africa and they all turn into blackie-lovers.'"

The second man had laughed as his friend's imitation of von Trotha's heavy Saxon shouting and then took a heavy drag on his cigarette.

"I never would've thought Herr Huber was a traitor," he said after a bit.

"Yes, it's always the meek ones you've got to watch out for," the first man replied. "Them and the pathetic ones like fucking Captain Abel. What I don't understand is how he just let Herr Huber walk out of his camp like he was taking the Negress for a damn walk."

"Pretty pathetic to send a telegram to the General's attention inquiring about his reward, too," the second man agreed. "There's a war going on down south, for Christ's sake. I bet Abel's likely to be sacked before the day's over."

"He'll be lucky if von Trotha doesn't toss his miserable ass into his own prison," the first man said as he flicked his cigarette butt into the ground. "As for Herr Huber, he'll be lucky if von Trotha's men find him first. At least he's likely to get a trial if the division catches him. His cousin's likely ordered the Schutztruppe to shoot him on sight, I'll bet. This cock-up is likely to bust Major

Huber all the way back to the rear ranks. His own cousin's been smuggling blackies out of the camps right under his nose!

"Noah from the 3rd battalion said that Conrad has been going to the Iron Palace every morning for over a month. Poor bastard must've thought he enjoyed his endless stories about Fat Black Mary. I bet Herr Huber was looking for this Nama princess the whole time."

"Why do you think he did it?" the second man asked.

"Who knows," the first man replied. "Maybe he really was seduced and kidnapped, and they'll find him dead in a ditch somewhere. That's the cover story Georg's been pushing on the General all morning. I don't think the Nama could've bribed him, but I wouldn't put it past the fucking British to have put him up to this. Bet those bastards down in Cape Colony are loving watching the Kaiser squirm over this revolt. Could've offered Conrad a million pounds just to stir up trouble for all I know."

"You really think he's a British spy?"

"Who knows," the first man said as he lit another cigarette. "Everyone knows the British don't want us getting a foothold in southern Africa. The bastards will be charming to your face, but don't ever think they won't jump on the first chance they find to get us out of here. It's been that way ever since old Bismarck first bullied them into giving up the DSWA.

"They could've offered Conrad a dukedom for all I know. Personally, though, I bet he's green enough he fell in love with the first pair of tits he got his hands on. Makes you stupid enough, that's for sure."

The two men talked and smoked a bit more before stomping out their last butts underneath their heels and turning back toward the Residence. When they'd gone, Petyr had crawled out from under the bush and run as fast as he could toward Conrad's apartment. His whole body throbbed, and twice he had had to stop to vomit, but he forced himself to keep running, praying that he would find Conrad and Sybille before they were caught.

By the time Petyr finished recounting what had happened, Sybille had managed to stop most of the bleeding. Conrad did not meet either of their gazes for a long time. He knew there had always been a risk for Petyr in being caught up in his scheme but seeing the boy's blood dripping from actual wounds shattered something inside Conrad.

Petyr was more than his charge; he was his friend. *Mein Gott*, he was younger than his cousin Frieda. And they could have killed him! Conrad did not doubt that they would have. They'd killed Berriz and his brothers, hadn't they?

All because they were looking for me, Conrad thought. I did this to Petyr the same as if I'd beaten him myself.

Damn Captain Abel! I knew I couldn't keep this charade up forever, but if that stupid fool hadn't been so vainglorious to send von Trotha a fucking telegram…

Conrad felt a gentle weight on his arm. He glanced up and caught Sybille looking at him. There was reassurance in her pale blue eyes, and Conrad clung to it desperately in the dark.

"Are you okay, Petyr?" Conrad asked, placing a hesitant hand on the boy's shoulder.

Petyr still looked as though he wanted to cry, but he nodded in response as Sybille continued dabbing at his arms with the handkerchief.

Conrad paused for a moment. The air in the basement had a foul taste to it. The thought of hiding here until dark made him feel sick and lethargic. He wondered fleetingly if it would not be better for Petyr and Sybille if he gave himself up. If he walked out in the streets of Windhoek and got himself arrested, perhaps the two of them could get away in the chaos.

No, he thought to himself. I can't leave them now.

Even if they had a chance of getting out of the city on their own, he knew they would never escape the division and the Schutztruppe so close to Windhoek. And he would never survive not knowing their fate. For better or worse, he was bonded to them both.

"Petyr," Conrad whispered as his thoughts swirled. "I need you to go find Erwin."

*

Conrad was too busy trying to find his footing to be worried about hyenas. He and Sybille had long ago slipped out of the city's back alleys and the pale glow of the street lamps. It would've been impossible for them to reach Schwerinsburg by the main road. Even at night, they could've been spotted anywhere along the well-lighted street. Even so, Conrad found himself wishing that they had risked discovery as he tripped over another root and stumbled once again on his hands and knees into a thorny sagebrush.

They could see the few lone lights of Schwerinsburg burning in the distance, yet the night was so dark that they could barely see one another as they trudged side by side. Any predator stalking the city outskirts might've found and devoured them with little effort, but no Schutztruppe or division soldiers would expect them to chance the bush at night.

At least, that was what Conrad was hoping.

When they emerged from the maze of sand and sage just above the Residence, they stood perfectly still and waited for Petyr to find them. In the dark, Conrad would never have found the way into Schwerinsburg himself. He was not fond of darkness. He'd lain petrified in near-total darkness when he'd traveled with Noko from Hochfeld to Okahandja, but at least he'd had the embers of their fire. Now, with the night sky cloudy and dim, there was no light at all, and Conrad felt as helpless as if he'd suddenly been struck blind.

When Petyr's hand brushed his own, Conrad nearly shouted in alarm. He could not see Petyr, but he felt the boy's hand wrap around his own as he led Conrad and Sybille slowly down the road the way he had come.

So far, everything seemed quiet. Conrad was still amazed that Petyr could see so well in the dark, but he supposed he shouldn't be. The boy had been sneaking in and out of Schwerinsburg for years for Sybille, carrying messages to her father's agents waiting invisibly in the bush.

Petyr led them past the dark outline of the main gate. They inched forward no more than a foot or two at a time, just beyond the sight of the two guards who chatted drowsily a few yards in front of them.

The three of them slipped past the main gate and edged their way along the compound's main wall. Conrad had lived at Schwerinsburg for a year, but without Petyr leading the way, he would have walked right past the decorated garden gate and never known that he had missed it.

The small gate hung half-open where Petyr had left it ajar, and the three of them crept inside and picked their way silently through Leutwein's garden. Once they made it through, they hurried quickly toward the stables. The last hundred yards were over an open courtyard, and there was no telling when a native staffer might step outside their bungalow to walk to the covered toilets or when a company of soldiers might return suddenly from a late-night patrol.

Inside the stable, they found Erwin nervously stroking the noses of four saddled horses. As soon as he entered the stable, Conrad knew something had gone wrong.

He smelled blood.

Sybille threw her arms around Erwin. She had not been lucid when Erwin had rescued her from the boxcar, and Erwin had not been able to risk seeing her since he'd brought her to the flat. He held her close to him for a moment before ushering her toward one of the horses.

"We got to go now," Erwin hissed to Petyr as he handed the boy the rest of the horses' reins. "They patrolling this whole area looking for them."

As Erwin helped Sybille onto one of the mares, Conrad saw the body.

It was Lucas, one of the Ovambo grooms. He was a young man, not much older than Conrad, and it looked as though his head had been smashed in with a blunt object. Conrad suddenly remembered Lucas's shy grin and his insistence to Conrad that Sybille must be a spy.

Erwin caught Conrad's stare.

"Lucas was a snitch," Erwin said matter-of-factly, pulling Conrad towards a gelding. "I told him to stay away from the stable tonight. But he come here to make trouble for us all. Dead man is no snitch."

Conrad was trying to remember if he had ever spoken to Lucas again when Erwin pressed a pistol into his hand. It was a rusted broomhandle that looked like it hadn't been fired in decades, though the gun itself could not have been two or three years old. The cold feel of it as it touched his hand made Conrad flinch as though the gun might go off at any moment.

"Where…" Conrad started.

"Don't matter!" Erwin hissed at him as he half-hoisted Conrad onto one of the horses.

Petyr was busy tying Sybille's reins together and looping them through the saddle. Her hands were still too raw to grip the rough leather straps, so Petyr notched them firmly to the cantle of her saddle. Petyr dropped the reins of the other two horses in his haste, and Erwin gave Conrad a violent push into his saddle as he dashed to retrieve them.

The horses were fidgeting. They had not been happy at being awoken in the middle of the night, and the smell of Lucas' blood was making them nervous.

Erwin took Sybille's and Conrad's bridles and began to pull the anxious horses out of the stable. The pistol was heavy in Conrad's hand, and he slipped it quickly into one of the saddlebags, praying that he might forget it was there.

As Erwin forced the horses out of the stable, Conrad saw out of the corner of his eye that Gustavus and Ivan were not in their kennel. Von Trotha had been happy to let the two dogs stay at Schwerinsburg since it would've been impossible for Conrad to keep them in his small apartment. Conrad still saw them occasionally through his office window, terrorizing the house staff as they ran wild across the courtyard. But he had not visited them in their kennel since he'd returned from Lüdertiz. It was hard to make out in the dark, but Conrad thought the door bolt looked as though it had been broken. Petyr emerged from the stable and looked at the kennel as well.

"They must've pried the lock open scratching at it," Petyr whispered worriedly to Conrad.

Conrad nodded, cursing their luck. The last thing they needed tonight was those two stalking around the Residence.

As Conrad thought this, he felt a warm, soft weight press on his opposite leg. He turned his head and looked down at his foot. Gustavus stared up at Conrad, his round, blockish head cocked in question, as if he were asking Conrad where he was going. Ivan's bulky outline sat a few feet away, sniffing questioningly in the direction of Lucas' body.

Gustavus had trod up to Conrad so quietly that Conrad's horse had not yet seen him. But Sybille's horse heard Ivan's sniffing and turned her head back toward the stable. When the mare caught sight of the two enormous dogs so close to her, she panicked and tried to break free of Erwin's grasp. The two dogs looked like leopards in the dark, and she whined a loud warning and pulled hard at the reins again. The leather sliced deeply into Erwin's right hand, and the mare's jerking nearly pulled him off his feet.

Conrad's horse turned around at the mare's panic, and when he saw Gustavus' head on Conrad's foot, his eyes went wide with terror. The gelding ripped its own reins out of Erwin's hands and in a wild fury, tried to launch a kick at Gustavus.

Conrad's glasses flew off his face as he was nearly flung out of the saddle. Gustavus dodged the gelding's kick and began barking furiously at the startled horse in retaliation. Ivan quickly abandoned Lucas' body and joined in Gustavus' barking.

Erwin managed to hold unto the mare's reins and frantically tried to calm her. The gelding's reins swung wildly around its face, spooking the horse even more as the dark leather straps struck at it invisibly. Conrad tried to grab at the reins, but he could not see and had to cling desperately to the horse's neck to keep from being thrown. The reins slapped the gelding's eye, and in panic, the horse aimed another kick at the barking dogs.

From somewhere near the Residence, Conrad heard frantic shouting and the sound of several men running. Petyr tried to help Erwin calm Sybille's horse, but the mare spun herself around trying to break free and knocked Petyr off his feet. Sybille pulled at the mare's mane, but the horse threw her head in response, ripping open Sybille's bandages.

Sybille cried out in agony.

The shouting grew louder and through the dark, Conrad heard the unmistakable sound of soldiers' boots and the cocking of weapons.

"*Stopp!*" he heard someone yell at him.

Gustavus, enraged by the gelding's kicks, launched himself at the horse's hindquarters and bit down hard on its flank. The gelding bolted, and the two dogs tore off after it. Conrad was nearly flung out of the saddle once again as the gelding broke into a desperate gallop. From just behind him, Conrad heard the group of soldiers break out into the open ground.

"Fire!" he heard their officer yell.

Rifle rounds tore through the air.

Two shots struck Erwin in the back, and another tore a large hole in his arm. His body crumpled as it caved in, and he fell to the ground, his mouth hanging open in fatal shock. Sybille screamed as the mare tore itself from the dead man's grasp.

Petyr's small body spun backward as a round clipped his shoulder and flung him against the stable wall. The gelding and the mare thundered past the boy, oblivious. Petyr, still on his feet, tried to run after them, one arm swinging limply behind him.

Conrad clutched uselessly at the air, begging his hands to catch the reins so he could turn the gelding around. Petyr ran lopsided, one hand clutching his bloody shoulder as he sprinted as fast as his small legs could carry him. Two Schutztruppe men tore after him and caught him easily. Conrad could see nothing in the blackness, but he heard Petyr scream as they grabbed him.

"Help me!" he wailed.

Conrad shouted and hit and kicked at the gelding, but nothing deterred it. The two horses tore out of the open garden gate as Petyr's cries were cut off by the loud *thump* of a rifle butt.

Shots cracked after them as Conrad and Sybille clung hopelessly to their saddles. There was a chorus of maddened curses and hurried shouts as several patrol men hurried into the stable to give pursuit. Lights flickered on all over the grounds as sleeping aides and staffers stumbled out of bungalows in their nightshirts.

Ivan and Gustavus tore after them, snapping at the horses' legs as the sound of their maddened barking echoed through the night.

But Conrad saw none of it. He could not see Sybille crying beside him or her mare galloping recklessly behind his horse. He did not see the bullet that whizzed past his side and tore a hole through his flapping jacket tail or the hurried saddles being thrown across the division's horses behind them. He did not even notice his own tears running down his face.

All he saw was the numbing blackness that stretched endlessly before them as the horses cut across the main road and hurtled unknowingly into the bush.

CHAPTER 16

DECEMBER 1904

Conrad woke up in the saddle. His joints began protesting before he'd even opened his eyes. The gelding had stopped moving, and the sounds of its labored breath echoed in Conrad's ears.

The sun blinded him as he opened one eye cautiously. He had to blink several more times to combat the fearsome glare. When his eyes finally adjusted, he found himself slumped over the gelding's neck. His body was drooping dangerously out of the saddle. It was a miracle he hadn't fallen off in the night. His hands were starting to turn blue from his vice grip around the horse's mane. Uncurling his hands sent a wave of pain down his arms as the blood eagerly rushed back into them.

They had stopped at a small stream bed that snaked its way defiantly through the endless plain of dried grass and sage. The gelding had buried its nose as far as it could into the shallow, murky water and was sucking down water madly, pausing only long enough to cough it back up as he struggled to catch his breath. Conrad did not know how his horse had found the pitiful stream, but he could see that it was not going to be persuaded to abandon it for a long while.

He slipped his legs out of the stirrups and swung his throbbing legs over the saddle, feeling the gelding shiver with relief as he did so.

His legs buckled immediately when they touched the ground. Conrad crumpled underneath his own weight, feeling as though Albert Witbooi had just struck him again. His wounded leg screamed in protest, and he lay prostrate in the orange sand until the throbbing subsided.

Once the worst of the pain had ebbed, Conrad rose to his knees and crawled to the tiny stream. The shallow water was so clouded that he could not see his reflection in it. His face was chafed from the wind and dust, and the water stung his cheeks as he cupped his hands and drank greedily. The water was mostly mud and covered in a thick layer of the gelding's froth. It tasted terrible, but Conrad drank handful after handful.

When at last he stopped, he felt his stomach roll over, and he vomited most of the water back up. He stayed hunched over on all fours, struggling to catch his breath.

After a while, he felt a heavy tongue licking at his face and turned to see Gustavus' nose hovering an inch from his face. The dog's saliva burned his blistered face, and Conrad lashed out at Gustavus, swinging a spent arm at the dog's head.

"It's all your fault!" Conrad screamed at him, his blow missing widely. "You stupid dog! This is all your fault!"

Gustavus retreated a few steps and whimpered softly.

Conrad stared heatedly at Gustavus for a moment, wanting to strike at the dog again. His whole body was heaving painfully as he continued to fight for breath, and he wanted to lash out at something, anything.

Then, as quickly as his anger had come, it fell out of him in a weak sigh.

"I'm sorry," he said to Gustavus. "I'm sorry, boy. It's not your fault."

He motioned for the dog to come back, and he scratched his large head with his blistered hand.

Conrad turned to look behind him. Sure enough, Ivan lay dozing a few yards away, his massive chest rising and falling slowly in the mid-day sun. The two dogs had managed to keep pace with the horses all night. Conrad could hardly believe it, but they'd chased them clear across the bush and now sat patiently waiting as if the whole affair had been a game, and they expected to head for home any minute.

Dried grass hills stretched before them in every direction, an endless patchwork of blistered rocks and windswept gullies. The horizon marched itself forever onward, and Conrad felt lost in the vast sameness that surrounded him. Each dune that rose and fell across the landscape was identical to the next one. Save for a few solitary camel thorn trees that rose like overturned pyramids from the sand, the desert lay vacant and empty, a vermillion sea broken here and there by the strained existence of mutinous brown-green grass.

Nothing stirred but the breeze and once Conrad regained his breath, he realized in a panic that he was alone.

"Sybille!" he called out as he forced himself up onto his wobbling legs. "Sybille! Where are you?"

He found her mare only a few yards away, hidden by a small bend in the stream. Sybille lay folded over her horse's back like a trophy pelt while her exhausted mare stamped impatiently for her to get off. Sybille did not answer him, and as Conrad approached her, he saw why.

Sybille was whimpering faintly, her voice little more than a soft mewing that he could barely hear over the wind. She lay sprawled across the mare's back as though her body did not have the strength to rise from where it lay crumpled in the saddle.

Her hands were stretched out in front of her, frozen in place where she'd clung terrified to the reins the night before. The rough leather had reopened the cuts on Sybille's hands and dug themselves deep into the flesh of her palms. A small group of flies buzzed eagerly around her clenched fists. Hours in the sun had crusted most of Sybille's blood over, embedding the reins into her hands.

"*Scheisse,*" Conrad swore out loud before he could stop himself.

It took all of Conrad's remaining strength to get Sybille off her horse. She did not scream as Conrad ripped her hands apart from the reins. Conrad doubted that she had any voice left to scream with. A good bit of skin stayed

327

fused to the leather, and Sybille's hands began to bleed freely once more.

Conrad managed to carry Sybille to the stream and dipped her hands into the slow-moving water. He knew the water must be filthy, but it was the only way he could think to stop the bleeding.

Leaving Sybille with her hands in the stream, he dragged himself back to where the mare was now also frantically slurping at the brown water, and he dug around in Sybille's saddlebags. He found a crumpled and well-worn shirt that Erwin had commandeered somewhere in Schwerinsburg, and he brought it back to the stream bank.

Conrad tore the length of the thin shirt into strips and used the rest to dry and dab at Sybille's hands. He tied several of the linen strips tightly around her hands, and teetering from his own fatigue, lay Sybille down beneath a nearby flame thorn.

The tree was much smaller than the grand one that had grown behind Maharero's bungalow in Hochfeld, yet it had somehow managed to survive in the rocky, orange soil. The tree offered the only visible shade, and its small barbs gave Sybille a tiny promise of shelter from whatever dangers might be lurking nearby. Gustavus and Ivan were still loafing lazily nearby, and with the added security of the dogs and the thorns, Conrad left Sybille and forced himself back to his feet.

There was no sign of anyone. No sign of a Schutztruppe patrol and no sign of a nearby village or hunting camp. Conrad recognized nothing about his surroundings and wondered in a daze just how far their horses had run in a single night.

It did not prove difficult to catch the two horses. After they had had their fill from the stream, both the gelding and the mare seemed content to let Conrad take their bridles and lead them away from the stream. He had no idea how to tie up the horses to keep them from running away, so he settled for looping their reins several times around one of the flame thorn's sturdier-looking branches and praying that nothing spooked them.

With the horses tended to for the moment, Conrad began to root through both sets of saddlebags to take inventory of their supplies.

He was disappointed to find that they did not contain much. In the mare's saddlebags, he found a faded red dress that he guessed was perhaps five or six sizes too large for Sybille, two hastily filled canteens of water, a loaf of hard bread, and a small length of rope. In his own, he found a spare bridle so worn it looked as though it might fall apart in his hand, a small knife, a wheel of cheese that had crumbled into mushy clumps from the jostling of the saddle, four apples, a blanket, and the pistol that Erwin had slipped him back in the stable.

If he had had the energy, Conrad would've cursed the world. Their plan had been to beg for food along the way, at villages that Erwin knew. They were going to head north into Damara lands before doubling back westward toward Walvis Bay. Erwin knew a few Ovambo folk along the northern coast, and Conrad had hoped that they would care for Sybille and Petyr while he and Erwin slipped down into the English port.

Conrad had dared to hope that he and Erwin might sneak into Walvis Bay and secure the four of them passage on a ship to the British Cape Colony.

But Erwin was dead. Petyr was either dead or imprisoned, and he and Sybille were stranded somewhere deep within the bush. He could not guess how far they'd traveled, only that they had woken up somewhere within the dreaded Kalahari.

Conrad felt bitter tears well up behind his eyes. Everything had gone wrong. He'd gotten Erwin and Petyr killed. It was all his fault.

He knew that neither Erwin nor Petyr would ignore the call to help Sybille. It had been Conrad's idea to try and steal the horses from the Schwerinsburg stable. He would never know what Erwin had thought about his plan or if he had even agreed with it. All he had known when he sent Petyr out of the apartment basement and back to Schwerinsburg with his half-hatched idea was that Erwin would make it happen for Sybille.

Conrad had known he was asking too much of them once again. Yet that hadn't stopped him.

Scheisse, Erwin had killed a man because of him!

And for all their sacrifices, Conrad had repaid Erwin and Petyr by getting them both killed and losing himself and Sybille in a uniform wasteland. They had, at best, two or three days' worth of food and water, and Conrad had no idea how to find the nearest settlement.

He thought of Erwin's dour face meeting him each morning in the Residence kitchen. He remembered Erwin taking pity on him in the aftermath of Conrad's fight in the alleyway with the two Schutztruppe, and the grim cook explaining to him so bluntly why Sybille hated him for it.

He thought of the day that he had taken Petyr with him to the swimming hole and they had had the whole place to themselves. He could see Petyr lounging comfortably on the sun-warmed rocks and remembered laughing as he listened to the boy imitate the female dove's nagging.

He started to cry.

Conrad fell to his knees. His leg shot a painful spasm up his side, forcing him to roll down onto his stomach. His mouth sagged open in the hot sand, which stung his face. Conrad coughed and spat out the sand, his heavy sobs choking him as he did so.

Somewhere within these hills were German patrols, men who had shot at him and labeled him a traitor. They were men he had drunk with, men he had sat beside playing cards late into the night.

And they had all turned on him in a single, terrible day.

Von Trotha would not stop hunting them. The man was not prone to forgiveness. Nor would he forget. Conrad knew that any Germans they encountered now would not hesitate to kill them. Conrad himself might be spared a bullet in the bush, but only for the final and more satisfying justice of a public hangman's noose. That was only, of course, if some other beast did not find them first.

Then, as the sand choked his tears and the breeze of the empty wastes whistled mockingly over his sprawled body, Conrad wondered if it would not be easier to beat them all to it.

He blinked away sandy tears, and his eyes fell on the pistol lying a yard or two away. The broomhandle looked smaller than Conrad remembered. It lay on its side in the sand where Conrad had placed it just a few moments ago. The steel barrel shone slightly through the thin layer of rust, making the pistol seem newer than it probably was. Conrad worked his hand over to the pistol and rested it cautiously over the worn handle. The gun was warm underneath his hand, though it had only been in the sun for a few minutes.

It would at least be quick, Conrad thought as his sobbing waned. Perhaps dying would not be so bad. And it would be far kinder to Sybille than to let hunger, the Schutztruppe, or a leopard get to her. They were practically dead anyway; it was just a matter of how they met their end. What was the point of stretching out their misery any further? Would it not be better to meet death on their own terms?

Conrad thought of his father, Ekkehardt. He had not thought of his father much since he had died nearly two years ago, but as he lay there in the dunes, Conrad could see the faded, puritan face of Ekkehardt as though he were back in Aschaffenburg, dutifully consigned to the back pew of his father's small church. He could see Ekkehardt's stern and sour expressions preening down over the edge of his pulpit, lecturing his flock in a droning voice.

What must he think of me? Conrad thought to himself. The minister's son turned Negro-lover and traitor. And committing suicide above all.

Conrad could feel his late father's disdain glaring down at him from his proud and righteous afterlife. If the man were not already in his grave, Conrad was sure the news of what his only son had become would have been enough to put him there.

All the more reason to make a quick end to it all, Conrad told himself. Let my father's ghost wash his hands of my embarrassment for good.

Conrad was sure he could get to his feet once more to shoot Sybille. He owed her that much, at least. But as his grip tightened around the stolen pistol, another thought thrust itself suddenly into his mind.

What would Maharero think of this?

It was an odd question to ask himself, Conrad thought. He had only met the man once and spoken with him for maybe an hour or two.

Yet Conrad could see Samuel Maharero in his mind as clearly as if the man now stood before him in the desert. Conrad could see Maharero's dark face smiling across from him in his clean-pressed cream suit, a wooden cup of cow's milk nestled casually in his large hands. Conrad remembered each of the carved wooden figures sitting on Maharero's window and the welcomed sanctuary the simple bungalow had offered from the hostile crowd and the hot sun.

He would not approve, Conrad answered himself, feeling more ashamed and more certain of anything since he first arrived in Africa.

The Herero man who'd welcomed a German into his home, bound hundreds of chiefs to a single cause, and charged an artillery battery with nothing but a sword in his hand was not a man who would understand such an acceptance of failure.

Maharero had lost his wife, and he had carried on. He'd been degraded, ignored, and persecuted at the point of a rifle by the Kaiser's government, and still he had carried on. And even when he had found himself and all his people brought before the military might of the German Empire, he had still carried on, leading a desperate, forlorn charge so that some of his people might escape.

No, Conrad thought. Maharero would not approve of this.

He clung to the pistol in the sand a moment longer, for that way would be easy, and getting back to his knees now seemed beyond him. Shame burned within him, a dark wave of fire that nearly forced him into oblivion once more.

But Conrad saw Maharero's lined face, and then he thought of Erwin and Petyr. They had carried on as well. Through trials and horrors that Conrad had never imagined might truly exist, they had carried on. And Conrad loved them for that.

His shame began to recede slowly, and bit by bit he was filled with an overwhelming desire to get back onto his feet. To live. Conrad uncurled his hand from the broomhandle and forced his screaming legs underneath him. Then he went to see what lay beyond the nearest dune.

*

Sybille did not stir until the sun began to set. She sat up slowly, her mind cloudy until the throbbing in her hands brought her out of her fog. Conrad moved closer to her and steadied her with one arm. He held out one of their canteens for her, and she drank clumsily from it, unable to grip it herself.

Neither of them spoke for a while. Sybille seemed to be taking stock of her surroundings, the tethered horses and the empty skyline, and Conrad did not possess the words to describe to her how they had managed to wind up stranded in the desert. They sat huddled together beneath the flame thorn, watching the sun begin its quick descent behind the dunes. It would be dark far sooner than either of them would have liked.

Outside their makeshift barrier of thorns and branches, Ivan had returned from his most recent excursion into the bush with a plump guinea fowl in his mouth. The big dog flaunted his prize in front of them as if expecting some admiration for his hunting prowess. He reminded Conrad of some of the housecats he had seen back in Germany, which did the same thing with mice that they'd plucked from their owners' gardens.

Gustavus had tried to snatch some part of the bird away, but Ivan growled harshly at him, and when it became clear that Ivan was not willing to share his meal, Gustavus got to his feet and slunk away into the dunes to find his own supper.

Conrad watched enviously as Ivan began licking away the guinea fowl's feathers. His own stomach gurgled loudly. He wondered if he should attempt to wrestle the bird away from Ivan.

Perhaps tomorrow, he decided.

He did not have the energy to try it tonight. Even if he could have gotten the bird away from Ivan, he knew that he would never be able to get a fire started. He didn't think there was enough dried grass or twigs around to build one, and even if he managed to get a small fire going, it would surely die out before the bird was half cooked. Besides, on the off chance anyone or anything was scouring the nearby hills, he did not want to have a fire betraying their hiding place.

"Are you hungry?" Conrad asked Sybille as he took his eyes off Ivan and his bird.

She nodded slightly. Conrad retrieved one of the loaves of bread from their saddlebags and what he could salvage of the cheese. He began to chisel away at the bread, surprised at how hard he had to work to free even a few small morsels.

He managed to pry off a few clumps, which he rolled in the remnants of the sharp cheese wheel to soften and then held out for Sybille to gnaw at. She could not bear to hold the bread in her hands. Conrad held a piece of bread up to her mouth, and after a moment's prideful hesitation, Sybille consented begrudgingly to being hand-fed.

It took the better part of an hour for Conrad to feed them both, and the sun was now dipping earnestly behind the horizon. Gustavus had returned with his own prized kill and had already consumed whatever it was before Conrad had slipped the last of the bread back into the saddlebags. The horses seemed content to nibble on the flame thorn branches and the small clumps of grass within their reach. Both the gelding and the mare kept a suspicious eye on the dogs, but neither showed any immediate signs of bolting. Very likely, they, too, were too tired to even consider it.

"Where do you think the soldiers are?" Sybille asked him as Conrad crawled back underneath their shelter.

"I don't know," he answered, glancing out at the dunes as he did so. "I couldn't see anything when I climbed those hills over there, and as far as I can tell, the wind blew away any tracks we might have left. As far as *they* know, *we* could be anywhere."

Gustavus yawned from his spot by the muddy stream and stood up to formally investigate their hiding place. He stuck his large head beneath the opening of the branches but paused when he saw Sybille's hands. She was resting them on her legs, her palms facing upward so they would not fall and get sand into her wounds.

Gustavus gave one of her hands a tentative lick. Sybille winced, and Gustavus drew back slightly. Then, as if it were the only other logical thing to do, the dog wedged the rest of his enormous frame beneath the flame thorn, pushing Conrad out of the way, and laid himself behind her.

Sybille hesitated a moment, then slowly leaned her back against Gustavus, sighing with relief. She lay her hands gently in her lap and relaxed her head against the dog's massive belly.

"Good dog," she said softly.

Conrad chuckled and rubbed Gustavus' ear affectionately. The two dogs really weren't so vicious when you got to know them.

"Well, wherever the patrols are, I don't think they'll be able to find us in the dark," he said. "And it doesn't seem that Gustavus is likely to turn us in either. He seems to like you."

Sybille smiled weakly.

Evening vanished as quickly as it had come. The last edge of the yellow sun was fading rapidly in the distance. The outlines of far-off trees and rocks turned jet black along the horizon, surrounded by half-shells of orange, red, and a thin line of indigo.

It was the most beautiful sunset that Conrad had ever seen.

Beside him, Sybille shivered, and so Conrad ventured out from under the flame thorn once more. As he retrieved the threadbare blanket from the saddlebags, he saw the shadows of five ostriches toddling along one of the distant ridges. He could see their long, powerful legs carrying them across the sand, and he laughed silently as they started to run along the dunes. They were the first signs of life that Conrad had seen all day, and though he could not quite place why, the sight of them gave him an odd sense of comfort.

He returned to their hiding spot with the blanket and draped it gently over Sybille, covering her hands so that the insects could not get at them. Gustavus had already fallen asleep behind her and had begun to snore slightly. Ivan lay asleep on his stomach a few yards from the flame thorn, unconcerned with whatever other creatures might come prowling around the murky water at night.

Sybille still lay with her head against Gustavus and turned to look at Conrad.

"Thank you," she said to him.

"I don't know that I've done anything worth thanks."

Sybille shifted slightly as though she meant to touch him but could not find the strength to move her arms out from underneath the blanket. She gave him a small smile instead.

"We're alive," she told him. "That's enough for now."

She fell asleep again soon after, but Conrad kept his eyes trained on the last light of the day, willing it to remain. When sleep finally took him as well, he hardly noticed, for the light had disappeared completely and he lay still in total darkness.

*

At some point in the night, Conrad's bladder got the best of him.

He tried to ignore it and force himself to fall back asleep, but after nearly half an hour of restlessness, he lost the fight with himself and slid his way slowly out from beneath the flame thorn. It was darker out in the bush than Conrad could've imagined. The stars shone somewhere up in the sky, but it was as if they were covered by a thick, black film that trapped all but the smallest sliver of light.

Conrad could not see his hand in front of his face, and the urge to relieve himself right outside their shelter and then scurry back underneath the thorns was overwhelming. But the ground dipped around the edge of the flame thorn, and Conrad did not think he could ever face Sybille again if she awoke to find that his urine had soaked their blanket.

Cursing loudly in his head, Conrad forced himself to walk out into the night.

The first thing he noticed was the sounds. During the day, the Kalahari had lain still, the only sound the occasional howl of the wind. But at night, a chorus rippled across the desert. Conrad didn't know if it was the buzzing of insects, the soft grating of shifting sand, or the frantic thumping of his own heart, but there was a vibration in the air that clung to him and made him pray for the certain loneliness of the day. With each step he took, he heard the same ambient noise and wished fervently that he knew where Ivan was.

When he'd walked as far as dared, he unbuttoned his trousers and began to relieve himself.

A chilling laugh behind him made Conrad jerk up suddenly, causing him to piss all over his shoes.

It was perhaps the most hellish sound he'd ever heard. Conrad felt as though he'd heard a woman trying to laugh coquettishly at a joke he hadn't told. The noise sounded feminine, but there was something not quite right about it, as though it came from a creature that was trying to sound human but was something else entirely.

Conrad forced his trousers up, ignoring the ache in his bladder, and turned to run back towards the flame thorn.

He froze as he spun around.

Between him and his thorny sanctuary stood a shaggy-coated hyena that eyed him with far too much interest.

At first, Conrad thought it was a wolf. The creature had long legs and pointed ears, yet its rounded snout and bristled hair made it look like some kind of bear. The hyena was tall and looked as though it must've weighed nearly as much as Conrad. Conrad had never been more frightened in his life.

The hyena's face was what terrified him the most. Its skull was massive, with powerful jaws that clicked together as it laughed. The creature watched him with brilliant, brown eyes that betrayed a ruthless cunning. In the dark, the hyena's eyes seemed to flicker as it moved, and Conrad thought he saw eager pride spread across its face. The hyena knew it was not going to go hungry tonight.

It laughed at him again. Conrad did not know if the laugh was a signal to the beast's friends that it had found easy prey or if the horrible thing was actually laughing at his helplessness. The hyena opened its wide mouth, displaying a jagged line of fangs in challenge. And then it charged him.

Conrad stood petrified. He could do nothing but stare at the terrible monster bearing down on him, too frightened to bother making a mad dash for his life.

Then something crashed into the hyena like a battering ram. The hyena gave a loud yelp of pain, and the air was filled with the sounds of gnashing teeth and sharp claws. Conrad heard a familiar bark as the hyena tried to fight off its assailant.

It was Ivan!

The realization brought life back to Conrad's legs. He stumbled backward at an awkward run toward the flame thorn. He could hear the terrible fighting as he fled and he couldn't tell if the hyena or Ivan were gaining ground. Ivan was strong and had taken the hyena by surprise, but Conrad had no doubt the hyena was a vicious fighter. Most natives called them cowards who only hunted the weak or the sick under cover of darkness, but Conrad could not imagine that a creature so horrifying would not put up a fight.

Both animals were enraged now, and by the awful noises each was making, Conrad knew they were both locked in a fight to the death.

Conrad's legs were burning. He should have reached the flame thorn by now. *Mist*, how far had he wandered away in the dark? Had he gone in a big circle?

At last, he saw the flame thorn's blurry outline in the dark, and he dove to the ground near the entrance of their hiding spot. He could feel his belly bruising from the impact, but he clawed his way beneath the briars, all the while expecting his legs to be snatched backward by hungry jaws.

Sybille did not wake up as he slid, chest heaving into their cover. She was dead to the world, and Conrad thought with a shiver that if the hyena had come sniffing by the tree instead of stumbling upon Conrad, it could have and dragged her off without a sound.

When Conrad returned, Gustavus shot out of the bush in a blind rage. As though he had been waiting for Conrad to watch over Sybille, he tore towards the sound of his brother's barking with anxious fury.

A minute passed, though to Conrad, it seemed more like hours. Then he realized that the manic sounds of fighting had stopped. He held his breath. How had the horses not spooked? Were they dead to the world as well or had something already carried them away?

Conrad thought about making a dash for the saddlebags to get the pistol, but he stopped mid-rise as he heard something heavy pushing aside the flame thorn's outer branches.

Gustavus pushed his way passed Conrad and resumed his sentry post behind Sybille. Behind him, Ivan's head and shoulders dug their way into the makeshift shelter, and Conrad threw his arms around him with relief. He had never been so happy to see Ivan.

The big dog could not really fit in the already crowded space, but he managed to lay down partially in the sandy root bed with his head facing out into the night. Ivan's mouth and shoulders were covered in blood, but Conrad could not tell whether it was the dog's own blood or the hyena's. Ivan let out a long sigh that Conrad could not interpret in the dark.

Gustavus whined softly. Conrad wished he knew whether they had killed the hyena or not. If it had only been run off, might it come back? And didn't hyenas usually hunt in packs? Could there be more of them waiting nearby?

He half-crouched and half-lay on top of Ivan, patting his thick neck and murmuring "*danke*" over and over again into the dog's course fur as he stared horrified out into the blackness.

It was not until morning that Conrad realized that he had pissed himself during the night and that Ivan was dead.

CHAPTER 17

JANUARY 1905

They buried Ivan underneath the flame thorn. The ground was hard beneath the sand, and it took most of the morning for Conrad to dig any semblance of a grave. He had pulled a sturdy branch off the flame thorn, and alternating between it and the small knife he'd found in his saddlebag, he managed to cut out a hole in the sand that he hoped would be deep enough. He was drenched in sweat and exhausted by the time he was done, but he could not bring himself to stop until he was sure that no nighttime scavenger would be able to find Ivan's body.

He owed the dog that much at least.

Conrad had found the hyena's body where it had attacked him. The creature's neck had been torn open, and it bore many deep gashes and claw marks along its back and chest. Conrad felt sure that the hyena had died first. Ivan had killed it, made sure it was dead, and then limped back to the flame thorn to die. Conrad couldn't quite explain it, but there was a certain satisfaction in knowing that Ivan had bested the hyena.

Gustavus guarded Ivan's body throughout the morning. At first, he seemed not to understand why Ivan would not get up or respond to his gentle prodding.

Then recognition poured over the big dog's long face and his entire demeanor changed in an instant. He became aggressive and would not let Sybille or Conrad get near Ivan's body. Gustavus barked at Conrad when he came to move Ivan into the grave, and when Conrad ignored him and tried again, Gustavus snapped at him. The dog missed Conrad's arm but had gotten close enough to give him pause.

After a moment's hesitation, Conrad gave up and sat with Sybille at the edge of the stream.

"*Gottverdammt* that dog," Conrad swore as he eased himself onto the sand beside Sybille. "Why won't he let me move the body?"

"He's grieving," Sybille said simply. "Leave him be for a while."

Conrad looked at her in surprise. She sat with her legs stretched out beside her, holding her palms on her knees to keep them clean, and she gave him a frank stare as though he had asked a rather foolish question.

"Dogs grieve?" he asked.

"Of course," Sybille said in a matter-of-fact tone. "Everyone grieves. Birds, dogs, elephants…everyone mourns the loss of a loved one. Just look at him."

Conrad turned back to study Gustavus. The big dog lay beside his brother, his head resting protectively over Ivan's neck. Gustavus made no noise as he lay there baking in the hot sun, but as Conrad looked more closely at the dog's face, he was astonished to see something remarkably familiar in his eyes.

Gustavus stared back at Conrad and in his mind, Conrad thought he could see the dog wrestling with something like guilt. Watching Gustavus pace in circles around Ivan's body, Conrad wondered if dogs *could* blame themselves for something. Gustavus had stayed behind to watch over Sybille and had not been able to help Ivan soon enough. When they had finally gone to sleep last night, Gustavus had woken up to a world where his brother was dead. The dog seemed almost human in the way that he tortured himself, and Conrad felt a surge of affection for him.

"I suppose they can," Conrad said to Sybille after a while. "How long do you think we should let him grieve?"

Sybille gave a slight shrug.

"He'll tell us when he's ready," she said quietly. "And I'd wager he won't let you near Ivan a minute before then."

It was sometime around midday when the sun had reached its sweltering peak that Gustavus finally gave in. He surrendered Ivan's body to Conrad and Sybille with a long, final whine as he moved to lay on the ground next to the small grave. Conrad picked up the heavy body and laid it in the grave with as much ceremony as he could muster under the dog's great weight. Sybille sat stroking Gustavus lightly with the back of her hand, cooing to him that everything would be alright.

When the grave was covered, Conrad shook the dirt from his trousers and stared down at the mound of dry earth. He felt as though he ought to say a few words. Conrad remembered his father mumbling a few words over the body of a neighborhood cat that he had found in the alley near their house when he was six. But his father's words then had been trite and forced. Ekkehardt had only performed the sad little funeral to keep Conrad from crying.

Conrad tried to think of something to say over Ivan's grave, but nothing meaningful enough came to mind. The dog had given his life to save Conrad's. Surely, he deserved more than a few hollow phrases?

Conrad's thoughts turned to Erwin and Petyr as well. And he wished them all peace, because that was all that was left for them.

Sybille came to stand beside him and looped her long arm around his. He was amazed that she was even able to stand. He shouldn't have been, though. She had survived Waterberg and Shark Island, and if will counted for anything, Conrad had no doubt that Sybille would last far longer than he would in the bush. The feel of her weight against him was comforting, and her sweat brought a sudden coolness to his hot skin.

"Thank you," he finally said to the hole filled with orange sand and dirt.

He turned to Sybille.

"Is that enough for a funeral?" he asked her.

Sybille nodded.

"It's enough for now."

With the sun beating down on them, Conrad refilled their canteens in the murky stream and untangled the horses from their make-shift knots. When he had rounded up Sybille's mare, he got down on all fours in front of her and had Sybille step up onto his back to swing her legs over the saddle. It was difficult, but between the two of them, they managed to get Sybille up into her saddle.

Conrad tied her reins to his own, and then he forced himself to jump up onto the gelding. The first time he did not jump high enough and landed hard on the saddle with his gut straddling it. His gelding gave a frustrated grunt from the weight, but after a few moments of pulling and straining, Conrad managed to haul himself upright.

Conrad turned back to Sybille and shot her a hopeless grin.

"Any direction in particular, do you think?" he asked her. Sybille gave him a small half-smile and shrugged.

Conrad nudged the gelding along the streambed and pointed his reins in the direction the water was flowing from. That seemed as good a plan as any.

The horses passed the hyena's gruesome corpse as they rounded the bend in the stream, and Conrad turned around to look back toward the flame thorn. Gustavus still sat by the grave, staring under the tree as though he intended to stay there forever.

Conrad whistled sharply once, but Gustavus did not budge. For a moment, he feared that Gustavus was not going to follow them. But after a long pause, the big dog let out a last, long whine and got to his feet to plod solemnly after them.

*

Two days later, the stream stopped abruptly. There was no obvious reason why; the stream was just no longer there. Conrad had read in Dias' work that sometimes in southern Africa's dry basins, water flowed beneath the ground. But Conrad could not see how that could be the case here. The water simply seemed to vanish.

It was still the rainy season, though that did not count for much. What little rain managed to reach the Kalahari often disappeared nearly as quickly as it had come. Finding this stream before it had dried up had been a stroke of fortune, and Conrad doubted they'd be able to find another in the sagebrush maze.

He swung himself down off the gelding to refill their canteens from the remaining puddle. His bowels ached from the dirty water, but they had no other choice.

Better to die of dysentery in a few weeks than dehydration in a few days, Conrad thought as he watched the muddy water gurgle into their canteens.

That was, of course, if they didn't starve first.

They had eaten the last crumbs of the bread the night before and had only one apple left between them. Neither of them had slept the past two nights. They'd hardly seen any signs of life since their first night, but the thought of Ivan and the hyena kept them both wide awake at night. Conrad doubted that he would ever be able to sleep again.

"Which direction are we heading?" Sybille asked him from atop the mare.

"West, I think," Conrad replied, though he had very little idea.

For the past few hours, Conrad had been trying to determine the position of the sun. When they'd left the flame thorn two days ago, he was sure they had been heading west. But every few minutes the sun seemed to change its mind. And when he would try to find the sun's position once more, the sky reflected so brightly off the dunes it was impossible to tell where the sun itself actually was.

"We could head back down the stream the way we came," Conrad suggested, though he knew that was not really an option.

They had already ridden up the length of the stream for two days, and they did not have enough food to make it back to where they'd started.

Sybille's stomach rumbled behind him.

"Do you want to eat something?" Conrad asked Sybille as he returned their canteens to the dwindling saddlebags.

Conrad's own stomach gnawed at him in protest.

Sybille shook her head.

"I can wait a little longer."

Conrad opened his mouth to insist. She needs it more than I do, he thought.

Her wounds won't heal if she doesn't eat.

But after a moment, he nodded and latched the saddlebag closed.

Sybille was wounded, lost, and hungry, yet enough of her old conviction survived to deny herself the last little bit of food they had left. She might be unable to mount her own horse or even feed herself, but enough of her pride remained that as long as Conrad went without food, she would too.

It was the last true piece of herself she had left, and Conrad could not bring himself to take it away from her. Even to keep her alive another day.

Conrad took the horses' reins and led them to the small stream for a last drink. Both the gelding and the mare sucked at the water eagerly, and Conrad wondered how long a horse could manage without water. He knew they were probably not getting enough to eat grazing at night on scorched shrubs and sage grass. Now they were about to leave their only water source as well.

When the horses give out, we're finished, Conrad thought.

As Conrad bent to gather their reins, Gustavus picked his head up off the ground and stared intently at the nearest hill. Conrad looked out at the hill after him, but he could not see anything. He looked back at Sybille and shrugged.

Then Conrad heard what Gustavus had picked up. Hoofbeats.

"It's a patrol!" Conrad shouted as he fumbled with the horses' reins.

The steady rhythm of at least a dozen horses echoed down from the nearest dune as Conrad wrestled the gelding and the mare away from the stream. Sybille's eyes grew wide as she tried to search for some way to help.

Conrad's fingers were fat from the heat, and the reins refused to knot as the mare sensed his sudden fear and struggled against him. Conrad tugged hard on the mare's reins, spooking the gelding, who sidestepped him and tried to break away. Conrad lurched backward and just managed to catch the gelding's reins.

It was no use trying to tie the two horses together now. The sounds of the patrol grew even louder.

"How the hell did they find us?" Conrad cursed aloud.

They were searching the whole miserable desert, and somehow, a patrol had still managed to find them.

He tried to jump onto the gelding's saddle, but the horse sidestepped him again, and Conrad missed. He smacked his chin on the stirrup as he fell to the ground.

"Go!" he shouted at Sybille through the pain in his jaw. "Go! Save yourself. Go!"

He rolled onto his side and saw, to his astonishment, that Sybille was laughing hysterically.

The "patrol" had stopped a few yards away from the stream as it crested the hill. Staring down at them from the dunes was a herd of small, quizzical-looking zebra.

The zebra eyed Conrad suspiciously while he gaped at them from the ground. They looked like donkeys that someone had meticulously painted with black and white lines. A few of the larger ones stepped out in front of the herd and made a high-pitched braying sound, as if debating whether the herd should turn away from the stream.

Yipyip. Yipyip.

They were much smaller than the two horses that continued to pull at Conrad's grip. Neither of the horses had ever seen a zebra before, and they were clearly unnerved by their smaller, striped cousins.

And then all at once, something seemed to settle the horses. The gelding and Sybille's mare still seemed unsure about the zebra, but they stopped tugging at their reins, and Conrad tried to follow their gaze to see what had calmed them. He looked out at the herd of zebra in front of them and, after a moment, was astonished to see a tall, black mare standing in the middle of the herd.

The black horse stood several hands taller than the zebra that surrounded it, and it looked at Conrad and the other horses with what might've been relief. The mare had a saddle mounted across her back and showed no signs of nervousness around either Gustavus or the humans. She pushed herself impatiently out of the herd of skittish zebra and walked right past the other horses to the stream and began to drink noisily.

Conrad and Sybille were too stunned to speak.

The zebra, for their part, did not seem to trust the big mare's ease. They were clearly thirsty but eyed the two humans skeptically. They waited a minute or so, their wide eyes darting back and forth between the confident black mare, Conrad, Sybille, and Gustavus. None of the zebra seemed to want to be the first to approach, in case the mare was mistaken and there really *was* danger.

But after a while, some of the zebra in the back of the herd became impatient and bumped a few of the zebra in front of them forward. The front zebra gave a few worried *yips*, but slowly the herd nudged itself toward the stream.

Gustavus watched the zebra with mild curiosity and gave a short growl that Conrad quickly shushed. The zebra gave the dog a wide berth and walked around Conrad and Sybille to where the black mare stood drinking. They crowded around the far side of the mare and put her between themselves and the humans.

A few of them bent their necks cautiously to the water, keeping their eyes trained on Gustavus while they drank. The rest watched the desert in every direction.

Sybille had stopped laughing now and watched the zebra with awed attention.

Each of them bore a soft, reddish-brown patch above their nose that gave them a whimsical, foolish look, and their short, cropped manes made them look fuzzy rather than wild. If it weren't for their stripes, Conrad might've believed they were ponies in the Kaiserin's stable.

Only their skittishness made them wild.

Conrad noticed that only a third of the zebra ever drank at one time. And while the big mare seemed at ease at the water's edge, every zebra seemed to be constantly moving, even when standing still. These were not trusting animals. They survived due to their wariness, and only the strength of their thirst had broken their skepticism of Sybille and him.

As Conrad watched the zebra, he noticed that one of them bore four long, faded scars on its flank that made him shudder. That zebra had hidden itself in the middle of the herd and only drank in swift, short slurps before it lifted its head again to scan the horizon.

It was only after the black mare raised her head from the water and snorted loudly that Conrad remembered that she was there. The big horse turned her head toward Conrad and looked at him expectantly.

A long rash roped its way under her belly. The saddle's cinch and stirrups looked as though they had been rubbing against the mare as she ran. The rash did not seem overly large, and the mare seemed more annoyed with it than in pain.

As Conrad slowly got to his feet and made his way over to the big horse, the zebra mirrored him. The whole herd moved backward as Conrad walked toward them, making sure that they maintained the same distance from him as he moved. Conrad could not help but laugh.

It was only when the mare stretched her neck toward him and sniffed his hand curiously that Conrad thought to wonder what had happened to her rider.

This was a German cavalry horse. He recognized the division markings on her saddle. Conrad could not imagine that they were anywhere near a village or town of any size that could've supported a garrison. And he knew the horse was not stolen, for no one would've been so foolish as to keep an obviously military saddle.

The horse had had a rider at some point, but where had she come from? The dunes that stretched before them could have hidden Windhoek or even Berlin itself just behind their horizon, yet Conrad did not think that the zebra would've come anywhere near where there might be people.

And if he and Sybille were truly as lost as Conrad thought they were, then the black mare could only have come to be this lost if some terrible misfortune had befallen her rider.

The Schutztruppe cavalry scouts often rode into the bush in search of fugitives, but Conrad could not imagine that they would be foolish enough to ride too far into the Kalahari.

Conrad stroked the big horse's nose.

The mare must've been part of the division's patrols, then. Or a part of some search party von Trotha had sent out after them. Her rider must've somehow gotten separated from his unit and been knocked out of the saddle by some accident. Conrad pitied the man. Wherever he was, he wouldn't have lasted long without a horse. He saw the scarred zebra take another drink out of the corner of his eye, and he suppressed a shudder.

The mare blew a long, hot snort onto Conrad's hand and turned her attention back to the muddy water.

"Well, she's managed to survive," Conrad said back to Sybille. "Maybe our horses have a chance too. She's a bit skinny, but she's still walking. We should probably get rid of her saddle, though. Might save the horses' strength a bit if we rotate the three of them every few hours."

Sybille nodded in agreement, neither of them having the faintest idea what they were talking about.

"Maybe our luck is changing," she added as an afterthought.

She hadn't meant it to be funny, but Conrad found himself laughing anyway.

It took him several minutes to figure out how to undo the mare's cinch and remove the saddle. He did not want to remove her bridle in case he could not figure out how to get it back on again. Conrad knew she could still eat with it on; he had seen the gelding and the mare manage alright for the past few days.

The big horse shivered with relief as he lifted the heavy saddle off her back. She went immediately down to her knees and fell onto her back with a loud *thud*, rolling in the hot dirt like a gangly puppy.

Both Conrad and Sybille laughed, and they let the mare roll around for a while, watching her ecstasy in being able to scratch at itches she must've had for days.

When the mare climbed to her feet again, Conrad tied her to Sybille's horse. The mare went amicably enough, though she flicked her ears several times in annoyance when she realized she'd been confined to the rear of their small convoy. The zebra watched uncomprehendingly.

Almost as an afterthought before he attempted to jump back on top of the gelding, Conrad decided to look through the mare's saddlebags. Her rider likely had an extra canteen in his bags, and if they were lucky, he might have kept an extra shirt or two that they could use to rebandage Sybille's hands.

The first bag was empty except for a length of frayed rope that Conrad took anyway. He didn't know if it would be useful, but it seemed wrong not to accept what little a dead man could offer them.

When Conrad opened the second bag, however, his face broke out into a senseless grin, and he nearly fell over backward from disbelief. The lost rider's bag did contain a spare canteen, as well as some assorted papers and a loaf of moldy bread. But buried beneath everything else were six cans of bratwurst sausages.

Conrad flung the spoiled bread aside and picked up one of the red and yellow tin cans. The label was faded and peeling, and a thick layer of dust coated the outside of the can, but its seal was still intact.

"What is it?" Sybille called to him.

"Sausages!" he shouted, startling the zebra who trotted another few feet away. "*Mein Gott*, it's six cans of sausages!"

Sybille's eyes went wide, and Conrad rushed clumsily to her and kissed her cracked lips. She bent down low over the mare's neck and kissed him back.

Her stomach grumbled, and they broke apart, grinning like fools. German patrols and the whole Kalahari be damned! Tonight, they would have a fire and a proper feast of army sausages. They'd have a can each! And tomorrow…a can each as well. And another each the next day.

Three whole days of food!

"Well done, *schatz*," Conrad said, patting the black mare on the neck. "Well done."

Conrad looked back up at Sybille and saw the faint glimmer of tears in her eyes. He felt the same tears welling up in his own eyes, and he hurriedly blinked them away.

They had three more days of food. Three more days of life.

Perhaps if we share a can each night, Conrad thought as he gathered up their newfound spoils, we might even have enough for six days.

He smiled up at Sybille, and she smiled back down at him. Conrad quickly forced himself back up onto the gelding, and they set off with the black mare trailing behind them, and Gustavus loping a few yards ahead.

If they were indeed heading west, six days might even be enough to find a small village. Such a thought was probably foolish, but it was the first hopeful one Conrad had had since he'd woken up in the desert, and he held it close to him, nurturing it over each of the gelding's slow, climbing steps through the orange sand.

They had ridden for several minutes before Sybille leaned across her saddle and whispered to him.

"We have company," she said, nudging him to look behind them.

Conrad turned and saw the herd of zebra following dubiously behind the black mare. He laughed and turned back to the horizon to lead their strange party over the next dune.

CHAPTER 18

JANUARY 1905

Conrad rose the next morning with the taste of grease still on his lips. The ashes of the tiny fire he'd managed to start with scraps of gnarled wood and brown grass had scattered in the early morning wind, and the pre-dawn desert felt cool and brisk against his sunburnt arms. Sybille was still asleep under their blanket, her head propped up dutifully by Gustavus's dozing bulk.

They'd found a camel thorn tree early the previous evening and had decided not to risk continuing. It was likely the best shelter they would find before the sun began to set, and they were both too eager to get at the sausages anyway.

Conrad had barely hobbled the horses before they'd pried open the first can with Erwin's small knife. They'd both been unable to wait for the sausages to roast over their tiny fire and had both eaten their first one raw. Sybille had even wolfed down the greasy water in the can when they'd finished. Conrad was sure they'd likely regret the half-cooked meat later, but as he tucked into a second sausage, he felt tears glistening in his eyes.

It was the best damn meal he could ever remember eating.

Now Conrad stretched his limbs and rubbed away the pain in his back from where he'd slept against a large root. The zebra had long since gone. After an hour or so of trailing nervously after the black mare, the herd had decided to abandon the mare to her new fate.

Conrad already missed their odd company and wondered fleetingly if he would ever get a chance to tell his cousin Frieda that he'd once ridden across the dunes in the middle of a herd of zebra. That would surely be enough to put the snobbish Ara Egger in her place for a month at least.

When the sun began to rise, Conrad woke Sybille gently and set about getting the horses ready. Gustavus trailed eagerly behind him, sniffing shamelessly at his pockets and licking Conrad's greasy fingers in the hopes of discovering some kind of breakfast.

Sybille rolled up their blanket with her fingers and slipped it back into her mare's saddlebag. Then the two of them set about re-saddling the horses. It was sloppy work, and the black mare eyed them with artisan disdain.

"Did you sleep alright?" Conrad asked as he tightened the cinch around the gelding's belly.

Sybille shot him a grumpy look, but then shook the dirt from her hair and laughed. It was such a sweet sound in the emptiness of the morning that Conrad could've wept for joy.

"Surprisingly well," Sybille replied. "I don't know that I'll ever taste meat that good again in my life."

"I'm sure the factory owner would love to hear you say that."

It was not very funny, but Sybille laughed anyway, and Conrad beamed at her gratefully.

"Perhaps I'll write to him once we make it to Bechuanaland," she said. "Make sure to save the cans so I'll have the address."

It was odd, Conrad thought as he helped Sybille into her saddle. They were on the edge of death every day now, and yet the bush had given them a sort of intimacy that felt even deeper than sex.

Perhaps it was the grease pumping new life into their limbs, but Conrad thought that something had changed within them both. He doubted whether either of them could pinpoint what it was, yet somehow, they both knew the other felt the same. Their resignation to their fate had been broken with a full stomach. And though they still might easily die, there was a chance, however slim, that they might live.

And that was enough to make both of them feel suddenly, and miraculously, human again.

Even though he felt refreshed and rested, it was more difficult than Conrad expected to keep a horse going in a straight line. He'd been too exhausted to notice it before, but now Conrad found himself growing irritated as they set off across a stretch of flat ground. Despite being hungry, the gelding still possessed a stubborn streak, which both mares seemed to feed off of.

The gelding stopped to nibble at every visible bit of thistle and grass strands, and Conrad found it a struggle to keep all three horses moving in a single direction. It was not as though there was any sort of trail or landmark to follow since they had left the stream, and with all the horses' sidestepping, Conrad was sure that they were moving across the Kalahari in a slow zigzag.

To distract them both from falling back into despair, Conrad devised a simple game. He and Sybille would each take turns asking one another questions, then when the other person had replied, they would have to guess whether the person was telling the truth or not.

"What's your favorite color?" Conrad began.

Sybille giggled involuntarily. It was such an unexpected sound that Conrad had pulled on his reins and turned around to check on her. Sybille's cheeks flushed with embarrassment and to compensate, she snorted derisively.

"Really, Conrad," she said. "We've slept together and are fleeing from soldiers across a desert, and *that's* the first question you want to ask me about myself?"

Now it was Conrad's turn to feel embarrassed. He looked away and replied sheepishly.

"Well, I just realized that I didn't know the answer."

Sybille rolled her eyes at Conrad's back but played along.

"Orange," she said neutrally.

"Is it really?" Conrad asked, turning around in the saddle as the gelding plodded along.

"I thought you were supposed to guess whether that was true or false," Sybille teased. "Isn't this your own game?"

"Fine," Conrad consented. "True."

"No," Sybille replied. "My favorite color is lavender."

"Lavender?" Conrad said. "I don't think I could've guessed that."

Sybille shrugged.

"Mind you, it's not a color you see very often in the villages. But when I first worked for Frau Grober, she had a vase full of stalks of lavender, and it was the most beautiful color I'd ever seen. Those flowers died within a week, and I've never seen another since, but I've never forgotten their color.

"My turn. What do you miss most about your home?"

That was a good question. Conrad thought for a long while listening to the muffled *clip-clop* of the horses' hooves as they continued to march across the dunes.

After another minute, he flashed a small smile and said, "The streetcar."

Sybille laughed with understanding. Conrad was surprised. There was no streetcar in Windhoek, though they had been running in places in British South Africa for over a decade. Perhaps Sybille had never seen one, but clearly she knew enough to understand the jest.

"I suppose you'd give up walking forever if you could, eh?" she asked, confirming Conrad's suspicion.

He smiled back at her.

"With my leg shot to pieces…you bet. You can push me around in a wheelchair for the rest of my life."

Sybille's smile faded slightly, but she resisted a strong retort.

"Your turn again," she said.

Conrad thought for a minute before asking his next question.

"What are your brothers like?"

"Ah," Sybille said. "Now that's a real question. Of all of them, Frederick is the most serious. He's always worrying over things that haven't happened yet. He reminds me the most of my mother."

There was a catch in her voice. It was the first time she had ever mentioned her mother to Conrad. She took a long pause to compose herself and then she added, "If he's still alive, he'll be the most likely to take over after my father."

Conrad was silent a moment, then he added hesitantly.

"Will you tell me about your mother someday?"

Sybille flashed him a look of mild reproof.

"That's two questions in a row."

Conrad turned his head back to face the horizon.

"Sorry. It just sort of slipped out."

Sybille rolled her eyes at the back of Conrad's head, but answered him.

"If we live to see the coast, then yes," she said simply. "I'll tell you about my mother then."

Conrad turned back to face her, and a daydream floated before him.

"It's a deal," he beamed foolishly. "When we are safe, eating *Streuselkuchen* and drinking coffee with cream in a café, without worrying about being hunted down in the streets."

Sybille rolled her eyes again.

"I doubt that any woman ever stops worrying about being hunted down in the streets, Conrad," she said flippantly.

Conrad didn't know how to answer that. There's so much I don't understand, he thought. Not just about Sybille, but about women – well, women and men come to think of it.

"Yes," she said, affirmatively. "If that day comes, I will talk to you about my mother, my childhood and all my secrets."

Then her mood changed again suddenly, and, despite the pain in her hands, she shot Conrad a playful grin.

"Did your German girls tell you all their secrets so soon?"

Conrad felt his face flush red beneath his sunburn.

"Er…no. I…never really had any German girls."

Sybille looked at him with a face that was unreadable.

"I've never had a sweetheart," he continued, "But in Germany, most girls – women – don't tell all their secrets. At least I don't think they do. It probably seems wiser not to."

Sybille thought about that for a long while, and Conrad thought she must've abandoned the game. He turned back to face the dunes, but Sybille surprised him by speaking again.

"I don't want that kind of romance," she said pointedly.

"Nor do I," he replied.

After another silence that filled Conrad with more hope than he'd felt in days, he smiled at Sybille again.

"I believe I owe you a question now," he said.

Sybille looked at him and gave him back a grin.

"You do," she said. "What is a *Streuselkuchen*?"

*

The sun had begun its rapid rise as they continued to talk, and only a few morning shadows still lingered over the dunes. Near midday, a faint breeze rolled over them when Conrad saw Gustavus suddenly stop.

The dark ridge of fur along his back suddenly straightened, and he whipped his head around to their left as though he'd caught scent of something foul. He flashed his teeth and uttered a low, terrible growl that startled Conrad and made him pull back on the gelding's reins.

"What's wrong?" Sybille asked from behind him.

"I'm not sure," Conrad told her, leaning back over the saddle. "Gustavus just stopped. I've never heard him make that sound before."

Gustavus' full attention was trained on a large cluster of sagebrush, and no matter how much Conrad called and whistled, the big dog did not respond. His growling grew louder and more urgent. Conrad sighed heavily, thinking that he would have to slide down off the gelding to pull Gustavus away from whatever rodent den he'd managed to find.

A second breeze blew over them, and suddenly the horses became agitated as well. The gelding's eyes went wide, and he took two pleading steps backward, bumping into Sybille's mare.

"What's wrong?" Sybille repeated as her tied reins caught her mare from throwing her head. "Can you see anything?"

"No," Conrad grunted as he tried to regain control of the gelding. "I can't see anything. The damn horses have just gone…"

Then Conrad saw what had spooked the horses.

Six lions lay on the other side of the sage. At the sound of Gustavus' growls, they had gotten to their feet and decided to investigate whatever was foolish enough to disturb them. They rose upwind from the midst of the dried grass like mid-day phantoms and turned their great heads towards the source of the growling. Then they smelled the horses, and six pairs of large, golden eyes turned their attention toward Conrad and Sybille.

They were far bigger than Conrad could've imagined. Each of them must've weighed at least five hundred pounds, and their shoulders rose in broad hunches that boasted immense strength and speed. Conrad saw at once that there was little hope that the horses might outrun them. He remembered the long scars down one of the zebra's flanks and a terrible shiver ran down his spine.

Gustavus became enraged now that the lions had shown themselves, and he bared his teeth as though daring one of them to fight him.

Oh please, God, Conrad begged. Please don't let him try and fight one.

Gustavus was big, but he might as well have been a newborn puppy for all it mattered. Leutwein had once told him that it took a whole pack of lion dogs to bring down a single lion, much less six.

But the lions paid little attention to Gustavus. They were much more interested in the horses and began to form a slow, even arc around their convoy.

It was impossible to watch all six of them at once. While half of the pride spread slowly to their right, the other half spread to their left. For a moment, the lions seemed puzzled, as if they could not quite figure out what the horses were or why they had not yet run away. Even elephants ran from them.

Conrad turned his head in a circle, trying to watch each of the lions and keep them all in sight. He was beginning to panic. Every time he took his eyes off one lion to search for the next, the first one would move, creeping steadily closer toward them.

"Conrad!" Sybille whispered behind him urgently. "Stop moving your head.

It's what they want you to do. Just pick one and stare directly into its eyes."

"What?" Conrad shouted back. "That's insane! What about the other five?"

All six of the lions moved in closer as he shouted, sensing his panic.

"Father once told me that a lion won't move if you hold its gaze," she hissed, making a great effort to keep her own voice calm. "I don't see a mane on any of them. That means these are lionesses. They're group hunters. They won't attack if one of them stops. You pick one and lock eyes with it on the right, and I'll do the same on the left. Please, trust me!"

Conrad could hear the pleading in Sybille's voice as he continued to whip his head back and forth. The lions were getting very close now, and blind terror was beginning to take over Conrad's limbs. He knew it was pointless, but his brain told him to run. The horses pulled against one another, trying to flee in different directions, but they only succeeded in further tightening the knots in their reins.

The lions were so close now.

"*Please*, Conrad!" Sybille yelled, her voice finally breaking into a shout.

Conrad could see one of the lions in front of him. Its muscles tensed as though it were ready to pounce, and it roared at him with a fierceness that shook his spine.

Conrad saw the lion half-leap forward, and then…she stopped.

The lioness had frozen where she was.

Conrad did not know how he'd brought himself to do it, but he found himself staring into the frontmost lioness' eyes. She was only five or so yards away from him, and her powerful body was still primed and taut as though she would leap and devour him at any moment. Yet she *had* stopped, and all the other lions had followed suit and frozen as well.

He could not believe it. Fearful sweat stung his eyes, but he forced himself not to blink it away. He was hanging on the edge of death, safe only so long as he could look his killer in the eye. He didn't dare look to see if Sybille was doing the same, but when he didn't hear the other lions attack, he guessed she must be.

The lioness was beautiful, Conrad realized deep beneath his fear. An undisputed queen of the desert, she was not accustomed to being challenged, and as close as they were, Conrad could see that his defiance infuriated her. She watched him with merciless interest, daring him to break whatever spell he'd cast upon her.

Her eyes were hypnotic. The two golden orbs watched him from behind small black pupils that drew him even deeper into their regal gaze. It was impossible not to be awed by the sheer power she possessed.

As Conrad kept his eyes locked with the lioness, he could still hear the frantic beating of his heart in his chest. He'd halted her momentarily, but Conrad did not think a lion gave up easily. His challenge had paralyzed her for the moment, but the lioness was in a far better position to be patient than he was. Eventually, he'd have to look away from her, and when he did…

"Conrad," Sybille whispered behind him. "Conrad, get the gun."

Conrad was so entranced by the lioness' gaze that it took a moment for Sybille's words to sink in.

The gun! He'd forgotten he still had it.

"How?" Conrad whispered back to her, forcing himself not to turn and look at Sybille as he spoke. "She'll jump us if I try and get it."

Sybille did not respond.

Conrad swallowed hard and slowly took one of his hands away from the reins. The gelding took another step back, and Conrad felt his hands clench over the reins. If the gelding chose this moment to make a break for it, Conrad wouldn't be able to stop him. With all his might, Conrad willed the damn horse to stand still, just for a moment.

The lioness watched him intently, but she still did not move. Slowly, Conrad traced his hand over his thigh and ran it gingerly along the gelding's back, searching for the familiar leather and canvas of the saddlebag. When at last his hand met the flap of the bag, he fumbled with the leather straps. They did not budge, and Conrad felt himself flinch in anguish as his fingers probed at a knot. The lioness saw the movement in his arm and drew herself even lower to the ground.

Please no, Conrad begged the great cat. Please.

It was so tempting to tear his eyes away from her. Sweat had begun to sting his eyes, and his right hand seemed to have gone numb fumbling with the straps. He was beginning to panic once more, and he could feel the lioness scenting his fear. She was tired of his boldness. Conrad could see the desire in her eyes overtaking whatever instinct had made her freeze under his gaze. She was going to jump him!

Conrad's hand wormed its way into the saddlebag, and his swollen fingers groped for the handle of the pistol.

The lioness' eyes widened. She tensed her broad shoulders, and Conrad knew he'd never be able to bring the gun around in time.

The lioness roared and lunged forward. Conrad ripped the broomhandle from the bag and squeezed the trigger.

The rusted pistol fired with a *boom* like a cannon.

All six of the lionesses froze once more. Conrad wondered if he had miraculously managed to hit one of them. His eyes were still locked with the same lioness, and he could not see the others around him or Sybille.

Something was suddenly different in the lioness' eyes, Conrad realized. The same golden eyes that had willed him to move so that she could devour him now appeared shrunken and anxious. She was afraid!

Conrad fired another round straight up in the air, and the six lions retreated several yards.

He felt a sudden surge of adrenaline rush through him. He'd been hovering on the edge of death, but now the tables had turned, and his tormentors were at his mercy.

Conrad squeezed the trigger again. As the loud crack of the broomhandle echoed across the dunes, the lionesses broke apart and fled like a pride of frightened alley cats back into the bush.

A surging warmth spread through Conrad. He felt powerful! He had looked death in the eye, inches from his face, and now it was running away from him. He fired the gun into the air again. And then again. He was laughing now, watching the lionesses flee and wishing he'd thought to aim at one of them. Even Georg had never killed a lion before!

He fired off another round into the sagebrush after them, and then he felt a gentle tap on his shoulder.

"Conrad…" Sybille said with concern in her eyes.

Conrad stared at her a moment, not understanding the look she was giving him.

"That's enough," she whispered.

Conrad looked at the warm gun in his hand and then back at Sybille. His adrenaline collapsed inward, and he suddenly felt ashamed of himself.

"Sorry," he replied quietly. "I don't know what came over me."

"It's alright," Sybille said gently. "They're gone now."

Conrad slipped the pistol back into the saddlebag and stared bashfully at the horizon. The lionesses had vanished as quickly as they'd come.

Conrad felt like a fool. He didn't know how many rounds a broomhandle held, but he could not imagine that it held very many. And he had just fired six. For all he knew, the gun was empty now. Conrad could see Erwin shaking his head at him in his mind.

Underneath him, the gelding was slowly coming back to life. All three of the horses shuffled their feet wearily as though they did not trust that the lions were indeed gone. The gelding stamped the ground once, and when nothing moved across the plain, his usual temperament returned, and he quickly began to grow impatient once more.

Gustavus had not moved from his spot when the lionesses had fled but stood shaking with anticipation. Conrad assumed he must've been waiting for some hunting command to tell him to give chase.

They all remained still as the silence of the Kalahari fell over them once more. At last, the gelding grew restless beneath Conrad and started out on his own, the other two horses following suit.

Conrad was too numb to notice and let the gelding have the reins for a bit. He whistled at Gustavus, and the big dog trailed after them, disappointed. When the horses crested the next rise, Conrad retook the reins and turned the horses westward, the piercing echo of the gunshots still ringing in his ears.

*

They made it over another three dunes before the Bushmen caught them. Though caught was perhaps too strong a word, for neither Conrad nor Sybille had much fight left in them. Much like the lions, the Bushmen seemed to appear out of thin air. The Kalahari had been empty a moment before, and then it was not.

There were twelve of them. As the horses had crested the ridge, the Bushmen had lain flat against the ground, their bodies completely motionless beneath a few patches of tall dry grass. Conrad had nearly ridden the gelding right over one of the wild men.

Then the man had risen from his hiding place with snakelike swiftness and brought the tip of a wooden spear against Conrad's chest. The rest of the Bushmen jumped to their feet as well, as quick and casual as if they'd each done it a thousand times.

Another of the Bushmen snatched Conrad's reins out of his hands, and two more lowered their spears on Sybille and Gustavus.

Conrad immediately raised his hands over his head in surrender and turned his head to look back at Sybille.

"Are they cannibals?" he asked, his voice shaking as he spoke.

Sybille shook her head.

"No," she replied. "They're San. Bush folk."

Conrad gave a frightened nod. That made him feel somewhat better at least. Over the past year, several Schutztruppe officers had told him stories of wild Africans who had never met Europeans. Crazed witchdoctors, devil worshippers, and cannibals who prowled the most remote dunes like vengeful shadows.

At least they won't eat us then, Conrad told himself.

The San who held the spear at Conrad's chest seemed to be in command. He was older than the rest of the Bushmen, and his skin looked as tough as an elephant's. Years of sun and wind had grated his wrinkled skin like sandpaper, and he glared up at Conrad with sunken, narrow eyes.

The rest of the San held small thin bows in their hands with only a few arrows clutched between them. They glanced from the older man to Conrad as if waiting for a signal.

"*Ju/'hoansi*," the man said gravely to Conrad.

He spoke in a series of loud clicks that sounded as though his tongue were rolling a marble around in his mouth. The clicks popped and echoed sharply, startling Conrad more than the man's sudden appearance.

"What?" Conrad replied stupidly.

The man stared angrily at him for a moment.

"*Ju/'hoansi*," the man repeated, this time more sternly.

Conrad looked back at Sybille for help, but she shook her head.

"I don't know," she said. "I don't speak the San language. I've never met one before."

The San elder looked between them and slid his spear slowly away from Conrad's chest.

"*Ju/'hoansi*," the man repeated in a raspy voice that was so low Conrad could barely hear it. Then the man thumped his own chest emphatically and pointed at Sybille as he raised his shoulders in question.

Conrad took a guess.

"Is he asking you your name?" Conrad asked Sybille.

"I don't know," she said as she turned to the San elder. "Sybille?"

The San elder appeared confused by her answer and turned to another of the Bushmen as if looking for confirmation. The second man shook his head and muttered something Conrad could not hear. The elder nodded and gestured at two of the San, who hurried quickly down the dune's far slope.

They returned a few moments later with a tall, young San who led a donkey up the dune. The man could not have been older than sixteen or seventeen, but he carried himself as though he were a man of importance.

He did not have a weapon. Instead he carried two large sacks swung over his shoulders. The donkey, a small, shriveled creature, followed obediently behind the young man, carrying six larger sacks across its back.

The San elder clicked at the young man impatiently. He gestured at Conrad and Sybille, and the young man nodded dutifully. He walked straight past

Conrad and looked curiously up at Sybille on her mare.

"We *Ju/'hoansi*," the boy said in broken German, gesturing at himself and the rest of the bushmen. "Who you?"

Sybille looked unsure for a moment, and then she made another guess.

"Herero," she said plainly. "I am a Herero."

The young man turned back to convey her response to the elder. The older man nodded as if that's what he had expected, and then he frowned at Conrad and clicked something hastily back at the youth.

"You German?" the young man asked him, pointing back to the San leader. "Chief. He say, you German."

The young man spoke slowly as though he had to think over every word before he said it. He was not simple, Conrad thought. It was miraculous he knew any German at all. Conrad wondered how he'd managed to learn the few words he had.

"Yes," Conrad admitted to the boy. "I am a German."

There was really no point in trying to lie, Conrad thought. For all he knew, the Bushmen might've thought all white men were called Germans. He doubted he'd be able to convince them he was anything else, lost in the desert of a German colony. And he decided it was probably best not to lie to the men who still had their weapons pointed at you.

The young man told the chief Conrad's answer and the older man clicked back at him hurriedly. They were both standing right in front of Conrad, discussing him with wild, animated gestures. Conrad felt ridiculous sitting atop the gelding, but he was afraid of being shot if he tried to get off the horse. After a few minutes, the young man pointed at Conrad again but spoke to Sybille.

"He catch you?" he asked Sybille with a hint of sympathy in his voice.

Sybille shook her head.

"No," she said. "He saved me."

The young man stared at her questioningly.

"He *saved* me," she repeated.

The boy clearly didn't know whether to believe her or not, but he translated it anyway. The chief scowled and muttered something back to the young man.

The young man paused, as if searching for the right word, and then turned back to Sybille.

"You. *Ondjamo?*" he asked. Do you need help?

He'd said the last word in Herero. The young man probably spoke less Herero than he did German, but he was trying to ask Sybille if she needed rescuing. Mainly, did she want them to get her away from Conrad?

"*Ayee,*" Sybille replied in her native tongue as she shook her head again. *No.*

The young man continued to study her as though he was hoping she might slip him some secret plea for aid. His eyes fell on her bandaged hands, and he raised an angry eyebrow again in question.

Sybille saw that the boy was still unconvinced and obviously thought she was Conrad's prisoner. Without waiting for him to speak again, she leaned over her mare's neck and kissed Conrad on the mouth.

She had to lean out of her saddle to reach him, and it was far more awkward than loving, but it had the desired effect on the rest of the San. The chief waved the bowman down, though he did not soften his gaze. Conrad looked surprised at Sybille for a moment and then caught an unmistakable flicker of jealousy in the young man's eyes.

Before Conrad could speak, the San chief clicked impatiently at the young man in front of them, and begrudgingly, the youth returned his attention to Conrad.

"Where lions?" he asked Conrad hostilely.

It took a long while for the young man to translate all the chief's questions and Conrad's replies, and the Bushmen eyed Conrad suspiciously throughout the interrogation. But piece by piece, he and Sybille learned why the San had been waiting for them.

The San were part of a small tribe of Ju/'hoansi Bushmen returning home from a long and unsuccessful hunting excursion. They had left their village several days before and had picked up the trail of a herd of gnu. At first, the hunters had been lucky. There had been several young and foolish bulls among the herd, and the San had been able to get close enough to the herd to bring down three on the first day.

But their fortunes had changed when a pride of lionesses suddenly appeared out of nowhere. The men had run, abandoning their kills to the lions.

The San continued to follow the gnu herd and made two more kills over the next few days. But the lions were crafty and had learned now that they could stalk the Bushmen for easy game. The same pride had evidently been a plague on the Ju/'hoansi for months.

The lionesses never bothered to hunt the San, but they continued to lie in wait and steal every kill they made. None of the San were willing to risk fighting the lions. Perhaps if there had only been one or two, but a full pride was far too dangerous for a dozen men to fight.

The San had abandoned the hunt two days ago and were returning to their village when they heard gunfire. The Schutztruppe rarely ventured so far into the desert, but a few of the Ju/'hoansi had encountered the German soldiers before in another part of the Kalahari and had watched several of their friends be captured and led away to the camps.

At this part in the story, several of the Ju/'hoansi eyed Conrad angrily, but their chief continued to wave them down.

When the hunters heard the gunfire, they were still too far away from their village to outrun a German patrol, so the San had hidden their donkey with the boy and laid an ambush.

"Where lions?" the San translator asked Conrad once more.

Conrad shrugged.

"They're gone," he said. "We drove them away."

Once this was repeated to the rest of the Bushmen, their demeanor changed slightly. They all still glared at him with distrust, but they were clearly impressed that he had driven off the pride of lions that had harried them for weeks. Conrad wondered if that would buy him and Sybille enough respect for his captors to let them go.

After a thoughtful pause, the chief muttered something to the boy, and Conrad saw the rest of the San stiffen.

"Chief wants to see gun," the young man said to Conrad.

Conrad felt a change in the air.

The San had relaxed slightly when they'd learned that Sybille was traveling with Conrad by choice, but the mention of the gun escalated the tension once more.

Conrad immediately sensed that this was dangerous. The chief had demanded to see the gun, and Conrad could not help but wonder if the chief was testing him to see that Conrad did indeed have a gun. It was impossible not to feel the implied threat and wonder at the consequences if Conrad revealed himself to be unarmed.

Conrad swallowed hard. Several of the San hunters looked nervous as well. They did not know that the pistol was likely empty, and a few stared at him fearfully. If he took the gun out, what was to stop him from shooting at them, too?

Conrad wondered how many of these men had ever seen a gun up close before. He wondered if he ought to try and shoot one of these men. The San might decide to attack them at any moment, and the chief had given Conrad an excuse to draw his weapon.

Would the San scatter the way the lions had if he shot one of them? Did he have it in him to shoot one of these men? He honestly didn't know anymore. He had never shot at a man before, but he was half-starved, and his nerves were frayed enough …maybe he would if it came to that.

If the damn thing even had any bullets left in it, that is, Conrad mumbled to himself.

The chief eyed Conrad restlessly, and two of his nearby men tightened their grip on their spears. After a moment's hesitation, Conrad relented.

He reached into the saddlebag and drew out the broomhandle. He tried to hold the gun innocently in his hand, but he saw a few of the Bushmen flinch nervously.

The gun was level with the San chief.

Maybe they'll run if I shoot their chief, Conrad told himself and shuddered as he heard his own thought. He was sounding like Major Baumhauer now, or perhaps even von Trotha.

"Small," the young man said critically to Conrad.

The young man and the chief looked from Conrad back to the broomhandle, as though they did not believe that the pistol was a real gun.

"Small gun," Conrad replied as levelly as he could. "Small gun, big bang."

The young man stared at him uncomprehendingly, so Conrad mimed an explosion with his free hand. Clearly, the San had some idea of what they thought a gun should look like.

The boy challenged Conrad again.

"No gun," he said, shaking his head and pointing a long, accusatory finger at the broomhandle. "No gun."

Conrad was growing angry with the boy now. He was exhausted. He'd already endured a battle of wills with a lioness, for Christ's sake. For a dark moment, he wondered if he ought to just shoot the boy and be done with it.

As soon as he thought it, Conrad felt ashamed of himself and let out a long, resigned sigh. Petyr's face came to his mind. Petyr, who was probably dead because of him. He pushed his anger aside.

Praying the rusted thing did indeed have at least one round left in the chamber, Conrad aimed the broomhandle straight up into the air and fired.

The shot echoed across the top of the dune, and the young man leapt backward as though he'd been hit. Two of the younger Bushmen dropped their spears in fright, and the rest quickly retrained their bows and spears on Conrad.

They would probably kill him now.

Conrad wasn't sure he cared. He wanted very badly to live, but if the Bushmen were going to kill him anyway, he wished they would just get on with it. Gustavus seemed to share his impatience and snapped at one of the San's ankles.

"Yes, gun," Conrad replied evenly.

The chief was the only one who seemed unfazed by the gunshot. He made an angry ticking noise at the young man and snarled at him until he regained his feet. Conrad had expected the chief to be angry at him for firing the gun, but instead, he seemed more concerned that the boy had been so frightened by it.

He clicked at the young man emphatically, and finally the young man got a hold of himself and turn back to face Conrad.

"What for gun?" he asked, taking Conrad by surprise. "Chief gun. Chief…"

He paused as if he were trying to think of the right word.

"Chief…*pay* you."

Conrad was stunned speechless. After a long moment, Sybille answered.

"Where is the nearest village besides yours?" she asked the boy.

The young man stared at her as though he did not understand and then looked back at his chief to translate. The chief clicked something in reply, and the young man turned quickly back to Sybille.

"Days," he replied, holding up six fingers and then pointing in the direction of the next ridge.

The San chief glared at Sybille. All at once Conrad wished they were facing the lions instead. He could see the man weighing his options beneath his furrowed brow, and he did not like the look he was giving Sybille.

"We want food," she told the young man, though she watched the chief as she spoke.

The chief scoffed when the boy translated what she wanted, and the young man shook his head.

"No food," he said, gesturing at the rest of the Bushmen. "No food to *pay*."

"Then no gun," Sybille replied tersely.

The chief did not need the young man to translate her tone, and he shouted something at her that Conrad was glad she could not understand.

The situation was becoming even more dangerous. Conrad did not want to give the chief the gun. The San did not know that it was likely now empty, and it was Conrad's only hope of deterring an attack. But on the other hand, he was afraid of what the chief might do if they did not hand over the pistol. Conrad thought about offering them the black mare instead, but he quickly realized that it was not wise to remind the chief that they had other things of value.

"No gun," Sybille replied over the chief's vile cursing. "Food for gun."

The chief stared up at her incredulously, but she matched his angry gaze with her own. The chief cursed her again, trying to intimidate her into giving in, but Sybille held her ground defiantly. Conrad suddenly remembered the night in the alleyway when she'd stared half-naked at Albert Witbooi's band of mercenaries and shouted at them as though they were children. She looked every bit as fierce and immovable now.

The two of them locked stares for a moment longer, until the chief spat at the ground near Sybille's mare in defeat. He clicked something at the young man in disgust.

The boy nodded and unwrapped one of the sacks from his shoulders.

"No food," he repeated as he offered her the sack. "*Otee*. From rooibos. You drink, no hungry."

He reached into his remaining sack and pulled out a handful of thin bark. The boy brought it to his nose to smell and motioned for Sybille to do the same.

She smelled it and passed the dried clump to Conrad. The bark crinkled under his touch, and Conrad realized that there were leaves in the sack as well.

"Redbush tea leaves," she explained to him. "But they're...different."

The young man seemed to understand her and nodded in agreement.

"Very, very strong. You drink at day start," the young man explained. "No eat all day."

"We've no water," Sybille said, gesturing at the empty canteens hanging lifelessly from their saddles. "We don't even have enough for our horses to make it beyond the next ridge. Let alone to brew tea."

Conrad doubted whether the young man understood this relatively long speech, but his eyes fixed on the empty canteens, and he gestured to a spot just before the next ridge and cupped his hands to make a deep V-shape.

"Water," he repeated to them. "Come from ground. Just there."

Conrad looked at Sybille.

"If the stream comes back out from the ground, the horses might just make it another few day," he said.

The young man seemed to grow impatient with their discussion. He pointed to his own sack and then at the gun in Conrad's hand, eager to confirm the trade.

"What do you think?" Conrad asked.

Sybille shrugged and gave the young San a hard look.

"Where is the nearest village?" Sybille repeated with a suspicious look in her eye.

"Days," the young man repeated, holding up six fingers again and gesturing to the same spot over the ridge.

Sybille looked at Conrad once more, silently asking him if he had any better ideas. He did not, so with a sigh, he took the offered sack and slid the pistol into the boy's hand.

The young man looked at the broomhandle with awe, and then he looked back up at Conrad. Conrad saw something in the boy's eye that made him tense. He recognized the grisly thrill he'd felt when he'd shot at the fleeting lionesses, and he wondered if the boy would try and shoot him now.

But before the boy could make up his mind, the chief snatched the gun from his hands. The chief made his own show of looking from the pistol back up at Conrad before letting the weapon fall harmlessly to his side.

As if confirming that their trade was complete, he clicked at the rest of the Ju/'hoansi, and as one, they disappeared back down the dune the way they'd come.

The young man was the last to leave, the thin donkey trailing obediently behind him. He stopped after a few yards and gave Sybille a last, hopeful look as if asking her to come with him. Sybille shook her head, and the boy shrugged and nudged the donkey forward. He continued down the dune after the rest of the hunting party, and Conrad felt his shoulders slump with relief.

In no time at all the Ju/'hoansi had vanished back into the Kalahari and, once again, he and Sybille were completely alone.

CHAPTER 19

JANUARY 1905

Conrad felt the wet cloth press gently against his forehead. The cool water jolted him awake, but his eyes remained shut behind heavy eyelids. Whoever was washing his face had strong, skilled hands, yet they traced his fevered forehead patiently, and Conrad could hear whoever it was humming softly under their breath.

"Sybille?" he asked through parched lips.

"*Ga tsoga e mosô,*" a woman's voice answered him.

Conrad pried one eye open hesitantly. A plump woman in a faded green dress smiled down at him. Her skin was dark, though not much more than Sybille's, and she wore a brightly colored scarf that matched her dress and covered all her hair and forehead. She seemed pleased that he was awake.

The woman finished wiping the sweat from his brow and set a new damp cloth over him. Conrad forced his other eye open and tried to sit up, but a wave of nausea met him immediately. The woman nudged Conrad back down onto the mat, and he gave in without a fight.

As his vision cleared, he saw that he was in a simple hut. There was a thatched roof overhead that looked as though it were woven from dried grasses, and the walls surrounding him were either clay or mud. Whoever the woman tending to him was, she'd done her best to make Conrad comfortable. He'd been given a mat to sleep on to keep him off the hut's dirt floor, and she'd piled several blankets over him throughout the night.

Conrad's throat was dry, and as though she could sense his thirst, the woman retrieved a small wooden bowl and dipped it into a pail of water. Conrad sucked the water down eagerly, spilling half of it down his chin in the process. The woman said nothing but blotted his chest dry with a ready cloth as if she'd expected the mess.

Conrad studied the woman as she worked. It was impossible to tell how old she was. She had an unmistakable matronly air about her, but her face could have as easily been twenty as forty.

"*Danke,*" Conrad said when he had finished the last of the water.

The woman smiled at him, but it was clear that she did not understand him. Conrad wondered what tribe the woman belonged to. She didn't look like most of the Damara women he had met, but they'd traveled so irregularly across the desert, perhaps they were farther north than he thought.

"*Okuhepa,*" he said, trying to thank the woman again, this time in Herero.

But the woman just smiled at him again, still not understanding.

He tried Ovango and then Nama. But the woman continued smiling at him and shaking her head.

Conrad was trying to think if he'd picked up enough Zwartboois in Windhoek to try and thank her when the woman finally spoke again.

"English, maybe?" she asked him as she refilled the bowl from the pail on the floor.

Conrad nodded with relief and accepted the bowl again eagerly.

"Alright," he replied through a mouth full of water. "English it is."

When he'd finished the second bowl, the woman took it from him and added another fresh cloth to his forehead. Conrad sighed with relief. "Thank you."

As he sank deeper into the mat, Conrad felt a cold nose press against his arm. Gustavus sat loyally beside him and inched his nose carefully onto

Conrad's chest. The big dog's weight hurt Conrad's ribs, but he laughed and scratched Gustavus' head with a tired hand.

"That is a very good dog you have," the woman said to him as she ran another cloth along Conrad's arms. "He hasn't left your side for days."

"Good boy," Conrad told Gustavus.

"Conrad?" Sybille called from the doorway. "You're awake!"

Sybille ran to him and flung her arms around his neck. Between Gustavus' weight and Sybille's embrace, he could hardly breathe, but Conrad smiled foolishly nevertheless.

"I'm awake," he said, his voice muffled underneath fur and cloth. "Where are we? What's happened?"

Sybille broke her embrace and kissed him gently on the cheek.

"You fell ill," she told him as she stroked his face. "I thought you were going to die. You caught a fever, and we didn't stop riding for two days straight. I couldn't pull you out of the saddle, and I was afraid that if we stopped moving to rest that you wouldn't wake up again."

She paused a moment, and Conrad noticed that she had tears in her eyes.

"But then we crested another ridge, and I saw this village in the distance. Two farmers from the village saw us and ran out to help us. They gave us to Mma Boitumelo, and she and her family have been nursing us both for more than a week."

Conrad blinked away the sweat from his eyes and tried to focus on Sybille. She was wearing a new dress. It was a deep, flattering red and looked as though it had been taken in to fit her. It was the first time Conrad had seen her in anything that suited her long frame. Even plagued with fever, he could not help but notice how beautiful she looked.

Sybille continued smiling at him and stroking his cheek, her eyes brimming with tears. Conrad was overwhelmed by her emotion and felt his own tears in his eyes. He must've been very close to death.

He didn't remember much of the days after they'd encountered the San. He remembered keeping watch all that night, too terrified that either the lions or the San would come back to prey on them if he fell asleep. He remembered brewing the rooibos tea leaves the next morning. He remembered the warm, strange sensation that flowed over him as he drank the San's concoction, and the feeling of relief as his hunger melted away.

But after that, he could not recall much.

He thought he remembered Sybille's voice calling to him once, as though she were suddenly afraid of something. He remembered feeling sluggish and dazed, in a dreamlike trance for hours. Or was it days? There had been nothing but the methodic, muffled clomping of the horses' hooves as they'd trudged through the heavy sand. And then he was falling, and Sybille was cooing over him, telling him that everything would be alright.

Sybille stroked his check once again and Conrad's eyes widened with recognition.

"Your hands!" he wheezed.

"Yes," Sybille said, still smiling. "Mma Boitumelo's a skilled healer. She made a paste for them. They're getting stronger every day now."

As if to prove her point, Sybille took up one of the wet rags by the mat and brushed it slowly over Conrad's cheek. It took a lot of effort for her to press the cloth against him, and her hands shook from the weight of the cloth, but she managed to wipe the latest layer of sweat from Conrad's brow, and he beamed at her through his fevered fog.

"Thank you," he said to Mma Boitumelo, who was diligently washing his arms on the outskirt of his and Sybille's reunion.

Mma Boitumelo nodded proudly, as though she did not really need his thanks, and drew back the blankets to sponge at his legs.

"Where are we?" Conrad asked, turning back to Sybille. "Outside Grootfontein? Surely, we haven't gone all the way to Gobabis?"

Sybille shook her head and laughed. She set the cloth back down to soak in the bowl.

"Bechuanaland," she told him.

"Bechuanaland?!" Conrad exclaimed.

He tried to rise in shock but sunk back down quickly as the dizziness hit him. Mma Boitumelo made a *tsk* noise from the end of the mat, and Gustavus squirmed himself behind Conrad to help him sit upright.

It was no wonder the Germans never found them or that they had never encountered a road or village until now. Instead of cutting northward and then west towards the Damara lands, as Erwin had planned, they had been heading *east* the entire time. They had crossed the Kalahari and reached the British protectorate!

"How…" Conrad started, but then stopped.

He knew how. They'd crossed the desert through sheer force of will, and Conrad doubted that he would ever be able to summon the strength to do anything like it again.

Mma Boitumelo's cloth felt wondrous against his hot skin, and with Sybille holding him up and stroking his face, Conrad allowed himself to cry. His eyes were dry, and he was still too feverish to weep much, but he gave a soft, joyful sigh, and a few salty tears managed to roll down his cheeks. Sybille wiped them away gently with her sleeve and kissed his forehead.

"He's awake!" a third woman's voice shouted from the doorway.

The woman hurried into the hut and knelt beside Sybille. It took Conrad a moment to recognize the woman's long face.

"Anna!" he finally said when he recognized her. "How did you get here?"

Anna scoffed with a half-smile.

"Same as you," she said. "We walked out of the desert."

"We?" Conrad asked.

Anna nodded.

"A group of twelve of us made it through," she said, and her face flushed a quick, grim frown that she quickly pushed aside.

"They'll be plenty of time for such talk later," she said. "You want to talk to Sybille right now, not me. I'll go make some tea to help your fever break."

"She's alive!" Conrad said dumbly as Anna left the room. "She's really alive."

"Yes," Sybille said evenly, running a bandaged hand through his matted hair.

"If Anna's alive," Conrad started, his mind sluggishly trying to work through the haze. "If Anna made it…that could that mean that…"

He blinked a few times to concentrate, attempting to force the rest of his thought out. But Sybille laid a gentle hand on his chest to stop him.

"Maybe," she said with the faint glint of a beggar's hope in her own eyes. "We will see."

Sybille eased Conrad back onto the mat and lay down beside him. Mma Boitumelo continued to wash Conrad's legs as she moved tactfully around Sybille and Gustavus.

Sybille cradled Conrad's head against her and nestled herself against him.

"Rest now, *omuingona*," she whispered to him. "We're safe. And that's enough for now."

Conrad's eyes grew heavy as he buried himself in Sybille's chest. Her hand ran along the back of his neck and the slow, patient strokes of the cold cloth felt so good on his legs that he felt fresh tears roll down his cheeks again. Sybille started to hum a song, but Conrad was suddenly too tired to understand the melody. He felt his eyelids droop and wondered fleetingly if Sybille were mistaken, and they were both already dead.

*

Conrad's fever broke two days later. He'd awoken with a ravenous appetite, and Mma Boitumelo had pronounced him well enough to handle a bowl of a thick, bland porridge she referred to as "pap." Several other families lived in the small Tswana village, but Conrad quickly learned that it was Mma Boitumelo's word alone that was law.

After two more days, he begged two of the women who looked in on him to give him some bread while Mma Boitumelo was away. They had both refused. Mma Boitumelo had instructed them to feed him pap, and that was what he would have until Mma Boitumelo decided otherwise.

At last, Mma Boitumelo decided that Conrad was well enough to take a short walk around the village. With Sybille and Anna taking his arms, Conrad got to his feet and was surprised to feel how little pain there was in his leg. It still groaned under his weight, but the pins and needles he'd felt jabbing at him for so long came slower, and the pain did not leave him as nauseous as it once had.

The village looked almost identical to Witvlei, though it was smaller. A three-meter-high wooden palisade surrounded the village, which Anna informed him was to keep lions away from the villagers' livestock. The palisade was made of sun-bleached, thin logs, and packed with mud and dried grass, but it looked feeble against the long sea of orange sand that stretched out in every direction.

"If we had crossed the next dune over, we would never have found this place," Conrad said in amazement as they reached one end of the village. "We might've kept wandering until we dropped dead."

Neither of the two women said anything, and Conrad thought better of continuing his thoughts. No doubt that was precisely what had happened to hundreds of the Herero. The three of them had survived, but the ordeal was still far too fresh to mention death so freely.

"How did you manage to cross it, Anna?" Conrad asked after a while.

He didn't know if he should ask the question or not, but he sputtered it out before he could think to stop himself.

The last time Anna had seen him, Conrad had been an emissary for Leutwein's government. Since then, the Schutztruppe had killed her brother and she'd been swept up in the Herero flight after Maharero's defeat at Waterberg. His question was impolite at best, but curiosity had bested him before he could gain control of his own tongue.

Anna looked at him though she'd been expecting the question and answered him with a mild shrug.

"There were twelve of us," she said practically. "I think it must be easier in a group. Two of the women with us had dogs to keep the hyenas away, and we at least knew we wanted to head east."

Conrad could not help but blush beneath his sunburn. He'd been trying to take Sybille west and had only succeeded in crossing the Kalahari by failing so spectacularly.

Anna looked thoughtfully out at the Kalahari for a moment and then turned back to Conrad and Sybille.

"I have no idea how the two of you managed," she said with a hint of admiration in her voice. "A bullet hole in your leg and open wounds on your hands…it's a miracle you both weren't eaten by lions."

Conrad felt a small shiver. He did not like to think just how narrow his escape from that exact fate had been.

"How long have you been here?" Conrad asked Anna, changing the subject.

It must've been several months at least. The battle at Waterberg had been in August, and it had nearly been Christmas when he and Sybille had fled Windhoek.

"A while," Anna replied as she turned to lead them back through the small village.

Mma Boitumelo had allowed Conrad some exercise, but only a short walk to the edge of the village and back. She had warned Sybille and Anna that the sun would drain his strength, and Mma Boitumelo would not have Conrad relapsing on her watch.

"We found this village by chance, same as you," Anna continued as they walked. "Many of us were sick. Everyone was hungry. We all stayed here until we got our strength back, and then most of the women continued to where Mma Boitumelo told them they could find British soldiers in the Tswana's capital. It's a city called Gaborone. Some of the women wanted to petition the English garrison there for help, but I think most just wanted to get as far away from the desert as possible."

"Did the other women reach Gaborone?" Conrad asked.

"I don't know," Anna said plainly. "Mma Boitumelo says it's a long way to Gaborone from here, and hardly anyone travels out this far into the desert. I haven't heard anything from the other women I fled with since they waved goodbye. And that was months ago."

"And you've stayed all this time," Conrad said in amazement. "Why?"

Anna shrugged and looked casually back over her shoulder at the Kalahari.

"There might've been more of us," she said quietly. "We made it across, so I thought maybe others would as well. Someone from their own people needed to be here for them when they made it."

Sybille squeezed Conrad's hand, and he felt her stiffen slightly beside him.

"Did anyone else make it out of the desert?" he asked, not catching Sybille's warning.

Anna shook her head.

"No. Just you."

Conrad fell silent as he paused to catch his breath. They'd walked only a short distance, but already it felt like he'd walked ten miles. Once he'd rested a moment, he decided to press his luck with Anna one more time.

"I was very sorry to hear about your brother," he said solemnly. "I don't think he liked me very much, but he was a good man who deserved better."

Conrad's condolences hung awkwardly between the three of them, and Conrad was afraid he'd struck a fatal nerve with Anna. But after a while, she gave him a half-smile and chortled softly.

"No, he didn't much care for you at all," she said, smiling as she remembered some private memory of her brother. "But Noko did say you were the only white man in the whole colony dumb enough to offer to shake hands with him."

Both Anna and Sybille laughed together, and Conrad laughed with them, not quite sure if he was a part of the joke or the butt of it.

None of them said much of anything as they finished their walk. Mma Boitumelo stood outside her hut, tapping an impatient foot as though they had broken curfew. She quickly ushered Conrad back into the shaded hut, fussing at him to lie back down and rest.

"Thank you," Anna whispered to Conrad as she helped him onto the mat.

Conrad nodded, unable to think of anything more to say.

Anna gave him another small smile and then left him to Sybille and Mma Boitumelo's care.

*

After another three days, Mma Boitumelo pronounced Conrad well enough to travel. There was an unspoken invitation that he and Sybille were welcome to stay in the village as long as they wished, but they both knew that the village would be hard-pressed to feed two more mouths for much longer. And Sybille was growing restless.

They had found Anna alive and well, and ever since Conrad had begun to recover, Sybille's thoughts had been flooded with a desperate hope that her father might have survived as well.

Conrad remembered the night he had returned to his flat in Windhoek to find her still awake and determined to travel to Bechuanaland to look for her father. That felt like a lifetime ago, though it must've only been a matter of weeks.

Conrad could see as Sybille helped nurse him back to health that despite everything she had endured, she was still just as determined to search for her father as she'd been that night in the apartment. It had seemed an impossible task to reach Bechuanaland, but now by some miracle, they had made it. And soon Conrad found himself eager to move on as well.

Mma Boitumelo truly was an adept healer, and Conrad soon felt better than he had in months. His leg still gave him some trouble, but it no longer throbbed as deeply when he walked, and when his fever broke, he felt flushed with new energy. They'd escaped the Schutztruppe and survived the Kalahari. The worst was behind them now, and Conrad had a promise to keep.

He had promised Erwin to get Sybille to safety, and they were very nearly there. And he would try to do one better. Once they reached Gaborone, Conrad could contact the British embassy and report the atrocities committed by von Trotha's army. He didn't know if his reports alone would encourage the British to intervene in the DSWA. They might not even believe him. He could be unlucky. The garrison commander might think him mad or discount his story because he did not particularly care what happened to native tribes in another Great Power's colony. The best Conrad could hope for was that the Gaborone commander would listen and wire Conrad's story to his superior officers in the British Cape Colony.

If he was lucky, the garrison commander's report might reach the ear of the colonial government, and if his luck stretched even farther, the Cape Colony governor might feel compelled to mention it in a report to the British Colonial Secretary in London. That man, whoever he was, might even tell the

Prime Minister. And if the Prime Minister was moved enough by the story, or if he saw some form of political advantage in broaching the subject with his counterparts in Germany, he might even suggest to the Kaiser that His Excellency should perhaps consider dissolving the Schutztruppe's camps to avoid worsening a humanitarian crisis.

And perhaps the Kaiser would consent to avoid losing face with the other European powers. After all, the Kaiser's main interest in empowering von Trotha in the first place had been to avoid political embarrassment, hadn't it? Perhaps Wilhelm would finally rein in his favorite general if the British made him think von Trotha was doing more harm to the Kaiser's reputation than good.

It was all a fool's dream, Conrad knew, but he still felt he owed it to Sybille to try. He had seen too much and watched too many suffer to do nothing.

Once they reached Gaborone, he would also find a way to provide a life for Sybille. He hadn't yet worked out how, but he would make sure she was provided for. He would track down the other Herero women who had fled to Bechuanaland, and if he could, he would find someone who could tell them for certain what had happened to Maharero. He would buy Sybille ten new dresses and find her a clean house where she could sleep every night in an expensive feather bed.

And if she wanted him to be a part of her new life, well…so much the better.

They gave the black mare to Mma Boitumelo. At first, the village matron refused. What would she, a simple countrywoman, do with such a big, powerful animal? But Conrad saw the faintest glimpse of excitement in her eyes when he first suggested that she keep the expensive horse, and after what he assumed was only ritual protest, Mma Boitumelo readily agreed to accept the mare.

Anna decided to accompany them as well. After a few more days of scanning the ridge of dunes, she admitted that anyone who had fled into the Kalahari after Waterberg and who had not emerged by now was likely dead. Noko was dead, and Anna had no idea what had become of his wife and children. She wouldn't find any answers waiting on the edge of the desert, and now that she had found Sybille at least, her place was with her and any other Herero they could find.

Four men from the village agreed to escort them to the largest nearby town of Mamuno. It took them only two days to reach the small border town where Mma Boitumleo's men saw them to the one dilapidated hotel.

The hotel manager, an old Tswana man in a dirty suit with a tear in the jacket, eyed them suspiciously at first but embraced one of the village men warmly as he came through the door.

Once Mma Boitumelo's men explained what had happened to the three of them, the hotel manager's gaze softened. Word of the Herero massacre must've reached Mamuno in some form, and once their guide explained that Mma Boitumelo would consider it a personal favor if the hotel manager would agree to help the refugees, the old man decided to take pity on them. Evidently, in Mamuno, the wishes of a country wisewoman carried weight. The hotel manager let Sybille and Anna share one of the vacant rooms, and he gave Conrad and Gustavus a pallet to sleep on behind the front desk.

The next day, the men from the village made inquiries around Mamuno to find a guide to take Conrad, Sybille and Anna on to another small town called Ghanzi. There were no railroads in western Bechuanaland, only a single dirt road that skirted around the worst parts of the desert until it reached Ghanzi. Once they reached Ghanzi, Mma Boitumelo's men told them, the road would fork south across the Okwa River towards the larger city of Kang, and then from Kang, they could follow the road all the way to the British garrison in Gaborone.

By the end of the day, Mma Boitumelo's men returned to the hotel with a Tswana rancher named Nyack. Nyack was a short, smiling man from Ghanzi who had come to Mamuno to purchase new cattle for his herd. He, too, had heard about what had befallen the Herero after Waterberg and gave the three foreigners a pitying look as he introduced himself.

Mein Gott, Conrad thought to himself. I wonder how word about von Trotha and the camps managed to make it across the desert.

He guessed that the San must've carried news from the German colony across the desert, and he felt a sudden surge of anticipation. If a lone hotel manager in Mamuno and a cattle rancher from Ghanzi already knew about what was happening on the other side of the desert, perhaps that meant the British authorities already did as well. Perhaps by the time the three of them reached Gaborone, they might hear whether the British intended to intervene.

Since Conrad, Sybille, and Anna already had two horses between them, Nyack agreed to take the three of them with him. From Ghanzi, he told them, he would have one of his nephews take them on to Kang. There, they could hire another guide to take them on to Gaborone.

It took Nyack two more days to purchase the last of his new cattle and gather up his hired cattle hands. Then, on the morning of their third day in Mamuno, Nyack drove his cattle down the main dirt street right past the hotel and waved to the three of them to fall in behind him. Conrad nudged his horse nervously into the sluggish herd, with Sybille and Anna riding together on the mare behind him. The cows shifted lazily around them in the tight streets, and the three of them were quickly absorbed into the cattle drive as effortlessly as if the cows had arranged it all months ago.

Mma Boitumelo's men waved goodbye to them as the cattle carried them eastward, and just like that, they set off along the bush road toward Ghanzi.

*

Traveling with the cattle herd was surprisingly pleasant. Nyack spoke English in a deep, affable voice, and he chatted with Conrad casually as if they had known each other for years. Nyack rode his horse with a confident air and whenever he he rode past Sybille and Anna, he always tipped his worn Stetson hat to them as though he were an American cowboy.

The other Tswana men were relaxed as well. They did not speak much, but they were friendly enough and did not seem overly surprised or bothered to have a white man traveling with them.

The Bechuanaland Protectorate was massive. Conrad had seen maps of the territory beneath the clutter in Leutwein's office, and he knew that it was nearly as large as the DSWA itself. Yet Nyack told him as they rode slowly along the road that Bechuanaland was home to only half as many natives.

Conrad wondered if that perhaps was the secret to ending strife in Europe's colonies. Simply spread everyone out so they were not on top of one another, and then leave each race to its own devices.

"Do the British soldiers ever bother you?" Conrad asked Nyack as he thought this.

Nyack laughed and shook his head.

"No sir, *Herr* Huber," Nyack responded, having great fun in addressing Conrad as "Herr." He had never heard the German word before and, for some reason, found it hilarious.

"We are too poor for the soldiers to bother. I give 'em a few cows for the garrison every now and then, and they let us be. It's too hot and dry in the Kalahari for white folks to bother themselves over our pennies."

All of Nyack's men laughed at that, and Conrad found himself chuckling as well. As their small party moved across the sun-baked road, Conrad relaxed too. Their pace was slow as the cattle hands nudged and pulled the more stubborn cattle along, and while Conrad was eager to get to Gaborone for Sybille's sake, he was enjoying their leisurely trek.

His muscles had strengthened from their toiling in the saddle, and he could now ride for hours without growing stiff. Having a road to follow after their blind blundering through the Kalahari seemed miraculous. They ate porridge and bread twice a day, drank bitter coffee that Nyack prepared over the fire in the mornings, and slept under thick, warm blankets under the stars while Nyack's men kept watch over the herd. Curled up on the hard ground next to Sybille with a wall of cattle surrounding them, Conrad had never felt safer, despite the vast wilderness around them.

Now that they were not at its mercy, the Kalahari seemed a far more majestic host. Nyack and his men pointed out leaping springbok, a pair of young, sparring gnu, and endless herds of gazelle, all of whom paid little mind to the boundaries of the road. They'd even come across a bizarre, scaled mammal with a long tongue that Nyack called a *kgaga*.

386

On the fourth day out of Mamuno, one of Nyack's cattle hands startled a family of warthogs from their den that all ran out onto the dirt road to escape the man's horse. Gustavus, delighted, tore off after them, but was stopped cold in his tracks when the mother sow rounded on him and charged at him like a battering ram.

She was half the big dog's size, but she squealed madly as she ran, and Gustavus yelped in fright and ran back toward Conrad's gelding with his tail tucked between his legs. The whole party had bent over their saddles laughing as the sow snorted in defiance and then turned up her skinny tail and trotted off back into the bush with her piglets.

On the fifth day, Conrad saw giraffes for the first time. Three of them walked across the road a few dozen yards in front of the lead cattle hand, as untroubled as if they did so every day. Conrad nearly fell out of his saddle in surprise.

He'd seen pictures of giraffes in books back home in Germany, and he knew Schutztruppe men who shot them while out on patrol. But he had never seen one himself. Now he sat in the middle of the road with his mouth hanging open, awe-struck, while the cattle waited unimpressed for the long-limbed giants to pass.

Nyack and all his men laughed at his expression while Gustavus stood frozen in even greater amazement than Conrad. The giraffes, utterly uninterested in either the humans or the cows, walked down the road ahead of them for a half-mile or so before they, too, disappeared back into the desert.

When their party finally arrived in Ghanzi, Nyack insisted that Conrad, Sybille, and Anna stay with him and his family. Nyack could clearly guess that the three of them were penniless, but Conrad thought that the man would still have insisted on hosting them in his home even if they'd been able to afford rooms in the local hotel.

Nyack's family lived on a small farm on the outskirts of town, and as his men drove the new cattle down Ghanzi's main road, Conrad was bewildered by the strange little town.

The first voice Conrad heard in Ghanzi spoke to them in Afrikaans. A tall, white Boer man greeted Nyack and tipped his hat to him, and Nyack smiled and waved back. Clusters of Boer women strolled unaccompanied down the road, and Conrad saw dozens of nearly naked San haggling over their string of plump guinea fowl with dark-skinned men in gray and navy suits.

The town was no bigger than Hochfeld had been, but there was an easy, comfortable air in Ghanzi that made the desert town seem far larger. At the city's center was a trading post decorated with so many skulls, antlers, and animal skins that it looked more like a pagan altar than a grocery.

As Nyack drove his herd past the trading post, a large, fat Boer man stood outside chatting pleasantly with a British officer. The fat man was dressed flamboyantly, despite the heat, and wore a three-piece tweed suit that barely contained his bulk. The two men smoked cigars while they chatted, the fat man leaning heavily on an elegant cane underneath a large wooden sign that read *van Zyl Trading Post*.

Both nodded pleasantly at Nyack as he rode past them and then turned back to their conversation.

"It was a damn goot shot, Captain. Damn goot," the fat man told the officer in a gravelly accent thick with smoke. "Sey are so tricky to fint in de trees sometimes, I almost didn't see him myself. But what a shot! Right in de lungs! You are truly a credit to His Majesty's service."

The British man nodded politely and tapped away some of the ash from his cigar.

"You are too kind, Mr. van Zyl. Truth is, I would have never seen the devil without one of your Negroes pointing it out to me. And you can have the skin delivered to the barracks in Gaborone?"

The fat man nodded graciously.

"Of course! We do dis all de time. We'll start working on him tomorrow and delifer your wife her leopart skin next month!"

Conrad was tempted to jump off his horse and rush over to the British captain, but Nyack caught his arm and stopped him.

"That's Willem van Zyl," Nyack told him as the two men disappeared back inside the trading post. "He's the grandson of the legendary Hendrik van Zyl, the man who made Ghanzi a rich town. He's a happy and harmless man most days, but he has a terrible temper when people interrupt him. Especially when he's conducting business. If you want to speak to his guest, I will bring you back here tomorrow."

Conrad was disappointed but nodded in agreement.

"What does Mr. van Zyl sell?" he asked Nyack.

"What are you buying?" Nyack laughed. "His family has a hunting empire in this part of Bechuanaland that keeps the British happy. He mostly serves bored garrison officers who want to shoot elephants and lions. The people here say that Willem and his grandfather were such deadly hunters that they once killed a hundred and two elephants in a single day."

Conrad heard one of Nyack's men scoff a few yards away.

"I thought it was a hundred and three elephants!" he called back to Nyack.

Nyack laughed and nudged along one of the slower cows with his boot.

"It will be a hundred and four the next time we ride through town!" he yelled back.

Sybille and Anna had been chatting pleasantly with one of Nyack's hands for a while at the back of the herd, but they rode up next to Conrad and Nyack as they passed through the town.

"This is such a beautiful place," Sybille said to Nyack.

Nyack beamed at her, and when Sybille and Anna weren't looking, he leaned over his saddle and shot Conrad a wicked grin.

"Do you know what 'Ghanzi' means?" he asked Conrad.

Conrad shook his head.

"It means 'swollen ass," Nyack whispered and then chuckled hysterically. "The animals here are so healthy that the old Naro folk who hunted here used to call this place 'the place with the fat-assed antelope!'"

*

Nyack's "family" were numerous, and Conrad struggled all evening to remember who was a child and who was a "nephew" or "cousin," come to see what presents Nyack had brought with him from Mamuno.

When Conrad was first introduced to the mass of people working at

Nyack's ranch, the swarm of Tswana children that flocked to Nyack were only briefly interested in him. But when Nyack told the children that Conrad had crossed the Kalahari, suddenly the German stranger became even more interesting than Nyack himself.

"They told me in Mamuno that this man stared down a pack of lionesses and rode a zebra," Nyack casually whispered to one of the younger children, and from then on, Conrad became the center of attention.

For hours Conrad answered a ceaseless barrage of high-pitched questions while Sybille and Anna smiled and laughed at his obvious discomfort.

The children also clustered around Gustavus, and several of the smaller ones clung to the big dog obsessively, petting the dark-lined fur on his back and hugging his massive neck. Gustavus, for his part, looked much like Conrad, unsure of how to entertain or tolerate so many children at once.

Nyack's wife, a plump, soft-spoken woman, served them large helpings of something she called *seswaa*, which she had prepared for her husband's return. The smell of roasted goat and fried dough quickly filled the small farmhouse, and everywhere around them, people were eating, talking, and laughing.

Nyack's wife hovered around Conrad all night. He had had to eat three platefuls of the rich dish before she was satisfied that he was full. Several of Nyack's "brothers" insisted on drinking a glass of beer with their German guest, and Conrad was quite drunk before the meal was half over.

Between the warmth of the cooking fires, the happy humming of the children, and the blissful ease of stretching out his saddle-sore legs, Conrad found his eyelids drooping, and he had to struggle to stay awake.

Well after midnight, when all the guests had at last gone home, Sybille and Anna were given a pallet in a small room with one of Nyack's daughters, and Nyack surrendered his own to Conrad.

As Conrad lay down on the hard bed, a jackal howled not too far away, but he paid it no mind. It was too warm under the blanket Nyack had given him, and the cool night air brushed soothingly against his permanently sunburned forehead. He felt full and lazy, and as sleep crept over his tired body, Conrad wondered if he and Sybille should stay in Ghanzi forever.

CHAPTER 20

MARCH 1905

After a few restful days of sipping thick malt beer in the shade outside his farmhouse with Conrad while his younger field hands tended to his new cattle, Nyack decided that his nephew, Mpho, would take Conrad, Sybille, and Anna south to Kang.

Unlike his uncle, Mpho was tall and quiet. But Nyack insisted that the boy was friendly enough and that he rode a horse better than any of his uncle's cowhands. During the rainy season, Mpho worked as a hunting guide for van Zyl, and Nyack boasted that he was one of the few Africans willing to lead insistent British officers further north into the treacherous wetlands of Okavango Delta to shoot hippopotamuses.

The wetlands were a water-logged maze even during the dry season, but Mpho was a skilled enough tracker to pick a safe path through the marshes and crocodile beds that even white folk could follow.

When the time came to say goodbye to Nyack and his family, it took nearly an hour to navigate the swarm of well-wishing and embraces. After only a few days of resting at Nyack's ranch, it seemed to Conrad that Nyack and his boisterous family had always been a part of his life.

Sybille and Anna had spent their days with Nyack's wife and her daughters, minding the droves of children that ran freely across the brown-green pastures and tending enough cooking fires to feed the regiment of workers and family members that drifted in and out of the compound like worker bees. The two of them laughed and talked with the other women, teasing the lazy young men and keeping one watchful eye on the children's chaotic games. They moved so freely among the crowd of strangers, smiling carelessly and working happily, that for a few moments, everything that had happened to them seemed like a distant nightmare.

Gustavus, for his part, looked well-rested, although he was clearly confused as to why he'd been able to hunt wild guinea fowl in the desert but now had to be restrained on a leash from chasing Nyack's wife's chickens, which were allowed to wander and peck wherever they pleased.

Even their horses seemed in better spirits. Conrad thought they had gained a little weight eating Nyack's grass. Perhaps there was something to the land of "the fat-ass antelope" after all.

Yet now it was time to leave. Nyack's home had been a veritable paradise, and suddenly Conrad felt more nervous about leaving the comfort of Nyack's family than he had when he'd first stepped aboard the deck of the *Calypso* and watched Hamburg disappear in the distance. He was in strange, new territory, and the moment they rode out of Ghanzi, it would be up to Sybille, Anna, and him to search for the Herero and make a new life for themselves.

Sybille was close to tears as she wrapped her arms around Nyack's wife. Conrad and Anna slowly gained ground in saying farewell to Nyack's collection of uncles, aunts, cousins, and friends. Gustavus had the worst of it, trying to nudge his large frame out of the children's grabbing hands, though out of the corner of his eye, Conrad caught his big tail wagging furtively.

Mpho was waiting patiently for them outside the farmhouse. He sat atop a small, gray gelding, absently stroking his horse's neck while he held the reins of their saddled horses in the other. Conrad doubted Mpho was more than eighteen or nineteen. Nyack's nephew sported a patchy beard of rough, black hair, and his long limbs hung awkwardly by his side through a worn and wrinkled brown coat. Yet he held the horses' reins and murmured to them with an expert air that made Conrad believe they were in good hands.

When, at last, he managed to separate himself from the pack, Nyack pulled Conrad aside, and the small man slipped a stack of pound notes into Conrad's hand.

"We sold some of the older cows. They were no good for meat anyway," he told Conrad with a wink. "Just something to settle the pretty ladies in Gaborone with."

Conrad stared dumbly at the faded money in his hand. It was nearly fifty pounds! Nyack could not have sold all his older cattle for half that price. The small rancher must've had to borrow on credit in town against the value of his future calves to get the money. Even with their apparent comfort, surely his family could not afford such a gesture?

Nyack's wife and daughters were still saying goodbye to Sybille and Anna, and no one had noticed yet that Nyack had pulled Conrad aside. Conrad looked from the women to the cluster of small children milling around underfoot. He wanted to refuse the money, but he did not want to insult the man by suggesting his own family would be better off if he kept the money for himself. And the truth was, he, Sybille, and Anna needed money.

"You let me worry about them," Nyack said with a soft smile as he read Conrad's thoughts and looked at his wife and children. "My father raised a family twice this big on far less. We will be fine when the calves come this summer."

"I will pay you back," Conrad replied quietly.

"You will or you won't, *Herr* Huber," the small man said with a grin. "But either way, those pretty ladies of yours will be taken care of. And if there's one thing old Nyack is known for, it is taking care of pretty ladies."

Nyack stuck out his hand to shake Conrad's, but Conrad ignored the offered hand and instead grabbed the small man and hugged him tightly. Nyack seemed surprised for a moment and then laughed loudly and hugged Conrad back.

"My God!" Nyack shouted so his grandchildren could hear him. "It is like hugging a giraffe!"

Sybille and Anna finally separated themselves from the group of women, and they both kissed Nyack goodbye, which pleased the old man immensely. Anna, who had picked up enough Setswana in the last few days to be polite, called him *Rre*, Father, which delighted Nyack even more.

Nyack helped the two women into their saddles, and as Conrad took his reins from Mpho and swung into his own saddle, another of Nyack's nephews came trotting down the road with a white man in tow.

Conrad recognized the British captain whom they'd seen at the trading post the day they'd first rode through Ghanzi. He'd gone back into town with Nyack every morning to try to find the man, but the captain had always been out hunting with van Zyl.

"Good morning," the captain said as he rode up to join them. "You must be Herr Huber, I presume. Captain Arthur B. Lawrence of His Majesty's Cape Mounted Rifles, at your service."

"Pleased to meet you, Captain Lawrence," Conrad replied.

Captain Lawrence did not introduce himself to Sybille or Anna, nor did he acknowledge Nyack or the young man who had presumably been his guide this morning.

"The pleasure is entirely mine, Herr Huber," Captain Lawrence said with a polite smile. "There's been talk all over Ghanzi these last few days of the German man who crossed the Kalahari on his own. I do hope you'll honor me with the tale along the way."

Captain Lawrence was a tall, good-looking man in his late thirties. His blond hair lay well-cropped beneath his officer's cap, and he smiled at Conrad amiably with dark green eyes and a roguish grin. In his colonial uniform, he looked the part of a gentlemen adventurer, and Conrad found his sudden company both astounding and reassuring.

"I haven't kept you waiting, have I?" Lawrence continued. "That van Zyl is a fascinating man, but if you give him an inch, he can talk your ear off until the dead rise again. I heard in town there was another man headed back to

Gaborone today, and I thought I'd end my holiday a tad early and tag along if it's no trouble?"

"Er, not at all," Conrad said, looking to Sybille and Anna a bit too late for their approval.

"Splendid!" Captain Lawrence beamed. "Now, which one of these Negroes is our guide?"

*

They made good time from Ghanzi. As they left the small desert town, the landscape changed quickly around them. The rains had brought life to the plateaus, and as they covered mile after mile, the Kalahari relaxed its sprawling dune-fingered grip. Green grasses sprouted on the edge of the dirt road and quickly gave way to long, skinny trees that grew fatter and darker the further south they rode.

Captain Lawrence proved to be a decent enough man. He had been surprised to learn that Sybille and Anna were accompanying them to Gaborone, but he had been polite enough to smile and at least attempt to swallow his disapproval.

In truth, Conrad did not think Captain Lawrence was a wicked man, just one who, despite his adventuring, had grown comfortable in an established social order that he saw no immediate need to reconstruct. Entitlement had a way of overexerting itself among many of the white men Conrad had met in Africa, and he was simply glad that the English captain felt confident enough in his own superiority not to assert himself regularly over Mpho, Sybille, or Anna.

The man was a skilled talker. He had gone to Ghanzi on a hunting expedition as part of a long-awaited and, in his opinion, very long overdue leave from the Cape Mounted Rifles. Captain Lawrence and his wife had spent a week in Cape Town in the Cape Colony to accommodate his wife's ardent infatuation with the ocean, which she had only seemed to develop after his company had been moved so far inland.

However, Captain Lawrence had managed to negotiate a few extra weeks' leave from his commander. It wasn't as though there was a war to fight now that the Boers were defeated, and so he had gone to Ghanzi to hunt with the legendary van Zyl family. His wife had been furious until he promised to bring her home a leopard skin, just like the one Queen Alexandra had worn over her shoulders at the opening of Parliament last year. After that, she'd practically saddled his horse for him.

"But enough about me, Herr Huber," Captain Lawrence finally said around mid-afternoon on the third day. "Let's hear some of your stories from the desert! They'll be all anyone will talk about for weeks once we reach Gaborone, and I insist on knowing every last detail first."

Conrad smiled nervously while Sybille and Anna, tired after two-and-a-half days of being ignored by Lawrence, rode further on ahead with Mpho by their own mutual, silent agreement. The midday heat was sweltering, and without Nyack's good humor to keep his mind off the sun, Conrad was painfully aware of each gob of sweat that fell from his face as he tried to concentrate and tell Lawrence all that was happening in the DSWA.

"Well…" Conrad started after a bit. "I'm really not sure how to begin…"

"Oh, no one likes a humble man, Herr Huber," Lawrence chided him. "Come now. The whole story. Out with it, man!"

It took Conrad twice as long to describe what had happened to the Herero and to him and Sybille than it otherwise might have. It seemed that every time he mentioned a particular detail or took a pause for breath, Lawrence would insert his own commentary on Conrad's ordeal, as though he and Conrad were merely swapping equally audacious stories.

"Hid in a basement, did you? My cousin and I used to hide from my older brother in the cellar back home in Cheshire. David was always a nasty brute, really. Constantly trying to pummel Robert and me whenever he got the chance. I'm sure it can't compare at all, of course."

Lawrence seemed to show genuine amazement at Conrad's story for a few short moments, during which he was blessedly silent. But then he would dive back into another of his comparisons that were so laughably out of place that Conrad was sure Lawrence had only really heard half of what Conrad had actually said.

"Poor beast," he'd said when Conrad had told him how Ivan had rescued him from the hyena attack. "I lost my beloved spaniel in a hunting accident just before I shipped out to join the King's Rifles. My father shot a low-flying pheasant on our Christmas hunt in Dumfries, and he didn't see poor Millie breaking out of the brush. Hmmm. Mauled to death by a savage beast, though. How dreadful."

Conrad was still struggling to get through telling their odyssey a day later. He was growing increasingly frustrated with Captain Lawrence's endless interruptions, and what truly shocked him was that Lawrence seemed utterly unfazed by any of von Trotha and the Schutztruppe's atrocities.

It turned out that Lawrence did have some knowledge of the German colonial government's prisoner camps, although he did not confide in Conrad how he had learned about them. And of course, he had already heard of von Trotha's arrival in the DSWA.

But Lawrence seemed uninterested in discussing the abuse of the native prisoners or von Trotha's war of racial extermination in Germany's desolate colony. And when Conrad tried to press the matter, Lawrence's face set in a brief, sour look, and he waved the subject away with appalling ease.

"It's uncivilized, of course. But I'm afraid it's not our problem, Herr Huber," Lawrence said as he patted his horse's neck affectionately. "God knows my Rifles and I have enough trouble on our hands keeping the Boers in line."

The only time during his story that Lawrence prodded Conrad for details was whenever Conrad mentioned von Trotha himself. Conrad thought that Lawrence understood at least partly that von Trotha and the Schutztruppe were responsible for why Conrad was riding beside him now in the Bechuanaland desert. And yet, Lawrence seemed to afford the famous general bewildering immunity.

He wanted to know every last maneuver von Trotha had accomplished at Waterberg, what the man thought about the current European political climate, and whether or not he thought cavalry would one day be supplanted by superior firearms. Conrad would not have been surprised if Lawrence had insisted on knowing what the man had eaten for breakfast every morning.

"A brilliant tactician, to be sure," Lawrence mused to himself several times. "I only wish I could have seen him in action at Langfang! They say he and his men faced the Boxers without fear, never giving an inch, and that von Trotha's train car headquarters came out of the war full of bullet holes."

Conrad grimaced as he thought about the sort of train cars that the General was using now. He said nothing as Lawrence recited more of von Trotha's career victories.

When at last Lawrence let him speak again, Conrad skimmed over his visit to Shark Island and his flight from Windhoek. He was sure that Lawrence would not have heard him anyway.

His hopes of British pressure on the DSWA diminished the longer he talked with Lawrence. If the Captain was any sort of judge of what his government would think of Conrad's story, then there was little chance that the British would bother goading the Kaiser on the Herero's behalf.

A few Methodists or Anti-Imperialists might choose to pick up the cause strictly out of solidarity. But Conrad's chances of reaching them seemed slim. He was on a long, dusty road in one of the most remote places in the world, and the only man he'd met so far who might've been able to carry the message for him was uninterested in hearing it.

Conrad was crestfallen. He felt as though he had failed. He couldn't even convince Lawrence to pay attention to him, let alone Sybille and Anna, and as the miles stretched on and Conrad listened to more of Lawrence's prattle, he began to hate the man. In the Kalahari, there were times that Conrad would have gladly traded his arm to hear another human's voice. Now he wished he might suddenly be struck deaf.

Yet with Sybille, Anna, and Mpho keeping their distance from Lawrence, Conrad had nothing else to do in the saddle the next day but to continue to tell Lawrence what had led them to Ghanzi.

The only thing positive that Conrad could say for Captain Lawrence was that he seemed equally unconcerned that he was traveling in the company of two fugitives.

From what Conrad could tell, Lawrence had either not realized that he,

Sybille and Anna *were* fugitives from the bits of Conrad's story he had listened to, or he simply didn't care.

Conrad had broken no laws in Bechuanaland and was not a dangerous man by any reasonable standard. He might've been a German fugitive, but he was in an English protectorate now, and that seemed to matter more than anything else. From time to time, Lawrence would shoot Conrad a conspiratorial grin, but Conrad could not tell from the man's expression if Lawrence suspected him of being a spy caught out on a secret mission, or if Lawrence was merely happy to have another white man accompanying him.

The only time he gave any indication that he had been listening to Conrad was around mid-day on their second day out from Ghanzi when he turned to Conrad and gestured ahead of them at Sybille.

"All of that for a Negress…you are *fascinating*, Herr Huber," he said evenly.

Conrad could not quite place Lawrence's tone, but before he could respond, Mpho suddenly pulled his horse to a stop ahead of them.

Conrad and Lawrence caught up with the others and looked at one another questioningly.

"I say, boy," Lawrence said, flustered. "Why the devil are we stopping?"

"Shhhh," Mpho breathed back in response. "Be very quiet. Elephants are coming."

"Elephants?" Captain Lawrence snorted. "Oh, come, now. I don't see any elephants around here, and it's not as though they're very good at hiding."

Beside Conrad, Gustavus' ears suddenly pricked up. The big dog sniffed the air once and then whipped his head in the direction Mpho was staring. A few thick trees stood clustered together beside the road in a narrow funnel of thorny foliage. The trees were tall and covered with dark green leaves, but they appeared empty, and Conrad could not see how even a single elephant could manage to hide among them.

Then he heard a large branch snap.

All at once the trees began rocking to life as their heavy limbs were pushed aside with little effort. Then an elephant emerged from the small grove and walked straight out onto the road in front of them.

Captain Lawrence's jaw fell open.

"By God, there was an elephant in there! How in God's name…"

Mpho reached across his saddle, clasped his hand roughly over Captain Lawrence's mouth, and held a finger to his own lips. Conrad saw the Englishman's face flush red in anger and heard Captain Lawrence start to protest this breach of conduct. But then the elephant turned its head toward them, and Captain Lawrence's objections died in his throat.

No one moved. The elephant stared blankly at them as if trying to concentrate on something far off in the distance. It rolled its big head, displaying two large, brilliant tusks. The elephant made a deep, exhausted grunt in annoyance and then threw a cloud of dust up in the air with its trunk.

Then the elephant turned away from them and lumbered on straight across the road. When the elephant reached the other side of the track, it disappeared slowly back into the brush, and Mpho slid his hand away from Captain Lawrence's mouth.

"Elephants do not see well," Mpho whispered intently. "They see the world as…fuzzy. They listen to what is near. And if they hear something that was not there before, they charge. And if they see something move they do not like… they will try to kill it."

Mpho's voice was higher than his uncle's, and he spoke in thick, accented English that Conrad had to focus hard on to understand. He had mostly kept to himself since they had left Ghanzi, and these were the first words he had spoken to either Lawrence or Conrad.

Lawrence tensed a moment as though still contemplating giving Mpho a stern reprimand, but then he nodded in reluctant acceptance.

"Is there only one?" Anna whispered to Mpho.

The young guide shook his head.

"Scout comes first. Babies come next with their mothers."

Sure enough, a few seconds later, a second elephant broke out of the tree line. And then a third. And then a fourth. These elephants were smaller than the first one, and one by one, they followed the lead elephant's exact steps across the dirt road before they disappeared behind the trees on the other side themselves.

At first, the elephants came single-file, and then suddenly, they were everywhere, crossing the road, three or four abreast in an endless procession of brown and gray giants.

Sybille reached over and touched Conrad's arm. She smiled at him and pointed discreetly at the middle of the herd. Conrad followed her eyes, and when he found what she was looking at, he smiled as well. Beneath their mothers' bellies, small, wrinkled elephants weaved playfully in and out of the herd. The young elephants were more than twice Gustavus' size, but they moved clumsily around their mothers like plump, plodding puppies. They flapped their ears happily and flicked their small trunks around haphazardly as though they were not quite sure how to use them yet.

Conrad could've watched the peaceful parade all day.

Then, without warning, a deafening roar erupted from the tree cover. Mpho's eyes went wide, and Conrad saw the man's color drain from his face.

"Oh no..." Mpho breathed. "This is *her* herd..."

"What?" Conrad asked, his voice trembling.

Mpho hesitated a moment as if too afraid to speak.

"Char-jar," he finally breathed.

Before Conrad could ask, the largest creature he had ever seen burst out of the tree line, uprooting two young trees as its massive shoulders ploughed through them.

It was an elephant, but one that dwarfed the rest of its herd. Its back rose nearly four meters above the ground, and its head alone looked larger than their horses. The elephant had only one tusk, but it stretched nearly halfway to the ground.

The elephant ran out into the middle of the road and thundered a loud trumpet that sent the rest of the elephant herd stampeding across the road for cover. Elephants waiting for their turn to cross now suddenly broke out of their cover in a panicked fright, tearing the small forest out of the ground and echoing their leader's trumpet of alarm.

"What in Christ's name is that thing?" Captain Lawrence shouted over the madness.

"Char-jar," Mpho repeated. "She is the grandmotha elephant in the herd. She is the meanest elephant in Africa."

As if hearing Mpho, Charger stomped the earth in front of them with one of her enormous legs and lowered her head in an angry challenge. If she could see them, the giant elephant did not seem concerned that she was outnumbered.

"Why does she only have one tusk?" Anna asked in a panicked voice.

"She killed a young bull that tried to mate with her last year. One of van Zyl's other guides found the male's skull with the tusk buried so deep in the bone that he could not pull it out."

Charger roared again, and Captain Lawrence made a grab for his rifle holster across the back of his saddle.

"No!" Mpho yelled at him. "You will not kill her. She has been shot many times, and she has killed seven hunters."

"Then what the hell do we do?" Lawrence shouted back, still reaching for the gun.

At the sight of the Englishman's rifle, Charger's eyes went wild, and she charged toward them with a loud roar.

"Run!" Mpho screamed.

The horses needed no encouragement and tore off in a mad gallop. Gustavus fled with them as well, flying back down the road as fast as his long legs could carry him. The horses ran wildly for their lives, and even Captain Lawrence could not get his mare back under control. Conrad's gelding ran for its own sake, indiscriminately knocking him into thorn bushes and tree branches.

Conrad could feel the earth trembling beneath them as the matron elephant bore down on them. He heard someone scream, but he could not tell who it was.

The gelding tore its reins from Conrad's hands and pulled him off the road and straight through a flame thorn tree. Conrad covered his eyes as the sharp barbs tore into him, and he squeezed the gelding's sides with his knees as hard as he could, trying desperately not to fall off. Leaves and twigs tore all around him, and he barely saw the large, low-hanging branch before the gelding plunged him straight into it.

Conrad heard the gelding scream in shock as the branch slammed into its chest, sending Conrad flying through the air. He somersaulted over the gelding and hit the ground hard as the wind was sucked right out of him. His head was spinning, and he felt a sharp pain in his leg that he hadn't felt in weeks. He could hear Charger trumpeting angrily nearby, and the ground shook beneath him as though the enormous elephant were just about to bear down on him.

He screamed with what breath he had left and waited to be trampled.

And then, all at once, it was silent. Conrad opened one eye and saw that he was alone. The gelding had stopped a few yards away and was now frantically trying to catch its breath. Its neck was bleeding from where it had run into the heavy branch, but it seemed more or less alright. The wound wasn't deep, and the horse was more scared than in pain.

They had stopped in a small opening of a grove of flame thorns that obscured Conrad's sight in every direction. The bushes formed a thick jungle of vegetation that had been invisible from the road. In this part of the Kalahari, there was enough water for some plants to grow, and these had flourished and grown large enough to conceal an army of elephants.

The sudden silence around him made Conrad's ears ring. There was nothing but stillness. He could not hear Charger anymore, and there was no sign of any other elephants or the other riders. Conrad suddenly remembered the terror of waking up in the desert after their flight from Schwerinsberg, and he felt the familiar panic start to well up in his chest.

His leg throbbed painfully, and he struggled hastily to get to his feet.

No, no, no, he cried to himself. I can't be lost again.

Then he heard someone calling his name.

"Conrad?" a woman's voice called. "Conrad, where are you?"

It was Sybille.

"I-I'm not sure," he called back as relief washed over him. "I'm in a grove of thorns. Are you okay?"

"Stay there, Herr Huber," Mpho called from the same direction. "I will come and find you."

After a few minutes, Conrad heard Mpho's muffled curses as he pushed his way through the flame thorns into the grove. Mpho pushed aside the large branch that the gelding had run into and, in the struggle, tripped in a large hole and fell headfirst onto the ground. He cursed and muttered something in Setswana as he got to his feet, shaking his head in disbelief.

"Your dumb horse ran you back into Char-jar's path," he said, giving the gelding a dirty look. "When we get to Kang, you can sell that stupid army horse for one that knows the bush. This horse will get you killed."

Conrad did not understand what Mpho meant until he looked more closely at the ground around him. Mpho had not stumbled in a hole but the divot of an enormous footprint. Dozens of them lined the long rows of flame thorns, carving the surrounding earth into broken trenches. Instead of running back down the road like the other horses, Conrad's gelding had turned completely around in a circle and bolted blindly back into the trees the elephants had just run through.

Mpho was silent a moment and then seemed to regret his harsh words about the gelding. He reached out, caught the frightened animal's bridle, and stroked its nose affectionately.

"At least you are not dead," Mpho consented.

"Er…where is Charger?" Conrad asked, half-expecting the matron elephant to come tearing out of the tree line again.

"Gone," Mpho said. "We got lucky. The horses all ran different ways, and so she gave up. Char-jar is old. She likes to catch you, but not chase you."

Conrad thought he heard a twinge of admiration in Mpho's voice as if he were almost proud to say that he'd crossed paths with the mystical Charger and lived to tell the tale. If nothing else, he was sure to have the best story at his uncle's next gathering.

"You've seen Charger before, then?" Conrad asked, massaging his leg while Mpho started to lead the gelding out of the grove.

"Once," Mpho said absently. "She killed my cousin Baboloki on a hunt last year."

The blood slowly began to flow again in Conrad's leg, and he limped tentatively after Mpho.

"I'm sorry," Conrad said.

Mpho was busy holding a heavy branch up for the gelding the slip beneath and didn't respond.

The gelding was skittish now, and Mpho had to give its reins a hard yank to get it to walk out through the flame thorn. Finally, the gelding slipped out of the grove, and Mpho let out a long sigh as he turned back to wait for Conrad.

"Is everyone else alright?" Conrad asked.

Mpho was quiet for a moment while he guided them out of the flame thorn's branches. Then he gave Conrad a small impish smile.

"Yes," he said. "But I think the Englishman shit himself."

*

They reached the Okwa River a few hours later. A modest obstacle, the Okwa moved westward in no particular hurry. Birds of every size and color flocked to the edge of its greenish-brown water, and when Mpho called for a rest, Sybille took Conrad's arm and pulled him over to where she'd spotted a small flock of bright pink flamingos wading nearby.

The odd-shaped birds bobbed elegantly along in the still shallows, dipping their beaks idly in the water and pruning away their old feathers. The nearby bank was covered in long, pink feathers as the sluggish tide pushed the discarded plumes ashore. Conrad scooped a handful of them up and placed them gingerly inside his jacket pocket.

It had been nearly two years since he'd sat in an open-air carriage in Hamburg while his cousin Frieda told him of her dreadful friend Ara Egger's boastings about the flamingo feathers her father had brought her from Africa. He suddenly missed Frieda and little Justus terribly. He doubted he would ever see them again.

Without realizing it, Conrad gave his jacket an extra protective pat.

Sybille saw and raised an eyebrow at him.

"Let Ara Egger gawk at these," he said playfully.

Sybille did not understand the joke but smiled back at him anyway. Gustavus, who had followed them to the water's edge, bounded into the shallows after the flamingos, scattering the vibrant flock in a swirl of pink feathers and startled honking.

Conrad and Sybille bent over laughing as Gustavus strutted back to the shore, proudly sporting a mouthful of feathers. Sybille leaned in close against Conrad, and he held her for a few moments, enjoying the first privacy they'd had for days.

Gustavus nuzzled against Conrad's other side, his wet fur soaking the leg of Conrad's trousers. Conrad chuckled softly and rubbed the big dog's head affectionately.

A bright coral feather washed ashore at his feet, and Conrad stooped to pick it up. It was a nearly perfect shade of bright pink. He plunked the feather from the water and handed it to Sybille.

"For you," he said shyly.

It was the first time the two of them had really been alone since the night they'd been interrupted in the Windhoek flat. They had been the only humans they'd seen for days as they crossed the desert, but their every effort in the Kalahari had gone toward surviving; neither of them had had any energy to explore anything else. And then Conrad had come under the watchful eyes of first Mma Boitumelo, then Anna, and most recently Nyack and Captain Lawrence.

Standing at the edge of the lazy river was the first time he and Sybille were truly alone since he'd told her he loved her.

Sybille smiled as she took the feather and tucked it into her hair behind her ear. It looked ridiculous against the faded brown dress she'd been given by one of Nyack's daughters, but she laughed and kissed him softly on the mouth.

"Thank you," she told him as she leaned back against him and listened to the chorus of birds around them.

It was hard to hear any one sort of bird above all the combined racket.

Sparrows gathered in the nearby trees by the hundreds, hornbills in the dozens, and even a few menacing-looking giant bustards prowled the edge of the riverbank looking for fish.

Egrets, skimmers, and snipes all crowded around the water's edge in a magnificent show of painted wings of every shade and hue. Browns, golds, whites, yellows, oranges, blues and greens. Sybille even pointed out two tiny lilac-crested birds hovering just above the water. But above all the chatter, Conrad heard a soft call from one of the trees that rose and fell in a familiar call.

Word, Har-der. Word, Har-der.

Conrad's voice caught in his throat as he heard the ring-necked dove's song. He thought of poor Petyr back at the Windhoek swimming hole, snatching the small bird out of the air, and then cooing its own song back to it.

"*No. Drink, La-ger. Drink, La-ger,*" Conrad called back quietly to the female doves.

"Did you say something, Herr Huber?" Captain Lawrence said as he emerged from where they'd tethered the horses.

Captain Lawrence was carrying a small sketchbook with him. He had been fully consumed in drawing a giant bustard when they had stopped, but he was an amateur artist and had already clumsily captured his version of the creature's likeness. Sybille shifted her weight slightly away from Conrad as Lawrence joined them on the riverbank. Conrad wished the captain would sense the moment and leave.

"No, nothing," Conrad replied casually.

Lawrence nodded and resumed talking to Conrad about the limited but admittedly adequate social circles of Bechuanaland that he would be happy to introduce Conrad into when they reached Gaborone. Charger's attack had quieted Lawrence for a time, but now the Englishman was back to his usual chatty self.

Mpho and Anna joined them at the water's edge a few minutes later with another Tswana man Mpho introduced as the ferryman.

A short, thin man with a scarred face and a half-cocked grimace, the ferryman stared at the water while Mpho explained that the man lived with his family in a nearby village and that their party needed him to guide them across the Okwa.

"The Okwa only comes with the rains," Mpho explained to them. "In the dry season, you can cross the riverbed without knowing it. But when the rains come, you need the ferryman."

Captain Lawrence scoffed.

"Why can we not simply ride across it?" Lawrence asked, irritated at the suggestion they would need to pay for a second guide. "The Cape Rifles have crossed the Okwa hundreds of times, and we've ridden right over it. I rode across this very spot not a week ago. It's not that deep at all!"

Mpho shook his head and insisted once again that they needed to hire the ferryman.

"The river is tricky and too dark to judge from the shore. One week it might be only a few inches deep, but the next, it is deep enough to swallow a giraffe."

He and Lawrence continued to argue for several minutes. Lawrence was growing angrier by the second, but Mpho would not budge on his insistence that they needed the ferryman.

"Fine!" Lawrence finally shouted in defeat. "Dare I ask how much this snake wants to take us all across?"

The ferryman, who had obviously not expected travelers today and looked annoyed at Mpho summoning him away from his dinner, mumbled something unflattering. Lawrence, thankfully, pretended not to hear the man.

The "ferry" turned out to be little more than a medium-sized canoe that would just barely hold them all. Lawrence fumed when the ferryman dragged the canoe out from where it lay hidden in a cluster of reeds and, through Mpho, casually demanded fifteen shillings per person for the trip across.

"Fifteen shillings?!" Lawrence shouted at the spindly man. "For a ride across a shallow ford in a damn hollowed-out log?"

The price was meant to be ridiculous, but Lawrence was furious now and in no mood to barter for a service he did not think he needed. He shouted at the ferryman, who did not understand, but stared back at him grumpily.

It took Mpho several minutes to negotiate and appease both parties in Tswana and English, and after a dozen or so rounds of back and forth, they finally agreed on the price of five shillings each.

Once Lawrence had calmed down somewhat, he decided that they would swim the horses across and carry their saddles in the canoe. As he and Mpho began to unsaddle the horses, the ferryman eyed Gustavus suspiciously and insisted that the big dog swim as well.

"Too big," he said plainly to Conrad in tattered English.

Conrad looked at the width of the Okwa. He did not know if Gustavus could swim or not. If the river was as deep as Mpho feared, then Conrad did not think the dog would make it across regardless.

"Can't he ride in the canoe with us?" Conrad begged the man. "I'll make a separate trip with him if it helps?"

The ferryman grimaced, unhappy at the thought of having to make two trips back and forth. He scratched at one of the scars on his face, mulling it over.

"We tie a rope to hold dog to the side," he finally said. "He flips canoe if inside."

The ferryman did not leave any room for argument, so Conrad consented and joined the others in unsaddling the horses.

It took the better part of an hour to get everything ready. The horses had to be hobbled together so they could swim but would not be able to run very far once they reached the other side. Captain Lawrence and Mpho managed to accomplish this without saying a single word to one another, while Sybille and Anna helped load the heavy saddles into the canoe.

Conrad took the rope they had with them and tied it around Gustavus' chest to make a makeshift harness. The big dog did not understand what Conrad was doing but stayed still out of curiosity.

The ferryman did not offer to help any of them, but sat by the water's edge and watched the lazy current. When everything was finally ready, the ferryman turned to Mpho, murmured something the others couldn't hear, and shook his head.

"He says we cannot cross today," Mpho translated for the group.

"Why the bloody hell not?" Captain Lawrence erupted. "The bastard's cheated us already, and now he won't keep his end of the bargain? Why the devil did he let us load the damn boat, then?"

The ferryman ignored Lawrence and instead turned to Sybille and Anna.

"No animals," he told them, gesturing all around the riverbank.

"He means that no animals have crossed here today," Mpho explained. "No antelope, no gnu, not even the elephants. No one has crossed the river here today. If the animals do not cross, then the ferryman says we cannot cross."

Captain Lawrence turned to Conrad, seeking an ally for his fury.

"Do you believe the gall of these blackie bastards?" Lawrence asked him indignantly.

He did not wait for Conrad to respond before turning to shout at the ferryman, who still did not understand a word the Englishman was saying.

"What do you think?" Conrad whispered to Mpho.

Mpho shrugged.

"Hard to say. The ferryman knows the Okwa better than me. The water looks calm, but if he says we should not cross today, then that is worth considering."

Conrad turned to Sybille and Anna, who both shrugged indecisively. They were eager to reach Gaborone, but they knew nothing about Bechuanaland, and Conrad could tell that they did not want to argue with the local man.

Captain Lawrence, however, had no such qualms, and after silently enduring the captain's tirade for several minutes, the ferryman finally furrowed his brow and tossed his hands up in defeat. He spat on the ground and picked up his long poling oar from where it sat in the mud.

"O-kay," the man said coolly.

"Goddamn thief," Captain Lawrence said to Conrad as the man reluctantly began to push the canoe into the water. "Trying to hold out for more money, no doubt. We've already paid him a bloody fortune for his lot."

It took Mpho another ten minutes to coax the horses down to the river, but once he got his own mare into the water, the rest of the hobbled horses gave in and began to wade out further into the river together.

Mpho hurried through the shallows and pulled himself into the canoe, keeping a firm grip on the lead mare's rope. Once the horses were more than halfway across, he would let go of the heavy lead line, but until then, he held onto it tightly so the horses could not turn around and swim back to the same bank.

Gustavus was far less agreeable with his arrangement. As the canoe pushed away from the bank, the water quickly grew deeper, and Gustavus began to squirm against his harness. The big dog did not trust the ropes to keep him afloat, and thinking he must be drowning, he tried to swim on his own, rocking the entire canoe in the process. Both Conrad and Sybille held onto him to try and subdue him, but he continued to struggle against them as the canoe slid slowly out into the river.

After only a few minutes, the ferryman's long pole slipped completely beneath the brown water. From the bank, the river had looked as though it might've been only a few inches deep, but the recent rains had flooded the Okwa, and Conrad was glad they had not tried to ford the river themselves. The horses swam reluctantly alongside the canoe, and soon only their heads were visible above the water.

No one spoke as they drifted across. Although there was little current, the canoe was weighted down with passengers and saddles and it moved precariously across the river, gliding only a few inches above the surface. Captain Lawrence sat in the front of the canoe with a large scowl on his face, as far away from Mpho and the ferryman as he could manage. There was little breeze away from the riverbank, and if possible, it felt even hotter out on the water than it had on land.

Conrad's attention was fixed on subduing Gustavus' continued attempts to escape his harness, but when he glanced up at Sybille next to him, he saw that her face had grown pale.

"What's wrong?" Conrad asked over his shoulder.

Sybille hesitated a moment and then gestured back at Anna.

"We can't swim," she admitted nervously.

"Oh," Conrad said. "Well, I'm sure the ferryman's made this trip hundreds of times. There's nothing to be worried about."

All of a sudden, the horses screamed in a wild panic. The lead mare leapt halfway out of the water with surprising violence and tore the lead line out of Mpho's grip, nearly dragging him overboard. The ferryman dropped his pole to grab Mpho, and the whole canoe tipped dangerously to the side. Gustavus broke free from Conrad's grip and thrashed about in the water against the tangled ropes around his body.

The horses swam back towards the near bank as fast as they could, abandoning the idle canoe in the middle of the water.

"What in God's name?" Captain Lawrence shouted as he tried to steady the tip of the canoe.

Anna screamed and pointed at a large, gray shape that had emerged silently a few yards away.

"*Kwena!*" the ferryman shouted, his eyes wide with fear. *Crocodile.*

The crocodile, nearly as long as the canoe, had appeared without warning. The horses had only escaped it by the mare's quick reaction, and they were now racing through the shallows to safety. The crocodile chased them for a moment but then swung its large body back towards the canoe and arrowed toward the stranded craft at an incredible speed.

For a second, it appeared the monster was going to ram the canoe, but then Conrad followed its eyes and saw what the crocodile was aiming for. While the horses had been spooked too early for the crocodile to catch them, Gustavus was too encumbered by his rope harness to swim. The big dog fought frantically against the binds, splashing and paddling wildly out of reach, trying in vain to reach the near bank.

Just a yard away from the canoe, the crocodile veered away and swam directly toward the helpless dog. Gustavus saw the crocodile coming for him and let out a desperate howl for help.

The sound pierced Conrad like a knife. In his mind, he saw Ivan's cold body sheltering him from the dangers of the bush and Erwin's lifeless form face-down in the dust of the Schwerinsburg stables. He remembered the sound of the gunshot that tore through Petyr's shoulder as he left the boy at the mercy of the Schutztruppe.

He thought of his mother back home in Germany and of Georg, whom he had betrayed and whose career he had very likely destroyed.

He had been beaten, shot, disgraced, hunted, and tossed out into the bush to the mercy of lions and Bushmen. He'd had enough of fucking Africa.

He wasn't going to lose this damn dog too.

Before the others knew what was happening, Conrad leapt from the canoe and landed hard on the crocodile's back.

Conrad hit the crocodile, heels first, and his legs buckled immediately against its hard scales. The impact drove both under water, and Conrad heard the crocodile hiss as it sank beneath him. For a moment, the giant reptile seemed stunned, as though it could not comprehend that something had struck at it from above.

The Okwa swallowed the crocodile and blinded Conrad in a swirl of mud and thrashing water. Conrad tried to open his eyes as he sank, but the sudden torrent clawed at his eyes. He felt the crocodile roll beneath him, and he grabbed limply at the water around him as if he could somehow take hold of the great beast and keep him from Gustavus.

His hands clutched at empty water, and his ears popped with the sound of the crocodile's large tail pushing it through the water. Suddenly Conrad's courage fled, and his lungs began to burn. He felt the crocodile's long body still twisting beneath him, searching furiously for what had attacked it.

The beast's tail hit Conrad in the gut, and Conrad felt as if he'd been struck by a cannonball. His mouth opened in pain, and water quickly rushed into his lungs. His heart was racing, and he felt his arms and legs flailing hopelessly on their own, pulling him frantically back upward.

When he finally reached the surface, he spun around in the water, gulping air as quickly as he could. He tried to tread water, but his clothes and boots hung heavily on his body, and he struggled to keep his head above the water.

He couldn't find the canoe or see Gustavus. Where was the crocodile?

Someone was screaming. Conrad could not tell where they were.

"Conrad!" someone shouted, and he flailed toward the sound.

Then he felt a sudden surge of water beside him as two powerful jaws snapped shut on his arm. Dozens of dagger-like teeth tore into his arm and dragged Conrad back underwater.

The crocodile thrashed its whole body, enraged, and Conrad felt a savage, white-hot burning that made him scream. The crocodile tossed him around like a limp fish with its jaws as water poured into his lungs.

Conrad punched and kicked at the crocodile, trying to beat the beast off him. But the crocodile held its grips mercilessly as it drowned him. Conrad saw blood in the water, and soon a thick, red cloud engulfed him.

Then, Conrad felt a horrible ripping sensation as the crocodile's weight suddenly fell away. Panicked, he kicked madly back toward the surface. He couldn't see the crocodile anymore, but he felt it thrashing near him, searching for him.

Conrad heard the crocodile hissing beneath him as he surfaced, furious that its prey had managed to break away. And then the crocodile broke through the surface beside him, ready to devour Conrad in its powerful jaws.

A rifle shot rang out across the water. Then a second one. Then a third.

Just before Conrad slipped back beneath the water, he saw Sybille holding the paralyzed Captain Lawrence's smoking rifle, firing round after round into the dark brown water.

CHAPTER 21

APRIL 1905

"You have a visitor, Mr. Huber."

Dr. Taylor stuck his worn, blotched face through the doorway, barely pausing as he continued his morning rounds. The old sawbones looked particularly put out this morning, and Conrad heard the barracks' surgeon grumble something under his breath about not being a damn footman for Krauts and Negroes.

Conrad sighed and used his good arm to prop himself up awkwardly on the hospital bed. Ordinarily, Grace, the lone Kalanga nurse who looked in on the British army's wounded would have trailed after Dr. Taylor to help him sit up. But today, Grace was busy in the army hospital's small kitchen preparing the morning meal for Conrad and the other five current occupants of the army hospital.

The "kitchen" was only a small wooden shack connected to the main brick-and-mortar recovery ward by a flimsy screen. Conrad could smell the smoke from the frying pan wafting through his open door.

Grace was a sluggish, heavy woman normally, but ever since Conrad had arrived at the hospital, lying half-dead in a wagon Captain Lawrence had requisitioned in Kang, she had shown surprising energy, bounding up and down through her daily chores. She was excited beyond measure that her mundane routine of mending drunken riflemen and being pawed by the crushed hands of railroad workers had been broken by a real, near-death German spy.

Where Dr. Taylor treated Conrad with only a barely restrained professional disgust, Grace treated him as a farmer back in Aschaffenburg might treat a prized pig. He was always her first visit on her morning rounds and the last in the evenings. She would constantly flutter in and out of his private room that the hospital usually reserved for officers, the folds of her enormous white uniform and headscarf bobbing haphazardly behind her as if her great bulk was somehow moving at a top speed.

Conrad could hear Grace singing loudly beside the cooking fire in the kitchen this morning. He knew she was doing so to cover the noise of her pilfering some of Dr. Taylor's prized stash of honeycomb. Grace had an insatiable sweet tooth, Conrad had observed, but every day she reserved some of the honey she frequently stole from the near-blind Dr. Taylor so that she'd have some left to slip into his morning meal.

Anything for her prized spy.

Conrad didn't feel much like a spy. He felt pitiful more than anything else, though Captain Lawrence swore he was bravest man he'd ever met.

Conrad did not feel brave either.

He struggled to shift himself upright with his left hand, refusing to look at the bandaged mess of his right arm. He could've called Grace for help—the woman could hear a crumb drop on the floor, even over her own deafening singing—but he didn't.

His right arm throbbed terribly. Taylor had given him something for the pain, but the bitter drug made him vomit, and Conrad supposed he'd have to get used to the discomfort anyway. Dr. Taylor had pronounced him stable a few days ago and was now eager to have the alleged spy out of his charge as soon as possible and handed over to the colonial authorities.

Captain Lawrence was Conrad's only visitor. Dr. Taylor was a mean man, but could not overlook Lawrence's authority and so he begrudgingly allowed the captain into the hospital wing each morning. Sybille, on the other hand, was a different matter. She had tried to come to the army ward every day for a week, but Dr. Taylor was not interested in allowing Conrad the comfort of visitors, let alone allowing a Negro free rein of his ward. Gustavus had managed to escape his leash once and bolt past the old doctor in search of Conrad, but Grace had produced a broom and wielded it at Gustavus like a garden scythe. Gustavus had withstood lions, warthogs and crocodiles, but being chased out of the ward by Grace's bulk and broom was too much. Now the big dog had to content himself with following Lawrence to the hospital every day and waiting across the street in the hope that Conrad would emerge today.

Lawrence always began his visits by assuring Conrad that he was not under arrest. Lawrence never seemed to tire of the joke, though it brought Conrad little comfort. Some bored British Colonial Office magistrate had heard of Conrad's arrival, no doubt from Lawrence's boastings, Conrad thought, and had quickly become suspicious as to why a German official had crossed into Bechuanaland illegally.

The colonial administrator assumed that Conrad was either attempting to sign a treaty with the Kalanga to challenge Britain's right to Bechuanaland or that he was on a mission to find some way to neutralize the local garrison. Why else would he have risked traversing the Kalahari so foolishly unless he was up to something sinister?

Conrad was more concerned, however, that someone in the Cape Colony government might think to ask their counterpart in the German Colonial Office if they were missing an official. Conrad knew that von Trotha would demand that the British hand him over immediately, but Lawrence told Conrad not to worry.

"Once you've recovered enough to travel, I'll escort you via train to the Colonial Office in Cape Town personally," he told Conrad on his last visit.

"You'll make an official statement of your escape through the desert, ask the Colonial Government for political asylum, and this whole thing will be swept under the rug. No one in the Colonial Office who has any *real* authority will want to make a fuss over this. We've already got enough trouble keeping an eye on those damn Boers. No one will mind an educated white man looking to emigrate. Why, I'd even wager those maligned magistrates will try to hire you in a month or two to sort out their problems with the Boers in the Orange Free State! You don't happen to speak Afrikaans, do you?

"In truth, I suppose King Khama, or whatever it is he calls himself these days, will also have to approve your asylum here. But he'll agree to most of our requests without too much of a push. He's a decent enough fellow for a Negro. His spearmen guarded our flank during the last war with the Boers, you know, and he's at least a Christian. It's all a formality until Bechuanaland becomes a part of the new South African Union of course, but we have to act out this play a bit longer until London stops dragging its heels and approves a formal annexation."

Lawrence then reassured Conrad that he had recovered the crocodile's skin for him.

"Blasted devil must be nearly five meters long! Took a team of four horses just to pull its wretched carcass out of the mud once the river dried up. I wouldn't mind having that Negress of yours as one of my mounted rifles, Herr Huber. She hit that thrashing monstrosity in the head with at least four rounds. Hardly any of my men can shoot that well. Small miracle she didn't hit you as well, really.

"I've had van Zyl's men skin the beast and mount it for you, and I won't hear of you trying to pay me for it. This is already the talk of the year in Gaborone, and I half expect every officer stationed from here to Cape Town will be flooding my home to take a look at the skin once it arrives. We'll move it to your home once we find you proper accommodations, of course."

Conrad could not have cared less about the crocodile skin and had no intention of keeping the damn corpse in his home, wherever that might be.

He spent most of Lawrence's lengthy visits nodding weakly in his bed and wondering how Lawrence's company managed with their commander absent for such lengthy periods of time. Mostly, Conrad just waited for Lawrence to tell him anything important.

Sybille and Anna had found a small home on the outskirts of Gaborone that

Lawrence did not care for. It sounded like the two were settling in well enough from the tattered glimpses Captain Lawrence gave him. Conrad could not tell if Lawrence had actually bothered to call on them, but Conrad gathered that they at least had a roof over their heads and enough of Nyack's money left to feed and clothe themselves for a while.

Lawrence was a poor go-between and an even worse substitute for Sybille, but he was kind in his own way, and Conrad was at least grateful for that.

Conrad heard the captain's voice coming down the corridor for his morning visit, and he tried to push down the nausea he felt rising in his stomach. He was not in the mood to talk to Lawrence this morning, but indulging the man was better than staring mindlessly at the white, chipped paint on the hospital walls and trying to ignore the phantom tingling of his missing hand.

"How is your arm?" a voice said from the doorway.

Conrad turned, expecting to see Lawrence familiarly adorned in his emerald jersey and riding spurs. But instead of the captain, a tall Black man stood stooped in the small doorway. The man's voice was deep and hoarse from fatigue. He wore a tattered cream suit that looked as though it had been torn and patched several times.

Conrad studied the man a moment, trying to place his face.

"Samuel?" Conrad finally asked the half-bent figure in disbelief.

The big man nodded and walked to the stool beside Conrad's bed.

"It is good to see you, Conrad," Maharero said with the shadow of a smile.

Conrad stared dumbstruck as Maharero eased himself onto the stool beside him.

"I thought you were dead," Conrad said dumbly. "During the battle...I saw you...I saw you disappear in the cannon smoke."

Maharero leaned back on the stool as though trying to make himself comfortable.

"I should be dead," he said matter-of-factly. "I was hit a few times, though not badly. My knees and shoulders ache when it rains now, but I am whole otherwise. How is your arm?"

Conrad looked down sheepishly at his bound arm.

"It hurts," Conrad admitted. "But the surgeon says I'll survive."

"That is good to hear," Maharero said with a brief nod.

Neither man spoke for a while. Conrad could hear Grace's horrible singing in the kitchen and the more distant sounds of the bored garrison riflemen playing cards outside on the parade ground.

Maharero sat beside him, reserved. He appeared to be waiting to say something, but Conrad could not tell what, and in truth, there was a part of him that was in no rush to hear what other horrible misfortunes had befallen the man.

Maharero was much thinner than the last time Conrad had seen him. His tall frame would still loom over most men, but beneath his worn clothing, Maharero's skin sagged over his joints. His features looked far sharper than they had once been, and Conrad could see the utter weariness behind Maharero's sunken eyes.

Conrad continued to sit in silence, unsure of what to say. Since they had first met, a lifetime seemed to have passed. Conrad's countrymen had fought Maharero, defeated him, and then sought to exterminate his people in their victory. And it was men such as Conrad's own cousin, Georg, who had risen so eagerly to the task.

Germans had killed Maharero's wife. His daughter had been hunted like a wild animal, captured, imprisoned and beaten to within an inch of her life. And even though Conrad had managed to free Sybille, he had nearly killed her by fleeing with her into the Kalahari.

To Conrad, it was a miracle that Maharero had not strangled him already. He would hardly blame Maharero if he decided to kill Conrad while Captain Lawrence dallied with Dr. Taylor. Germans had already taken so much from Maharero, it would be some small measure of justice if he could kill a helpless German for a change. And Conrad would even be almost happy to give Maharero that gift.

But Maharero sat idly beside him, rubbing his large hands together as if in deep thought.

"Sybille never believed you were dead," Conrad said, searching for something to fill the silence with. "She wanted to come here and search for you. I told her she was crazy."

Maharero nodded.

"She told me something similar," he said.

"You've seen her, then?" Conrad asked hesitantly, wondering how much Sybille would have told her father about all that transpired between them.

"I have," he said plainly. "And I understand that the two of you are *fond* of one another?"

Conrad felt his face flush a deep crimson.

"Yes," Conrad admitted as he squirmed slightly on the bed.

"I'm very fond of her…I love her."

Maharero was silent a moment, and then he surprised Conrad by patting his knee.

"That is good," he said matter-of-factly. "She loves you too."

Conrad did not know what else to do, so he gave Maharero a foolish half-smile.

"Good," he said.

Maharero nodded.

"It is."

"Are she and Anna well?" Conrad asked. "I haven't seen them since…since I woke up in this hospital.

"They are fine," Maharero answered plainly. "The house they found is old but sturdy. When I left them this morning, they were going to buy some paint for the shutters."

Maharero coughed once and then fell silent once again.

Conrad shifted his weight uncomfortably. He felt as though he were talking to a ghost. The Maharero sitting before him was not the chieftain he remembered from Hochfeld. Strains of gloom and suffering hung around him like a shroud and made the proud man seem to shrink the longer Conrad looked at him.

Conrad could not bear the renewed silence and began searching again for anything else to say to the man.

"How did you survive?" he finally blurted out when he couldn't think of anything else to ask.

Maharero did not answer immediately. He continued to slowly rub his large hands together, tracing over them as though he were inspecting one of his wood carvings.

"I am not sure I did," he said after a while. "I am alive, yes. But in many ways, I feel as though I am dead."

Conrad did not know what to say, and he felt himself shifting uneasily on the bed again.

"I suppose I feel like you must, Conrad," Maharero continued. "You are gone from your people, without a way to return. Surely, they would arrest you if you tried to return to Germany?"

Conrad hadn't thought much about what the Imperial government would do if he tried to return to Germany. Von Trotha would want his head, but he was now the Commissioner of a distant colony, and he very likely thought that Conrad was already dead. If he went south, Conrad might catch a boat from Cape Town or Port Elizabeth and sail to England. And from there, he could easily slip back into Hamburg as if he'd never left.

He could not return to Uncle Johannes' house, of course. He'd all but disgraced his family, and he'd likely never see his cousins or his mother, Georgina, again. He'd be penniless and back to splitting rails for a few marks here and there, but he *could* go home. If he could outrun the Schutztruppe and cross the Kalahari, he could manage to slip back to Germany if he wanted to.

He could attend church, order a pint at a pub, or catch a train to the coast for a long weekend and no one would bat an eye. True, some might notice his missing hand, but they would assume he was a discharged, wounded solider or some poor factory worker who'd been mutilated in an accident.

I could go home, Conrad thought to himself. But would it be my home anymore?

"I suppose I am gone from my people," Conrad admitted. "If I wanted to, I could avoid arrest. But I suppose there wouldn't be much point. I don't really want to go home, to tell the truth."

Maharero nodded slowly.

"There is the difference," he said. "I *do* want to go back. But my home is gone. My people are gone. A few of us may survive the desert, but what we Herero once had is gone forever."

"You are gone from your people, Conrad…and my people are gone from me."

Maharero went quiet once more, and Conrad could not think of anything else to say. They sat in a solemn silence, absently listening to Grace's destruction of a Kalanga hymn that neither of them understood.

"I'm sorry," Conrad breathed finally, his voice scarcely above a whisper. "I-I could've stopped this somehow…If only the Colonial Office had sent someone else…I shouldn't have ever come here….I…"

Conrad felt a strong hand grip his shoulder. He looked up to see Maharero staring at him, his expression unreadable for a long moment. Then he slowly shook his head as though he'd made up his mind about something.

Conrad felt tears begin to flow freely down his face. Without thinking, he grabbed for Maharero, pulling the man fiercely into a tight embrace while he sobbed into his dirt-covered jacket. Maharero hugged him back, and Conrad felt a few of the man's own bitter tears fall against his shoulder.

They stayed like that for several minutes, crying softly together beneath the roaring Kalanga gospel.

"I killed Erwin and Petyr," Conrad cried. "They were good people, and they would still be alive if I hadn't asked them to help me."

Maharero held Conrad upright against him, weeping freely.

"*Yandje omuzandu,*" Maharero told Conrad in Herero between sobs. "*Ami pandjarisa yandje omuzandu.*"

My sons. I lost my sons.

"*Nokokure ye ovantje koka. Ye omakazendu okuyepa.*"

Noko's children died. And his wife is missing.

Conrad held onto Maharero, listening to the great man's grief. Then, a sudden howl of pain erupted from the kitchen.

Grace, in her honey-gobbling spree, had accidentally stepped into her cooking fire with her bare feet. The big woman screeched as though she'd been shot and began to curse everyone and Jesus Christ, even louder than she'd been singing.

For a moment, Conrad and Maharero fell silent, Grace's cursing echoing down the hallway like rolls of thunder.

Then Maharero let out a booming laugh that spread a wide smile across his face. The man wheezed as he laughed, as though a lifetime of sand and dust were lodged within his chest. Yet as he laughed, he began to look more like the man Conrad remembered. Conrad laughed as well, just as Dr. Taylor came shuffling past the doorway, led by Captain Lawrence, swinging his loaded pistol around in his hand, utterly terrified that the garrison must be under attack.

Conrad's whole body shook so much with laughter that Maharero had to catch him before he fell out of the hospital bed.

When Grace's curses finally simmered, and Dr. Taylor and Captain Lawrence had retreated to the doctor's office in an infuriated huff, Maharero wiped his eyes and turned to Conrad.

"I came here to wish you luck, Conrad," he said. "And to give you my blessing to marry my daughter, if you wish, before I go."

Conrad, who was trying to dry his own eyes with his good sleeve, was stunned.

"Marry?" he finally stammered, his ears flushed with embarrassment. "I… er…well…."

Conrad fumbled awkwardly with his bedsheets, trying to think of something to say.

"Thank you, Samuel," he finally decided on. "But I'm a German…"

Maharero shook his head.

"You two are already married, in a way. Though you have yet to say any words, you have been intertwined by this war. It's not my nor anyone's place to keep you apart if that is what you wish."

He paused a moment and then smiled again.

"And I doubt I could force Sybille not to marry you even if I wanted to."

Conrad returned Maharero's smile, still trying to steady himself on the bed.

"Where will you go?" Conrad asked him. "Sybille can't lose you again now that she's found you. She and Anna should go up north with you. I'll follow the two of you as soon as I've recovered."

Maharero smiled at him again as if he were imagining that very possibility. But then his smile faded, and he gave Conrad a look of weathered regret.

"Sybille's people are as gone from her as they are from me," he said. "To be Herero now has become a challenge to live on. We must live the lives that evil men tried to take from us. There are a few hundred or so of us camped in the grasslands in the north, waiting to see if King Khama will grant us asylum or turn us over to the Germans and march us back into the desert.

"For all I know, that is all that remains of us, and that is all that there will ever be of us. I am a pauper now, unsure of whether this land will accept me or take me prisoner and hand me over to von Trotha. There has been too much suffering and death for our people for me to let Sybille throw away a chance at a happy life here to bake in a tattered tent and worry after her father.

"She was Herero, and you were German. But now, you are each other's people. Together, your place is wherever you decide to find it. I pray that it is a good place. One that will give you a new life away from all the blood of the past."

And with that, Maharero stood up and stuck out his hand. Conrad shook Maharero's hand, trying to find the words to say to the man.

"We'll find our way," Conrad said when he could think of nothing else.

Maharero gave him one last approving look, and he left the hospital room without another word, disappearing just as Captain Lawrence rounded the corner in his usual huff.

"Good Lord!" Lawrence exclaimed as he unbuttoned his cavalry jacket and slipped his pistol back into its holster. "That woman is an absolute menace to everyone in this garrison. How she hasn't managed to carelessly lop off your head when she's been shaving you is beyond me. She's just lucky Dr. Taylor has a taste for large women."

Lawrence pulled up Maharero's recently vacated stool, completely ignorant of its warmth.

"Sorry I'm late, Herr Huber. But I have wonderful news! I spoke with Dr. Taylor in the corridor, and he says you can be discharged in the morning."

When Lawrence finally looked at Conrad, he found his charge sitting upright with fresh tears in his eyes.

"Are you alright, man?" Lawrence asked him with genuine concern in his voice.

Conrad smiled at Lawrence and wiped his eyes clumsily with his sleeve.

"Never better," Conrad told him as he stuck out his good arm. "I was just wondering if you think the Cape Colony office could really use a man with one hand?"

EPILOGUE

BLOEMFONTEIN,

FORMER-ORANGE FREE STATE,

BRITISH CAPE COLONY

SEPTEMBER 1915

The train was late. Very late. Conrad unfolded his newspaper again and tried to calm his nerves by re-reading the headlines.

The Great War was at a standstill. Germany had launched a new offensive against the Russians at Dvinsk, and in response, the Tsar had declared that he was now personally taking control of the Russian armies. The United States had recalled its Austro-Hungarian ambassador, and Bulgaria and Greece had begun partial mobilization. Despite early British optimism, it looked like the war in Europe was doomed to continue well into another year.

In their African colonies, the British had renewed their attack on the Mora mountain range in German-held Kamerun, where the remains of the last stubborn unit of Schutztruppe had retreated. The paper predicted the capital, Yaoundé, to fall within the month. Conrad was not so sure, yet they had said the same thing about Lomé in Togoland, and the Schtuztruppe had surrendered there in a matter of weeks.

Conrad put the paper down. He could not bring himself to focus on the articles. Beside him, Sybille felt his uneasiness and took his hand in her lap, giving it a soft squeeze. The other passengers and families occasionally gave them odd, disapproving looks, but today at least, no one had made any disparaging remarks out loud. Mixed couples were common in the Cape Colony, if socially undesirable, and there were far more mixed-race children playing near the train platform than white ones.

Conrad turned to look at his children sitting next to their mother on the bench. Their daughter, Wilma, sat lovingly stroking the hair of the new doll he'd bought her in town yesterday. She was nearly six now, and her big, brown eyes had gone wild with excitement when he'd handed it to her off the shelf in the store and told her it was hers.

Their son Petyr, only four, sat staring eagerly down the tracks, one of his small hands curled tightly around Sybille's. Ever since they'd arrived at the station an hour ago, the boy had become infatuated with trains.

"The train come soon, Papa?" he asked Conrad with a big smile on his face.

Conrad smiled back at him.

"Yes. Any minute now."

Petyr turned his attention eagerly back to the empty track. He was lighter-skinned than his sister, and the other children on the platform treated him with a warry acceptance, unsure exactly where he fit into the confusing social hierarchy described to them by their parents.

Conrad reached a phantom hand for his pocket watch and then caught himself. He still did that on occasion, though he'd gotten better about it over the years.

"What time is it?" he asked Sybille, not wanting to take his hand from hers to search his own pocket.

"Still half-past twelve," she said with a faint hint of amusement. "Same as it was a moment ago. Don't worry. It shouldn't be too much longer now."

Conrad nodded and kissed her cheek.

Gustavus felt him shift his weight on the bench above and let out a long, bored sigh. The big dog's muzzle had turned almost completely gray, and he had a stiffness in his hind legs that took him several moments to shake off whenever he stood up. But still, he pouted at having been confined to a leash and made to wait patiently amidst the interesting smells and sounds of the Bloemfontein station.

So much had changed since they'd stumbled out of the Kalahari ten years ago.

In the end, it was money that had brought an end to madness in the DSWA. It had taken three years for the Kaiser to notice how loose von Trotha had been with the Imperial purse. While the DSWA under Leutwein had brought in a respectable fourteen million marks a year from its mineral trade, von Trotha's army and the upkeep of his new camps was costing the Empire nearly 600 million marks.

On top of that, Conrad's first cable to the Cape Colony office about von Trotha's vicious tactics and campaign of extermination against the Herero had somehow found its way onto the desk of the British prime minister, Lord Asquith.

When the newspapers had gotten wind of the cable due to a hapless clerk's gossip, London's evangelical and missionary societies had made an even greater nuisance of themselves to the prime minister. They'd launched a series of public protest campaigns, and after enduring months of attack articles on his government's lack of attention to the natives' plight in Africa, Asquith had been forced by public opinion to formally address the issue with the Kaiser's government.

Embarrassed on the national stage, the Kaiser had no choice but to restrict Germany's ongoing war with the Nama, and von Trotha had been made to close nearly all his new camps, including Shark Island.

After that, however, the British had not particularly cared what became of the natives outside of Walvis Bay. The evangelicals had sung their triumphs for a few days and then gone right back to badgering Asquith to get involved in the atrocities of the rubber plantations in the Congo Free State. And after being made to heel for a few months or so, von Trotha's leash was once again slackened.

But then, a year ago, the Great War changed everything once again.

For the past year, every journalist from London to Cape Town craved reports of atrocities. And the longer their soldiers sat rotting in the muddy trenches of Europe, papers, both white and Black in Africa, seemed to want more and more narratives to paint the Germans, Austrians, and Ottomans in an even darker light.

Conrad and Sybille had been interviewed more times in the past few months than they could count. A few of the white papers had even started printing Sybille's accounts.

Maharero and the remaining Herero were now considered martyrs in Bechuanaland and had finally been given free rein to travel within the protectorate by King Khama.

Maharero now lived with them during his brief respites between trips to the border to help look for and settle new refugees. Each time he came home, he told Sybille how much Wilma looked like her mother, which always made Sybille beam with pride.

Most of what Conrad and Sybille knew about the few Herero who had survived the camps in the DSWA came from these visits, when Maharero would tell them the stories of the small trickle of people who continued to survive the desert crossing.

Von Trotha had distributed any surviving Herero to German farms as free laborers. They were given a registration number by the colonial government, and every Herero over the age of seven had been forced to wear a crude metal disc displaying their number.

Maharero had shown them the disc of a runaway laborer on his last visit. The poor man had been forced to cross the Kalahari, unable to break the metal ring around his neck, and the heat and glare off the collar had rendered him nearly blind by the time he reached Bechuanaland.

The Nama had fared little better in the ten years since the Witbois had rebelled.

Hendrik Witbooi had been shot and killed in a skirmish with the Schutztruppe in 1905. Conrad and Maharero had both half-expected the Nama's rebellion to die without Witbooi, yet the Nama had continued to fight on sporadically for three more years.

When the European scrutiny over his methods had finally abated, von Trotha had threatened the remaining Nama chieftains with the same extinction the Herero had suffered. The Nama rebels, leaderless and unaware of the European politics that had first restrained and then released von Trotha, had dithered for a few months but were ultimately too exhausted by war to continue the fight. One by one, they all surrendered.

Von Trotha, fresh off another Imperial victory, was recalled to Germany just before the war in Europe had broken out. Conrad had gathered from Arthur Lawrence's gossip that the General had been given a high field command in the Imperial Army. Conrad did not know if he was still involved in the fighting in the war in Europe, but he certainly hoped so. If the European theatre was as bleak as the newspapers made it sound, von Trotha could get himself killed.

The Imperial division had pulled out of the DSWA after the Nama surrender, and only a reduced number of Schuztruppe were left to keep the peace. When war was declared, the British Cape Colony had wasted no time in launching an invasion of the DSWA. The South African forces, including the now-Colonel Lawrence's Mounted Cape Rifles, had advanced quickly across the DSWA, and the last outmatched Schutztruppe company had officially surrendered two months ago.

A thin whistle blew in the distance, and Conrad slowly got to his feet. Sybille and the children stood with him. She squeezed his hand once more and looked at him from beneath the new hat he'd bought her yesterday. She wore an elegant, fitted green dress and covered the scars on her palms with light brown gloves.

"Are you alright?" she whispered as the whistle grew louder in the distance.

Conrad looked at her and their children.

"Yes, of course," he said.

The train lurched into the station without much ceremony. It had taken

Conrad weeks to track down Lawrence in the field and even longer to arrange for the parole. He'd called in half a dozen favors from officers he'd never met, and he had no doubt the South African Colonial Office would be expecting him to single-handedly annex Bechuanaland to repay the debt.

Only a few dozen passengers disembarked from the train, and Conrad scanned the scant crowd anxiously.

At last, a man in stained khaki climbed down onto the platform. His shoulders bore a long shadow as though he might've once been a plump man. But now his frame was thin and sagged, hunched with hunger and defeat. The man saw them after a moment and looked hurriedly away, busying himself with the canvas bag he had been carrying on his shoulder. It was plain that the man was not sure what he should do.

Conrad and Sybille glanced at one another as though deciding what they ought to do themselves, until young Petyr rushed forward to the man happily. The man saw the mulatto child running toward him, and a slight grimace crossed his face.

Sybille took a step forward.

Petyr reached the man in the uniform and, without fear, outstretched a curled fist and dropped something into the man's hand.

"Papa said you like these," Petyr announced happily.

The man looked down into his hand and saw the tiny nara fruit the boy had given him.

He stared at the fruit for a moment as though unsure of what it was. Then Georg looked back at the boy, and a disgusted look spread across his face. He heaved his bag over his shrunken shoulder, knocking Petyr's small hand in the process. The nara fruit fell onto the platform with a soft squish.

Petyr's young eyes filled with tears, and he began to whimper, frightened, as Georg headed for the dusty depot, stalking off the platform without meeting Conrad's eye.

Wilma, sensing the sudden tension, cowered behind her mother and clutched her new doll tightly to her chest. Sybille put her arms around her and shot a black look at Georg's disappearing back.

Conrad hurried over to Petyr and knelt beside his son, who was rubbing his small hand where Georg's heavy bag had hit it.

"Are you okay, Petyr?" he asked. "Are you hurt?"

Petyr said nothing. He continued to rub his hurt hand, tears rolling down his round cheeks.

"Are you frightened?" Conrad asked him.

Petyr nodded but still said nothing.

"Do you know what I do sometimes when I'm scared?" Conrad asked him.

Petyr shook his head and looked up at his father.

"I like to count to a hundred," Conrad told him. "By the time I'm done, I've forgotten what it was I was scared of. Do you want to try it with me?"

There were still tears in the boy's eyes, but he nodded slowly and began to count with Conrad.

"*Eins...zwei...drei...*"

AUTHOR'S NOTE

The very first editor I showed this novel to shocked me by saying that Conrad was "a real piece of shit." And I confess, I was more than a bit offended at first, because I have always had a soft spot for gangly and awkward "nice guys," having spent a good many years considering myself one. But as the drafts continued, I realized that responding to that editor's comment is probably the most accurate way to address the difficult nuances of this book.

It's important to remember the context of when *The Sands Shall Witness* takes place. As Conrad sets sail for modern-day Namibia, the German Empire was just barely thirty years old and industrializing at a breakneck pace. As the Kaiser sought to establish Germany's place on the world stage, he did so amidst the sharp-elbowed competing narratives answering the (highly problematic) question: which European empire truly deserved to follow its "manifest destiny?"

From the experienced realms of Great Britain and France to the relatively new empires of Germany and Italy, each country's leaders believed that they were destined for greatness through exploration. It was up to the white man to bring God and glory to the "dark continent" (and if they made a tremendous profit simultaneously, so much the better), but just which *specific* breed of white men should reign supreme remained an open contest of perpetual rivalry.

Too often when Western novels thrust Africa onto the main stage it is to play out the white savior trope. A good-hearted man (usually) who, through trial and tribulation, is shown the error of his ways before rising to heroic heights to save some poorly specified tribe from the evils his own kinsmen have wrought. One only needs to read the first few pages of Binyavanga Wainaina's *How to Write About Africa* to see how ingrained these tropes have become in our everyday lives. "Africa" in our western imaginations, is a single, backward place full of half-starved masses waiting for salvation.

Yet that depiction of a sudden "enlightened change of heart" for the heroic white savior was never a reality. As a young German stepping onto a steamer bound for "the colonies," Conrad's perception of his own importance cannot be overlooked. He is of a time when few young European men would have questioned their right to rule over other peoples. A few, like Conrad, might've protested against cruelty and violence when forced to confront it, but far fewer would have *ever* paused to consider whether the people they ruled over might just be their equals.

As much as we might wish to assume the best of men like Conrad, we shouldn't get to ignore the historical context within a "nice guy's" soul. Commissioner Leutwein was widely referred to as the bloodless governor of German Southwest Africa. Yet it was he who ordered the construction of the deadly concentration camps, and he who led the mission that butchered Andreas Lambert's Khaua. We might wish to consider him the foil to von Trotha's genocidal rampage, yet nothing is ever that simple. To von Trotha's tactics of ethnic elimination, Leutwein objected, but not on a humanitarian ground — on an economical one. He was once quoted after his removal from office saying:

"I do not concur with those fanatics who want to see the Herero destroyed altogether...I would consider that a grave mistake from an economic point of view—we need the Herero as cattle breeders...and especially, as laborers."

Colonialism is a brutal and exploitative narrative in our history as human beings, and to assume "the best" of any one individual without addressing the harmful mindsets of imperialism would be, to put it extremely mildly, unfair.

And therein lies my difficulty as an author. My job is to entertain you and provide you with a compelling story of love, loss, adventure and redemption — while hopefully teaching you a little about a corner of history often ignored.

For, if we are honest with ourselves, that is the kind of book most of us will pick up over a nonfiction account of horrendous atrocities. And I would be dishonest if I said I hoped that you were not entertained by this book. I certainly hope you were.

But as much as I might wish that I could claim the Battle of Waterberg or an island camp guarded by sharks as the terrifying fruits of my own imagination, they are, in fact, undeniably real. And into this backdrop of a beautiful land about to be torn apart by war and genocide, I have dropped Conrad Huber, the shy "white knight" come to save the beguiling African princess.

Conrad is a trope. And while I've spent countless hours and drafts deleting, rewriting, and again deleting his personality, in the end I've come to accept that he is the only lens through which I can claim to try and capture this tale. Conrad looks like me, talks like me and, at times, is probably as utterly ignorant as I am even where I believe I am doing the right thing. I considered up to the very last minute of publishing this book of rewriting it from Sybille's point of view, from Maharero's or Petyr's, or simply scrapping the whole narrative altogether.

But the truth is, that's not my history to tell. I don't possess the skill to tell you what Maharero's version of this tale would be, let alone that of a woman who (although fictional) is as resilient and determined as Sybille. My history with this narrative is the history of Conrad. The history of those who thought they were doing the "right thing," no matter how many times they were, to use that first editor's word, being shitty.

So, perhaps in retelling a version of this story, I am a piece of shit of myself. I certainly hope not. I have attempted to use my own lens to turn the white knight trope upside down and show how utterly helpless, out of place and unwanted such a "hero" is. Most every decision Conrad makes, no matter how "well-intentioned," leads from bad to worse — for himself and everyone around him.

I have also taken great creative license in the telling of this tale, both in the literary exaggerations of landscapes and the depictions of real historical actors. Regarding places within Namibia, I owe you, the reader, a few points of clarification. While there were rebels who opposed German rule in Tsumeb and Grootfontein, there is no rail line connecting the two. The only rail line that reaches Grootfontein is from the small town of Otavi, which is about 60 kilometers southwest of Tsumeb. Beaunard's railway extension is thus, to my knowledge, entirely fictional. If such a railroad was ever built, it has long since been lost to the landscape.

And speaking of landscapes, it is impossible to Google "Namibia" without seeing countless photos of its spectacular orange sand dunes. These dunes are picturesque and can be found in the Namib desert that stretches along the western coast of the country. The Kalahari Desert, where Conrad and Sybille escape through, is not home to the same topography. In most places, the Kalahari is home to grassy woodland. However, in my own travels through the Kalahari, I felt mesmerized by the orange-tinged sand (a very different shade of light brown-orange), and, to this day, cannot think of its sloping landscape as anything other than dunes. Thus, I have knowingly superimposed my own impressions on you, however confusing they might be.

And now for the people.

This novel focuses on the darkest chapter of Namibian history, and there were countless perspectives that I might've chosen to explore it through. This novel could just as easily have been focused on the Nama, whose history is as unique and terribly troublesome as the Herero. However, I decided it would have been impossible to do both the Nama and the Herero perspectives justice, and so I chose to focus this novel on the Herero.

Samuel Maharero and Hendrik Witbooi are two of Namibia's most prominent historical heroes. And like all literary depictions of historical heroes, I have taken great license in my description of their thoughts, feelings and actions. They were real people, brilliant and flawed, whose lives were doubtless completely different from how I have portrayed them.

Sybille is a fictional daughter of Samuel Maharero. To my knowledge, although Samuel Maharero did have children, he was never married to a white German woman. An interesting concept but, again, to the best of my knowledge, purely a literary fantasy.

Although in this novel Maharero is unsure if any of his sons survived the war, at least one did. In 1920, an aging and still exiled Maharero empowered his son Frederick Maharero to choose his successor. Frederick chose Hosea Kutako as the man who would go on to form the first nationalist political party of the new country of Nambia and whose hundred-year-old life was as fascinating as it was long.

In summary, this is a flawed novel. I believe any novel that would try to do justice to such horrific atrocities while also entertaining its readers is bound to be flawed. Still, I have tried my best, and I hope that if you have read this far you have enjoyed the story for what it is: a work of fiction based *loosely* on the complicated and cataclysmic history of one of the most fascinating places on Earth.

Thank you for reading my book.

Kara nawa. Auf Wiedersehen. And until next time.

Walter Hurst Williamson

ACKNOWLEDGEMENTS

I have often heard it said that it takes a small army to finish a book. Luckily for me, a small army is precisely what I had. This book began as an outline on a yellow legal pad where I would hurriedly jot down ideas between work meetings. And many times, the story proved to be smarter than me. This is a difficult tale to tell, and as the story continued to morph and evolve, there were countless moments where I considered abandoning the project and throwing the whole thing away.

In that respect, this book really belongs to my family. My loving parents Mark and Sally, my sisters Katie and Gwen, my wonderful wife Emma, and my grandmother Calista (who consistently demanded to read a fresh draft). *The Sands Shall Witness* would never have been finished if it had not been for them. For all the love, support and gentle nudges to get back to work, thank you.

But as every writer knows, finishing the book is not an act that ever really concludes. It's more an endless screaming fit of rewrites, false hope, and further rewrites until the printer pries the inevitably flawed "final" product out of your white-knuckled grip. It takes a skilled hand to be able to move an author off their own alleged brilliance, while at the same time keeping their ego on enough life support to sustain a book. For that and much more, I thank my editors, Meghan Pinson and Margaret Diehl. And for the heroic task of turning my vague ramblings into artwork, I thank my brilliant designer, Mark Thomas.

Perhaps most importantly, I offer my profound thanks to The Embassy of the Republican of Namibia in Washington, D.C. and to my new friends at the Otuvawa Cultural Institute in Windhoek. Fenny Tjiriange and Dr. Metusalem Nakale: thank you.

WHO IS REAL?

In any historical fiction novel, readers are bound to be curious who is fictional. For the curious, here is a list of real people in *The Sands Shall Witness*:

Namibia (German Southwest Africa):
Samuel Maharero, chieftain and leader of the Herero revolt
Hendrik Witbooi, chieftain and leader of the Nama revolt
Andreas Lambert, chieftain and leader of the Khaua revolt

Botswana (Bechuanaland):
King Khama III, Ruler of the Bangwato people
Hendrik van Zyl, Transvaal politician

The German Empire:
Kaiser Wilhelm II, Emperor of Germany
Theodor Leutwein, Commissioner of German Southwest Africa
Lothar von Trotha, General of the Colonial Army, later Commissioner.
Eugen Fischer, eugenicist
Theodor Mollison, eugenicist

Great Britain:
Herbert Henry Asquith, Prime Minister

ABOUT THE AUTHOR

Walter Hurst Williamson is a communications consultant and professional storyteller. *The Sands Shall Witness* is his debut novel. Hurst graduated from Rice University with degrees in African History & International Relations.

WHWILLIAMSON.COM